SAINT

Mark Bailey

JOVE BOOKS, NEW YORK

SAINT

A Jove Book / published by arrangement with
the author

PRINTING HISTORY
Jove edition / November 1997

The Putnam Berkley World Wide Web site address is
http://www.berkley.com

ISBN: 0-515-12173-8

A JOVE BOOK®
Jove Books are published by The Berkley Publishing Group,
a member of Penguin Putnam Inc.,
200 Madison Avenue, New York, New York 10016.
JOVE and the "J" design are trademarks
belonging to Jove Publications, Inc.

PRINTED IN THE UNITED STATES OF AMERICA

10 9 8 7 6 5 4 3 2 1

THE AWAKENING

"Nicolao?" Dr. Andrew Shepard called, a rescuer guiding the lost from a dark forest of unconsciousness. "Nicolao? How're you feeling? You're in the BioGenera lab and everything is fine. Nicolao?"

The man's eyelids twitched. Eyes darted left, then right, then rotated in a circle beneath the lids. Finally they opened and coaxed order from the brightness.

The man who returned Andrew's searching stare was clearly not the same man who had laid down on the table two hours earlier.

"Nico-lao?" repeated the man, scowling ferociously.

"It's Dr. Shepard, Nicolao. Are you all right?"

"*Quod?*"

"Nicolao?"

"'*Quod,*'" repeated Giuliana. "He's speaking Latin. '*Quod*' means 'what.'"

"Nicolao, do you know where you are?"

"*Nullus,*" he said, his voice a growl. "*Nullus—Pietro!*"

"Peter?" asked Giuliana.

The man nodded affirmatively and tapped his chest. "Peter, *ita*. Peter," he smiled. "I Peter—eh, I am Peter."

SAINT

A scientific and spiritual thriller in the tradition of Jurassic Park *and* Neanderthal

For Lenore

Acknowledgments

Thank you:

Mary Jane and James Lincoln Bailey for inspiring an appreciation for the refractive powers of faith.

Ted Chichak for impassioned professionalism.

Margaret Wander Bonanno for insight and inspiration.

Leslie Gelbman, Susan Allison and Anne Sowards for adopting the tale.

PROLOGUE

Imperial Rome—18 June 64

THE VAST PIAZZA OUTSIDE THE CITY WALL FELL QUIET. ONLY Petros' agonal groans broke the stillness. Eventually, gratefully, he surrendered to unconsciousness and, a short time later, death.

Rome's bright sun dimmed to a luminous rose color. Normally frenetic swallows and starlings fell silent. The land breeze eased and wildflowers bowed under their own weight.

After satisfying themselves that their prisoner was dead, the soldiers tried to take Petros' body down from the cross. But the weight of his large frame had wedged the long, square nails solidly into the wood. Several attempts to extract them failed. Finally one of the soldiers found an ax and cut the body down with one powerful stroke of the blade through Petros' ankles. Spared the weight upon them, the nails through his wrists were then readily pulled free. The soldiers carried the long corpse over to a pyre between the River Tiber and the city wall.

It wasn't much of a fire. An afternoon shower had reduced the pyre to a steaming mound of smoldering, half-incinerated corpses. More fuel was needed, but the soldiers were in no mood to chop down more trees at this late hour, so they took a chance that no one would check their work so late in the day. They hoisted Petros' body onto the head-high pile of foul, simmering death. Then, their work completed, they picked up their tools and walked back to the garrison.

New religions were a constant in the life of Rome; this one would be no more enduring than any of the others. No one would ever know that Petros or his people had lived at all. His life was just one more story to be lost in the mists of time and memory.

Three shadows stole up to the pyre in the ebbing daylight. They lifted Petros' charred body and swiftly disappeared along the bank of the Tiber.

A short time later, in a pagan necropolis outside the city wall, three men delivered Petros' corpse to a wealthy Roman freedman at his family's pagan mausoleum. Working according to a prearranged plan, they carried the body into the burial chamber, where they bathed it in milk and wine, carefully washing the head and hair, working down to the raw stumps just above where his ankles had been. They closed all of the body's orifices with pure bleached cotton.

At this point, working quickly but respectfully, they cut seven *minae* of mastic and fifty leaves of myrrh, aloes, and Indian leaf and wrapped the corpse in purple cloth—the purple reserved for gods and prominent Romans. Inappropriate use of the specially dyed fabric meant the death penalty if they were caught.

Finally, the owner of the vault poured some Attic honey into his own marble coffin, laid Petros to rest, and sealed the compartment. He marked the tomb with a simple white pagan marker. For Romans, white stone commemorated a joyful day. It was a clever cover. No one would think of this as anything but the final resting place of a fellow pagan. When they finished, the three hurriedly left to avoid suspicion.

Thus the three citizens—who, if their actions had been known to the authorities would surely have been put to death —helped their patron in one more obscure act in the esoteric life of a Roman.

A.D. 253

Smoke hung over the seven hills and glowed from blazes set by the invading persecutors. Screams filled the air and hoarse pleas to pagan gods floated on wings of certain death in every section of the city.

At the crypt of the freedman, two men and a woman deftly gathered dozens of bleached bones in a partially decomposed purple cloth. Even as marauding hordes plundered nearby graves for jewels, they carefully placed the bones in a niche in the wall beside the grave. They then plastered up the niche so expertly that the owner himself would not recognize the modification that had been made to his own crypt.

The woman pulled a stylus from her waistband and paused for strength. The men averted their eyes as her face twitched violently and her lips whispered the prayer. They admired her courage but couldn't bear her defect. Finally, she reached up and carefully scratched two words in the hardening plaster. The men then added their own coded requests for prayers, as was the custom at every Roman grave.

ROGA CHRISTUS JESU (Pray Jesus Christ), wrote one man several times. IN HOC VINCE (In this, conquer), wrote the other. They scratched their words over and around the woman's words in such a way that people who came there would need to know what they were looking for to see the words, to understand their meaning.

In 313 A.D., Emperor Constantine ordered construction of his basilica-martyrium over what tradition indicated was the tomb of Peter.

More than eight centuries passed. Calixtus II built a larger marble altar directly over Constantine's *memoria*.

In the year 1300, two million pilgrims visited the *memoria* in response to a rumor that those who visited this place where Saint Peter's remains were believed to be interred would receive full absolution from their sins.

In 1506, Pope Julius II ordered that a Christian basilica "in the Renaissance style" replace the deteriorating Constantine basilica.

Urban VIII commissioned Giovanni Bernini to create a *baldacchino*, or canopy, over the high altar. Bernini sculpted his ornate *baldacchino* in brass and raised its roof ninety-five feet above the altar.

Above this soared Michelangelo's dome, the largest of its

kind in world history. Above the dome, Catholics believed, Peter's spirit watched over it all.

All these layers upon layers of human tumult were motivated solely by the inherited tradition that the remains of Peter, Christ's most trusted Apostle, were there. No one could be sure, however. Certain tenets of the Church were supported by faith alone. Until science developed tools to confirm the tradition, faith would have to suffice.

28 June 1968

More than fifteen years after her first glimpse at the tangle of scribbles on the excavated plaster wall, another Italian woman, the noted cryptographer Dr. Anna Aldobrandi, stood beside Giovanni Battista Montini, Pope Paul VI, as he made the most electrifying announcement in the history of the Roman Catholic Church: The skeletal remains of Saint Peter, Prince of the Apostles and the Rock upon which the Catholic Church was built, had been identified.

Dr. Aldobrandi, along with an international team of specialists, had proved beyond any doubt that Peter had been found. The crucial last piece in one of the greatest puzzles of all time had fallen into place when she deciphered the two words scratched into the plaster over the niche by another woman nearly two thousand years earlier: *Petros Eni.*

Their meaning: "Peter is within."

1

Città del Vaticano—Rome

GIULIANA SABATINI STOOD AT THE WINDOW OF HER tiny office overlooking St. Peter's Square, her glance inevitably drawn toward the iron cross atop the obelisk that dominated the piazza, trying to calm her quick Italian temper. Once again, Cosa was toying with her. The cardinal had demanded her presence at an urgent early-morning meeting, only to have her informed by an aide once she arrived that the meeting had been postponed "until sometime later in the day."

" 'Later in the day,' " Giuliana had repeated the obsequious voice's words into the phone with a small frown. "When? An hour from now? This afternoon? Early or late? Have I time to return home to retrieve the notes I was working on, or must I wait here all day at the cardinal's convenience? How soon is 'later in the day'?"

"I'm sorry, *Dottore*; that is all I can tell you. His Eminence will inform me, and I will inform you."

She had hurried her morning run, rushed from the Metro at Stazione Ottaviano with the rising sun in order to have time for early Mass, and had been pacing the confines of her cell of an office, too keyed up to concentrate on her work, ever since. It was now past noon. Nor was this the first time Cosa had done such a thing to her.

Adeodato Cardinal Cosa was one of the most powerful men in Rome—and her immediate superior. Giuliana had snapped at his aide because she could not snap at him. Now, as the soft Roman breeze teased her fiery chestnut hair, she calmed herself. She was well aware of how fortunate she, a laywoman, was to be in the place she was in the hierarchy of the Church. If Cosa wanted her to wait, she would wait. It was the province of those in power to exercise that power by making those who served them wait.

Her senses alive to whatever this summons might mean, Giuliana waited.

BioGenera Laboratory—La Jolla, California

Andrew Shepard stood disbelieving in the cool limbo of 3:30 A.M., hands gripping the edge of the table, knuckles whitening. A gust of wind teased the window blinds while outside, eucalyptus leaves rattled the air. Sensing a shift in polarity, he fingered a tuft of Niko's black simian hair.

His thoughts slowed and awareness buckled in the vacuum of failure. He felt himself sinking, a drowning man observing his own descent. How could it be happening again?

• • •

He had planned the experiment in three stages. Before he could even begin the first stage, he and his lab assistant Will Austin had to invest considerable time in getting acquainted with Niko and Lucy, a pair of adolescent chimps. Both chimps had been well trained before BioGenera acquired them, a fact of which CEO Mike Gindman could not resist reminding Andrew at nearly every budget meeting. They were docile, housebroken, able to communicate their essential needs in the gestures of American Sign Language. Even so, they required almost as much attention as a pair of energetic children.

The nature of Andrew's experiment required that he treat these animals not as mere lab specimens but almost as friends. The more he knew about Niko's personality, in particular, the better he would be able to measure the success of his experiment.

Stage One had consisted of injecting a solution of Niko's DNA into the bloodstream of the rhesus monkey, R. H. There had been no adverse effects following the first injection; in fact, there had been no effects at all. Forty-eight hours later Andrew had ordered Will to administer a second injection. Nothing.

R. H. had evidenced no physiological changes, no alteration in behavior or activity throughout six weeks' observation. Stage One was a failure.

Andrew knew he could hardly walk into the next staff meeting and say as much to Gindman. His boss ran BioGenera on success, not failure. With a silent prayer, he had worked all night to prepare Niko for Stage Two.

Now he traced the hollow below Niko's ribs, felt the slackness of the diaphragm, its readiness for breath. Bending down, he blew onto the chest, caressed the muscled forearm and elongated hand. *Where was the life that had surged through these limbs?* Andrew felt Lucy's dark eyes observing him. Trust still shone in her expression as she also waited for movement on the table. She glanced at Andrew for understanding, then back to the still form of her mate. A shadow darted across her gaze and wrinkled her brow. A muted whimper sounded from deep within her, and she reached out between the bars to touch, to calm herself.

Andrew swallowed. He had to accept responsibility. Placing his hand on the small chest, he held his breath and listened. It was useless; the rush of blood in his own veins was too loud for him to hear anything.

"Niko . . ." he whispered.

Niko had become more than just a monkey, more than merely another subject for experimentation. He was Andrew's link between species, an eloquent reminder of nature's complexity who both humbled and inspired the biogeneticist.

Science was Andrew's religion, the search for truth in the maze of genetics his mission. Angels dancing on the head of a pin, the legacy of his Catholic boyhood, had long since been displaced by the cryptic dance of genes along the spiral microcosm of DNA. Niko had been his last hope of rising out of anonymous scientific mediocrity and making a lasting contribution to the betterment of his species. And because Andrew treated him as a friend, Niko had overcome his distrust of men in white lab coats and showed interest in his keeper.

He would watch Andrew sit at his desk making notes, absentmindedly pulling on his earlobe, constructing double-helix DNA models from colorful plastic sticks and spheres, drifting into thoughts far, far removed from the lab, staring unblinking out the window for an hour. Niko followed the suspended motion for as long as a minute or two. Beyond that his self-control would crumble and he would take to distractions, flinging tennis balls out of his cell, clapping noisily, rattling his toys against the bars. He had once beaned Andrew with a teddy bear from across the laboratory, a direct hit, and was immensely proud of it. Even Lucy, usually the quieter of the two, had applauded that one. Still, they had both finally learned that nothing could command Andrew's attention once he was absorbed in his work.

Andrew's ex-wife, Margaret, had learned as much too, though it had taken her considerably longer.

Every morning Andrew let Niko and Lucy out of their large cell so they could sit at the window overlooking Torrey Pines Golf Course and the Pacific. They drank in the fresh air, dozed in the sun, studied the flights of sea birds and the seasonal migrating of whales. Neither Andrew nor Will worried about the chimps' getting into serious trouble or ingesting anything harmful. They avoided everything but fruits and vegetables; anything else made them sick. They found Andrew's steady diet of coffee and bagels with peanut butter downright repulsive.

Niko would curl into Andrew's lap when the sun traveled beyond the window and insist on play. When he didn't get enough hide-and-seek or wrestling or even simple grooming, his tantrums would be heard all the way to Mike Gindman's penthouse office.

The phone would ring. Always Gindman's executive assistant, Delphine. Always the purred taunt: "Who's running that asylum, Dr. Shepard?"

Always Andrew would laugh. Watching him, Niko would throw back his head in perfect imitation and, silently, laugh too.

She hurried from the Metro at Stazione Ottaviano under the penetrating gazes of idle merchants and women who looked closely before averting their eyes. Through Porta Angelica and across the vast piazza, she walked on stones that remembered the birth of faith, pausing in the morning light to stand quietly on the piazza floor.

She looked up at the basilica and listened. It was her way. To listen to the stones, remembering the birth of faith before practicing it. When she ascended the steps from Rome's teeming *vizio* into the muted radiance of San Pietro in Vaticano, she felt instantly closer to God.

Two of the five massive bronze doors were open. The others, with the exception of the Porta Sancta, would open in time for the rush of tourists and pilgrims at midmorning. By papal decree in the year 1300, only the pontiff was permitted to open the Porta Sancta, and only during a Holy Year. A brick wall behind it was loosely assembled to enable the feeblest of popes to destroy it with a few hammer blows.

Giuliana walked across Maderno's seventeenth-century atrium and felt her heart quicken as she approached the nave, the vast main aisle of the basilica. Michelangelo's architectural vision was impressive by any standard, but it assumed miraculous significance when she remembered that the maestro had executed it in his seventy-second year with the technology of 1547.

The church stretched out more than six hundred feet from where she stood, down the nave, beyond the papal altar, all the way to the wall of the apse behind Bernini's Cathedra Petri. The ceiling hovered 150 feet above her, soaring 390 feet to the lantern in the dome above the altar!

A visiting American priest's Latinate chant drifted quietly from the far corner. Giuliana followed the voice to the Chapel of the Crucifixion of Saint Peter where early Mass was under way.

"Hoc est enim corpus meum. . . . This is my body . . ."

She was surprised and pleased to hear Latin again. It had been banned for thirty years, but there were still many Catholics like her who cherished the mystery of the Mass in Latin and sought it out. She offered a prayer of thanks for the American priest's courage. He would be disciplined, she thought sadly.

The ring of sanctus bells floated on the scented air, and Giuliana prepared to receive the body of Christ. Despite the grip of crisis in which the Church had struggled since Vatican II, including a dizzying array of seemingly insoluble dilemmas—polarization between individual freedom and church authority, erosion of the priesthood, alienation of the faithful, and the Holy See's credibility in sexual matters—Giuliana found comfort in the Eucharist. It was a constant in a life in which she had experienced violent change.

"The body of Christ . . . ," proclaimed the priest in his broad American accent as he held up the Eucharist for her to receive. *Chicago,* Giuliana guessed.

"Amen," she whispered and gratefully accepted the unleavened wafer on her outstretched tongue.

Crossing herself, she turned and found an empty pew in which to thank God for his blessings and for his forbearance in her weaknesses. She knelt, eyes closed to better see Christ, hands folded as the nuns had taught her so long ago, heart open to inspiration to be a better Catholic. She wished she could stay there forever, lulled by Gregorian chant and the padding of pilgrim feet.

Above her, gray stone ascended to form graceful arches,

the Gothic metaphor for hands joined in prayer.

After an appropriate pause she rose and walked north across the centuries-old mosaic-tiled floor. Her heels clicked crisply, but the sound was lost to all but the shifting chalk of the saints' bones beneath the floor and in the walls. Even sound lost itself in this place.

When she reached the statue of Saint Peter near the entrance to the sacred grotto, Giuliana touched his smoothly worn foot, genuflected and crossed herself. Mornings like this, on which she was about to participate in the Vatican's holy work, refreshed her spirit. She had prayed for the opportunity to develop her talents. And now she prayed to Saint Peter, asking him to deliver her gratitude to God's ear.

Stretching out before her, twin marble stairways descended into the *confessio*, the devotional area over Saint Peter's tomb, which lay directly below the highest point of the dome. Ninety-five sanctuary lamps, perpetually lit, flickered along the stairwells to light the way to grace near Peter's final resting place.

There could be no doubt that the bones were those of Saint Peter. It wasn't just the weight of archaeological and forensic evidence that made Giuliana certain, it was an act of faith, inspired by the faith of those who had gone before, the faith that, as much as genius and skill and years of labor, had fashioned this place.

Michelangelo had designed this largest of all cathedrals so that its highest point, the dome that rose above so much of Rome, perched four hundred feet directly above Peter's remains, one foot for every year until 1951, when technology enabled man to positively identify Peter's bones. Giuliana basked in the cascading fall of light and felt herself fully restored. The spirit of Peter touched her with the light, as if acknowledging that he had successfully completed his errand. It was amazing how good life could be when one surrendered to the blessings of a faithful life.

This morning Giuliana was to have met with Special Pontifical Adviser Adeodato Cardinal Cosa regarding a matter of utmost concern to him. Therefore, she had wanted to be at the pinnacle of her physical and mental powers.

She ran an extra two kilometers above and beyond her

usual five along the River Tiber, crossing the Ponte Palatino into Rome proper, around the Circus Massimo, the Palatine, and back across the Tiber by way of the Ponte Angelo.

At thirty-eight, Giuliana was just beginning to feel the effects of running on her knees. Her legs were perfectly proportioned, not muscular like those of some runners. She was careful to avoid that. But her knees tired more easily now.

To most observers, Giuliana was simply an attractive Italian *signorina* with luxuriant hair, neat proportions, the grace of a royal, and an earthly gaze that seemed ready to sparkle into delighted laughter at the slightest prompting. Despite her apparent beauty, however, she felt awkward within. Even clumsy at times. Why, she did not understand. Perhaps her childhood experience had left her with some residual strangeness, a sense of unreality. But she was as aware of her own awkwardness as she was of her need to overcome it.

And now Cosa had thrown her off balance again, as he seemed to take a perverse pleasure in doing. The reason for postponing their meeting until the afternoon, as Giuliana had finally managed to wring out of the obsequious aide, had something to do with the availability of Monsignor Kleiman.

Monsignor Kleiman was the guardian of the Vatican reliquaries, the keeper of the bones of saints and presumed saints, an antiquity among the antiquities. What could the need for his presence at a meeting that Cosa had deemed "of greatest importance" possibly mean?

Puzzling over this, Giuliana had essentially squandered the greater part of the day. Now, as the midday siesta ended and the rest of Rome resumed its daily activities, she returned to the basilica to bask in the light for a moment, then crossed herself once more and continued out of the nave en route to Cardinal Cosa's office.

Andrew forced himself to dictate notes, each word a reproach: "Time of death"—he looked at the wall clock—"three thirty-two A.M. . . . ."

He dutifully recorded the volume of blood drawn from his own vein, the clear gelatinous texture of his purified DNA, Niko's acceptance of the injection, the drift into sleep, then the seizure and expiration. His voice tightened as memories of Niko played across his mind.

He carefully, respectfully bagged Niko's small body and rolled it toward the refrigerator as Lucy watched stoically. Andrew heard a small, plaintive cry and turned to comfort her. But the cry hadn't come from Lucy. She was silent, focusing wide-eyed on the bag.

Andrew pulled on the wide zipper even as the bag began to move. The zipper jammed, and he struggled with it, finally getting it open all the way. First two overlong furry arms emerged, the almost-human hands grasping at Andrew's, then Niko in his entirety clambered out of the bag and bounded to the floor, mouthing sounds as if trying to speak.

Too shocked to react, Andrew simply stared. Lucy leaped and shrieked and gesticulated, then as suddenly quieted, studying her mate.

Niko walked. Not lumbered or toddled, but *walked* on two feet to Andrew's desk. He "spoke" in an entirely new pattern of intonations and rhythms. Andrew imagined words.

"Niko?" He found his voice.

"Hm?" Niko answered without looking around. He found half a bagel thick with peanut butter amid the clutter on Andrew's desk, tested it with his index finger, then bit into it and began to chew.

Andrew's shocked expression melted first into a dull suspicion, then into the openness of discovery.

Niko strode over to the coffeemaker, puzzled for a moment over how to reach it from chimp height, then moved the desk chair to the counter, clambered up, and poured himself a cup of coffee, which he placed fastidiously on the desk. He then moved Andrew's chair back over to the desk, sat down, and sipped distractedly.

Lucy shrieked her surprise, but Niko didn't seem to notice. Smacking his lips, he studied the double helix on the desk. He pulled a red ball off the model and replaced it with a blue one to complete a chromosome—a refinement that had occurred to Andrew just moments before he had stopped work on it to give Niko the injection. Niko set the model down, studied it from multiple perspectives, and showed his teeth.

After another sip of the steaming coffee, he settled, chin

on hand, and gazed out the window into the night. His eyes soon glazed over and he became the image of thought.

Lucy watched closely, calm now, intensely curious.

Andrew stroked Niko's head. He was rewarded with a pleasant, distracted sigh.

Seeing Niko this way, mimicking his own gestures and behaviors, Andrew had a sense of being in two places at once, as if he were looking into a mirror and seeing an ancient parallel reflection of himself.

"You exist!" he whispered. "It works!"

Niko heaved another sigh. It took Andrew's listening heart and lifted it to a new place.

"We did it!"

He leaped up and down, danced around the lab tables, rattled the bars of Lucy's cell, ran into the next room and back to the window. He shouted and sang, a high-pitched wail. He had accomplished what he had come to believe couldn't be done.

After several minutes of frenzy, he settled—chest heaving, heart racing—into the chair near Niko, who remained focused on his distant mystery.

Moonlight shone in silvered patterns. Distant chimes rang 4:00 A.M. from the village tower and stopped. Waves from Japan thundered on Black's Beach below, and Andrew turned deeper into the spell of his discovery.

The last time he had felt this way was when he first saw a cell subdivide. He felt as if he'd seen God, as if he could invent a religion.

"We've crossed the Rubicon, Niko, my friend," he breathed. "... My ... self."

2

Città del Vaticano

TWO SWISS GUARDS OUTSIDE CARDINAL COSA'S OF-fice snapped to attention as Giuliana approached. Sergente Meola reached over and opened one of the seventeenth-century carved doors that had been coaxed from a tree predating the Renaissance. He did so blank-faced, as he had been taught. Giuliana enjoyed his formality. His passion for his military career was equal to her own dedication to the Church.

In Michelangelo's time, there was psychological and tactical significance to the bright, even flamboyant appearance of the orange, red, and blue-striped jumpsuits that the maestro had designed in the 1550s. Today, they delighted tourists in the same way British Guardsmen did outside the queen's palace in London. The menacing long-handled halberds with evil-looking ax blades and spears had been effective medieval weapons for unhorsing knights and dismembering them. Now, they like the uniforms, were more theater than security.

Despite appearances, the Swiss Guards were expert in counterterrorist tactics, crowd control, close-quarters combat, and the other counterinsurgency skills required of a player in world politics.

Since the attempt upon Pope John Paul's life by Ali Agça, many of the Guards had received extensive additional training, quietly, beyond the eyes of all but the most aggressive intelligence organizations. Such involvement in the realities of a terrorist-ridden century did not sit well with the Vatican's image of love and otherworldliness, after all.

Then again, the Vatican had survived the Borgias.

Tourists were unaware that Swiss Guard Special Ops soldiers existed. Romans heard rumors but had never seen a single clue to support the stories. And the superpowers were so preoccupied with each other and the annoying activities of restive Third World terrorists that they were largely unaware of the units' day-to-day whereabouts or operations.

If Special Ops team members were the royalty of the Swiss Guard, Jurgen Rindt was the undisputed king of Special Ops. The two sentries now on duty at Cardinal Cosa's office portal were not even in the same league with the shadowy Rindt.

No one knew who he was. It was possible that Rindt was not even his real name. Although no one had any specific evidence, most suspected that it was Rindt who had secretly defused the situation involving the Carmelite nuns at Auschwitz, who had mediated between Washington and Tehran for the final hostage releases, and who, some insisted, had single-handedly prevented World War III by the distinctively un-Christian-like termination of the international hoodlum known popularly as Ricardo.

Dr. Sabatini would recognize someone with the potential to be a Special Operations Officer, thought Sergente Meola. He stole a sideways glance at her. *Ringraziare Dio io essere italiano!* he thought. *Thank God I'm Italian!* Extraordinary she was, a *madonna*. Fine-boned, long-legged, with deep brown eyes and soaring cheekbones, the current of a Roman morning. She was dressed simply, in a pleated skirt and a trim blazer that would have looked extravagant on a woman less *femminile*, less *sensuale*. Her hair, a fiery chestnut, just missed being red. Her voluptuous figure missed nothing at all.

Sergente Meola made an attempt at gentility as she paused for him to pull on the massive door handle, but he knew he was grinning in spite of himself. The effect of her dark eyes sparkling into laughter at his awkwardness made him feel strong, chivalrous.

"Grazie, Sergente."

Her fragrance, a fragile balance of blossoming violets and provocative spices, hung in the air for a moment before it dissipated like hope. She reminded Meola of a Veneziana stepping out of Venice's exotic *nebbia* and into married men's wet dreams.

"Prègo, Dottore." He flashed a bright, uncharacteristic smile and reluctantly closed the door behind her. *"Prègo."*

Sunlight filtered through the boughs and danced on his sleep-blurred corneas. His feet were winged messengers, barely touching the carpet of needles on the trail that clung to the windswept cliff.

As the sun gained altitude, its rays found the Pacific's horizon and swept in toward him as he ran. He was right on his seven-minute, twenty-second pace, and he thrilled at staying lean and competitive and being in tune with the greater powers of nature. Unlike so many of his colleagues at the lab, he recognized that life on the planet went to those willing to work for it.

His wristwatch beeped politely. It irritated him, and he

quickly silenced it. He slowed to a walk to begin his cooldown.

"You're a sorry case, Shepard!" he huffed, then chastised himself for feeling so empty when surrounded by so much beauty.

A rustle sounded from a stand of gnarled pines to his left. A coyote poked its head out.

"S'just me, girl," he whispered.

He should have been more cautious. Coyotes were usually too smart to get close to man. This one must have been caught by the speeding sunlight, which just now reached where the two of them stood.

She lowered her head under a bough. When she looked back up, a furry body with a cottony tail swung heavily between her jaws. She looked directly at Andrew and, despite himself, he returned her glance. He knew better, but it was such moments of connection that sustained him in his other life at the lab and at home. The coyote seemed to understand his breach of etiquette, or at least she tolerated it in favor of her morning catch.

She woofed softly, then turned and vanished soundlessly into the canyon on the other side of the pines.

After watching her go, Andrew began walking again and drifted over to a boulder on the far point that afforded the best view in Torrey Pines State Park. From there he could see Dana Point sixty miles to the north and south to La Jolla Cove.

These ninety minutes before the city awakened were his. No one could reach him here. No one could claim even a corner of his soul. This was his time.

"Top o' the morning, Doctor Sabatini!" Monsignor Murphy greeted her in his lilting brogue. Waves of red hair began high on his brow, offering a sharp contrast to the green eyes behind wire-rimmed glasses. Giuliana always noticed Murphy's contrasts; he was an attraction in the subdued Mediterranean tones of Rome. "His Eminence is waiting. He was wanting a moment with you before Monsignor Kleiman arrives. Tea or coffee?"

"Tea, *grazie*."

The cardinal's door opened, and a large, ageless man, a

gleaming pectoral cross resting on his ample crimson chest, strode soundlessly in, filling the room with his presence. Small, sharp eyes in the fleshy face gave him the alert, charismatic gaze of a courtier, which first swept a room, then focused like the gaze of a fox on the smallest opportunity. Giuliana could tell by his assured movement that Cosa was engaged in some new crusade. With him, even routine tasks assumed significance. Perhaps this afternoon's meeting would give her a clue.

Refreshed and confident, Cosa moved his great weight easily. One could sense that he had long ago gotten over being shocked by human weakness. In fact, Giuliana secretly wondered if he wasn't occasionally fascinated by corruption. Perhaps the burdens of his office had slowed the flow of God-given goodness in this man.

"Ah! Giuliana, dear! Welcome, child, welcome!"

Cosa generally refrained from extending his ring hand for men to kiss, to spare them the humiliation of having to genuflect. Women, he thought, enjoyed the custom, and he allowed it.

Giuliana stiffened. She secretly loathed the custom but could not let Cosa know it. A few drops of tea spilled over the rim of her cup. Cosa noticed as he extended his ring. To spare herself further embarrassment, Giuliana executed the briefest curtsy, her runner's knee not quite touching the floor, and kissed the cardinal's ring.

"Sit, my dear."

Cosa gestured to a hand-carved chair from the seventeenth-century reign of Pope Innocent XI. His voice never rose above a deep-chested whisper, sonorous enough to fill a room. Was there a bit more smugness than usual in his tone? There was none in his expression. Wary, Giuliana sat.

Adeodato Cardinal Cosa, Chief Pontifical Adviser to His Holiness Pope Luke John I, the 302nd successor to Peter, and Special Liaison to the Roman Curia, was the gravitational force that held the satellites of the Catholic galaxy to their orbits around the pope. These "assets" of the Church strained more or less constantly at their leashes. They had been brought into its sphere of influence through centuries of sacrifice, proselytizing, and discipline, and still they threatened to spin out of line and destroy the fragile coalition of forces known as Holy Mother Church.

It was Cosa's personal mission, he believed, to hold that universe of believers together. In the long and at times turbulent years since he had received the crimson vestments of cardinal, it had been Cosa's capable hand on the helm that had saved the barque of Saint Peter more than once from foundering in confused seas. It was he, as the power behind the throne, who guided the ship that was the Church along its steady course toward a new world of cooperative ecumenism. Popes might come and go, but Adeodato Cardinal Cosa endured.

"I want to thank you for the way you clarified our relationship with the Pontifical Academy of Sciences," he told Giuliana as he seated himself in an equally ornate chair, leaning toward her confidentially. "His Holiness is pleased with your unique contribution to the difficult task of helping him bring the Church into the future. As our liaison with the sources of scientific knowledge in the lay world, your contribution has been invaluable."

"*Grazie*, Your Eminence," Giuliana replied. She wanted to tell him she was only doing her job, but she had learned with Cosa that it was sometimes better to say too little than too much.

"God bless you, child," he said before she could say anything further, and he raised his jeweled right hand to give her his blessing.

Nonplussed, Giuliana reflexively crossed herself. What *was* he up to?

The door opened and Monsignor Murphy entered with a coffee service. "Monsignor Kleiman has arrived, Your Eminence."

"Thank you, Kevin. You may show him in."

"Certainly, Your Eminence." The monsignor ducked noiselessly back out the door, closing it behind him.

The juxtaposition of Kleiman, keeper of antiquities, with Cosa's mention of the Academy of Sciences still puzzling her, Giuliana opened her notes.

Above and to the left a campfire beside the hang-gliders' shed collapsed with a sigh, and a thousand embers floated into the ebbing darkness. Three young men laughed easily in its warmth, no doubt sharing tales of other cliffs on other mornings. They were free spirits perched four hundred feet atop the sheer cliff, waiting for the land breeze that would fill in shortly after dawn. They would capture the wind and ascend to a thousand feet over the sleepy Southern California coastline before most residents had risen to their first cup of coffee.

Just beyond the glider port stood the monumental Salk Institute, with its countless medical mysteries. Andrew imagined the building as sculpture, a unique interpretation of Auguste Rodin. Beyond it he could see million-dollar homes, the Scripps Institution and the oceanographic pier to the south. The research ship *Melville* rode the tide lazily at the end of the new pier, awaiting its crew of marine biologists, geologists, and graduate students for its upcoming voyage to Christmas Island to study El Niño.

Andrew thought of Juan Cabrillo and his 1542 voyage along the California coast. Was it only the headiness of the pristine morning, a residual runner's high, that gave him the conceit to consider himself as much an explorer as Cabrillo? He could relate to blazing new trails as he explored the frontier of the next century: the human gene. He was as determined to unlock the secrets of the human genetic landscape as Cabrillo had been to "civilize" California. Perhaps his own work could someday have as much impact on human history as Cabrillo's.

Obsessed with the idea, Andrew was determined to use all of his talents, intellect, and imagination to enrich mankind's psychological potential. He wanted to unlock the secret that would enable every man, woman, and child to tap into their unused mental power.

The superstitions and fears of his ancestors were alive and well, however, in the age of science and technology. The human mind was fast becoming the last bastion of personal privacy. Any hint of tampering with the final taboo was quickly met with strident calls for more governmental regulation of science.

BioGenera, Incorporated, was not alone in fearing encroachments upon its business by fundamental religious groups, the media, and government regulators. More than one hundred biotechnology research and development laboratories had evolved since the early 1970s, when the scientific community had developed the tools and the understanding to advance science faster than humanity's ability to absorb its benefits. The battle for control of America's newest defining industry had been under way before Andrew realized that he was on the front lines.

And so he gazed out to the horizon, a sharp border between where he was and where he could be. There were people and places and processes in motion over there in the distance, in the outposts of his imagination. He was missing it all. He hadn't learned to cut stone, bend wood, or navigate by the stars. He didn't know how to write a sonnet or inspire a song in the heart of a woman. Even now as he sat waiting for his pulse to settle and bring his body back into equilibrium, he longed for what wasn't here. He wanted to break the bone and suck out the life-giving marrow.

It wasn't adolescent dreaming. He had outgrown that long ago. No, it was more elemental. He had lived in anticipation of the beginning of his life, and only now, at age forty-five, was the realization dawning upon him that life was half over.

A part of Giuliana, the poor girl who had grown up on the hillsides of the Val d'Elsina, still believed there was such a thing as supreme goodness. The rest of her, the educated adult struggling to reconcile her religious faith with the realities of everyday life, sometimes had her doubts.

Her parents, Giovanni and Angelina, had wrested a hard living from their olive groves by day and celebrated their little girl as a princess by night. Giuliana was an only child, a rarity in the fecund Italian countryside, born after a difficult labor to a mother who had miscarried more than once. The village doctor had been stern with Angelina. Caressing Giuliana's small newborn head with one hand, he shook the fingers of the other at her mother: "After this one, no more!"

Giuliana was precious. She was all they had.

But something terrible had happened to her on one anvil-heavy summer afternoon in the Val d'Elsina. Giuliana had died.

Yet Giuliana was alive, grown to maturity decades later—urbane, educated, sophisticated, beautiful. Returning to visit her parents in the countryside, she found wonder in their eyes. How had this remarkable stranger grown out of their little girl, their little girl who had died?

None of them could speak of it among themselves. Giuliana never spoke to anyone else about what had happened, not her girlfriends in school, not her teachers or *professores*, not the several men who had passed through her life. How could she tell her unbearable secret to anyone? She carried her burden alone and grew strong under its weight.

Where as a child she had lived in a universe of infinite possibilities, she now existed within a circle drawn tightly around herself, ever cautious, ever controlled.

The princess was dead. Giuliana was alive.

Since then, learning had provided little victories that sustained her. Yet she deprived herself of many of the normal experiences that inform the adult personality about itself. She was almost totally unaware of her beauty, for example. She mistook the lingering gazes of men, priests included, as male aggression, the male instinct to possess. It never occurred to her that she inspired simple pleasure in them.

A by-product of her purity of spirit was a stunning résumé of advanced credentials. She had degrees in history and medicine by age twenty-two. By twenty-four, her M.B.A. By thirty-one, her Ph.D. Yet, despite all the career opportunities available to this overachiever, Giuliana was content to serve the only institution that meant as much to her as her dedication to her parents: the Roman Catholic Church.

The Church responded by rewarding her for her insights. It needed her. Whereas medieval convents had flourished with women of intellect, the Church had done little to foster the minds of its women in recent times. Once again Giuliana was a rarity.

She need look no further than Monsignor Kleiman for an example of the traditional attitude of the celibate male toward women. The old dinosaur, member of the Pontifical Academy of Sciences, archaeologist and specialist in forensic pathology, dry as the bones he labored over, thought little of Giuliana's presence here in the stratosphere of the Vatican's power elite. The rasping smoker's cough with which he greeted her evidenced his disapproval. Giuliana had always wondered how a pathologist, knowing what he would know about the long-term effects of nicotine, could possibly be a smoker.

Well, dinosaurs eventually went extinct.

Monsignor Murphy, by contrast, admired Giuliana greatly, though if pressed he'd have to admit it wasn't only for her intellect. She gave form to his fantasies. He tried, yet failed, to keep his eyes from drinking in the sight of her rounded breasts and honeyed complexion in Rome's filtered late-afternoon light. It occurred to him that indulging his imagination might be more than his weakening resolve could withstand.

Cardinal Cosa gazed in turn on each of the three sitting across from him. If he knew the other men's thoughts, it was because he knew their weaknesses. Kleiman made no more attempt to hide his disdain for Giuliana than Murphy did his admiration. As for Giuliana . . . perhaps the gravest disadvantage to a man who lived his entire life among men, Cosa thought, was that he never truly understood the hearts of women.

"Very well, then, let's get to it, shall we?" he began, clearing his throat. "His Holiness is expecting a brief on the progress of genetic science and Mother Church's role in guiding that progress before he departs for his African tour. Contrary to the *cautela*—some are calling it resistance— expressed in the Church's latest encyclical regarding gene therapy, genetic engineering, and particularly recombinant DNA, I believe we are obligated to keep pace with science."

"To control it, Your Eminence?" asked Kleiman in his most innocuous tone, though his cynicism was too deeply rooted to be disguised.

Cosa didn't blink. "On the contrary. To participate as a full partner in responsible development of this controversial science."

The cardinal's preamble and response to Kleiman reinforced his leadership. Giuliana noticed its reassuring effect on her. She still responded to authority, although that was her secret and she would never tell another soul.

"While I am aware that breakthroughs are occurring almost daily all over the industrialized world, it is essential that we keep abreast of every new development." Cosa allowed his fox's eyes to linger on each of them. "What do you have for me?"

"*Scusi*, Your Eminence, before we begin . . ." interjected Giuliana, gathering her thoughts even as she spoke them. "So much of genetic research is initiated in the attempt to prevent, if not eliminate, birth defects. There are now also any number of genetic defects that can be corrected by surgery in utero. What answer does the Church have for the faithful, particularly in America, where so much of this surgery is performed, who have an opportunity to treat a genetically damaged fetus?"

She wasn't prepared for an argument, but Cosa had touched upon a sensitive topic.

"Personally, I can understand their confusion," Cosa replied evenly. "They see reform moving their way and assume the Vatican will move with the developed nations. And we are not insensitive to the sufferings of parents whose child has such a defect. Nevertheless, such matters are the will of God. Those who would say otherwise are, simply, wrong."

"What will happen to them?"

"They can follow the guidelines drawn by the Church, or, if they believe they know the will of Christ better than His Holiness, they can leave." Complacently, the cardinal emptied his coffee cup.

"Leave?"

"Yes, *Dottore*." Delicately for such a large man, Cosa poured himself another cup. "They will most assuredly be considered excommunicate."

"That is your solution, Eminence?" Giuliana fought to keep her voice from rising. "That is your answer to a sincere difference of opinion in the faith?"

"My 'solution'?" the cardinal asked tolerantly. "My child, we are in a contest for souls. Perception is everything. Our flock wants to know that we know the true Word, that we have power greater than the mosque or the temple. Someone must stand up for the Church, for truth! It is my . . . our . . . calling to control the influences on truth. Surely you see that."

Giuliana met the cardinal's gaze, determined not to be overpowered by him. She thought she detected a minute twitch that vanished as soon as it arrived on his skin. Her trained eye was skilled at discerning the slightest constriction of the mouth or jaw or, most telling of all, the inferior oblique strand of muscle beneath the eye. Such minor movement could betray the meanness of a soul.

Finally she looked away and allowed Cosa the respect he expected. She did not like what she had seen.

The analytical side of Andrew's brain alerted him when it registered that his heart rate was back down to seventy-two beats per minute. He stood, noticing the ocean responding to the caress of the rising sun. Massive thermals generating over the inland deserts were stirring the breeze.

A faint buzz sounded from his waist. He reached irritably for the pager and tried to read it, but couldn't hold it far enough away to bring it into focus.

"Dammit."

His ice-blue eyes weren't getting any sharper. In addition to experiencing creeping farsightedness, they were becoming increasingly light-sensitive. He would have to put on his sunglasses before long, just when the morning was coming into full color.

Setting the pager down on a rock, he stepped back to try and read the small LCD display. As he backed up, a tree root caught his heel and he fell unceremoniously on his backside.

"Jesus Chr—!"

It was still too dark.

Finally, frustrated by the damn LCD screen and his failing eyesight, Andrew headed home.

3

THE HABIT OF RISING WITH THE SUN, FORMED DURing Andrew and Margaret's honeymoon on Maui, had outlived their marriage. So did his memory of the way she used to affect him: her readiness to explore their imaginations, her swaying laughter when she forgot herself, her eyeshine as she bent down to prod a fire.

They'd been a handsome couple when they started dating

in college—hardly the jock and the homecoming queen, but they seemed to "fit," to belong together.

"You look more like a cowboy than an egghead!" was one of the first things she'd said to him, straightening his shirt collar proprietarily, brushing the unruly curls back from his brow. Andrew hadn't thought about it, taking his broad-shouldered height and easy way of moving for granted. Most women wrinkled their noses at his unkempt look—his clothes looked slept in because they frequently were—and never gave him a second glance. Margaret's cool eyes had appraised him from across the room and lingered for a second look.

Her own looks were unconventional—fresh and natural, athletic rather than pretty, as much at home on a cross-country hike as at a faculty tea. She was all cool colors, blue eyes and fair hair. Cool emotions, too. She seemed to think before she spoke, weighing the outcome of her words, keeping herself to herself. It was perfect for her job, but it had taken its toll on their marriage even before the crisis that had shattered it.

She had the TV on in the kitchen and the paper open on the table in front of her, getting her daily saturation in the day's news before she left for work. She didn't look up from the *Tribune* when Andrew entered and poured himself a cup of coffee. There'd been a time when she would have fussed over him after he pulled an all-nighter and then went running, lecturing him about how he should get more sleep, eat a decent breakfast instead of subsisting on endorphins and caffeine. Back then Andrew would have grinned sheepishly and said, "Yes, Mother!" and Margaret would have laughed her dry laugh.

He hadn't heard her laugh in a very long time.

Golden light warmed her cool features as she sat by the window facing the neglected garden, the late-season roses. Hummingbirds rippled the light just outside the windows as they thronged the blossoms, lured by memories of passion blooming in this house.

The angle of Margaret's downturned face made her nose seem wider than it was, and her eyebrows arched like wings. Her hand, weighted by a waterproof black UDT watch, lay pressed flat on the page. Dressed for work in khakis, starched blouse, sensible shoes, her badge hanging from her breast pocket, she filled the kitchen with an official presence. A blunt-nosed .38 resting on the counter in its shoulder holster with her keys and cuffs completed the effect.

My wife the police officer! Andrew thought wryly. He noticed that her job's paraphernalia no longer irritated him as it had in the dark year leading up to their divorce. Then her job had seemed an affront—she was all action, he was all talk, all brain, the intellectual hiding in his lab while she kept the streets safe for the rest of humanity. Thank God he'd grown past that.

So this is my life. I sleep on a hide-a-bed, a guest in my own home, living with my ex-wife. Christ, I can't even get a divorce right!

At least he had done the hard thing and ended a failed marriage. Yet here he was: living with Margaret until the beach house he'd bought was made habitable. When the electrician scraped away some old paint to check a wiring conduit, exquisite hardwood joinery surfaced for the first time in half a century. Quite by accident, Andrew had acquired a priceless Charles and Henry Greene Craftsman bungalow. Built in the teens, it had a stone foundation, oversized beams, and wood no longer available anywhere at any price. Before he knew it, architectural students, Greene and Greene devotees, and historical society experts were materializing out of nowhere, poring over the renovation. He could have sold tickets.

The restorer in Pasadena wasn't yet finished with the lighting fixtures. Dusty plastic sheeting still flapped where the windows should be. And the contractors wouldn't take their equipment away from the front yard for at least six weeks more. It was a circus. Andrew couldn't wait for it to be over. Meanwhile, he had nowhere to live.

Margaret said it was ridiculous for him to spend the extra money on an apartment, and she offered him the spare room for as long as he needed it. She seemed sincere, and he couldn't afford the distraction of camping out in a distant apartment while trying to keep his experiments on track. So he accepted. Despite their mutual concerns about aggravating their grief over the demise of their marriage, they settled into amicability with only occasional moments of friction.

How could life get so complicated? And what difference did any of it make with Anna gone?

The day before, she had been uncontainable. She had every minute of her sixth birthday planned: a waffle breakfast with strawberries and whipped cream, Pirates of the Caribbean at Disneyland with her three girlfriends ("Maybe we'll actually meet the Little Mermaid!"), then cake and presents back at home. Andrew had gone in to wake her at dawn with the kitten he'd picked out for her. She lay still as sculpted marble, not even a whisper of breath.

Deep in the underside of Anna's brain, an unforeseen congenital tangle in a branching artery, already weakened during her rapid growth over the summer, had shuddered and ballooned. A mortal rending collapsed at a critical turn and blocked the supply of oxygenated blood to the brain.

It happened so abruptly that her vital functions halted before she awoke. She felt no pain, saw only sudden light in her dream, grew weightless, and soared into the starless night.

The pathology report listed cause of death as a "berry aneurysm." Andrew and Margaret had read it together with the objectivity of their separate professions, trying to fathom what these cold words had to do with the absence of their little girl. Dead in the night. No cause was sufficient, no explanation adequate. No relief from the nightmares.

Margaret's precinct captain had recommended therapy and she'd gone; Andrew had buried himself in his work. When they emerged from their separate worlds, they no longer recognized each other.

They were too friendly to be lovers, too different to be good friends. Courtesy bound them. They shared a common history that had begun while at university, when a lifetime seemed infinite. Then Anna died and they became refugees.

In the Apostolic Palace, the conversation had strayed far afield. Cardinal Cosa spoke ad rem, returning to the matter at hand.

"I am not ignorant of the appeal of recombinant DNA. Although narrow minds might consider it Satan's ingenuity, I see instead God's grace . . . properly managed, of course."

He paused to let his statement penetrate. His words had a life of their own, insinuating themselves through subtle cracks in logic, tracing fragile connections through the faintest neural firings, intensifying as they got close to new understanding. A brilliant scholar, Cosa didn't expect answers. What he did expect was clear thinking.

"The Pontifical Commission for Reliquiae has received a request for tissue samples," he announced with a nod toward Monsignor Kleiman, who acknowledged the statement with a nod of his own.

"These are not formal requests," Kleiman clarified. "Only preliminary queries about Vatican reliquiae and policy regarding their disposition."

He ended his statement with a dry cough. Cosa's small eyes focused on Giuliana.

"Tell me, Dr. Sabatini, what you suppose this might signify?"

"I would speculate that whoever made this query is getting close to the breakthrough we anticipate," Giuliana voiced her thoughts.

Monsignor Murphy handed the cardinal a note from the small leather portfolio he held open on his lap. Cosa retrieved a pair of half-glasses from his desk and slipped them onto the end of his nose. "The request is from a facility in America. BioGenera."

"Ah, *si*, in Southern California," Giuliana confirmed. "I have been expecting news from the San Diego area. The best work is being done there."

Cosa removed the glasses, raised his eyebrows, and looked expectantly at her.

"Particularly at BioGenera by the geneticist Dr. Andrew Shepard. He is doing impressive work," Giuliana finished somewhat nervously. She was certain that Kleiman would not appreciate her dominating the conversation. Further, Cosa was a relentless and ungenerous interrogator whose mind plotted constantly. He lived for unending calculation, for tactical operations as complex as the alignments at Anzio, and he delighted in setting his subordinates against each other.

"Work of what kind, *Dottore*?" he asked her.

"We don't know for certain, Your Eminence. Like so

many brilliant men, Dr. Shepard prefers to labor in obscurity and let his work speak for him when it is ready. He is one of the key facilitators of the Epidermal Growth Factor (EGF), which . . ."

Cosa raised his hand to stop her. Too much information could cloud his incisive mind.

". . . 'skin' growth hormone, Your Eminence," Giuliana persisted. She considered this particular bit of information worth the risk. "This is to the treatment of severe burns what Salk's vaccine was to polio, a great medical advance. All the world is watching to see what Dr. Shepard will discover next."

Cosa accepted this. "Do we know where his interests may be taking him? What do his articles tell us? More gene therapy? Recombinant DNA?"

"I do not know, Your Eminence. He publishes little, the last article more than two years ago."

"Well, then, what does his request for the Church's holy relics tell you?" Monsignor Kleiman interjected. This was his bailiwick, after all.

Giuliana could only imagine what a scientist of Dr. Andrew Shepard's proven creativity could have in mind for ancient bones.

"Perhaps an exemplar, an archetype with which to gauge genetic mutation over a known period of time?" she suggested to Kleiman.

The cardinal nodded thoughtfully. "Why a relic from the Church? Why not from a museum?"

"In the short history of genetic research, science has discovered that DNA is fragile, easily damaged by chemical treatments and preservatives, Your Eminence. Most specimens in museums have been chemically preserved with no understanding of their potential value as sources of genetic material. Christian relics, on the other hand, have been preserved in their original condition."

"As they should be!" Kleiman added unnecessarily. Cosa gestured to silence him.

"So the Church holds a precious natural resource," the cardinal summarized.

"*Si.*" Giuliana appreciated his succinct analysis. "I expected such a request, Your Eminence, although I do not know the specific objective or scientific rationale. Biotechnology growth is racing.''

''Do you infer then that Dr. Shepard is researching a commercial use for relics?'' asked Cosa.

''No, Eminence. I only meant that biotechnology is becoming a major industry. Sources of insight are the raw materials of this new science. The Vatican may be a rich source for such raw materials.''

Kleiman winced at the choice of words.

''Go on,'' the cardinal prompted.

''Mike Gindman's assistant called,'' Margaret said without looking up. ''Better call back. She said he's upset about something.''

Where was the future he'd envisioned for himself? Andrew wondered. In his entire life he had done nothing that really frightened him. He hadn't tested himself, except in the forge of science. Even Anna's death, while it destroyed his faith in any but an arbitrary God, distant and indifferent, had been something he'd locked away inside himself, unexaminable, hence unexamined. In the laboratory of theorems he had succeeded beyond all expectations, including his own. As his private life withered, he farmed his mind and harvested enough discoveries to make it seem worthwhile. He had become quite accomplished at substituting work for life.

Despite the gaping void in his love life, he'd never permitted himself to fantasize about other women when he was married to Margaret. Even now, the idea of getting back into the flow of life, meeting women, going through the motions of a social life, seemed like too much trouble to be worthwhile. But the need was always there, like the hum of wind outside trying to find its way in through cracks in the walls. He ignored it, willfully.

Something on the small tabletop TV screen caught his attention.

''Mind if I listen to this?'' he asked, reaching past Margaret to turn up the volume.

''*Sources at the Pentagon report that General Genetic of California will supply Epidermal Growth Factor therapy to*

U.S. Armed Forces. EGF is a genetically engineered therapy for treating combat traumas and victims of severe skin damage.

"General Genetic had been competing with another California company, BioGenera, the inventor of the process, for the first contract of its kind.

"BioGenera first identified Epidermal Growth Factor in human cells and developed the process to manufacture the factor in volume.

"Apparently, General Genetic's Washington connections paid off..."

"Christ," Andrew groaned. "Oh, Christ!"

Now he knew why Mike Gindman was so upset.

He dialed the office number quickly and leaned against the counter, shoulders hunched, braced for trouble.

"Delphine? I just caught the bad news on CNN."

"Dr. Shepard!" Her assured tone sounded through the receiver. "Mr. Gindman has called a meeting for eight-thirty. Can I tell him you'll be here?"

"Sure. I'll be there in twenty-five minutes. How bad is it?"

"Bad. He's watching news on the satellite. Everyone is predicting we can't survive. It's so unfair, after all your brilliant work!"

"And everyone else's," Andrew said generously. He considered mentioning last night, then hesitated. No one knew yet about his memory resurrection (MR) experiment. Not even Will Austin realized how far he'd taken his theory.

"Sorry, Doctor, I have to go alert the others," Delphine said abruptly, and the line clicked dead.

"Gindman's furious," Andrew said at Margaret's inquiring look. He took a swallow of cooling coffee. It tasted flat; he poured it in the sink.

"What about royalties on the patent?" she said. "Won't that be enough to satisfy him?"

"Small change compared to the profits from a Pentagon contract. Gindman's notoriously impatient. What if he sells BioGenera and moves on to something he can win at? It couldn't be a worse time for my research."

"It'll work out," Margaret said. It was touching how she tried to encourage him even now. "If BioGenera folds, somebody will recognize the value of your work.''

"Any disruption now could set me back years," Andrew muttered, refusing to be encouraged.

He went upstairs to shower. He needed the curative, mind-clearing indulgence. Theoretical conundrums melted into tangible solutions under hot running water.

The sun hadn't yet found his window; his bathroom was still as cool and gray as his brain matter. He turned on the hot water, and steam billowed as he stripped off his sweats. Stepping into the needle stream, he let the hot jets open up the veins in his head. The hot water on his work-sore body reminded him of the pain after running, after winning, like the old days. He had lettered at Harvard in the distance events. He'd kept in shape, working out every morning in spite of his schedule.

While toweling dry he caught his reflection in the mirror. He studied his image for the damaging effects of forty-five years. Crow's-feet and weathered skin told the years, many of them under Southern California's sun on salty swells. Eighteen years as Margaret's husband were there in the trusting eyes, an expression acquired in the good times. Two years of second-guessing himself and agonizing grief since Anna died had drained his face of its vigorous color. Deepening furrows on his broad forehead and a narrowness about the eyes were the armor of his divorce war combat. He wondered if they were permanent features like scars, or if they would heal. It had been seven months and the image in the mirror still reminded him of a reluctant witness caught in a lie.

Finally, a powerful jaw, aggressive chin, forearms wound spring-tight and efficient, and purposeful legs spoke of the evolving Dr. Andrew Shepard, biochemist, pioneer scout on the biotechnical frontier. The bulge in the midsection annoyed him; he couldn't seem to work it off no matter how much he ran. But overall he saw a body lean from too many missed meals and too much coffee, hardened by the sacrifices of intense periods of discovery. Not bad, considering the way most of his contemporaries had gone to seed. Running would help. But work was more important now.

Was he fit enough for the crucible of this morning's news? Could he cope with the collapse of the project upon which he had built his hopes for a second life?

The memory of last night dawned as he set the razor to his jaw, narrowing his farsighted eyes to see what he was doing. Then elation crackled through him like lightning. The procedure worked!

Giuliana read from her notes. "Sales of biotechnology products were $5.8 billion last year, an eighteen percent increase over an eighteen-month period. In America, Japan, and Europe, biotech stocks have been driven to record levels by investors eager for returns that are by any measure phenomenal."

Beside her, Monsignor Murphy consulted his own notes and silently confirmed her statement. One of his duties as the cardinal's secretary was to monitor wire service reports for just such economic information.

"The Thousand Oaks Company in America saw its profits soar twenty-four hundred percent on the strength of two products—EPO, an anti-anemia drug, and G-CSF, the cancer-fighting medication . . ."

Giuliana detected a glimmer of pride in Cosa's expression as he listened. She thought there might even be the beginning of a smile lifting one corner of his mouth.

"Our projections are for $50 billion in biotechnology business in the U.S. alone by the end of this decade," she concluded.

"*Grazie*, my dear. Most impressive," Cosa complimented her.

Giuliana knew she was being patronized, but she disregarded Cosa's tone. "Your Eminence, evidence indicates we can further expect America to lose its domination of biotechnology after a brief but intense period of business development. In this way, America may suffer from shortsightedness, as it did in electronics and semiconductors . . ."

"Biotechnology research is obscenely expensive, Your Eminence," interjected Monsignor Kleiman, sensing that he was losing ground by remaining silent too long.

"A curious choice of words, *Monsignore*," Cosa observed drily. Monsignor Murphy suppressed a smile.

". . . and while American firms are the pioneers and present leaders, they are already selling valuable rights to Japanese investors in return for capital to fund the research," continued Giuliana, as if there had been no interruption. "This, combined with a tentative world economy, has resulted in a plateauing of biotechnology advances. History tells us we may expect a breakthrough at any time."

The cardinal's eyebrows lifted again.

"A major advance, in my opinion, Your Eminence," Monsignor Kleiman added.

"Where?" Cosa wanted to know. "Where can we expect this breakthrough?"

"It's impossible to say, Your Eminence," answered Giuliana, leaving Kleiman farther behind. "Scientists all over the world are cooperating to decipher the genetic script in the Human Genome Project. So far, the greatest surprise is how rapidly science is learning which genes perform what functions. Many experts believe that practical application is still years away. I am not convinced. When the breakthrough happens . . ."

"What kind of 'breakthrough'? Can you be specific?"

"I can only speculate."

"Speculate, then. I will not hold you to it."

Giuliana took no comfort in the cardinal's assurance. She knew he would remember her answer long after she had forgotten this conversation. "This is only a guess, Your Eminence, but if history is instructive, I think brilliant minds like Andrew Shepard's would be drawn first to the cure, then the prevention of disease. His Epidermal Growth Factor attests to the cure; preventions cannot be far behind and, in fact, are already coming."

"Then—?" Cosa prodded her.

"Then perfection of the species, Your Eminence. Evolution is a slow process. Biotechnology can accelerate and direct its course in ways we could not have imagined just five years ago."

"Can we trust any individual doctor or scientist to decide the future of human evolution?"

"That is not for me to say, Your Eminence," Giuliana demurred. "I merely point out the likelihood that this will be the third phase of biotechnology. It is human nature. Repairing a human defect is one thing, but once we can do so routinely, it will become more difficult to argue against adding genes that confer desired qualities. Who among us would define the boundary between repairing inherited defects and improving the species?''

No one responded. Giuliana had placed herself at risk again, broaching the one topic that no one in the hierarchy of the Church wished to have raised, the issue of biogenetics on the reproductive level.

Why is it, Giuliana could not help thinking, *that it is always the issues that affect women—reproductive rights—that are the chronic sticking point among these dry old men?*

The thought was disloyal to the Church that nurtured her; she banished it. Besides, she was not entirely sure that Cosa couldn't read her mind.

Margaret had picked up her revolver and was nearly out the door when Andrew came through the kitchen looking for his car keys. ''Listen, um, Andrew—?''

He turned. ''What?''

''I know I said you could stay until the beach house is ready . . .''

''There a problem?''

She glanced at the floor, at the roses through the window, back to him. ''I want to get on with my life.''

''I know. Me, too.''

''How much longer?''

''I can move into the lab,'' he offered. ''It should only be a couple more weeks.''

''No, no, that's all right.''

''Margaret, I'm sorry this is so awkward.''

''Me, too . . .'' she agreed, and closed the door behind her.

''It works,'' he said as her retreating footsteps faded into the garage and her car started down the drive.

The second stage of his interspecies test had succeeded. He'd wanted so much to tell her. He had transferred awareness, memories, his very *consciousness* from himself to Niko! He had proved that memory is eternal, as indestructible as pure energy. He had proved it could be transplanted, and he was now certain that his protocol would work with DNA from deceased cells.

He remembered the way Niko had tried to speak. A chill raced down his spine.

Where was Niko's consciousness now?

4 TRAFFIC ON TORREY PINES ROAD SURGED LIKE THE tide below. Andrew coaxed his aging Porsche through the gears to a familiar crawl and tried to turn off his mind, but it was useless. Forces were gathering.

The sky was cloudless to the horizon, cobalt and uplifting. Wind ruffled the ocean surface yet didn't raise a single whitecap as far as he could see. God was shuffling his feet. Andrew sighed and double-clutched into second.

To the west, between the view and himself, was the Scripps Institution of Oceanography, with its long, slender pier. The light changed. He passed behind a wizened Torrey pine. Then the sun appeared again and filled the spare Porsche interior with light.

How many cells in the sea and sky held secrets to be learned through a process like memory resurrection? After last night anything seemed possible, at least theoretically.

It occurred to him that all he knew, he knew in theory and little if anything in practice, in life as much as in work. He had a desire for love, yet little in the way of experience. Margaret had been content to play at the act of the flesh only insofar as he insisted. She never truly participated, only lent him her body, almost as a favor.

He tried every way he knew to please her, but her response remained unchanging. The only time she'd expressed the least bit of enthusiasm was when they were trying to conceive Anna. Afterward . . .

When he realized that Margaret was incapable of sharing herself with him or anyone, Andrew had given up trying to please her and surrendered to de facto celibacy. A part of him thought that he would someday plumb the depths of his sexual being, but as he slipped into his middle years it became increasingly difficult to believe.

His Catholic upbringing had brought him this far on childhood's residual faith, but his childhood religion balked and withered in the dark vacuum that followed Anna's death. Nowadays Andrew found bitter amusement in hearing the pope's latest encyclicals quoted on the evening news. The Church's insistence on its own infallibility was so far removed from what he understood as reality that it seemed almost comical.

Since his teens, pontifical pronouncements were no more worthy to him than Delphic utterances. Ironically, science had done more to convince him of the existence of God than everything the Dominican nuns had taught him.

"Morning, Dr. Shepard!" Gus, the calcifying ex-Iowan guard, greeted him in his whiskey voice as he turned in at the BioGenera security gate. Andrew waved and accelerated toward the BioGenera compound, which hugged the cliffs and crouched shyly behind evergreens, out of sight from the road.

Andrew had come into his own here in La Jolla years before biotech flourished. He had followed his intuition and excellent training to identify the foundation for growth factors, marvels produced by the human body in minute quantities. They were so important that even a trace amount could compel a cell to replicate itself within moments.

Andrew had pioneered this field alone in the early days when it was virtually unknown outside research laboratories and theoreticians' offices. The footpath he had blazed by trial and error was now dense with followers who saw opportunity. More than one hundred growth factors were now known.

The Roman afternoon was waning, casting long shadows across the floor of Cosa's office.

"Is there a fourth phase, *Dottore*?" he asked Giuliana after a small eternity.

"*Si*, Your Eminence. In my view, given that we humans are curious and romantic, we will naturally be tempted to recapture what has been lost to us."

The three men waited expectantly.

"The recapture of extinct species is an obvious target for such skills. Just as Rome re-created Greek temples and extinct traditions, today's musicologists reconstruct musical instruments of the Renaissance to their original specifications, and movie makers re-create the Jurassic, can other means of recapturing what has been lost be far behind?"

"Such as—?" Cosa prompted.

"I cannot say for certain, Your Eminence," Giuliana again demurred. She had notions, but was reluctant to share them just now. Why risk her standing with the cardinal?

"Oh, please, *Dottore*!" Cosa offered magnanimously. "Surely you can . . . speculate?"

"It would be strictly conjecture."

"A guess, of course. If I were Dr. Shepard, to what grand vision would I apply my genius?"

Giuliana faltered, spreading her hands in a particularly Roman gesture. "Perhaps to the unknown, the great mystery on the other side of consciousness . . ."

The cardinal leaned forward and listened intently.

". . . to explore the secrets locked in the human genome," Giuliana continued, "the genetic text on which is written the entire history of mankind. It might be like a *biblioteca*, a library in which the Almighty has registered with unerring fidelity the records of being."

"Do you mean . . . memory?" Cosa asked.

"*Si*, Your Eminence."

The verdant reception area welcomed Andrew in its cool embrace. He walked down the maze of subterranean laboratory suites and considered the facts:

First, there was pressure on the entire BioGenera staff from R&D to Marketing. So desperate was Mike Gindman for success that he was pushing current experiments dangerously. His recent policy requiring daily morning briefings by all departments had been cutting into Andrew's work time, risking the integrity of his experiments, and he'd said as much. Gindman backed down; Andrew won that one.

What could this morning's bad news possibly do to the admittedly fragile momentum of his autonomy? *It can't help*! he thought as he nodded good morning to a passing lab technician.

His current experiment was also in danger. It would live or die depending on Gindman's response to the news. All those extra hours in his laboratory, and now the breakthrough so significant that he was reluctant to talk about it with anyone!

He dreaded the inevitable chain of events that would follow: Marketing would push applications of his process before it was refined. Finance would counsel budgets and complain about what were sure to be high development costs. Legal would cower before the liability risks. Operations would block adequate resources to give his process a fair trial.

He couldn't blame them. He was the one pointing to miracles and dreams, while his employer fought for survival! Still, he knew he was onto something important. He had discovered an entirely new avenue of science. He had opened a door that he knew would soon reveal a greater reality. And he strongly suspected that he would soon see the face of time itself, whatever lay out there beyond the mists of memory, behind the curtain of death.

Pretty grandiose results from such a simple experiment. By means of a deceptively straightforward splicing of the gene from one species (*Homo sapiens*—Andrew Shepard) into the cells of another species (*Pan paniscus*—Niko the chimpanzee), he had transferred the consciousness of one into the other.

Had it really happened? Had he actually seen what he thought he saw? He had been working hard lately.

C'mon, Shepard. You're not Superman . . . or Frankenstein. You've mucked up everything else in your life. What makes you think you could transfer memory, consciousness?

But I saw it. Niko became me. Lucy saw it, too.

Oh, great. Try that on Gindman. Go on, Lucy. Tell the nice man what I did. Tell him how Niko just isn't himself anymore . . . He's me!

Right.

It works. I'm not sure how it works. But it works, dammit!

The exact mechanism of the memory exchange was still a mystery, but he would learn that soon. The critical point was that he had manipulated DNA, taken the basic building block of heredity, from one species and applied it to another living form. His consciousness lived in Niko's mind!

If that was possible, as he now knew it to be, why not restore a deceased consciousness to living form?

The reality of his success would be hard enough for the other scientists to comprehend, not to mention BioGenera's lay administrators.

There were an estimated 100,000 genes in the nucleus of each human cell, each composed of DNA. In those genes was the essence of the plant, the animal, the person, the instruction manual for life itself.

He would need to carefully, patiently bring Gindman and his board of directors up to date on the state of the science. That would be difficult, considering Gindman's restive personality.

He rehearsed the facts: The first success with bones was the extraction of some DNA text from a thighbone found in a seventeenth-century English Civil War cemetery. That was followed by a 750-year-old upper-arm bone from a medieval cemetery. Then a 5,400-year-old thighbone from a Judean cave.

Andrew and other scientists remained uncertain as to why this was possible. The best theory to date was that the DNA came from the osteocytes, specialized cells deep within the bone. Whatever the specifics of the mechanism, the FBI had for years used polymerase chain reaction DNA amplification to obtain DNA sequences from minute traces of blood at murder scenes—a hair, even a single spermatozoon. Forensic pathologists could determine whether there was DNA in the subject's tissue by testing minute samples of bone.

It was a short jump to the Human Genome Project, the international effort to map the millions of genetic strands in human DNA.

Andrew took a deep breath, for here was where he found himself at the crossroads of his career. How he said what he was about to say would determine his success or failure.

"I have discovered a reliable means of restoring 'life' to deceased cells . . ." he rehearsed, waiting, imagining the response of his audience. Gindman would grow restless, tell him to cut to the chase. The others would either voice their skepticism or simply laugh. Maybe, just maybe, they would listen and catch a glimpse of what he saw, scientific history and possibly the salvation of BioGenera.

If it worked so successfully, so reliably, so predictably on nonsentient organisms, and then equally well with sentient creatures, there was no reason to expect that it would not function identically in human beings!

"Memoria." Cosa savored the concept. "In our genes, eh? *Memoria genetica*?"

The thought seemed to require a moment of silence, almost of reverence. It was Monsignor Murphy, finally, who broke the silence.

"What Karl Jung called the collective unconscious. A theory, until now. Unless these geneticists can prove it . . ."

His voice trailed off. He seemed to realize he had spoken out of turn. It was Giuliana, with newfound confidence, who rescued him.

"The inexplicable riddle of life, memory," she suggested quietly. "All of the memories of the dead, which until now have been lost to the grave and to history."

"Nonsense!" Kleiman sneered. Once more Cosa gestured him to silence, his fox's eyes only for Giuliana.

"Is such a thing even thinkable, *Dottore*?"

"Probabile non, Your Eminence. However, you asked where humankind's scientific curiosity might lead it," Giuliana hedged. "Whatever the breakthrough, after the cure for AIDS or cancer, I think it will involve the mind. The essence of experience that we share with our forebears. I personally believe that, if it is possible at all, it is most likely to come from a laboratory working on associated DNA technology."

"Would you hazard a guess as to where we might be watching?"

"The technology was born in the UK, but the greatest progress is taking place in the United States."

Cosa leaned back in his chair, as if aware that his intensity might be too revealing of his intent. "America is a vast country," he suggested intimately, to her alone.

"Yes, it is," Giuliana concurred. She had restored the momentum of the meeting and was sure that the cardinal recognized it.

"Are there many laboratories we must watch?"

"Twenty-one, Your Eminence." Giuliana suppressed a smile. It was exhilarating, this game of wits with one of the world's most powerful men. He was testing her, putting up progressively higher hurdles for each one she overcame. Kleiman and Murphy had been left behind and could only watch. "But we may expect the major advance from one of only two or three: Cold Spring Harbor, Scripps, and BioGenera."

"Dr. Andrew Shepard at BioGenera, perhaps?"

"There is every possibility, Your Eminence."

"Very good, Dr. Sabatini," Cosa nodded his approval.

They had been at it for hours. Murphy had replenished her tea some time ago, but it had long since grown cold. She lifted the cup to her lips all the same, savoring the triumph.

Cosa turned to the others. "In the meantime, how would you advise His Holiness on the Church's position in these matters?"

Monsignor Kleiman saw an opportunity to reinsert himself into the debate at last. "The Church would be wise to support genetic research," he ventured, "including the Human Genome Project, Your Eminence. Comprehensive understanding of the miracles of the human being will be a blessing, of course, unless it falls into the wrong hands."

Or unless it is used to give women more control over their reproductive lives and the health of their children! Giuliana thought.

"That is why the Vatican's participation is critical . . ." Kleiman went on, interrupted by his smoker's cough. ". . . to protect the miracle, guide it according to God's wishes."

"And what would his wishes be, *Monsignore* Kleiman?"

Kleiman turned scarlet and coughed again.

"No answer is necessary, *Monsignore.* I understand what you intended. But there are many suffering and angry souls who would not understand. Remember, we live in contentious times. I counsel temperance in thought and words."

"Of course, Your Eminence," Kleiman rasped.

Andrew turned a corner that opened into an intersection of four main arteries of BioGenera's lab wing. Uproar drifted down the hallways in the aftermath of the morning's bomb-shell. Televisions and radios blared from every laboratory and office.

The receptionist for his wing was watching CNN. A white-coated technician in the pathology lab was hidden behind the *Christian Science Monitor*. Dr. Orin Sharpton, Andrew's particular nemesis, was absorbed in the *Wall Street Journal*.

When he turned into his own lab, he spotted Will Austin's lanky frame tilted back on his lab chair, his cowboy boots propped comfortably on the black marble counter, one hand holding a cup of coffee, the other whirling the tuning knob of a shortwave radio. The Voice of America sounded through the static:

"General Genetic, a United States genetic engineering company, has advanced medical science in the world's fight for better treatments for victims of burns and other skin injuries.

"Scientists have speculated that this may be the first step toward limb regeneration for amputees . . ."

"Bullsheeet!" growled Will, shaking his head in disgust. Then he noticed Andrew was listening. "Can you believe all this hype?!"

"Seen Gindman yet?" asked Andrew.

"Not yet, Doc," Will said, tilting his chair forward, getting up to stretch his long legs. "Probably fit to be tied, what with all this."

"How's Niko?"

"Acting strange. He's . . . thinking."

"Thinking?"

"Yeah, thinking. Just concentrating. Except for trying to take away my coffee every time I get near him. That's a new one."

"How can you tell he's thinking?"

"It's like he's got a problem to solve. Hell, he's been trapped in that lab with you for so long he's started impersonating you! Mimicking your gestures, even down to that faraway stare of yours. All I can call it is thinking.

"Lucy doesn't know what to make of it. His color is fine and he seems okay otherwise. But he hasn't been himself since I arrived. Occasionally he looks up as if to speak and mouths something. But only noise comes out.''

"He's trying to speak?'' Andrew asked slowly, making sure he understood.

"Yeah, exactly. Trying to speak,'' Will paused and stared at Andrew thoughtfully. "Is there something I should know?''

"Tell you in a minute,'' Andrew replied and went into the other room to check on Niko. He found him deep in thought, just as Will had described. When he saw Andrew he stopped, climbed onto the door, and reached in a conspiratorial manner for Andrew.

"What the hell is going on?'' Will asked from the doorway. "That isn't the Niko I know. What have you done, Doc?''

Andrew looked carefully at Will and back at Niko. He unlocked the cell door and lifted Niko up into his arms.

"Morning, fella.'' He scratched under Niko's ear, avoiding Will's gaze. "Well, ah . . .'' he began as he crossed to his desk, temporizing.

He poured two coffees, split a bagel and piled it high with peanut butter, and served Niko, who settled into Andrew's chair as if he belonged there. Niko took a sip of coffee, set it down, and immediately began to work with the double helix DNA model.

Will stared in disbelief, first at Niko, then at Andrew. "Doc—?''

Andrew looked calmly at Will. "It works,'' he said.

Will gawked at him. "Come again?''

"Listen,'' explained Andrew, "I extracted some DNA from my blood, multiplied and cultured it, then injected Niko. He went to sleep for a while, then he suddenly had a seizure and his life signs stopped altogether. I thought I'd killed him. Then he just . . . came back. Except he wasn't alone. He was . . .'' He gestured at Niko, as if his sheer presence would say more eloquently what Andrew couldn't put into words. "He's been . . . aping me . . . ever since.''

Niko looked up at Andrew, bared his teeth, and nodded in amusement.

"No pun intended,'' Andrew finished weakly.

"Jesus Christ!'' Will said under his breath, squinting intently at Niko. "Does Gindman know?''

Andrew shook his head.

"Does anybody know?"

Another shake of the head.

"Jesus Christ!"

Will's cowboy *whoop* reverberated off the walls of the laboratory. He started to hug Andrew, slapping him on the back and yelling, "You did it, son! You did it!" until he remembered Andrew was his boss. Both men looked at Niko like boys whose match bomb actually worked.

"You did it!" Will said a final time, awe in his voice.

"I have to take care of some business and then get upstairs for a meeting," Andrew said, damping down his own enthusiasm. It was only Stage Two of a three-stage experiment; there was no telling now if he would even be allowed to attempt Stage Three. "Try to keep Niko calm, all right?"

"Try to keep myself calm, you mean!" Will scratched his chin and studied Niko as if seeing him for the first time. "Sweet Jesus Christ!"

"It works, Will. Now I want to try it with ancient DNA."

"That why you contacted the Vatican?"

"And a few other sources. The Vatican's taking its own sweet time, naturally."

"Didn't it take them three and a half centuries to acknowledge that the world was round?" Will mused, glancing sideways at Andrew. "Sorry. Didn't mean to step on anybody's toes. You're not Catholic, are you, Doc?"

"Not anymore!" Andrew said with more vehemence than he'd intended. "Anyway, back to cases. The principle's the same—using ancient DNA to attempt regeneration. It worked on Niko and it will work on a human host. All I need in order to prove that is some fresh, ancient DNA."

"Whoa! What about protocol? Aren't you missing a few steps?"

"I know. Live human DNA to live human, then recently post mortem human DNA to live human . . . ," Andrew rattled off the ordered sequence of tests that would maintain the integrity of scientific method. "No time," he said bluntly.

"Wait a minute! That's not what you've been hammering into me for the last year. 'Systematic, exacting, repeatable, verifiable results.' What happened to all that?"

Andrew waited for his assistant to calm down and then spoke evenly, "Listen to me, there comes a time when experience and instinct intersect. Then every once in a while—not often mind you—maybe once in a lifetime, certainty about what you know inside and an outside need come together. This is that time, Austin. I know memory resurrection works. And BioGenera has one shot at saving itself from history's trash heap. I've got to take the chance . . ." He waited for Will's reaction.

" 'Fresh ancient DNA,' " Will mused as Andrew searched for his copy of the brief memo he'd faxed to the Pontifical Commission for Reliquiae weeks ago. "Isn't that what they call an oxymoron?"

"Trust me, Will," answered Andrew as he gave Niko another close look. "Niko—?"

Niko was still pondering the DNA model. "Hm?" he responded without looking up.

A soul divided in two, Andrew thought, feeling a pang of something like guilt. He shook it off; there wasn't time for second thoughts. It worked, didn't it?

"We must know more!" Cosa continued forcefully. "We must be there at the moment of discovery. Who are the best candidates for this breakthrough? May we assist them?"

"Assist them?" repeated Giuliana, caught off guard by this new twist of Cosa's Machiavellian mind.

"If the advances of genetic science are to be as dramatic as you say, then there may be confusion if the science is not framed by the Church's vision and moral leadership," Cosa explained, as if it were self-evident. "That is why the Church embraced Leonardo, Galileo, Marconi, and other geniuses in the Pontifical Academy."

"The Church was ready to burn Galileo," Giuliana gently corrected him. "It freed him only when he denied the science that we now accept as truth, Your Eminence."

"A minor aberration in the Church's long record of promoting truth, *Dottore*," Cosa dismissed history easily and forgave his predecessors. "We recognize that progress is inevitable. The best means to manage it for the man in the pew is to become integral to the science rather than remaining an impotent observer."

"I see," Giuliana said warily. Something in his tone registered with her, making her distinctly uncomfortable.

"We are in regular contact with all the researchers participating in the Human Genome Project," Kleiman pointed out feebly.

"The Human Genome Project is merely a starting point," Giuliana suggested, "a barometer of the research climate." She sensed that Cosa's interest was waning with the afternoon light, and so she gathered her notes. "The advance will almost certainly occur at one of the laboratories I have identified. I will compile the appropriate information for Your Eminence."

Cosa motioned for her to remain seated as he stood, alerting the others that they were expected to leave. "Stay, *Dottore, per favore.*"

Murphy rose and left directly. Kleiman followed but couldn't resist a glance over his shoulder at Giuliana, as if searching for a clue to the cardinal's purpose in keeping her there.

As the door closed behind them, the cardinal turned quickly to Giuliana. "My child," his tone was suddenly warm and confiding, "I wish to pursue this request from Dr. Shepard. There is much to consider and I will need your help."

"Of course," she said warily. "Your Eminence?"

Cosa seemed absorbed in his own thoughts. "Hm?"

"Please, do not take my comments too seriously. Everything I said here today is purely speculation."

Cosa smiled warmly. "You have confirmed my own thinking, my dear. I have known that the time for risk, the time to explore this new science, was approaching. It is nigh!"

"There are risks, Your Eminence. Many risks. As in any exploration, the outcome is unknown."

"*So che*; we must be brave. If not we, then who?"

"The results may reveal more questions than answers."

"There is always that potential," Cosa said thoughtfully, "particularly in our ministry to the world. I have faith."

"May I suggest some foundational research, Eminence? To give you a more factual base for your deliberations?"

"No, my dear. The fewer who know my thoughts, the

better. *Dio mi guiderê*. God will guide me. But *grazie*, Giuliana. *Grazie*.''

''*Prègo*,'' she said sincerely, wondering at this change in character.

Cosa's smile was unguarded and spontaneous, childlike. He was focused on some distant thought that she could only guess at. When he felt her gaze, he gave his blessing and escorted her out into the hall, where he uncharacteristically took her hand in his and thanked her again. The Machiavellian prince seemed to have vanished, and in his place she saw a true believer. Cosa seemed to glow with an enthusiasm she'd never before seen in him.

Giuliana turned away before he could notice her surprise and walked down the soaring Baroque hallway, her steps metronomic against marble. She replayed the cardinal's strange behavior, the lifting of worry, the sudden intimacy.

By the time she emerged from the Apostolic Palace into Rome's warm evening, she had identified the sensation that stood the hair on her neck on end. For the second time in her life, she sensed that it was dangerous to be alive in this world. She couldn't understand why, but she was overshadowed by misgiving.

She rushed for the 4:50 train back to her apartment, carrying this disquiet like a sudden evening chill.

5

ANDREW TOOK THE PRIVATE STAIRWAY TO GINDman's office suite. Every employee at BioGenera knew that Gindman considered those cherrywood steps with the plush charcoal runner to be his personal access to the penthouse. Was he high enough on the food chain, Andrew wondered, to be allowed to walk here?

The air seemed better at the top. Even sound was different, muffled, nothing extraneous. Andrew couldn't shake the sense that he had arrived in a different realm, in the place where the real decisions were made, where things happened.

Then, of course, there was the challenge of getting past Delphine.

Delphine Havel ruled the huge glass-walled reception area the way Mike Gindman ruled the executive suite. She had arrived with Gindman when he'd taken over BioGenera, his executive assistant, his right arm. Young and exotically attractive, she was no mere office fixture. Rumor had it that she was the power behind the throne, the one Gindman bounced the agonizing decisions off of after hours, the one who really ran BioGenera.

The other staffers were arriving by ones and twos, using the regular stairway. Mike Gindman glowered at a television beside his desk, watching *EC Times*, the BBC afternoon news. A panel of Swiss, French, British, and German scientists was discussing the impact of General Genetic's contract announcement.

"C'est magnifique!"

"... but shouldn't an EC member country have made this advance?"

"... our time is coming, I assure you."

"... who else but America with its Pentagon can afford such research right now ..."

Gindman muted the volume, rose to his full six-foot-two-inch height, walked to the window behind his desk, and stared at the horizon. He was a fit fifty-six-year-old, balding slightly and the picture of health. This mystified Andrew when he thought about his boss's round-the-clock schedule of teleconferences, the constant stress, his apparent complete disinterest in any sort of physical exercise. Mike Gindman seemed to live his life in a never-ending hurry-up two-minute offense, stopping to huddle only when forced by the dictates of an ever more competitive business culture or the need to bring his subordinates up to speed on the game plan.

"I can't wait for General Genetic's official announcement tomorrow morning," he announced, turning back toward those assembled around the table. "We've got to act now."

For a long moment no one spoke.

"Well, Mike, there's still the Asian market if we move quickly," Marketing Vice President Ward Rauch suggested optimistically.

Gindman rubbed his jaw and clenched his teeth. Sinew

rippled under the skin. "EGF's a dead issue. It's time to move on to other things."

Dr. Orin Sharpton shifted in his chair and cleared his throat. "I may have something," he suggested tentatively.

Sharpton's presence at BioGenera was a matter of economics. Gindman had gotten him as part of the package when he purchased the faltering laboratory. He was an odd duck. Old money, Ivy League, he gave the impression that biogenetics was a kind of hobby for him and that he was decidedly slumming at a facility like BioGenera. He was a man wasted with passions he would never have the courage to express.

"Let's hear it," Gindman growled.

"Uh, it's a little complicated."

Gindman sat at the head of the table, the BBC still nattering away sotto voce on the tube behind him, and gave Sharpton his complete attention. "Try us, Dr. Sharpton. We're all good listeners."

If Sharpton heard the sarcasm, he ignored it. "Well, it's sort of a genetic approach to an area of dermatology."

" 'Sort of'?"

"Yes. You see, I have found a way to program skin pigmentation."

Andrew saw some of the others exchange glances. Not only had none of them heard anything about any such technique until this moment, it was hardly a significant avenue of genetic research. Pigmentation experiments had been around since Gregor Mendel.

"It's only temporary," Sharpton was saying, oblivious to the stares he was getting. "But it works on my drosophila."

"On fruit flies?" Gindman was incredulous. "How the hell can you tell? What do you do, examine them under a microscope?"

"There have been significant changes. I've documented all of them," Sharpton said with a touch of self-righteousness. "I sent you a report last week. I suppose you haven't had time to read it . . ."

"Cut to the chase, Doctor," Gindman said stonily.

"I believe, sir, I have developed a tanning technique."

"Tanning," Gindman said slowly. Someone suppressed

a snicker. "I see. What's involved here? Shots, pills—what?"

"It's a little early to be sure, sir," Sharpton said. "But I think once I've perfected it, we can launch a marketing campaign that—"

"Let's let the marketing people worry about that." Gindman leaned back in his chair, hands clasped behind his head. "I want your vision on the technique itself. Where are you going with this?"

"Intravenous, sir," Sharpton admitted sheepishly.

Everyone shifted to stifle laughter. Gindman snorted in disgust.

"Intra—!" He couldn't even finish the word. "Sharpton, there are pills on the market already . . . some kind of vitamin complex . . . God knows what's in them, but one of my sons is into fitness—for the life of me I can't remember which one it is—four kids, two ex-wives; I can't keep track . . . But you take these things at night and you wake up with a tan. For all I know it's simple beta carotene. Probably kills your liver in the long run, but it's already out there. And you're talking about intravenous—!"

"But on an outpatient basis!" Sharpton defended himself.

Gindman's gaze held on Sharpton. He could've been watching the death throes of a drosophila.

"And how long would the effects last, Doctor?" he asked, a little too calmly.

"A week or so. I want to test it on rhesus monkeys. Uh, tan them, then autopsy them."

Gindman threw up his hands. "Oh, I can just see it! Women lining up at fat farms and the Betty Ford Clinic to get their tanning shots before they leave for home. Jesus Christ! General Genetic is saving human lives with EGF and you want BioGenera to sacrifice primates for a goddam tanning technique?"

Sharpton had gone deadly white; even his own tanning technique couldn't help him now.

"Get out of here, Sharpton." Gindman waved his hand dismissively. "Get the hell out of my sight!"

Sharpton stalked out with as much dignity as he could muster.

Gindman was back at the window. "Anyone else got anything to say?"

Andrew wanted to explode. How could he possibly make a reasonable presentation with Gindman in this state of mind?

"There may be cutbacks," Gindman announced finally. "I don't know who or how yet, but we'll have to tighten our belts and suck it in. But goddammit, BioGenera is going to come out of this on top! Anyone who isn't in this to win can clean out their desk and get out, now!"

The meeting was over. Everyone else began to trickle out. Andrew hesitated, then decided to leave well enough alone and followed the others.

He stopped at the top of the stairs. Was he going to let ten years of work, ten years of minor victories, but victories nonetheless, get shot down in the crossfire of a corporate feud?

Time to fly. He inhaled deeply—and decisively pivoted toward Gindman's door.

6   GINDMAN WAS ON AN OVERSEAS CALL AND DIDN'T see him at first. Andrew could still leave unnoticed. As he was thinking this, Gindman's left arm reached out and dropped the receiver into its cradle.

"What is it, Dr. Shepard?" he asked, looking up at Andrew.

"There's something I want to talk over with you. Got a few minutes?"

Gindman seemed calmer, transformed from the brittle character that Andrew had seen a few minutes earlier. He gestured toward two chairs crouched by the corner window. Andrew lowered himself into the whispered hush of Italian leather.

"You're a bit of a enigma to me, Shepard, if you don't mind my saying so," Gindman began before Andrew could say a word. "You're brilliant, you've added essential patents to BioGenera's asset column, but except for staff meetings I never see you."

"No mystery there," Andrew started to feel more at ease. "I work. Take it a day at a time."

"Balls. Don't believe you. You're not as relaxed as you'd like me to think. That's what I like about you, Shepard. No neutral gear. You're effective."

Andrew wanted to laugh. He doubted if Margaret would call him effective.

"The way I see it," Gindman continued, "you show up in my office, it's important. What's on your mind?" Suddenly he grinned like a cobra. "Hasn't got anything to do with tanning, has it?"

"No," Andrew laughed. "No, I've discovered a way to tap into intellect and experience, the stuff that makes beings sentient. I believe that I can capture and transfer memory genetically."

There, he'd said it, just like that. Let Gindman rip his head off the way he had with Sharpton. He had nothing left to lose.

The phone on the desk buzzed. Gindman ignored it. It persisted.

"Not now, Delphine!" he shouted toward the door. The buzzing stopped.

"All right, you've got my attention, Doctor." Gindman leaned forward. "Genetic memory, huh? Explain it to me in words I can understand."

"Until recently scientists believed that DNA was fragile, that it broke down and was destroyed shortly following the death of the organism. It had been proven that the enzymes of a cell break up the DNA into smaller and smaller pieces in the initial postmortem days. Add to that environmental factors such as radiation, airborne contaminants, and moisture—"

Gindman held up his hand. "I'm still with you, Shepard, but barely."

Andrew nodded. "I know, sir—cut to the chase."

"You got it."

"In spite of these factors," Andrew went on, "archaeologists are finding viable DNA in ever more ancient sources: the frozen remains of a 4,600-year-old man in an

Italian glacier, a 7,000-year-old human brain in a Florida bog, blood on a 100,000-year-old Neanderthal stone tool in Australia, 17-million-year-old flowers, and now 25-million-year-old bees and gnats preserved in pine sap.''

"How is that possible?" Gindman wanted to know.

"It's due to the abundance of DNA bases, two of them in every cell of our bodies," answered Andrew. "However, even though trace remnants of DNA are being found in ancient remains, the samples are so minute as to be insufficient for experimentation. That is, until the development of polymerase chain reaction.''

"PCR," Gindman interjected, proud of himself. "What the FBI uses for forensic evidence.''

"Exactly," Andrew said. "The convergence of technology, understanding, and newly discovered genetic resources opens up a wealth of possibilities.''

"That's why I'm in this business, Doctor. That's why I bought BioGenera. But when you say 'viable DNA,' what are you getting at? Cloning? Are we talking *Jurassic Park*?''

"Not exactly. My process is simpler. Since nearly every cell contains the complete genetic blueprint of the animal to which it belongs, in theory a well-preserved cell could yield an intact gene set. It's conceivable that we could clone all the properties of that animal from that gene set, including its genetic memory.''

"And that's what you're proposing to do." Gindman leapt ahead.

"Exactly. I've actually done it, using one of our lab chimps.''

Briefly, he told Gindman about Niko, deliberately skipping any mention of the failure with the rhesus. Gindman didn't want to hear about failure.

"You're serious!" Gindman said, a look of boyish delight on his usually stony face. Andrew had surprised him, presented him with a new toy. It excited him. "I'm gonna have to come down out of my ivory tower here and see your chimp for myself. However"—here he recovered himself, the businessman reasserting himself in lieu of the little boy—"we're not in the freak show business here, Shepard. Tell me what practical application this has for humanity, and by that I mean: What practical application does this have for BioGenera?''

Here it comes! Andrew thought. *This is where I either catch the wind or run up on a reef.*

''The third phase of the experiment would be an attempt to recover the memory from ancient human tissue. Specifically, ancient bones.''

''A mummy?'' Gindman's imagination caught fire again; Andrew saw the flash in his eyes.

''Possibly. We've got a call in to the Ministry of Antiquities in Cairo, but—''

''—but you haven't heard back yet,'' Gindman finished for him.

Andrew looked surprised. ''No, we haven't. How did you—?''

Gindman laughed. ''I've done business with the Egyptians, Shepard. They have an expression to cover every contingency—*malesh*. There's no English equivalent. Closest they can come to a translation is 'no problem,' 'don't worry about it,' something like that. You ask me, its closest analogue is *mañana*. They're an ancient people; you can't hurry them and very little surprises them.''

''Well, that explains that,'' Andrew said. ''However, we'll wait on them. There are also limited but excellent samples in tombs all over the world. Since moisture and air are the major enemies of preservation, I'm looking for ancient tombs in historically dry regions.''

''Historically dry regions,'' repeated Gindman. ''That narrows it down to the Arctic and equatorial regions. Since the odds of finding a sample, not to mention a viable sample, at the North or South Pole are smaller than my chances of winning the Irish Sweepstakes, that leaves the Mediterranean and the Middle East.''

''I've already contacted Rome several times. The Vatican has remains dating back at least to the first century.''

Gindman looked uneasy. ''What'd they say?''

''Haven't received a response from them yet either.''

''I'm not a religious man,'' Gindman said, ''but when you say the Vatican, I hear problems. Political, theological, and, most especially, legal problems. Yet something even more fundamental is bothering me. Isn't human memory a living, transitory, and ultimately perishable phenomenon? I mean, isn't it a shadow that's—you'll pardon the expression—all in our minds?''

''According to quantum theory the biochemical engrams of mental processes stored in our brains are no different than tangible objects,'' Andrew offered.

''You mean my memory of the first time I got laid in the backseat of my dad's Buick is a *thing*? Something that can be seen, touched, held in my hand?'' Gindman pantomimed with his outstretched palm. His expression glowed with the thought of it.

''According to quantum theory, it's as concrete as the thalamus, the cerebellum, or the occipital lobe that contains it.''

''Jesus H. Christ on a raft!'' Gindman whistled softly. He seemed to be turning it over in his mind. Andrew waited respectfully. Finally Gindman said, ''Bottom-line it for me: You get your viable tissue samples and you do what with them?''

''Centrifuge them down into solution, clone it by inserting it into a plasma or phage vector that can replicate in bacteria. Or, since it's genomic, we can clone it by using a restriction enzyme to cleave it into fragments, then join them to the cloning vector by using restriction enzymes to generate sticky ends—''

Gindman leaned forward, his expression indicating that he was reaching for comprehension but not finding it. His face collapsed into a blank stare. Mercifully, Andrew paused.

''Sorry. We recombine—splice—the ancient DNA with the subject's DNA.''

''But how is that possible? Two-thousand-year-old DNA must be different from ours, isn't it?''

''Actually, no. Genomes are relatively static. They change on the leisurely timescale of evolution.''

Gindman seemed to find that interesting. He nodded, accepting. ''Then what?''

''We inject the recombinant DNA solution into a human volunteer. The host accepts his modified native cells back into his body with hardly a notice.''

''And then—?''

"We wait," Andrew answered simply. He didn't consciously decide to lie about the subject's death and resurrection. It just seemed like too much for Gindman to absorb.

"Wait," repeated Gindman.

"Right. To see if the memory of some ancient man will evidence itself in our volunteer the same way my behavior is evidencing itself in Niko."

Gindman shook his head. "*Now* you're talking science fiction, Dr. Shepard. You're going to have to walk me through that part in stages."

And so it went for the next forty minutes. The two of them sat huddled in the corner, drenched in morning sunlight. Andrew spread out his theory in just enough detail for Gindman to appreciate the solid scientific foundations that buttressed the procedure. Gindman listened carefully, interrupting only when he was unclear about a finer point. When Andrew reached the end of his presentation, he didn't know whether he could expect Gindman's support.

"The procedure would require approval of the NIH Recombinant DNA Advisory Committee," Gindman pointed out. "As for the legal ramifications—I can't even begin to sort those out. Our subject would have to sign releases out the wazoo . . . medical coverage, notifications of next of kin . . . We'd need security tighter than the Pentagon's . . . and how the hell do you get liability insurance for something like this? On top of all that, if it leaked we'd find ourselves fielding calls from the ACLU and every loony group on the planet claiming we coerced our subject, infringed on his rights, the whole nine yards." Gindman looked at Andrew incisively. "That's quite a *megillah*, Shepard. I'll have to think about it."

He returned to his desk, started shuffling papers. Andrew realized he'd just been dismissed.

"Sir, there's not much time. If I do get a response from Cairo or the Vatican . . ."

Gindman looked at him from under his eyebrows. Andrew had seen more warmth in a shark's eyes. "I said I'd think about it, Dr. Shepard. Tell you what you do. You work up a formal presentation for the entire committee, present it at the next meeting, and we'll take it from there. Right now, I've got work to do, and so, I presume, do you.''

Mike Gindman marshaled his thoughts as he watched Andrew disappear. He'd changed rhythm on him neatly. Now he'd let him wait. Best way to build commitment to the cause.

Memory resurrection! Gindman thought. It gave him chills. *It could change everything. We could defeat the grave and learn all the secrets from the other side—scientifically! Find the answers people have been consulting mediums and fortune-tellers for all these centuries. Communicate directly with Lee Harvey Oswald, Jack Ruby, John Lennon, Gandhi, Schweitzer. Determine whose body parts are buried in the Tomb of the Unknown Soldier. We'd have to rewrite history, rethink government, reexamine the meaning of life itself.*

Victims could testify against their oppressors, against the lies of history, against our false notions of the spirit world and eternity. Gindman's mind raced. *There'd be no more hiding place for the wicked. Anyone who possessed our procedure could possess the truth!*

He walked to the window to get away from the sharp feeling of panic in his chest, but he couldn't run from his own incisive analysis. It came to him that humankind could destroy itself in a struggle to control such power.

Gradually his fear turned to fascination. The entrepreneur in him focused on the procedure's commercial potential. Just a hint of such a capability would put BioGenera in the international spotlight. Memory resurrection would appeal directly to everyone's questing spirit. It was universal. Everyone on planet Earth would do anything, pay any price to discover what awaits them beyond this life.

What if there is no "other side"? Nothing beyond? Then again, what if there is? Will the force that created the universe allow us to glimpse the ultimate truth? If so, at what price?

Gindman shuddered and then stared out the window. It was too much. On the one hand, he knew that his reaction was the same human reaction he could expect from others. That was good.

On the other hand, his initial fear, which by now had

settled into a cautious respect, told him that he, or Andrew, might be on the brink of unimagined danger.

He pressed the intercom button. "Delphine?"

"Yes?"

"What have I got on for tomorrow?"

"A teleconference with the Lengnau group at six-thirty A.M., the usual until eleven, when you're giving the *New York Times* half an hour. Then lunch with Bear Sterns, golf at two, and dinner with NIH director Francis Wilson."

"How'd I get suckered into doing the *Times*?"

"You got sweet-talked by their financial editor. He's interested in your take on the EGF contract. Whither Bio-Genera now that General Genetic's done an end run around us, that kind of thing. Your side of the story."

"I don't know. I've got a lot on my plate." The thought occurred to him that he wasn't sure he could trust himself to keep quiet about memory resurrection under questioning by the *Times*.

"It could stem our slide in the market, Mike," Delphine suggested. She never advised, merely suggested. It gave Gindman the sense that he'd arrived at his conclusions on his own.

"All right. I'll talk to him, but cancel the lunch and golf."

"Cancel lunch and golf, check."

Gindman paced to the window, hands deep in his pockets and chin forward. He rotated his shoulders to work off the tension.

Memory resurrection. Jesus Christ!

The call from Cairo came during a slow afternoon in the lab.

"It's almost midnight their time!" Will mouthed to Andrew as he handed him the phone.

Following the usual fits and starts and misunderstandings with the multilingual overseas operator, the call finally came through. Andrew had to clamp his hand over his other ear to hear Dr. Fawzi at the other end of the satellite call. Still, it was a good connection; the echo was only half as loud as usual.

He tried not to notice that Will and Niko were watching

him with equal curiosity as they each pretended to be busy with other things.

"You will forgive me for taking so long to return your call," Gamel Fawzi began. "My office is so chaotic I must often wait to make calls from home. This is not to mention that the overseas lines are frequently down. *Malesh*, I am still here. You will forgive me also if I speak softly. My family are asleep. I am making this call from my living room so as not to disturb them."

"That's quite all right, Dr. Fawzi." Andrew had to fight to keep from shouting against the echo himself. "I appreciate your getting back to me at all."

"Very well. Let me see if I can answer the questions in your letter in the order in which you listed them. To begin, the oldest mummies of which we are aware date from about 2600 B.C. The process continued until Muslim Arabs conquered Egypt in A.D. 641."

"Excellent," Andrew said. "The later ones might be exactly what we need."

"Could you please describe the tissue sample you are seeking?"

"Skin or internal organ tissue would be optimum. If that's not available, then certain bone tissue may be okay."

"May I ask the precise nature of your research?"

"Sorry, Dr. Fawzi, I can't go into specifics. It's a matter of company policy, concern about security. Not that I don't personally trust you, but—"

"Please, Dr. Shepard!" Fawzi's voice cut through the echo on the line. "You are speaking to an Egyptian. If I may be blunt, we invented court intrigue and industrial espionage while your European ancestors were still emerging from their caves."

"That's fair!" Andrew acknowledged with a grin. "Okay, then, all I can tell you is that we're investigating DNA survivability."

"I see." Fawzi was as fascinated as most scientists with the rapid pace of molecular biology and its stunning achievements in genetic science. "Why mummified tissue specifically?"

"Because it's so well preserved," Andrew replied.

"Yes, the techniques of my ancestors are impressive in-

deed. It is an amazing process. At its height in the Twenty-
first Dynasty—and we are speaking of three thousand years
ago—the most advanced mummification procedures required more than seventy days to complete.''

"Wow," Andrew said appreciatively.

"It is important that you understand the chemical processes to which the remains were subjected, as they may
affect your research," Fawzi continued. "First the priests
made a four-inch incision near the hip of the deceased and
removed the internal organs. These were cleaned in spiced
wine. The abdominal cavity was then thoroughly flushed
clean with cedar oil."

"What about the brain?" Andrew asked hopefully.

"It was also removed, because it contained moisture that,
left untreated, would supply bacteria and fungus during subsequent aging. The brain was removed with a pointed tool
that was forced through the soft nasal passage and then
scraped around inside the cranium."

"Ouch! I suddenly have a headache."

Fawzi laughed softly. He liked this American. "Stay with
me, Dr. Shepard, please. I am almost finished. The cleaned
organs were then packed in natron to dry them—"

"Natron?"

"A rock salt composed of sodium carbonate and sodium
bicarbonate. What you would call washing soda and baking
soda. Each organ was then wrapped and replaced inside the
body cavity. The remaining space was filled with linen, tar,
sawdust, whatever was non-acidic and available."

"I've always been impressed by the retention of facial
features," Andrew said. "How was that done?"

"The priests were quite accomplished. The face and body
were sculpted from the inside out, using very small wads of
linen inserted under the skin to restore the remains to their
living appearance. Finally, each limb, each digit, was meticulously wrapped in resin-treated linen. I have unwrapped
more than a mile of linen from a single mummy."

Andrew whistled soundlessly.

"The dried tissue—is it intact? Or does it fuse with the
resin and create some kind of biological alloy?"

"Good question. I am not a chemist, but I understand that

mummified tissue samples are no longer effective biological specimens.''

"Damn!" Andrew rapped the desktop with his knuckles.

"I am sorry I could not be of more help," Gamel Fawzi said sincerely. "But, you know, Dr. Shepard, everyone assumes that Egypt holds the patent on ancient remains. This simply is not the case. There are limited but excellent samples in tombs all over the world. Have you considered contacting Rome? The Vatican surely has remains dating back at least to the time of Constantine.''

"As a matter of fact, we have investigated that potential already," Andrew admitted. "Unfortunately we never received a response.''

"Malesh!" Dr. Fawzi said sympathetically. "Perhaps in matters of policy, the Vatican is even more dilatory than Egypt.''

He and Andrew shared a laugh. "Perhaps it's time to try again.''

"Good luck, Dr. Shepard," Fawzi said sincerely. "I will be looking for the results of your research.''

"No go, huh, Doc?" Will had seen Andrew's entire body deflate as he heard the bad news from Cairo.

"No go," Andrew repeated. He ran both hands through his unruly hair. "Damn! Did I give Gindman the sales pitch of the century for nothing? What happens now?''

Will had Niko in his arms. The chimp had become increasingly restive as Andrew talked to Gamel Fawzi; now he seemed inconsolable, hugging Will until he felt strangled. Will pried his arms loose and handed him over to Andrew. Let them comfort each other. Hell, they shared the same mind!

"Well, son, cheer up!" It amused Andrew the way Will tended to call him "son." "We've still got one last shot at it. Looks like it's going to have to be the Vatican.''

Apostolic Palace, Vatican City

"THE CHURCH IS TAKING A DRUBBING IN THE WEST-
ern press over His Holiness's encyclical, Your Eminence,"
observed Murphy, setting a fresh cup of espresso before the
cardinal. His boss was finishing the last of six prominent
dailies he read each morning. "One has to wonder if reaf-
firming the Church's rigid stand against birth control when
people are suffering so is wise."

"It is a risky strategy, *si*," replied Cosa thoughtfully.
"And there is no denying the numbers in the Third World,
nor the negative voices in the Commonwealth States. However, His Holiness takes the long view, Murphy."

"Why now, Your Eminence, when revenues are falling?"

"The future of the faith is in souls unborn." Cosa sat
back comfortably in his leather wing chair. Generally not a
man who tolerated interruptions easily, he enjoyed testing
himself in dialogues with the Irishman. "Wealth is a renew-
able resource, harvested and reinvested in a more or less
constant cycle. A soul exists once. If it is lost, it is lost
forever."

He let that thought float. Examined too closely, it was
terrifying. It was what drove him.

"That's one way of seeing the thing," acknowledged
Murphy, sensing the cardinal's mood and jumping into the
dialectic with enthusiasm. His was a sunnier disposition than
Cosa's; to him, the conversation was a mental exercise, not
a matter of life and death. "As one of my countrymen observed, however, the great danger of conversion is when the
religion of the high mind is offered to the low mind, which
feels its fascination without understanding it, drags it down,
degrades it."

"Shaw again, eh?"

"Aye, Your Eminence. I fear that the souls we attract
with the narrow view, we may attract for the wrong reasons.
They oversimplify and radicalize the high precepts."

"But now is exactly the proper time, don't you see, Murphy? This is the dawn of a new age—socially, politically, economically, and religiously. Even political leaders presume to redefine morality. Consider the number of theocracies that have arisen in the Arab world alone in recent years.

"Strong voices draw the uncommitted to their causes. The dispossessed recruit armies of poor, yearning foot soldiers. Humanity hungers for answers on this Earth, which will show them the way to the next life. Governments race to keep up with their subjects' needs, expectations, demands, but they cannot. The only true government is the government of the soul.

"Change, that is the only constant. It brings opportunity. The Church has an advantage in this chaos—two thousand years of experience at change. It must reach out and proclaim in a voice louder than all the others, now when uncertainty stresses the soul."

"It's wonderful in theory," Murphy acknowledged. "But may I be candid, Your Eminence?"

"Certainly, Kevin."

"It's just that sometimes I wonder if His Holiness isn't going about it the wrong way. Taking the narrow view, shouting against thunder."

"*Si*, sometimes it seems that way. He is only our second non-Italian pontiff, not one of us. He sometimes does not appreciate the complexities, the nuances . . ."

Cosa stopped suddenly. He had gone too far, admitted too much to his trusted aide. He had allowed himself too much candor. Machiavelli lived in the details, and he had revealed too many details, he feared.

"No offense to Ireland or to you, my friend. I only mean to say that Stephen Parnell is perhaps too gentle a spirit, too trusting for our times."

Murphy's eyes twinkled. "I'm not forgetting my history, Eminence. How many centuries was it that the Romans themselves elected the pope? Old habits die hard."

Cosa had to smile. "You forget, Murphy, that I am not a Roman. I was raised in Trastevere, but I was born in Siracusa."

This seemed to amuse Murphy all the more. "Sicilian, eh? Well, that explains it. Your country's been conquered more often even than mine. It makes for a certain strength of character, a will to survive.''

"Even so," Cosa acknowledged.

"As for our Irish pope . . ." Murphy knew he was bordering on irreverence, but he'd take the chance. "Irish Catholicism has always been a different breed. It's the difference in climate, I'm thinking. Beware trying to transplant a religion nurtured in a warm, sunny clime to a place of creeping damp where it rains every afternoon at three. The end result is a certain dampness of soul."

Cosa's smile turned brilliant. "And how is it you manage to escape this . . . dampness of soul, Monsignor?"

Murphy gestured at the Roman sun streaming through the tall windows.

"Very simply, Eminence. I've relocated to a warm climate." He glanced at the time; it was his duty to make sure Cosa met his appointments on time. "In sum," he concluded, "it's no surprise to me that you find our lad Parnell a bit difficult to—manage, shall we say?"

Cosa found himself wondering what might have happened if Machiavelli had been an Irishman. To counter any perception of disloyalty, he said seriously: "His Holiness is our one supreme teacher on this Earth. I will serve his wishes in whatever way I can."

He was relieved when Murphy nodded agreement.

"It's time you're off, then. He'll be waiting," said Murphy.

How could Cosa discuss his pain with Murphy, with anyone? He wanted to share it with the pontiff, but Stephen Parnell possessed a faith seemingly genetic in its roots. How could he burden him with his despair, his desperate need to resurrect faith in the world and himself? Genocide was on the rise on every continent; tribal feuds in Africa . . . ethnic cleansing in the Balkans . . . cult perversions in the Americas. And in the soul of Adeodato Cosa there grew not a dampness as Murphy described it but despair.

"Honest confusion among human beings of goodwill," Parnell would remind Cosa when confronted by the murderous evils of the world beyond the Vatican's walls. He no doubt experienced some pain at these evils, but despair? No, not despair. Not Stephen Parnell.

Cosa, on the other hand, managed evils on behalf of the Church. It was to him that the Special Ops division of the Guard reported, in the person of Jurgen Rindt. Rindt was a murderer. Cosa knew. It was to him that Rindt came for confession, and Cosa could not but give him absolution, even as he wondered if Rindt believed in God, much less religion. But how could he deny his Special Operative absolution for his sins, when it was he, Cosa, who most often assigned Rindt to the commission of those sins?

He had never officially ordered Rindt to take the life of another. He had simply pointed out the advantage to the greater good of having a particular individual removed from a position of threat or power, by any means necessary. It was Cosa, in fact, rather than Luke John, who took the long view.

How could a man in his position deny reality? His Church was built as much on the bones of those it had martyred as it was on the bones of the early Christians slaughtered by pagan Rome. How did a man of his knowledge and gifts respond to the persistent evil of the world if not with doubt and despair? How was he to do his part to make the modern Church a purer entity, absolved of the sins of its past? How did a soul remain pure when confronted by the silence of God?

Cosa had not determined the answer to these questions. While he worked publicly for the soul of mankind, his private struggle for his own soul intensified until he trusted no one, not even Saint Peter's successor. Stephen Parnell possessed an innocence of soul that Adeodato Cosa had never known.

Cosa did not know whether to envy or despise him.

Pope Luke John I waited patiently, his senses alive to the motions and sounds of faith in the house that Peter built, his moist eyes grateful for all they saw. Cosa was late, again.

There was nothing to do but wait. Every aspect of a pope's life was managed for him, from the moment his valet came to help him out of bed at dawn until he returned to that bed at night. It was a wonder, thought Stephen Parnell wryly, that he was even allowed the privacy of his dreams.

Since his idleness was enforced, he meditated, this time on the mysteries of faith and redemption, the recurring riddle that wound through his mind in an endless Möbius strip of thesis, antithesis, synthesis. It never failed to comfort him.

It also provided escape. Stephen Parnell had been escaping for his entire life.

Until he entered the priesthood, he'd never even had a bed of his own. The seventh of twelve, he'd slept between two of his elder brothers on the sagging mattress of what had been their parents' marriage bed twenty-odd years before.

His father had died of overwork and drink, the principal killers of middle-aged men in Derry, when young Stevie was eight, leaving his mother with two still in diapers and no support except what any of her older children could bring home between bouts of unemployment, the chronic cancer of Catholic Belfast. It wasn't until a man of indeterminate age, a man without a name who kept his face always in shadow, began to come around on rent day to hand Maeve Parnell a folded wad of currency, origin unspecified, that supper became more than bread and gravy again and there was enough coal for the grate.

When both twenty-year-old Brian and eighteen-year-old Tommy began to put in longer and longer hours at "work," most of it at night, Stephen began to understand the way the world was made.

No one breathed the words "Provisional Army"; everyone knew there was no such thing.

The older ones had tried to protect him. Stevie was the delicate one, the bookworm, the one who might amount to something if he could ever get off the streets. His best-kept secret was that books were his escape, the place where he went to hide from the dirt he felt accumulating on his pale skin from those streets—not physical dirt so much as spiritual dirt, the dirt of a place too imbued with blood and old feuds ever to be washed clean.

He'd been lost in a book the day Tommy was shot in the back of the head along with two of his fellows in an empty field; the news never even made the evening papers. When the faceless men brought the body home, Brian and their ma had a terrible row. He wanted vengeance; Maeve wanted peace.

"I've lost the one son already!" she shrilled. "It's my own fault for turning a blind eye to your activities, but I'll not stand by knowing another's turned killer."

"Then I'll relieve you of the responsibility!" Brian raged. They never saw him again.

That spring Maeve was standing outside the church, her two youngest by the hand, talking with some of the other women about the shame of it all, about how the menfolk would never see past their own stubbornness and perhaps it was up to the women to make an end to it. A car bomb went off in front of the pub across the road. Maeve and the little ones were killed by flying shrapnel, along with eleven others. That not only made the evening papers, it made international news.

Trembling and terrified, twelve-year-old Stephen Parnell had bolted from the funeral home to run after the priest who had just said the rosary over the one full-sized coffin and the two tiny ones. One of Brian's cohorts, come to pay his respects, had hinted to the lad that it was time he paid his dues as well.

"Father, take me with you!" Stephen pleaded. "They're after me to join the Provos. In conscience, I cannot."

It was a terribly adult statement made in the voice of a boy, and the priest was wise enough not to refuse him. With the help of his superiors he cut a swath through the red tape necessary to take a boy too young but academically gifted out of the city and away from the Troubles, spiriting him away to a Christian Brothers' secondary school in the countryside. Stephen Parnell grew and flourished. It was no surprise to anyone, least of all himself, that he should apply for Holy Orders on his graduation day.

He never set foot in Belfast again. Now, fifty years later, his scholarship and his spirituality had taken him as far from that world as he could come. His escape, thought Stephen Parnell, now Pope Luke John I, had been complete.

Luke John glanced at his wristwatch, a twenty-year-old Gruen that was more accurate than comfortable. He had noticed recently that he was waiting more often at Cosa's behest. Cosa had asked for a private meeting, which meant that the matter was something of great importance to him, yet he was late. Cosa's requests were often veiled and frequently ominous; he made the punctilious Stephen Christy Parnell uncomfortable. Not tense or guarded, or even irritable—merely uncomfortable. The more Cosa pretended to straightforwardness, the more he could be suspected of hidden agendas.

The cardinal's charisma, his sharp mind and magnetic authority, outweighed any eccentricities that someone in his position was prone to exhibit. Previous popes had always had at least half a dozen *a latere* cardinals—high-ranking clerics with the ear of the pope who enjoyed nearly unlimited access to His Holiness. Parnell had one.

Although Cosa was a political man, a skillful predator in the wilds of government, his temperament was reliable, even cool, judged the pope. He had risen to his position, now second only to Parnell, without having offended anyone too grievously. The result was that his rise had appeared to be uneventful, inevitable even, an ideal backdrop for the final step up to the throne of Catholicism. And his penchant for intrigue was no more pronounced than that of any ranking diplomat, thought Parnell. Such personal attributes were essential to the profession these days. Cosa was worth waiting for.

When the cardinal at last entered the Hall of the Savior in the Apostolic Palace, he found His Holiness seated peacefully in the gilded Guaccarini armchair between the *quattrocento* vase and the tall window overlooking the piazza. Even he had to admit there was something undeniably saintly about the small, round, balding figure bathed in morning light, his mild eyes partly obscured by the rimless glasses he always wore.

Luke John was a strong believer in the soft, defenseless body of an aging man; he had allowed his spirit to prosper at the expense of health and vigor. Foreign journalists, particularly the antagonistic British and Americans, delighted in commenting on his deliberate public persona, which gave the impression of someone sleepwalking. Some of the tabloids even hinted that he was drugged. They did not appreciate how the office weighed down the man.

"*Buon Giorno*, Adeodato," the pope greeted Cosa, simultaneously raising his right hand in blessing. "What subject is so critical that you would deny an old man his siesta, eh?"

"I apologize, Your Holiness." Slightly out of breath, Cosa eased his great bulk into the chair offered him. "But a matter I raised with you earlier may prove to be of greater import to the Church than even I first realized."

Luke John smiled at the cardinal's admitted egotism. "And what matter might that be?" he asked, his voice still holding a trace of Belfast.

"Last week I brought to Your Holiness's attention the request of a biogenetics laboratory in America for access to certain relics—"

"BioGenera," the pope said, reminding himself as much as Cosa.

"Just so."

"I'm listening."

"Naturally I am aware of Holy Mother Church's stated policy against providing relics to scientific research, a policy that you yourself have reemphasized in recent years."

"True enough," Luke John admitted. "However, I will remind you that we permitted scientists to carbon-test the Shroud of Turin."

"The request from BioGenera is somewhat different, Your Holiness."

Luke John visibly relaxed then, as if he knew something Cosa did not.

"Adeodato, as you know me, you know I am an avid reader. I enjoy a good science fiction tale as well as the next man. And that is precisely how Dottore Shepard's research seems to me, as the basis for a good science fiction tale."

"Holiness, I have provided you with ample evidence—"

"I should not wish to hazard the Church's dignity by lending credence to science fiction," Luke John concluded, as if Cosa had not spoken.

Undaunted, Cosa held his ground. "Holiness, I believe that Dottore Shepard's experiment may provide an unprecedented opportunity for the Church."

"Do you? Then by all means, go on. But quickly, please. I have a busy afternoon."

"I suggest that in this instance science can work in tandem with faith."

This caught Luke John's attention. "I've never known you to be cryptic, Adeodato. What are you saying exactly?"

Cosa allowed himself a conspiratorial tilt of the head. "Dottore Shepard may have it within his power to penetrate mankind's most impenetrable barrier to understanding."

"What barrier is this?"

"Time, Your Holiness. Time itself. If we allow him access to our most treasured relics, and if his experiment is successful—"

"—A great many 'ifs'—"

"—Shepard may be able to utilize those relics to reveal certain facts that have been denied us by the grave."

"Of which relics are we speaking?" Luke John asked carefully.

Cosa drew himself up. He had rehearsed this moment.

"Those of your earliest predecessor, Holiness."

The suggestion struck Luke John with the force of a bullet. He fell back against his chair and signed himself.

"And what benefit do you foresee that this might have for the Church?"

His wording was deliberate. Of course he knew the unimaginable advantage of communing with the soul of Saint Peter, though his mind reeled at the possibility. What he needed to know was not the objective advantage to the faith but what Cosa saw as the advantage.

"*Exempli Gratia,*" Cosa suggested calmly. He could see the fever of discovery in Stephen Parnell's eyes, and he played to it. "We could at last answer the riddle of the missing years. Hear the actual words of our Lord Jesus, not as they were recorded in the Gospels decades after his death but as he spoke them. His specific instructions to the Apostles. The potential is . . . incredible."

"Potential cuts two ways, Adeodato. The voice of ancient bones may not be the voice we expect to hear. What if it contradicts Church teaching? What if the experts are wrong and the relics we revere are not those of a saint but of a tyrant?"

"Did Galileo tremble before truth? Do we truly know the

reality of existence?'' asked Cosa. "Or have we grown up in a cave where we know only shadows?"

"What if shadows are all there is?"

"Then we will know that, too."

Stephen Parnell felt his heart pounding, as it hadn't since the day his mother died. He saw no escape this time.

"You can afford to be brave, Cosa. It is not your name that will become a synonym for ridicule and despair if the truth is not as you and I believe."

"Nor is it my name that will join Peter's alongside the Holy Trinity," Cosa countered. A bit of flattery helped wash down the bitterest pill. "There is no doubt in my mind that God speaks through the Church."

"Was it God, then, who nearly executed brave Galileo?"

"In a sense, yes," Cosa answered boldly. "Galileo's ordeal was necessary to enlighten human understanding. Need I remind Your Holiness that truth prevailed? I believe truth will prevail in this instance also. If Dottore Shepard's experiment is against the will of God, it cannot but fail."

Luke John hadn't considered the matter in this light. It was why he needed men like Cosa.

"Very well," he said after a moment's deliberation. "Because I know you as a realist, Adeodato, I will put my trust in your evaluation of this experiment. You would not validate such science to me if it were fiction."

The pontiff ended with just enough question in his expression to remind Cosa that he was the pope and took his responsibilities seriously.

"Of course not, Your Holiness. I have considered this request with my usual diligence." He paused long enough to lend extra credence. "I would not ask for your time if I did not believe the experiment had merit."

"Science is a human work, genetic 'miracles' notwithstanding," Luke John pointed out.

"Christ was also human, Your Holiness. How can we say what is God's work and what is man's work? Are they not sometimes one and the same?"

"What do we know of this Andrew Shepard?" Luke John wondered. "Yes, I have read the background material you provided me regarding his credentials, his accomplishments. But what do we know of him as a man?"

Cosa took out his reading glasses, producing a folder from the small leather portfolio he had brought with him. Luke John did not recall noticing it when Cosa came in.

"How much do you wish to know, Holiness?" Cosa looked over the rims of his glasses at him, then began to read. "He is forty-five years of age, degrees from Harvard and the University of Chicago, married and divorced . . ."

Cosa watched as Luke John shook his head. He himself gestured, as if to say, *Americans! What can one expect?*

"He and his former wife had one child, a daughter, who died at a young age—"

"Cosa, enough!" the pope protested. "I will not ask you how you know so much, but it is more than sufficient. Thank you!"

Better that you do not ask, Holiness! Cosa thought. *I should not wish to be placed in the position of making someone like you aware of the existence of someone like Jurgen Rindt.*

"Such information is easily obtainable, Holiness," he offered aloud. "The proliferation of computer networks—"

"—the end of any hope for privacy," Luke John finished for him with a sigh. He glanced out the window at a black cloud forming over the piazza, at a world that grew more menacing each day.

"Do we need this, Adeodato? Do the benefits outweigh the dangers?"

Cosa cast his lure into the pope's stream of consciousness. "Consider, Holiness, the benefit of being able to prove conclusively that Jesus in fact rose from the dead on the third day . . ."

Instantly there was a catch on the line. The pope looked back to Cosa.

"The Church teaches that this is so. But still there is doubt among the faithful." Cosa now worked the line carefully, steadily, allowing his catch to swim at his own pace, in his own chosen direction.

"This is true!" lamented Parnell.

"Yet even the most skeptical biblical scholars concede that something extraordinary occurred in Jerusalem a few days after Good Friday," Cosa continued. "The Apostles fled to their homes fearing arrest. When they emerged, they preached fearlessly to the very same people who just three days earlier had crucified their Christ. Why? What happened? Until now, no one has been able to shed any more light on this mystery.''

Cosa spun the familiar facts with verve.

"Until now.''

"Dottore Shepard's memory resurrection may hold the keys to the kingdom.''

"Such a miracle would benefit God's presence on earth.'' Stephen Parnell was allowing himself to invest his emotions in what had been until moments earlier an administrative matter.

"Such proof could aid you in your mission, to bring souls out of darkness into light.''

Cosa sat back, confident he had his quarry in the shallows near his landing net, ready to be taken.

"And if the proof were not to our benefit?'' His Holiness reflected. "I would be disgraced. Don't misunderstand, Cosa. I have faith that ours is the one true way. It is my concern for our flock. Are they ready to understand the price of enlightenment? It is my duty to consider these things.''

The pope darted a few yards away in the rushing waters. Cosa watched helplessly as he escaped.

"Give me some more time. I must have more time.''

8

EVERY GENETICS LAB HAD ITS SCIENTIFIC ADVISORY panel, and BioGenera was no exception. As Andrew entered the conference room, he nodded to his peers around the conference table. The senior member was Dr. Barton Beale, white-haired, patrician, a self-styled "old warhorse.'' Beside him sat Dr. Veronica Olson, forty-something, beautiful as an ice sculpture and about as approachable, blond hair pulled back severely, exaggerated horn-rims defiantly marring her high-cheekboned beauty.

Neither Linda Hajib nor Stephen Carlson looked old enough to have a doctorate. From Andrew's perspective, they could have been high school students, she with her riot of black curls, generous figure, and infectious giggle, he trying to look older than he was behind a gingery beard.

His glance lingered on Orin Sharpton. *Know thine enemy!* he thought, keeping his expression blank, wondering as always how secure these meetings were. Each of these people was a molecular biologist with a specialty in genetic science, and a sterling résumé impressive enough that he or she could easily jump ship for a rival lab at any time. He could only hope that his memory resurrection procedure would intrigue them enough to ensure their confidentiality.

On the other side of the table, chatting up the out-of-town board members, Lauren Griffiths looked more like someone's grandmother than BioGenera's consulting psychologist. The four board members themselves were a mixed lot. Malin Hartwick, CEO of First Pacific Bank, was right out of Central Casting, down to the understated pinkie ring and the precision cut of his graying sideburns, which exactly matched the color of his suit. To the unpracticed eye, Caroline Davies, president of DMI, the international market research firm, might seem to be just another woman executive in a power suit; only the startling purple-black of her arching manicured nails hinted at the free spirit within.

Stewart Washington, Ph.D., dean of the Harvard Graduate School of Business, might have played center for the Bulls in his salad days; now he stifled a yawn behind his elegant fingers (''Jet lag!'' he smiled at Delphine) and shifted his long frame in a chair that was just like half a dozen chairs at half a dozen conferences that would demand his attention this week alone. Only Karol Sliwa looked as if he'd wandered onto the wrong soundstage; the juxtaposition of his military haircut and the one-thousand-dollar suit tailored to his wrestler's frame suggested a robber baron or perhaps a spy, rather than the chief financial officer at Royal Essen Pharmaceuticals.

These were the individuals who would judge the scientific merits of Andrew's memory resurrection project. Delphine moved gracefully among them, offering coffee or tea, greeting each as if he or she were the most important person in the room.

The scientific advisory panel met essentially as a seminar to discuss a project's merits. Logistics and marketing tended to overshadow science; a meeting was usually considered a success if the participants managed to focus on the details of the project itself long enough to form an educated opinion. Consensus was the ideal; agreement to disagree was the reality.

When Gindman entered the room, the temperature dropped a few degrees. Small talk trickled off. All eyes were upon the CEO as he strode to the head of the table.

"Good morning," Gindman greeted the assembled and took his place. "Thank you for accommodating this unscheduled meeting. I've asked you here for a couple of reasons, both relating to time, or lack of it.

"Doctors, ladies and gentlemen, BioGenera is in the fight of its brief life. This market environment is unlike anything any of us has experienced. All the rules have changed. Competition is transforming the marketplace; BioGenera has to do better. The Pentagon's decision to award the contract for Epidermal Growth Factor to General Genetic makes a serious situation critical.

"Change is so constant and unrelenting now that, frankly, it's a bitch just keeping up, not to mention breaking out and getting ahead. So I'm changing the rules. Monthly meetings aren't cutting it. From now on, we'll meet when I see an opportunity that warrants our consideration. This morning is such a time."

He looked at Andrew and handed the meeting over to him.

"Dr. Shepard—it's all yours."

Andrew rose, his ears buzzing and vision narrowing in waves. He detested public speaking.

"Thank you, Mr. Gindman. Ladies and gentlemen, I'll try to get to the point. There is some background, however, that may be helpful to those of you outside the immediate realm of molecular biology and genetic engineering."

He arrived at the head of the table as Gindman pushed his chair to the side. The CEO's expression was courteous but opaque, revealing nothing. It occurred to Andrew that he wouldn't be here this morning if Gindman weren't sufficiently interested to call an unscheduled meeting of the advisory panel. That was a good sign, but it was a thin reed to hold to while confronting the group of aggressive and energetic intellects staring back at him. Some of them had flown across several time zones to be here; he had to make it worth their while.

"In many of the great human challenges, we have envisioned the goal before the means to achieve that goal were available," he began. His tone was one he had heard a hundred times from experts at symposia; his own conviction surprised him.

"In genetics, this situation is reversed. Only as recently as 1953 did the discovery by Crick and Watson of the double-helix DNA structure teach us that our bodies, our intellectual potential, and our susceptibility to disease were governed by a genetic text. Our experience with DNA has progressed from discovery to exploration in a single human lifetime. We are learning to read the script much faster than we thought possible. Progress in deciphering DNA script has outpaced even the most optimistic projections. Where we once thought it would take us until at least the year 2010, we now believe we will 'crack the code,' so to speak, before the millennium."

There were appreciative murmurs from the board members. As far as the scientists on the other side of the table were concerned, this was mostly old news. Andrew waited a long moment for the undercurrent to subside before he continued.

"The GENBANK computer data banks in Los Alamos, and European Molecular Biology Organization's banks in Heidelberg presently house more than fifty million DNA characters," he went on, gaining confidence, "and researchers have already diagnosed genetic disorders such as Down's syndrome from simple blood samples."

Karol Sliwa nodded knowingly. "That was Royal Essen's principal business last quarter," he reported.

Andrew's confidence climbed further.

"Amniocentesis is on its way into the medical history books," he continued. "We no longer need to insert needles through the placenta, risking spontaneous abortion. Now we can take a blood sample, screen it for fetal blood cells, and then survey chromosome pairs. If an extra copy of the X chromosome is found, it confirms the presence of Down's.

"In October 1991, doctors at the National Institutes of

Health attempted for the first time to immunize a terminally ill cancer patient against his own widespread melanoma by injecting two hundred million live, genetically altered tumor cells into the thigh of the forty-six-year-old man. This caused the man's immune system to generate lymphocytes that were attuned to attack the melanoma cells.''

"Like a vaccine?" interrupted Washington.

Andrew had to remind himself that not everyone in his audience was a scientist.

"A vaccine usually prevents disease," he explained. "Through gene therapy, we can actually treat advanced cancers after they occur, even after conventional methods have failed. With this particular patient, the lymph glands that drain the thigh area were removed three weeks later. From those glands, lymphocytes sensitive to the gene-modified cancer were extracted, cultivated in huge numbers in the laboratory, then reinjected to boost the patient's own immune response to the cancer."

"I remember that case," Sliwa noted. "The success of that procedure was a benchmark for NIH policy, the same policy that enabled—correction, *would* have enabled—BioGenera to move into producing Epidermal Growth Factor commercially."

Andrew nodded. "That's right, only it did more than that. It opened the door for use of the procedure in other ways, and our progress continues to build momentum. My method of decoding the genetic texts, based initially upon Dr. Kary Mullis' DNA amplification, or polymerase chain reaction (PCR) method, and Fred Sanger's dideoxy, the chain termination method of sequencing, have enabled me to read up to five hundred bases' worth of sequence daily for the past six years. Now we have the Hood automated gene sequencers. These machines have accelerated the pace of my work by a factor of twenty.

"The Hoods are new, and we're lucky to have eight of them. Unfortunately, they haven't been placed on our government's export restriction lists. It's entirely possible, even likely, that certain regimes looking for a better weapon against their enemies are also collecting Hoods."

Nobody had to say the words "ethnic cleansing," but everyone was thinking them.

"Delphine—?" Gindman interjected quietly, the fir.
time he'd spoken since Andrew began.

Delphine had been leafing through a manila folder on the
polished tabletop in front of her. "We've just learned from
a source at the Commerce Department that Israel has—let's
see, where was it? Oh, here it is—thirty-six Hoods. Libya
has twenty-eight, Iraq up to sixty, Pakistan six, China
twenty-four, North Korea eighteen, and Japan seventy-
eight."

Andrew grimaced. "As you can see, the pressure is on
for us to accelerate our research. The autoradiographs used
in my work have been reverified by other specialists, and I
am pleased to announce to you today that I have patents on
the DNA sequences of more than one hundred viruses. Of
course, these data cannot be regarded as proprietary or used
for profit, in my opinion. I reference these patents only as
a measure of our relative progress . . ."

As he'd grown more comfortable with his audience, Andrew's mind had bifurcated. Half of it was on automatic
pilot, explaining his work with the confidence of someone
who knew what he was talking about and wouldn't make
mistakes; the other half was gnawing at him. What if this
entire presentation was for nothing? If he didn't hear from
the Vatican, in the affirmative, and soon, would Gindman
and the board lose interest? If the Vatican refused him, was
there any other source left?

There was only one solution: the Vatican had to say yes.

Thousands of tourists filed through St. Peter's basilica,
oblivious to the inner workings of the city-state surrounding
it. For most, fulfillment came in the sights, sounds, and
scents of the Vatican. Merely being present in such a holy
place made them feel closer to God.

In the nearby Apostolic Palace, Luke John worked quietly
in his office and apartment quarters. His eyes scanned the
magnificent surroundings, the Berninis, Raphaels, and Buon-
arottis as he padded through the private rooms praying, de-
liberating.

He tried to concentrate upon vespers and pray for guidance, yet couldn't finish one of the prayers he had recited
thousands of times before. He had been unable to stop think-

ing about the memory resurrection procedure since Cardinal Cosa first mentioned it. New possibilities of this wondrous experiment continually occurred to him and sent his imagination soaring heavenward.

Surely, it cannot hurt to engage BioGenera, he thought to himself. *I will insist that Cosa make our involvement sub rosa, of course. If it fails, we lose nothing. If it succeeds . . .*

"May I remind you that this organization exists to make a profit, Dr. Shepard?" Malin Hartwick pointed out. He was gracious about it, but there was no mistaking his concern about profitability.

"I understand that, Mr. Hartwick," Andrew said. "All I meant was that it's a guiding principle of science to share findings."

"Listen," Gindman spoke up finally. He'd been leaning back in his chair, hands clasped behind his head, now he leaned forward, wound tight. "We know this, but maybe we need to hear it again: We can get farther with a good idea and a profit motive than we can with just a good idea. Where, then, is the opportunity in these genetic texts for BioGenera to make a profit?"

"In the applications of our knowledge of those texts," Andrew suggested. "In the way we apply that expertise to marketable products."

"I think I understand. Please go on," Hartwick acquiesced.

Andrew took a deep breath. "Everything I've given you so far is background, and I thank you all for bearing with me. We are on the threshold of the most exciting era in science history. The Human Genome Project's goal—set here in San Diego at the first meeting in 1989—was a complete reading of the human genetic code within twenty years. We're well on our way. A variety of commercial applications are already taken for granted."

"For example?" prompted Caroline Davies.

"General Genetic is marketing insulin, Factor VIIIC— which has revolutionized the treatment of hemophiliacs— and human growth hormone." Andrew ticked them off on his fingers. "BioGenera has several proprietary technologies available for application. The fact is, BioGenera has always excelled in pushing the theoretical envelope while developing spinoff processes that will be the seeds of tomorrow's applications. Gene therapy. Genetic engineering. Molecular biology and genetic science are in their infancy.

"We will no longer be limited to merely treating the symptoms of disease. We will work directly with the cause of disease before it can become a problem. Rather than living under the dark cloud of cancer and autism and AIDS, we will learn to alter the design of the human DNA strand to *preempt* problems.

"My point is that we are privileged to be here at this paradigm shift, but I also want all of us to realize the significance of what I am about to propose. Now, let me segue to a parallel subject: the human brain."

Flickers of recognition flashed across faces around the table. The scientists, at least, had heard rumors about what Shepard and Will Austin were up to in that lab of theirs.

"Our brains contain, by a rough estimate, seventeen billion cells. These cells manage a hundred million messages per second, all day and all night, around the clock, for the entire seventy-plus years of our lives. They transmit and receive these millions of messages perfectly most of the time. It's a communications process. But how can one cell communicate to another? Psychology, biology, chemistry all try to explain it, but we're still not sure. If a cell can't communicate, at least in the sense that we think of as communication, then another possible explanation is that each cell must possess a consciousness."

He paused deliberately, giving his audience time to digest what he was saying.

"The theory that each cell has a consciousness is satisfying to psychology and psychiatry because it explains such problematical disorders as schizophrenia. It is an extraordinarily fragile process, this system of intercellular communication. How, for example, does our consciousness remain intact after trauma, after scrambling of the cells by some terrible blow? Why don't football players' personalities change after every hit, as one cell's consciousness is replaced by another's? This theory also offers us an extraordinary opportunity."

"What opportunity is that, Doctor?" Stewart Washington asked quietly.

"If we can graft bone, hearts, lungs, skin, why not memory cells? If, as we now understand, all life is composed of the same DNA building blocks and each cell carries in its nucleus the entire history of its species in its DNA double-helix strand, why can't we graft memory?"

Everyone took a breath.

"What I propose today is a conservative therapeutic approach as a test of my concept. Simply put, I intend to restore the life experiences and sense memory of a deceased human to active, living form. In so doing, I believe we can accelerate our pace of learning in a variety of scientific disciplines."

There was silence. Lauren Griffiths, the psychologist, was the first to speak. "It sounds as if you're talking about a kind of engineered reincarnation."

"Like most people in the Western world, I don't believe in reincarnation," Andrew said. "There is simply no compelling evidence. However, my experiments have convinced me that there is some sort of awareness—or consciousness, if you will—that can be transmitted genetically, just like hair color or body type.

"I am proposing consciousness resurrection. Researchers have shown that DNA can be obtained from 7,500-year-old human remains. Experiments are currently under way to extract DNA from a Neanderthal fossil."

"Let me see if I understand this," Dr. Griffiths said slowly. "You're proposing to extract viable DNA from an ancient source and 'graft' it—upon whom? And how?"

Andrew swallowed. Here was where the panel would make or break him. "The 'how' is explained in the proposal that will be distributed to each of you at the end of this meeting. The 'whom'—well, we're in the process of seeking a volunteer host right now."

"Is the effect permanent?" Lauren Griffiths wanted to know.

"My results are so far inconclusive. The effect seems to be long-lived."

"If your subject is, say, twenty or so, and the effect remains permanent . . ." Dr. Griffiths raised her hands helplessly, unable to finish her thought, but Andrew could see that it appalled her.

"Then I've committed the volunteer to sixty years with a stranger's consciousness," he completed the thought for her. "I know."

"Whoa!" Stewart Washington sat back in his chair as the full impact of what Andrew was suggesting reached him. "We're talking serious alteration to the host's quality of life here. How do you propose to find a volunteer willing to—quite possibly—lose his mind?"

"That's in the report, Dr. Washington," Andrew said. "We're weighing age versus such factors as terminal illness, someone for whom the procedure would represent a new lease on life, a second chance."

"But you'll want someone as vigorous and healthy as possible," Linda Hajib interjected earnestly. "The immunosuppression necessary before you can even begin injecting a host with antagonistic DNA—"

Suddenly the scientists' side of the table was alive with debate. Andrew didn't know whether to try to regain control or let them have their heads. He glanced helplessly at Gindman, who just grinned at him.

You started this, Shepard! he seemed to be telepathing. *Just think of what the world at large is going to make of your procedure!*

"No offense, Dr. Shepard," Orin Sharpton's strident voice suddenly cut across everyone else's, "but I must point out to Mr. Gindman and the others that your experiment seems weak in the commercial development area."

He turned to address Gindman directly. "I mean, isn't our mission here to develop as quickly as possible whatever will sell?"

"You're half right, Dr. Sharpton," responded Gindman, on his feet, taking command. "Because of competitive market conditions, we're forced to develop protocols and products as quickly as we can . . ."

Sharpton began to gloat, sure that he had stolen the momentum from Andrew's presentation.

". . . consistent with sound and preferably proprietary science," Gindman continued. "Our goal here is to give our product a unique position in the marketplace."

"Well, then, shouldn't we go with a product that has proven market appeal?" Sharpton was warming up his most unctuous tone. "Just make it better and faster than our competition? You said earlier that we don't have time—"

Gindman had reached the head of the table; he was in charge again. "No, Dr. Sharpton. It's that kind of short-sighted thinking that is dragging American business down. BioGenera will focus on market creation, not market sharing. It's the bottom of the ninth, people. We either suck it up as a team right now, or we lose. I won't lose. We've got too much talent and opportunity right here to look for reasons not to create something important. I for one think Dr. Shepard's memory resurrection procedure has possibilities."

He began distributing copies of Andrew's proposal. "I want you all to think about what you've heard this morning, read over Dr. Shepard's proposal, and return with your input for the final phase of our review. I expect clear thinking on all procedural aspects, including ethical and legal. Now, unless anyone has anything else to say, we're adjourned."

He strode out without another word, Delphine in his wake. The rest of them dissolved into chaos, everyone talking at once as they filed out. Andrew watched them leave and looked for clues as to how they would vote, but the skeptics seemed to outnumber the enthusiasts. He didn't know what to think.

9
NOW WHAT CAN STOP THIS, STOP ME? ANDREW asked himself over and over, a mantra to shout down his new fears. The Vatican had to say yes, it had to. Otherwise he'd have to resort to requesting remains from rare Bronze Age finds—bodies melted out of glaciers, susceptible to decay and bacterial contamination and a host of bureaucratic and jurisdictional problems. How long might that take? How long would the board sit still, if the Vatican refused him?

That's not your concern, Shepard! he castigated himself. *Just do the work. Let events sort themselves out.* The Vatican would say yes; there was no point in considering other alternatives. His request was no more radical than the request to study the Shroud of Turin. The Church had nothing to lose, and everything to gain in terms of public relations if it honored his request. He would proceed on that assumption, regardless of how frustrating it was to wait.

The emerging potential of memory resurrection both frightened and sustained him. *Just do the work!* He wanted to talk with Niko, but Niko could only listen, a strange intelligence that was not his own glowing in the back of his eyes. So Andrew had to be content to observe, to reassure himself that Niko's consciousness was still his own, to touch and be touched. More often than not, Will slipped out at the end of the workday leaving the two of them staring off at the horizon, barely noticing his departure.

Preparations had a force of their own. Everything Andrew did, every calculation, every theorem produced new insight. There was no wasted effort. Momentum built with incredible power; pieces fit together. He was in his prime, incapable of stupidity or mistake. This almost godlike ability to create terrified the other side of him; he didn't believe he would be able to sustain such exquisite precision for very long. Sooner or later he would err. Had he missed anything? Was there anything in his procedure that would harm others?

In the meantime he worked and simultaneously watched from outside himself, amazed that a life in science had produced such extraordinary skills.

"There's a logistical problem that's been bothering me, Doc," Will said.

Andrew sensed a faint disturbance at the extreme edge of his concentration as he and Niko experimented with a new chromosomal mutation model. He was about to connect two letters in parallel when Niko caught on to what he was thinking and inserted the blue ball where Andrew visualized it.

"Doc?"

"Sorry!" Andrew stirred and turned to listen.

"What if the procedure is permanent?"

"Then we've committed our volunteer to a lifetime of hosting a stranger's consciousness," Andrew completed the thought. "I know. The issue was raised by the advisory panel, too."

"And—?"

Andrew studied Niko; he was only nine, still a youngster. Had he been doomed to live with a man's consciousness for life? They didn't have the luxury of observing him for six months, a year, a lifetime, to determine how long the effect would last.

"We decided to trade the specimen's age for the security of minimal risk to the host's quality of life," said Andrew.

"An older volunteer," Will thought aloud. "Someone who has lived out most of his life span, but as vigorous and healthy as possible."

"The older, the better," they said in unison.

"Or someone with a terminal illness," Will suggested. "Even a death row inmate? Now that some states have reintroduced the death penalty . . ."

He didn't finish. Medical lost causes, sociological complications were things that pure scientists shouldn't have to deal with. Unless they lived in the real world.

Andrew felt suddenly deflated. "Difficult choices. But medical miracles have come out of similar cases in the past. Why not genetic miracles now?"

He refused to be defeated; he was in no mood to waste time. The Vatican's silence had him hobbled. The project was still on track, but if he needed to find another source of viable DNA, that would take valuable time. He decided to accelerate his work on the elements he could control. He shifted his focus from DNA sources to finding precisely the right host. He and Will reviewed several host candidate profiles before midmorning.

They hadn't expected such an overwhelming response. A few quiet inquiries to local medical facilities had them swamped with applicants. There were scores of volunteers from the nearby VA hospital, some homeless men from the UCSD research hospital and medical school, some terminal patients from the Cancer Institute, some prisoners from the federal prison, and a handful of AIDS patients. All the regulars showed up; none of them qualified. They were little more than upright dead men, hoping for one last hurrah before the grave. Andrew wanted a healthy male with a healthy attitude.

Then they found Nicolao Soares.

In his office at the opposite corner of the Apostolic Palace from Luke John's apartments, Cardinal Cosa intensified his research into the availability of tissue for Dr. Shepard. In the event that His Holiness chose to honor BioGenera's request, Cosa would be prepared; if not, there was nothing lost. Cosa needed, always, to be prepared.

He had asked Dr. Anna Aldobrandi to reschedule her morning graduate seminar in archaeological technique at the University of Rome and come directly to his office.

"Tell me about the bones from the niche, *Dottore*."

Dr. Aldobrandi was surprised by his request. "You know everything there is to know already, Your Eminence."

"Humor me, *Dottore*," replied the cardinal cryptically.

Dr. Aldobrandi had participated in a dozen meetings with the cardinal in as many years. Never had she sensed genuine warmth from him. He was as cool and efficient about his business as she had become about her own. Today he was different.

"Very well," she began formally, slipping into her accustomed lecture rhythm. "As you know, Your Eminence, one hundred and thirty-five bones—some of them full length, the rest fragmented—were removed from the niche in what is known as the Graffiti Wall—so named because of the previously indecipherable inscriptions roughly carved into its surface—beneath the basilica during the 1939-to-1949 excavations and were ignored for a decade due to an accident of human oversight.

"Fortunately, however, they were carefully preserved in the storeroom behind the chapel of Saint Columban, then moved to dryer storage in the basilica's main offices. In 1962, Professor Correnti proved them to be the skeletal remains of a powerfully built man of about seventy years who had lived an outdoor life. On June 28, 1968, after several years of intense theological, academic, and scientific scrutiny, His Holiness Pope Paul . . ."

". . . announced to the world that the skeletal remains had been identified," Cosa interrupted.

"Yes." Dr. Aldobrandi concluded her report. "The remains were then returned to the Graffiti Wall, where they have stayed to this day."

"As they should," Cosa interjected. "These relics are the spiritual anchor that holds the basilica to its moorings."

"Metaphorically speaking," Dr. Aldobrandi frowned. "As a scientist, I am far more concerned with the fact that the bone fragments were placed in airtight plastic cases to preserve them under less than optimal conditions."

"What do you think, *Dottore*?" Cosa asked. "Are you convinced of their authenticity?"

She paused, drawing a finger to her lips in reflection. She was a conscientious scholar, scrupulous about separating fact from opinion. It was well known throughout the Vatican that when Dr. Anna Aldobrandi delivered a judgment, it was supported by research, scientific method, and personal restraint.

"*Si*, Your Eminence. Without a doubt."

"Such faith is a comfort," Cosa observed dryly, looking away into some private inner distance.

"More than faith, Your Eminence," Aldobrandi presumed to correct him. "Confidence supported by scientific evidence. Yet, am I correct in assuming that you question these conclusions?"

The cardinal made a noncommittal gesture. "Just another two-thousand-year-old doubt to keep me awake at four in the morning. I pray for guidance."

"Guidance in what, may I ask?"

Cosa leaned his great bulk back in his chair. "Thank you for meeting with me on such short notice. You have been most helpful," he said abruptly. "Please send my apologies to your students."

Dr. Aldobrandi knew that there was no use in pursuing the subject. She had been dismissed. Still, her curiosity had been aroused. Those bones were the specimens that had helped establish her international reputation as a bold, uncompromising scientist. Of what possible use could they be to the cardinal?

"*Prègo*, Your Eminence. Please call me if I may assist you further."

"God bless you." Cosa raised his hand.

Dr. Aldobrandi lowered her eyes and crossed herself. No matter what else one felt about the cardinal, his blessing was several steps closer to God's than her parish priest's was.

A retired second-generation Portuguese tuna fisherman and devout Catholic, Nicolao Soares was at first glance as healthy as a breeding bull. Everything about him bespoke a dynamic, explosive character. Recently, however, the fire had been damped. His wife of forty years had died the year before. His two grown children were a disappointment to him. And there was a demon in his brain.

A short man, or rather a large man of short stature, he was compact and thick-chested. His hands were calloused beyond healing, plated with years of hardened armor that rasped whenever they brushed against anything. His leathery face glowed with an earthy dignity, and his coal-black eyes glistened sadly. They were eyes accustomed to trusting and appreciating and laughing, but recent events had dimmed the reflection of inner light.

According to Will's screening interview, Soares's son and daughter, thoroughly modern Californians, had no interest in joining him on the fishing boat for which he had mortgaged his future. So he had cut his losses and cashed out. He and his children were now living off the proceeds of the sale of his last boat. Andrew found that he liked the man.

"The fisherman's always had a tough time of it, hasn't he, Mr. Soares?"

"Ach, the stories I could tell you!"

"I see on your profile here that you have children," Andrew said conversationally. He was leaving the medical profile until last.

Nicolao shifted angrily in his seat and growled, holding up two thick fingers.

"Grandchildren?"

"Also two. My daughter, Marie's."

"Well, there you go. Do they work with you?" Andrew knew how close-knit Portuguese families tended to be, how a family business was passed down the generations.

Nicolao sighed and slumped his broad shoulders. "You're a good man, I can tell, Doc. Your papa raised you to be a good son. I tried with my Tony, but he don't want to fish.

He ran off to Alaska, makes big bucks as foreman on the pipeline.''

"A foreman? But that's great, if it's what he wants to do—''

Nicolao held up his hand. "You got kids, Doc?''

Andrew started. How could he answer that, especially to a stranger? Nicolao wasn't waiting for an answer.

"One way or the other, do me a favor and don't tell me how I shoulda raised mine. With Tony, I did something wrong. Must have. He's got no respect.''

"What about your daughter?'' Andrew persisted. He had to get a solid psychological profile on this man. He felt a strong resonance in Nicolao, a gut feeling that he was the right one, but he had to be sure. "Marie?''

"Marie.'' Nicolao nodded, a brief pride warming his bleak face. "She's a wonderful daughter, a good mother. She tries to help, but her heart's not in the business. Her children and husband come first; I know this.''

"And your wife?''

"Passed away last year.'' He crossed himself. "The only woman who could ever have kept me out of trouble for so many years, a madonna. You probably couldn't tell that I was a terror, a real man at sea and ashore.''

Andrew grinned. "I might have guessed.''

"But since my Teresa passed on . . . I thought that was the reason at first . . . why I started having the dreams, and then the headaches . . .'' He squeezed his eyes shut, as if against a terrible pain. They were filled with tears when he opened them. "I didn't know then about this thing . . . this thing in my brain that's eating me alive . . .''

"Get a load of this one, Doc,'' Will had said, dropping the file folder lightly on Andrew's desk only that morning. "Courtesy of UCSD.''

Andrew gave him a bemused look. "I thought we covered all of those.''

"Only the walk-ins from the shelters,'' Will pointed out. "This one's private.''

"How'd you happen to come by it?''

Will managed to look sheepish. "Oh, a friend of a friend.''

It dawned on Andrew slowly. "Sharon, the cute little resident from Neuro."

Will was suddenly defensive. "I want you to know that this was acquired at great personal sacrifice. It was a goodbye gift. She told me she was breaking it off because I 'lacked commitment.' Or maybe it was because I ought to be committed—I wasn't really paying much attention to that part. But she'd heard on the grapevine that some of their terminal cases were being referred to BioGenera and wanted to know if we were 'playing Frankenstein up there,' was how she put it. I assured her we weren't, and then she told me about this rare tumor case that had turned up on her rotation, and, well, I think this guy may be the answer to our prayers."

For the next half hour Will managed to shut up long enough for Andrew to study the file. The patient had presented complaining of confusion, violent mood swings, short-term memory loss, occasional loss of vision, and "not being myself." Exhaustive neurological testing had ruled out Alzheimer's disease. MRI scans had revealed the real culprit: an inoperable tumor in the postcentral gyrus of the cerebrum, the part of the brain that controlled sensation and virtual recognition. Cannibalizing healthy tissue in both the gray- and white-matter layers, it was quite literally stealing Nicolao Soares's soul.

"I'm sitting in Marie's living room with the baby on my lap," Nicolao told Andrew. "She's one and a half, cute as a button, and she's standing up pulling on my eyebrows, calling me 'Popi,' and all of a sudden I push her away from me. Almost threw her on the floor, Marie tells me afterward; I don't remember any of it. And you know why? *Because I don't know who she is!* I look up at Marie—the baby's screaming, she's taking her away from me, staring at me like I'm a murderer—and I don't recognize her either! After a while it goes away, I come back to myself, but it's happening more and more, and there's no telling when it's going to happen or what I'm going to do next.

"I don't care anymore, Doc. I sit around the supper table with Marie and the kids, my son-in-law; everybody else is laughing and having a good time—I don't feel anything.

There's a little *taverna* by the docks, I been going there for years to have a glass of wine, shoot the breeze. I've known some of these men thirty, forty years; we been through life and death together. I don't feel nothing for them anymore. One of 'em passed on last week. I went to the wake, his wife's going on about how we loved each other like brothers—nothing. I'm standing there thinking, *I don't care. I didn't care if he lived or died. I don't care if I live or die.*"

Andrew listened silently. There was nothing he could say in the face of such despair.

Nicolao was staring down at his hands. "I don't even recognize myself anymore. God help me, I never used to believe that stuff about the devil stealing your soul. Now I know better. This thing is eating me alive!"

The prognosis in his medical file had said essentially the same thing. Nicolao Soares could live for years—the tumor was nonmalignant and not affecting autonomic function—but his "self" would disappear, devoured by this growing mass that would eventually leave him an unresponsive hulk, a lost soul.

"That's why I volunteered, Doc. Any kind of life's got to be better than that. I figure we can help each other, right?"

"We're certainly going to try, Mr. Soares," Andrew said sincerely, still not ready to commit. "Aside from the tumor, your overall health looks good. Any complaints?"

"A little rusty in the joints, but show me an old buck who ain't and I'll show you somebody who didn't live."

"This is a purely experimental procedure, Mr. Soares. Are you absolutely sure you want to volunteer for it?"

"What else have I got to lose, Doc? 'Sides, I've always been a curious guy. I like to learn new things, see what's on the other side of the squall, y'know?" He hesitated for a fraction of a second, not out of fear, merely weighing the situation. "How risky is it?"

"We don't believe there's any physical danger to you. But there are other aspects that frankly we don't know about yet."

"Uh-huh," considered Nicolao. "And what 'aspects' would those be?"

Andrew had to laugh at himself. He did sound pompous.

"Mental aspects," he explained. "Psychological, emotional."

"I never put much store in that psychological stuff," Nicolao remarked. He tapped his forehead with two fingers. "Besides, I figure there's plenty of room for improvement."

"It could change your life forever," Andrew cautioned him. "Improve it, or destroy it. Or, it might not work at all. I can't offer any guarantees."

"I like straight talk, Doc."

"If it works with you, then we'll refine the procedure and provide it to others. You'll be famous."

"Yeah, well, I can take or leave that. Never saw much good come from fame. When do we start?"

"A day or two if you're selected. But we still have to look at a few more candidates."

Nicolao gave him a canny look. "Oh, sure! I seen that sorry bunch of sad sacks and alkies out there. Ask me, you found your guinea pig." He rose to leave. "You go ahead and do what you have to do. I'll be ready when you are."

"Thank you, Mr. Soares."

"Call me Nic." He shrugged. "And I ain't done nothing yet."

Andrew shook hands with him, noting the old man's vise-like grip.

Nicolao turned and walked down the hall, shaking his head at the sight of the other waiting men. He shuffled past them and disappeared into the sunlight quietly, almost invisibly.

As Andrew watched him depart, he was impressed by Nicolao's fierce nobility and gruff acceptance. He saw himself as he might be in twenty-five years and felt infinitely sad.

"There must be millions of dormant genes, evolutionary genes waiting for exactly the right conditions to reactivate," mused Will as he lowered the objective lens to the glass slide, glanced into the eyepiece of the microscope, and focused. Hundreds of Niko's T cells bloomed into view. "Maybe, just maybe, we can tap into them, too."

"The possibilities are endless," agreed Andrew. "Just think: If we could find, say, one of Einstein's eyelashes that had fallen into the pages of his favorite novel . . . or Dickens's or Aristophanes' or Hitler's . . . anyone's . . . theoretically, we could re-create its owner! We could resurrect that personality from the dormant cells in the sliver left behind.''

"Books as time capsules . . ." added Will.

"Precisely."

"Imagine all the lives, all the secrets, all the history in a well-circulated library volume! In a library of volumes—!" Will's imagination began to run away with him.

"—in the rare-volume room of a library." Andrew added more fuel to the fire.

"A Gutenberg Bible! Medieval copyists . . . marauding Huns . . . crusading knights . . . kings . . ." Will was babbling.

"Why stop there?" Andrew continued. "Why not Cro-Magnon, Neanderthal, *Homo erectus, Homo habilis*! Jesus, we could go all the way back to the earliest hominids, find the exact set of circumstances where we as a species parted company from Niko and his . . ."

Both fell silent, each on his own frontier of possibilities, the far plains of scientifically retrievable history.

"We'd be playing God!" Will suggested breathlessly.

"Or maybe proving that there isn't one," Andrew countered, taken aback by hearing out loud what had only been a vague mental exercise until now.

The procedure was now real. It lived in the thousands of problems he deliberated as he pushed the project from theory to application. Final approval wouldn't arrive until the scientific advisory panel held its second and final meeting to debate the ethics of memory resurrection.

He still didn't know yet where his source DNA would come from, but Andrew knew into what host he would inject it. He visualized the experiment repeatedly, always with Nicolao Soares receiving the injection.

Cardinal Cosa arrived in the pope's private library at 4:59 that afternoon, precisely ten seconds before his scheduled appointment.

He had walked the long way to the meeting to allow more time to consider his situation. He carefully weighed the pros and cons and concentrated on avoiding any conclusion that would leave him wanting for morality or good judgment in the pontiff's eyes.

Fortunately he had gotten it right in the past, always managing to align himself just in time with each new direction the papacy chose to take, calculating the pope's probable decision in every instance and thus being in a position to capitalize on the benevolence of an appreciative papacy and Curia. It had nothing to do with luck. Opportunity was a commodity in which Cosa had made his own wealth.

Luke John looked up from his reading—le Carré's newest thriller—and greeted Cosa warmly.

"A good day, I trust, Adeodato?" The pope dog-eared a page and set the book on a nearby table.

"*Si,* Your Holiness." Cosa settled himself in his accustomed chair somewhat breathlessly. "Not as good as some, but better than most."

Luke John smiled comfortably. He appreciated Cosa's restrained mood. It signaled that the world was intact; no immediate crisis lurked outside the Vatican walls to disrupt the unique peace he was feeling, the peace of having made a decision.

"Well, then, what do you think about this experiment? Any new developments about which I should be aware?"

"*Non,* Your Holiness. All that is left to you is to decide the merits of the project, risks versus rewards, that sort of thing. At worst, doubt will be cast on the authenticity of the remains."

"That would be a serious development," the pope acknowledged. "And at best?"

"At best they will confirm the identity and perhaps even add new information to our understanding."

"It occurs to me, my friend, that we may be servants caught in an historic moment, hm?"

Cosa waited for him to go on.

"Where there is the technical skill to move a mountain, there is no longer any need for faith to move the mountain."

Cosa's face whitened. Of course the thought had occurred to him, but not in such succinct terms. He saw in memory resurrection the potential for more control and hence more power. But he had not fully considered the effect that the realization of such power would have on all of mankind.

What would be the reaction of mankind when it looked into the face of undeniable historical truth?

"The candidate these scientists will select to be the subject of their experiment . . ." Luke John mused, "do we know how he will be chosen?"

"It is my understanding, Holiness, that they are seeking someone with a terminal illness," Cosa said somberly. "Someone who has not long to live."

"A brave man, whoever he may be!" Luke John pronounced. "Willing to give over his body for the greater good, like a Crusader, even a saint."

"Perhaps," Cosa demurred.

"Forgive an old man's failing memory, Adeodato," the pope said. "The man's name again who has created this technique?"

"Shepard, Your Holiness. Andrew Shepard. A good man, according to our sources, as well as a brilliant scientist." Cosa waited for the pope to comment.

"Peter was very much a man," the pope thought aloud. "The fact that he rose above temptations and carried on Christ's message is proof of the power of the Word. Proof enough for some. As a scholar, however, I must seek facts, the truth. For me, truth is a form of beauty, even when it offends. I suppose we have little to lose."

"Only the Church, Your Holiness," Cosa suggested ironically.

"A bit like Pascal's wager, isn't it? Your understatement aside, Cosa, I think we have leapt out of this world. I hope the world to come is kind to us."

Cosa was touched by the pope's courage. He didn't dare speak.

"Now, if the consciousness is not our saint's, then we end our involvement quietly. No harm is done," the pope continued.

"If the consciousness in the bones is the authentic saint we believe it to be, we have encouraged truth, perhaps participated in a miracle," Cosa suggested.

"And what if the consciousness is your saint's and he contradicts the Church's teachings?" asked the pope. "That could be . . . complicated."

"That would be very bad indeed, Your Holiness. But I have faith that the Church is in the right."

"You may need it, Adeodato."

"You have decided, then?" Cosa asked carefully.

The pope nodded slowly. "We will proceed."

"*Bene!*" Cosa said quietly. His spirits lifted. He would get to work immediately, as soon as he could leave the room without offending the serenity of his old friend's kind temperament.

Luke John graced Cosa with his abbreviated blessing, his left hand scrolling a vague ampersand in the scented air. With that, the cardinal bowed and made a silent, respectful exit.

Andrew had seen enough of corporate politics to know that things were rarely as they appeared. A straightforward man, he had found that the ways science advanced on the frontiers of human understanding were as Machiavellian as they were unpredictable. Therefore he knew he shouldn't have been surprised when Gindman called him in the middle of the night with the news that the Vatican had reconsidered: The relics would arrive the day after tomorrow.

Alone in the silent house—Margaret was on nights this week—Andrew stood in the darkness, his hand lingering on the phone after he'd replaced the receiver.

It was almost anticlimactic.

10

THE MEMBERS OF THE ADVISORY PANEL ARRIVED AS a group this time. Andrew could picture the in-house scientists waiting in the main lobby to greet the four board members as they arrived en masse from their hotel. Everyone chatted amiably, but it was clear that they were all intent upon their purpose for being there. Each had notes, readings, and reference materials with them, including Andrew's update on the choice of candidate for the procedure.

The air in the room suddenly crackled. Andrew looked

up to see Gindman enter. "Let's get started," he said tautly. As he sat down, Orin Sharpton stood up.

"Three billion chromosomes," he announced weightily, his eyes boring into Andrew. "In each of two sets, duplicated to make six billion. That's more than ten times the number of letters in the entire *Encyclopaedia Britannica*! And those letters are at least broken into legible words, sentences, paragraphs, and pages. At best, only a few pages of the material in each of the billions of cells in our body have been interpreted!" He waved his arms in mock dismay for the benefit of his audience, zeroing in on Andrew. "Aren't you the least bit afraid of what we don't know yet?"

"I wouldn't be much of a scientist if I let my fear interfere with my work," Andrew responded patiently. "Besides, we know how to control the process. We won't be creating any monsters here."

Linda Hajib raised her hand as if she were still an undergraduate. "Dr. Shepard, will your procedure require the five-day dose of toxic radiation therapy that we use on bone marrow transplant recipients? Given your host's age, wouldn't that put him at excessive risk?"

"We intend to try the procedure on the candidate without radiation first. However, I assume that in most cases we will have to weaken the immune system to some degree until we understand the mechanism of gene communication better."

"Is there a reason why we have to be the ones to do this?" asked Dr. Cooper Stephens, the staff researcher who had become BioGenera's de facto ethicist. A high-strung, wiry man with a permanent five o'clock shadow, he was known as the Inquisitor behind his back. "Why not just pass on it? Do nothing, at least until someone else clears the way."

"Because only *we* have the technology, the experience, and the facilities to move ahead," Andrew pointed out. "Look, Dr. Stephens, I know your role is to look out for the welfare of your—of *our*—patient. But Nicolao Soares understands the risks. He wants to try. And, given the present state of his health, we are, regardless of the outcome of the experiment, improving his quality of life."

"You're suggesting a qualitative departure from humankind's entire history," Barton Beale broke in. "Until now, each organism has lived a separate and distinct life. Is guaranteeing our betterment as a species a decent trade for relinquishing our individuality?''

"Our subject is already in the process of losing his individuality to an invidious and incurable disease,'' Andrew pointed out reasonably. "Besides, it's too late for this discussion, isn't it? The genie is out of the bottle. Who here can criticize the benefits that genetic therapy and engineering are making possible? If we are convinced that what we're doing is in the interest of creating a better future, then this discussion is disingenuous. We're committed.''

Dr. Lauren Griffiths, the consulting psychologist, leapt in. "Dr. Shepard, I don't think Barton is suggesting that it's a genetic tendency toward cystic fibrosis or leukemia that defines our uniqueness as individuals. Our concern is for those intangible qualities that separate mankind from all other beings—memory, sentiment, compassion, imagination, love. These things are of the mind and consciousness. Your project is the first to attempt to engineer those essential and uniquely human qualities.''

"Ladies and gentlemen?'' The speakerphone sparked to life in the center of the long table.

"I was wondering if you were still there, Dr. Wilson!'' Gindman responded, then explained to the panel: "I thought it would be a good idea for Francis Wilson, director of the National Center for Human Genome Research at the NIH to listen in this morning and give us his opinion. Go ahead, please, Dr. Wilson,'' he prompted.

"Thanks, Mike. I'd just like to say that it is precisely a concern for our very humanness that compels me to support Dr. Shepard. Earlier in this nation's history, miscegenation laws sought to prohibit intermarriage between humans of different color based upon mistaken notions of the 'superiority' of certain races. More recently, the Nazis, the Iraqis, the Serbs, and the Croatians have attempted to 'purify' the genetic pool by means of highly selective genocide. All of these attempts were halted, as they were an offense to our humanness.

"Now we are presented with a low-risk therapeutic opportunity to learn more about what makes an individual a human being. I don't think this discussion is about making judgments or placing at risk our humanness. It's about the ultimate goal of the human race: Have we reached an acceptable level of self-understanding? Is *Homo sapiens* a fully realized species? Or, do we keep seeking out every dimension of the human experience to discover, understand, and improve? To me the answer is clear.''

Andrew was stunned, and elated. Francis Wilson, Nobel laureate, one of the founders of modern genetic science and an international leader in scientific thought, had just delivered his unequivocal support for the memory resurrection procedure. No other endorsement could carry more importance.

''Thank you, Dr. Wilson. I appreciate your taking such valuable time from your schedule to assist us this morning,'' said Gindman.

''Thank you, Mike. And, Dr. Shepard—?''

''Yes?''

''Keep up the good work!''

''I will, sir,'' Andrew answered, suddenly feeling nervous.

When Giuliana arrived at Cosa's office, he was waiting for her. He began without ceremony. ''I have a special assignment for you, my dear.''

Giuliana used the ceremony of kissing his ring to collect her thoughts. ''An assignment, Your Eminence?''

Cosa motioned for her to sit across from him. ''How much do you know about the Academy of Science's involvement in genetic engineering?''

Giuliana was genuinely surprised. ''I was not aware that the Church even approved of genetic engineering.''

''You are now one of only a few who know differently, my dear. It is all most confidential.''

''I understand.''

''What it comes down to is that certain—progress—has been made. Nothing as sophisticated as what is going on in America, but impressive, nonetheless. For example, the members of the Academy believe that it may be possible to duplicate personality traits. It is only theory and there are many obstacles to overcome, but they believe that in time they will be able to design a better human.''

Giuliana said nothing. The information Cosa had just imparted was startling enough in itself, and she would puzzle over its implications in private, but for now it was smoke screen, part of the cardinal's characteristic knack for obfuscation. Giuliana kept her mind clear, waiting for Cosa to get to what was really on his mind.

"On a not-unrelated subject," he said now, "it seems your Dottore Shepard at BioGenera has developed what he believes is a method of resurrecting the memory of the dead, by a unique procedure of injecting DNA from deceased remains into a living host."

Giuliana stared, waiting for the cardinal to tell her he was joking. She realized he was not.

"Dottore Shepard has requested access to certain relics, and His Holiness has approved his request. There are some conditions, however."

The cardinal rose ponderously and walked slowly toward the corner window. Was it because he did not want to see the look of wonder and confusion on Giuliana's exquisite face or because he did not want her to see the smug smile on his own?

"Relics? Sacred relics, Your Eminence?" she stammered, trying to take it all in.

"Perhaps," Cosa said mysteriously.

There were ancient tombs all over Rome, but each presented certain problems. Imperial Rome had been replete with Cities of the Dead, but the great mausoleums that had survived were not strictly representative of these ancient burial grounds. The rows of tombs that flanked the Appian Way had been looted and probably modified over the millennia. Further, pagan Romans had traditionally cremated their dead; there would be no viable DNA in such long-cold ashes.

Only in the necropolis discovered beneath St. Peter's basilica in 1939 were there tombs from Imperial Rome protected and meticulously maintained under the vigilant guardianship of the Vatican. The *Grotto Sacre* beneath St. Peter's was a time capsule, much like Pompeii, a first-century necropolis inadvertently sealed intact beneath hundreds of tons of earth by Constantine's architects, who were less concerned with ancient bones than with building an edifice worthy of their emperor.

The Sacred Grottoes, just below the floor of the basilica

but above the sacred necropolis, held the remains of popes and kings, the oldest of which were those of Emperor Otto II, who had died in 983 A.D. at the age of twenty-eight. If the scientists at BioGenera wanted truly ancient remains, Otto II would not help them.

In the necropolis itself lay the mausoleum of Popilius Heracla, a wealthy pagan about whom little was known except that he wished his tomb to be constructed "in the Vatican, near the Circus." When secret excavations beneath the basilica had been begun during World War II, it was decided to leave Popilius's tomb intact as a scientific "control." Would the pope reverse that decision and violate Popilius's tomb now? Giuliana doubted it.

That left the seven first- and second-century popes who had been hastily interred, their remains literally stacked one atop the other in shallow graves around the Graffiti Wall, the supposed burial site of Saint Peter.

Lastly, there was what were believed to be the remains of Peter himself.

"Dr. Shepard?" It was Caroline Davies. "Assuming the Vatican does come through for us, do we have any idea whose remains they intend to provide?"

"No," he said. "We don't. And I don't want to know. Any prior knowledge of the identity of 'Subject X' has the potential to contaminate our findings."

"You want a blind experiment," Caroline Davies supplied.

"Exactly."

There were nods of acceptance, some more hesitant than others, around the room. Mike Gindman rapped his knuckles on the tabletop.

"Wrap it up for me, people. Ethics first. Cooper?"

"Dr. Shepard assures absolute openness with the living host," Cooper Stephens said solemnly, referring to his notes and the proposal before him. "That, combined with Bio-Genera's policy of lifelong medical, psychological, and whole-person care regardless of the experiment's outcome, goes beyond accepting liability, it assumes responsibility. It answers to any ethical concerns I might have had."

Gindman turned next to Edwin Harding, BioGenera's

public relations consultant, who had slipped unobtrusively into the room during Andrew's rebuttal of Orin Sharpton's argument. "What about the PR angle, Ed?"

"BioGenera's image and reputation will be put squarely on the line, Mike. If the experiment produces tangible benefits for the average American, then BioGenera will benefit. Even if the experiment fails, BioGenera will enjoy at least a temporary boost in prestige as an innovator."

"What if we simply kept the project secret until we have confirmed results?" asked Karol Sliwa. He and his employer, Royal Essen Pharmaceuticals, were renowned for their discretion in a business characterized by secrecy.

"I'd recommend against trying that, Mr. Sliwa," Harding replied. "The public is suspicious of its institutions, and justifiably so. The cost of a leak is incalculable compared to the cost of controlling an ostensibly open information flow."

"Mr. Gindman, there's just one last thing," interjected Orin Sharpton. "We're talking about altering a fundamental precept of the human condition. That precept is death. The limits imposed by the natural order."

"We're also talking about the life and death of this institution!" Gindman stated. "And maybe we'll be the ones to alter those limits, alter that 'natural order.' Before the discovery of penicillin, it was the 'natural order' for humans to die of opportunistic infections. An untended cut on your finger could lead to septicemia and death. Science is *about* altering the 'natural order,' and that's good enough for me. Further, if the Roman Catholic Church decides to participate in this project by providing reliquary samples, then I think the support of the moral and theological leader of nine hundred million people should be enough for you, Dr. Sharpton."

Sharpton subsided at last.

"Anyone have anything else to say?" Gindman demanded, as if daring them. "All right, then. Ladies and gentlemen, Ray Bradbury said, 'The human future is not for the fainthearted.' If human DNA-related consciousness restoration is viable and useful, then it is our responsibility—no, our duty—to press forward.

"I've decided to give Dr. Shepard free rein on this." He

looked carefully at every individual in the room. The quiet was overwhelming. "Subject to the board's concurrence, of course."

He waited.

Stewart Washington straightened in his chair and said, a little too loudly, "I support the project, on the condition that the Vatican comes through."

"So do I," added Cooper Stephens.

"Me too," Caroline Davies agreed.

Karol Sliwa raised his hand and nodded.

Dr. Lauren Griffiths inhaled, then said brightly, "I approve."

"Approved," Malin Hartwick followed.

Gindman rose, looked into each face around the table.

"Good. We're agreed." He turned to Andrew. "Make it work, Dr. Shepard. Don't make us look bad, or I'll make sure you never get another chair in science for as long as you live." He paused for effect. "In the present sense of life as we know it, of course."

There was uncertain laughter around the table from everyone but Andrew, who met Gindman's gaze and held it.

Was it possible that the Vatican would lend a group of American scientists the bones of Saint Peter himself? Giuliana wanted to cross herself, but to do so would reveal her vulnerability to Cosa. She would not surmise, she would wait, pretending to a control she did not feel.

"You mention certain—conditions, Your Eminence," she said quietly.

"The first condition is absolute secrecy," Cosa said without looking back at her. "The second is that no damage is to be done to the relics the Church will provide."

"Of course, Your Eminence. What else?"

Cosa returned to his chair across from her and watched her closely. If she lacked the discipline of a true servant of the Church, it would betray her now, at the moment when her childlike faith would be tested by a very adult sacrilege. He had evaluated Giuliana's readiness for this carefully. He would now discover whether he had misjudged her.

Giuliana returned his gaze without faltering. There were

both fire and steel in her expression, the fire of enthusiasm, the steel of self-control.

"BioGenera should be capable of determining whether there is viable DNA in the relic's tissue by testing a sample of bone weighing only one hundred-thousandth of a millionth of a gram," she concurred, businesslike.

The cardinal suppressed a smile of self-satisfaction. "Next, and very important, BioGenera must report the experiment's findings first to the Vatican, to me. Dottore Shepard will not be permitted to publish his findings without first briefing me and obtaining the Church's permission."

Giuliana began to take notes. It was clear that the cardinal wasn't wasting time, and she wanted to be certain of herself, certain that she omitted nothing.

"Next, the Vatican shall have sole authority over disposition of the report," he continued.

"BioGenera should be willing to accept that, because if the experiment is successful, subsequent results can be reproduced from other, less proprietary, tissue," Giuliana suggested.

"And if the experiment fails, it won't matter anyway," Cosa added.

He beamed, so pleased was he with his judgment about Giuliana's readiness for this special mission. His pride in her was almost paternal. He had taught her well and, like the best of students, she had surpassed his teaching.

"Lastly, it is absolutely essential that cloning be prohibited, for two reasons: primarily because it is a sacrilege to imitate God but also because, frankly, it would take too long."

"*Scuzi,* Your Eminence. So far we have been speaking of relics in a generic sense. Have you a particular relic in mind?"

The cardinal didn't answer for a moment.

"*Si,* Giuliana. His Holiness has agreed to provide Dottore Shepard with samples from the *Grotto Sacre.*"

"*Madonna!*" This time Giuliana did cross herself. She had guessed right, then. "I am honored, Your Eminence. Thank you for placing your trust in me."

"*Prègo*, Giuliana. I have anticipated this day for several

years. The Lord brought you to us for some very important reason. Perhaps this is it, eh?''

Giuliana flushed deeply. "And what is to be my role in this wonderful project, Your Eminence?''

"I am assigning you as Special Papal Liaison,'' he said with appropriate importance.

Giuliana caught her breath. There had been no more than four individuals granted the title of Special Papal Liaison in her lifetime! Two of them had been old men, white-haired and arthritic, diplomatically vetted. The other, for reasons she did not understand, was the mysterious Jurgen Rindt, colonel in the Swiss Guard and, she suspected, a great deal more.

"*Grazie*, Your Eminence. I am doubly honored.''

"Nonsense, my dear, you have earned the pope's special trust.'' Cosa extracted a crimson folder from his desk drawer. The papal seal gleamed in gold leaf in the corner, and a small note in the Holy Father's handwriting was clipped to the top. When Giuliana saw that the note was a personal blessing, her heart skipped a beat.

"It is all in here, Giuliana. Your mission, essential contacts, and rules of engagement. You will accompany Colonel Rindt and the relics to BioGenera in La Jolla, where you will deliver them personally to Dottore Shepard. You will be the Vatican's eyes and ears throughout the experiment. You will oversee *everything*.'' He paused significantly. "Do you have any questions, my dear?''

"Not at this time, Your Eminence.''

"Good.'' He rose, signaling the end of their meeting, and escorted her to the tall door. "You may reach me at any time. Anytime.''

"I understand. *Grazie*.''

"One more point, Giuliana, and this is important.'' The cardinal grasped her arm and looked at her directly. "A special dispensation by His Holiness has granted Dottore Shepard access to these sacred relics. No one—I repeat, *no one*—is to be told the source of these remains.''

"Not even Dottore Shepard?'' Giuliana ventured.

Cosa shook his head, holding her eyes.

"As you wish, then, Your Eminence. No one is to know the source of the bones. I promise you, no one will.''

She somehow found herself on the streets of twilit Rome

and began the long walk back to her apartment, hugging the crimson file to her breast like the baby she had never had.

Long after the last pilgrim had left the massive nave of the basilica, the darkened area under the dome had gone silent, and Rome's late-night strollers had vanished from the streets and alleys into their apartments, three shadows moved down the central nave and noiselessly descended the narrow four-hundred-year-old marble stairs into the *Grotto Sacre*.

Wherever their flashlight beams swept the darkness, alabaster statues of the saints and gilded architectural details swam into view for a moment, then were embraced again by the night. Their torch beams stretched into the blackness, most of the time exhausting themselves before alighting on anything. They simply traveled as far as they could in the void and disappeared, messengers sent into space and forever lost. Their frenetic reaching as the figures walked took on a surreal rhythm as visions presented themselves in the fickle light, then dissolved as it passed.

The three specters paused at the bronze grillwork doors that closed off access to Saint Peter's grave beneath the high altar. The area was still as it had been for nearly seventeen centuries, except for scars in the masonry left by the excavators.

A large-framed older man with a golden cross resting heavily on his chest waited patiently while the second man, the supervisor of the *sampietrini*, nervously worked the ornate antique padlock. The third, a tall, lean, catlike man in his early forties, simply glared at the lock. His gaze was so sharp, so intense, that the supervisor wondered if he could will the stubborn lock to fall open just by staring at it.

"*Scuzi*, Your Eminence. I'll get it," the supervisor assured the cardinal over his shoulder as he continued to struggle. Perspiration streamed down his neck. He hadn't been called out in the middle of the night to this crypt since the bones were first discovered. Why tonight he couldn't know. Neither did he particularly want to know. The cardinal had his reasons for everything that happened in this place.

"Take your time, Antonio," Cosa calmed him. "There is no hurry," he said, not entirely truthfully.

The lock opened just then, filling the small space with a shrill metallic screech. The chain surrendered easily from the place where it had rested since 1968, and the supervisor shouldered the door inward. The scraping of the bronze door hinges was muted by the preservative oil Antonio insisted that they regularly receive, but the ancient bronze doors that had waited so patiently for so many years would not be denied a little protest.

The slender man squeezed past Antonio and approached several heavy plastic boxes cradled in a repository in the Graffiti Wall. He inspected them without any apparent emotion, calmly registering the layout of the bones inside the boxes. When Cosa arrived immediately behind him, the man pointed to two of the boxes as if in inquiry, and the cardinal nodded assent.

"Antonio, I want you to provide to Colonel Rindt the bone fragments he indicates."

"*Si*, Your Eminence," Antonio acquiesced, his voice cracking.

First he broke the vacuum seal on the second box from the left, put on the latex surgical glove that Rindt provided him, and extracted the upper portion of the right humerus, passing it to Rindt.

Rindt crouched down, placed the matte-black Haliburton attaché that he had been carrying on the floor, opened it, and lifted a sterile white cloth. Underneath, there were two vacuum-seal plastic bags. He put on latex surgical gloves, accepted the bone from Antonio, inserted it carefully into one of the bags, sealed it, and pumped the air out of the bag with a small plunger. Satisfied that the vacuum was holding, he folded the corners of the bag and nestled it in a pre-cut depression in the foam interior that fit the dimensions of the bone fragment.

Although it was only a fragment, it was easy to accept that it was a part of the large bone that connects the clavicle to the radius and ulna at the elbow. Certain bones in the human skeleton look familiar even out of context.

Rindt then pointed decisively to a large fragment in the last box on the right. Of the three fragments of the right tibia, it was obvious that this lowermost one was selected for its mass and superior condition. Superior, that is, except for the forceful cut through the ball joint at its lower extremity.

A loud hiss sounded when Antonio broke the seal on that box and lifted the largest bone.

Again, Rindt carefully prepared the fragment for transport in the attaché, fitting it securely into its mold. When he was satisfied that all was as it should be, he spread the sterile cloth over the wrapped bones, lowered the lid, and secured a series of three latches. Finally, he attached the nozzle of the vacuum plunger to a small valve under one of the latches. Without any sound at all, he pumped the plunger several times until even his bulging forearms could not extract another molecule of oxygen from the interior.

Cosa turned to the supervisor. "*Grazie*, Antonio. You will reseal the boxes."

"*Si, immediatamente*, Your Eminence."

"You will not speak of tonight to anyone, Antonio." The cardinal looked directly at the frightened *sampietrini*. "Anyone."

"*Comprendere*, Your Eminence."

"*Bene*," Cosa bestowed his approval and a deliberate blessing. "*Molto bene.*"

He and Rindt then disappeared, out the bronze grillwork door and into the darkness of the basilica.

As Antonio resealed the boxes, he listened to the retreating tempo on marble. He couldn't be sure, but he thought he heard one of the departing men speak.

"Votto begins . . ." were the words the *sampietrini* thought he heard, but which man had spoken them and what did they mean? Neither man spoke again, and soon the tapping of their footsteps was overtaken by the stillness of the saints.

11 *Los Angeles*

GIULIANA OPENED HER EYES AS THE PLANE BANKED over the San Gabriel Mountains on approach to LAX. She wondered how long she'd slept. After an interminable night in first class, during which she'd half watched and only partly understood an American comedy, and had failed several times to engage Jurgen Rindt in conversation, they and their sacred cargo were in California.

They were met by the papal nuncio, whose diplomatic immunity gave him the right, after the usual searches, to board the plane and escort first Giuliana, and then Rindt, carrying the black attaché case, directly through Customs. The American immigration officers nodded them through. No one so much as touched the attaché, much less asked to examine its contents. Giuliana had watched Rindt secure it to his wrist as the plane landed and wondered if the melodrama was his idea or Cosa's, and whether it was entirely necessary.

They followed the nuncio through the sprawling airport into a private lounge in the vicinity of the Admiral's Club. He escorted them to a secure phone, where he dialed and then handed the receiver to Giuliana. The ring sounded familiar. Giuliana gave him a puzzled look. When Monsignor Murphy answered, she understood.

"*Monsignore?* This is Dr. Sabatini."

"Oh, yes. You're now in Los Angeles?"

"*Si.* We just got off the plane. Is everything all right, *Monsignore?*"

"Of course, Doctor. His Eminence only wanted to know that you'd arrived safely."

"We have," Giuliana said evenly, feeling oddly like a wayward child.

"And Colonel Rindt, as well?"

"Of course. He is right here," Giuliana said, not adding what she was thinking: *Where else would he be? He's been with me everywhere but the lavatory since we left Rome!*

"Excellent!" the monsignor said. "I will inform His Eminence. Thank you for calling, Dr. Sabatini."

The line clicked off.

Rindt was on his cellular phone, browbeating a clerk at the rental car company. They would be driving down the coast to San Diego rather than taking a shuttle flight. Cardinal Cosa, unaware of the distances in a country the size of America, had deemed this necessary to the secrecy of their mission. To Giuliana it seemed foolish, but it was

Rindt's problem, not hers. Perhaps she could sleep in the car while he drove.

At the moment, however, it seemed that the specific car Rindt had ordered was unavailable. Whatever vehicle the rental clerk was offering to substitute in its place was clearly unacceptable, and Rindt was making his dissatisfaction heard. He never raised his voice above a whisper, but it was taut and vaguely threatening.

Rindt, Giuliana had discovered, was in the habit of giving orders to anyone he perceived as being beneath him, just as he took orders without question from those he perceived to be his superiors. In his own mind, apparently, he had no equals. Giuliana was also amazed at his accentless English. Hers, she knew, was uneven—sometimes too formal, sometimes hesitant as she searched for the right word. She was vaguely aware that Rindt was multilingual—as a Swiss he would have to be—but apparently he had additional talents that she did not want to begin to guess at.

She didn't like Rindt. She realized that she didn't have to, but it would have helped to make the journey, and the weeks ahead, a bit more pleasant.

When Andrew opened the door to a beautiful and smartly dressed young woman followed by a compact, tightly wound man, his initial impulse was to shake hands with the man. But the woman smiled brightly and extended her hand.

"Dottore Shepard?"

Somewhat befuddled, Andrew returned her handshake. "Yes?"

"I am Dr. Giuliana Sabatini," she said with practiced Continental graciousness. "His Eminence Cardinal Cosa asked me to convey his greetings." She gestured toward Rindt. "This is Colonel Jurgen Rindt of the Swiss Guard."

"I see," Andrew said, although he didn't see at all. He vaguely returned Rindt's nod, barely able to take his eyes off Giuliana.

"Please—come in."

Rindt passed the attaché to Giuliana, and they entered. Andrew's confusion must have shown on his face.

"You were expecting someone else?" Giuliana asked

lightly, still smiling, but as if to suggest that his reaction was one she had encountered before.

"No . . . yes. I don't know what I expected," he admitted, thinking, *Whatever it was, it wasn't . . . you!*

"Not a woman. Not from the Vatican." It was more a statement than a question.

Andrew flushed.

"I am sorry. I should have explained." Giuliana searched his expression directly, sympathetically, sensing his embarrassment. "I am the cardinal's associate and a Special Papal Liaison. I am here to deliver this to you, of course."

She offered him the attaché. Andrew didn't actually see Colonel Rindt move, yet somehow he was suddenly standing closer, protective.

"I am also here to help you," Giuliana added pleasantly.

"Help me?" Now Andrew was irritated. The Vatican handed over the remains but slipped in an assistant to "help." What kind of game were they playing?

Giuliana's smile was unflagging. It was bright, confident, and exasperating. Didn't she—didn't they—realize the significance of his experiment? The Special Papal Liaison clearly read his mind, yet his annoyance didn't affect her charm. On the contrary, it amused her, which only made Andrew more irritated, more inclined to be obstinate.

"You should not take offense, Dottore Shepard. You see, the Vatican authorities have investigated your credentials and hold you in extraordinarily high regard—"

"I appreciate that, but—"

"But why have they chosen to send me? I am not precisely sure, *Dottore*. Perhaps Cardinal Cosa sees a particular use for my skills. Whatever the reason, I am happy to be here."

"Pardon me, Doctor. I don't mean to be rude. It's just—I really don't need any help. And this is a bit of a surprise."

"For me also. But—forgive my English, *per favore*—did not Pasternak say that surprise is the greatest gift life grants us?"

That smile again. She challenged Andrew with her uncomplicated joy. He felt smaller with each word.

Fortunately, Dr. Sabatini was sufficiently gracious to compensate for his lapse of manners. His disgruntlement faded as he watched her move around the laboratory.

Her gaze was alert, and her hair tumbled like sunlight on rapids. As she paused at the window to take in the view, she shook out her thick hair, then roughed it upward with the back of her hand in an unmistakably feminine gesture. She was astonishing. Andrew would remember the way she breathed new life into his existence in that moment. They were the only two people in the room, perhaps in the world, the chill presence of the silent Rindt forgotten.

Giuliana. Andrew tried the name out in his mind. She was dressed superbly in tissue-thin suede and matching silk. Her trim navy blazer testified to impeccable Italian taste. Her skirt countered her movements and heightened Andrew's interest. Silk strained gently against her provocative breasts and revealed occasional lace wisps when she moved. A thin gold cross suspended by a nearly invisible golden chain rested against her bronzed skin.

She was irresistible. Andrew experienced the irrational force of his desire for her at once. When she turned past his peripheral vision he caught another glimpse of lace.

"As for my own credentials, I am a business analyst with a specialty in the biotechnical sciences," she explained, offering him her résumé dispassionately. "I also have a doctorate in philosophy, some expertise in international law, and other rather unique skills and contacts that may be useful to you. Now, perhaps you would tell me about the procedure."

Knowing she had already been briefed on his advanced degrees in molecular biology and biochemistry with a specialty in genetics made it easier. Andrew hated to talk about his accomplishments, never sure if he was striking the correct note between arrogance and false humility. It was far easier just to talk about the present, about the procedure. He quickly found himself on the comfortable terrain of science again, secure.

Giuliana listened with interest and asked questions that revealed insight into his esoteric work. He was grateful that she was scientifically competent. They had been talking for nearly half an hour when Will poked his head in the door.

"Dr. Sabatini? Well, howdy!"

Giuliana hesitated before responding. Andrew guessed she'd never seen anyone like Will before and wasn't sure if he was authentic. Perhaps she thought he was making fun of her.

Will, with his Tony Lamas and his string ties and boisterous manner, was used to people not knowing how to take him at first, and he sensed her discomfort. He grinned his most disarming grin. "I'm Will Austin, Doc Shepard's assistant and hired hand here at the BioGenera Ranch." He offered her his hand.

Caught up in his infectious spirit, Giuliana laughed and introduced herself.

"Are you a real cowboy, Will Austin?"

"Well, I am from Montana, ma'am, but there's some good ol' boys up there who'll tell you I'm about as handy on the trail as a one-legged blind man."

"I don't think I would believe these boys," Giuliana said sincerely, but her eyes were dancing.

"At your peril, ma'am." Will went to the coffeemaker and poured her a fresh cup of coffee. "Here you go. I made it extra strong. It's not espresso, but it's dark."

"*Grazie.*"

"*Prègo!*" Will answered, pleased with himself for knowing the right word. "You want some, dude?" he asked Rindt without waiting to be introduced. Rindt silently declined.

Andrew cleared his throat. "Will has been integrally involved in the memory resurrection procedure," he explained, trying to stick to business. He could feel Rindt's eyes on him and decided it was time to assert his authority. "He refined the technique for obtaining viable DNA from ancient remains and will be responsible for doing as little harm to your samples as is scientifically possible."

"Excellent!"

"May I see what you brought along, Dr. Sabatini?" asked Will, trying not to sound too eager.

Giuliana began to work the locks on the attaché. The cellular phone in the trench coat that Rindt had not bothered to remove chose that moment to beep. Wordlessly, Rindt handed it to her.

"*Prègo?*" she said, listening. Whoever was on the other end apparently had a great deal to say. As she listened, Giuliana's courtesy grew darker.

"*Si, Monsignore.* You may inform His Eminence that we

are now presenting the relics to Dottore Shepard,'' she answered in a controlled tone. Again her expression clouded and Andrew was sure he saw annoyance in it.

"... *Buon Giorno*, Your Eminence. I was telling Monsignore Murphy that we are now presenting the relics to Dottore Shepard and his team ...''

Andrew, Will, and Rindt waited.

"... I have everything under control, Your Eminence. *Si*, Rindt is here also. *Si, si* ... ''

She shifted, one hand on her hip, looking out the window. A brittle smile brightened her features, but her body language expressed something else. It was as if she were playing several roles at once. Andrew noticed Rindt observing her, reading her.

"*Addio*, Your Eminence. *Si*, we will keep you informed ...'' She found her lighter voice again near the end of the conversation, relieved of the cardinal's oppressive supervision. She pushed the disconnect button, folded the telephone, and returned it to Rindt, who pocketed it.

It was he who then assumed possession of the attaché, spinning a small valve until a muted hiss sounded as the internal air pressure equalized with the room's air pressure. Deftly working the three locks, he snapped each open with a precise metallic click.

He stepped back again and watched as Giuliana lifted the lid and revealed the two bone fragments to Andrew and Will.

The bones gleamed in the morning light. Will let out a low whistle. Then he leaned in and scrutinized them before taking a dental pick from the nearby counter and gingerly lifting one end of the smaller fragment out of its foam mold.

"They're in good shape,'' he observed. "How old did you say these are?''

"Nineteen hundred years, approximately,'' Giuliana temporized. She must not reveal anything more specific that might give clues to the bones' origins.

This was the first time she herself had seen them, and she couldn't take her eyes off them. She had never been so close to Catholicism's most sacred relics before. She wanted to cross herself.

Andrew noticed that she was staring.

"They look to be in good condition, all right," he agreed with Will. "That grayness at the edges indicates long-term exposure to moisture, but the other surfaces are calcified and seem to be petrifying normally."

"Yep. Hard to know for sure, but I'd say these are viable," Will announced.

"You are pleased, then?" Giuliana asked.

"Oh, yes, Dr. Sabatini," Andrew assured her. "Thank you!"

There is a force in old bones that grips the human imagination. In some it restores awareness of our fragility and urges us to live more completely. In others, it confirms the futility of aspiring to anything beyond the moment. And in a rare few, it inspires faith.

Images of rain-washed cattle skeletons occurred to Will. They were scattered in the badlands, sun-bleached, having long since nourished animals lower on the food chain with the meat that once gave them form. He wondered whether man had a right to expect a better fate.

Rindt cut off his own thoughts about the soul that had once resided in these bones. As far as he was concerned, anything less than total dedication to the safety of the bone fragments constituted self-indulgence. He didn't know or care who once occupied them. Years of discipline took over before he could become distracted. He had a job to do.

Andrew felt an unexpected anxiety. The arrival of the bones restored the dangerous edge to his work. There could be no turning back now.

Giuliana was one of the rare few. She offered a silent prayer.

The saying that all roads lead to Jerusalem has real meaning for every Zionist.

No effort could be spared, no sacrifice was too great to assure the continued safety of the Jewish state. Therefore it was to be expected that those responsible for the preservation of the state would stop at nothing to learn all they could about any scientific development that might have an impact on state security. No matter where in the world a potential threat was taking form, the Mossad or Mossad-run agents were listening, recording, and transmitting back to Tel Aviv the bits of information they had collected for evaluation.

There, analysts added the rumors, lies, little slips, and careless leaks to the constantly building body of information. They measured the resulting conclusions. Then they presented the facts to policymakers, who, in turn, requested more information requiring new avenues of research. Already aggressive, this process intensified whenever a threat began to assume an identifiable form, however vague or amorphous its outlines.

By extension, the activity had meaning for other governments, particularly the self-styled theocracies, but it was fair to say that no nation on the planet could leave such resources unaccessed. Thus it was an anonymous source, a civilian who provided occasional source material to the Mossad's invisible network, who was the first to alert the network to BioGenera's memory resurrection procedure.

It might have been the quiet premed student from UCSD who had worked as an intern for a week in Andrew's lab. He'd asked a lot of questions about the work going on in the other labs as well. It might have been, as Edwin Harding suggested with an uncanny prescience, a friend or relative, spouse or client of any of those present at the decisive final advisory meeting. Even the custodial staff was suspect. Anyone could rummage through a wastebasket, "accidentally" overhear a snatch of conversation in a hallway or on a phone extension. Scientists were told to shred all their research notes, secure their files under classified passwords, but there were invariably slipups.

When Mike Gindman was personally contacted by an officer from the Israeli Consulate in Los Angeles, he went ballistic. He sent for Andrew at a time when he could least be spared from the lab.

"This isn't just coincidence!" Gindman raged as Andrew scanned the fax, on official letterhead, suggesting a strengthening of ties with Israel's fledgling biomedical research industry. "It was the timing that tipped me off. I've been courting these people for two years, and suddenly they can't live without me? They're offering 'assistance,' but that's smoke. They want direct access to 'Subject X,' and they know our research involves bone tissue secretly provided by the Vatican.

"Now, how do they know that, Shepard? You tell me."

"I don't know, sir." Andrew let the fax fall gently onto Gindman's polished desk. "My team is secure. It's the rest of this place that's full of holes. And we have no way of knowing how secure the Vatican sources are. That colonel from the Swiss Guard, for one—"

Gindman grimaced. He wouldn't admit it aloud, but Andrew was right. Gindman relaxed his aggressive stance.

"All right, then, why? What business is it of the Israelis—aside from obvious profit motive, of course? What do they care what we're doing here?"

Delphine suddenly appeared in the doorway, a sheaf of printouts in her hand. "Well, if anybody was asking my opinion . . ."

"We aren't!" Gindman shot back. "Dammit, Delphine, I told you this meeting was confidential!"

"You could keep it that way, too, if you weren't shouting loud enough to be heard on the golf course," she said primly and set the printouts on his desk.

"Research," she announced over his scowl. "I've been surfing the 'Net, especially the religious chat rooms, to get a feel for what's out there. Conservative factions in the Israeli government are becoming increasingly hypersensitive—and vocal—about any scientific development that sheds new light on either the Old or the New Testament. Most Judaic scholars consider certain authors of the New Testament, certain interpretations of Apostolic utterances, to be anti-Semitic. If there's to be a reinterpretation of the Bible, based on scientific discovery, these scholars want a hand in authoring that revision."

"What's that got to do with us?" Gindman asked, though he'd juggled politicians all his professional life and had a fair idea.

"Much of the State of Israel's claim to legitimacy is based upon the Old Testament," Delphine explained. "Portions of the New Testament challenge that claim. The consensus of the online debate is that if the Vatican's 'Subject X' turns out to be someone who lived during the time the New Testament was being written—"

"Or before," Andrew interjected. Where had he read that the Gospels were written decades after Jesus died? Certainly not in the catechisms of his youth; the nuns would have had him believe that everything in the Gospels was a direct quote from the master himself, not some later scribe's journalistic license.

"—then he or she could be manipulated, used as a political pawn to speak for the enemies of Israel," Delphine finished.

"Politics and religion!" Gindman muttered, rubbing his forehead as if it pained him. He hadn't bothered to thank Delphine, but she was used to that. He looked at Andrew grimly. Already the phone in the outer office was ringing; this morning's fax was only the beginning. "So much for pure scientific inquiry! You tend to that part. I'll practice putting the toothpaste back in the tube."

Politics and religion. The words kept echoing in Andrew's head. Those seemingly dead fragments of bone now reposing in a locked vault in his secured and monitored lab (a security guard posted at the door after hours, closed-circuit TV monitors eyeing the hallways around the clock) were more than just the subject of a scientific experiment. They had suddenly taken on a life of their own, remnants of historic conflicts that had carried from their century into his own.

And, to exacerbate matters further, Cardinal Cosa had his nose in everything.

"Is the cardinal serious about my having to obtain his personal permission at every step?" Andrew asked Giuliana. He had calculated the half-life of the culture from the bones and saw that the culture would be viable for only hours, not days. "He gave me permission when he delivered the bones. Isn't that enough? There's no time for me to call and check with him at every step of the procedure. It's also a violation of security, and there've been enough leaks."

"His Eminence carries history on his shoulders, I think," Giuliana suggested mildly.

"What is he worried about? I'm a scientist, for chrissakes . . ." He stopped suddenly, embarrassed. "Sorry."

She let his breach of propriety go. " 'Concerned' is a better description. He wishes to be a full participant. He does not wish anything to go wrong."

"I understand that. But the culture is fragile. When it's ready there may not be enough time to wait for his okay."

"His order is explicit," Giuliana reminded him firmly. She didn't pull rank on him, but it was clear where her loyalties lay.

"I'll do my best, Doctor," Andrew relented, equally clear in his commitment to the procedure.

Delphine helped Nicolao get his personal affairs in order: Did he have a will? A living trust, maybe? Were his wishes known to a responsible family member? Was his insurance coverage appropriate to his current wishes and responsibilities? Were his beneficiaries clearly assigned? Any emotional loose ends that he'd like to tie up?

"I never worried about that stuff when I was living," he growled. "Why should I let it worry me now? I'll sign one of those forms that says you can have my body for research if I don't make it. Other than that—I sold my boat, my kids got equal shares; I got nothing else. I've said my good-byes."

"Just don't forget to say good-bye to me when the time comes, Nic!" Delphine patted his scarred hand gently. She was the first one he'd allowed to call him Nic; for her part, she couldn't help mothering him.

"Far gone as I am, I'd never forget to say good-bye to a pretty girl!" he growled in return, his calloused fingertips brushing her cheek.

Meanwhile, Will examined bone fragments under Jurgen Rindt's vigilant scrutiny. Whenever the bones were removed from the vault, Rindt was by their side. Whenever Will touched one of the specimens, Rindt folded his arms and focused his unblinking stare on each and every movement, no matter how slight.

The colonel was frequently in his way, but Will managed to work around him. He allowed Rindt to carry the sealed attaché case to the UCSD med school to use the X-ray and magnetic resonance imaging equipment there. With it he was able to identify bits of dried marrow nestled within the crusty shard of the tibia as his most promising target. He let Rindt carry the bones back to the lab too. If he was going to be underfoot, he might as well do something useful.

Rindt, for his part, responded to Will's instructions as he had to everything since his arrival—with a superior half-smile and an almost Trappist silence.

"Takes all kinds!" Will had shrugged. He'd always thought he could get along with anyone; in Rindt's case, he decided it wasn't worth the effort. He concentrated on his work.

First he drilled a microscopic pilot hole in the fragment of tibia, then guided a titanium probe just .087 millimeters in diameter into the bone, precisely to its target. He then siphoned out a grain—.0648 grams—of the precious calcifying tissue.

Giuliana was in and out of the lab and so left the security of the relics up to Rindt. She asked questions only occasionally, which Will readily answered. The rest of the time she got to know Nicolao Soares, the BioGenera compound, and Andrew.

Andrew noticed that he felt uneasy when she was near. Whether it was the pressure that the Vatican's Special Papal Liaison added to his already full schedule or something else, he didn't know or bother to worry about. He needed to focus on every one of the thousand minute details of the experiment if it was going to succeed. Besides, the work was easier than confronting the strange feelings he had been having.

The first sample was a dud. Moisture and exposure to pollutants going as far back as 160 A.D. had destroyed the genetic material, leaving it shattered, incomplete, and truly "dead." It was useless to attempt sequencing or duplication.

The second sample had parts of a double helix that appeared to be viable. But there were so many missing elements that Will and Andrew decided it should be retained only as a backup source.

Finally, after going back and reevaluating the MRI films, they identified another possible site, embedded in a difficult-to-reach nexus in the tibia. Again they took multiple samples to minimize the handling of the bone.

This sample proved to be almost perfect. There was some damage to the text, but Andrew had seen genes from medical school cadavers in worse condition. He decided they could work with it.

The next phase was to bring Nicolao to UCSD for complete medical exams and baseline testing. The most difficult part was persuading Rindt not to tag along.

Will had told him he wasn't needed at the lab the next day. There would be no further work done on the bone fragments for now; in fact, they wouldn't even be removed from the vault.

"Why don't you take the day off, dude? Sleep in, watch golf on cable. Hang out at the beach and work on your tan."

Rindt, whose iron self-containment suggested that he no more needed sleep than he needed a tan, had merely smiled tolerantly. The next morning he arrived at the lab just as Andrew and Will were about to leave the grounds with Nicolao, ready for the walk to the medical school.

"Where do you think you're going?" Andrew demanded quietly as Rindt fell into step beside them. He stopped and turned on the colonel, drawing himself up to his full height. He was a good two inches taller than Rindt—why did he feel outmatched?

"I am here to observe the testing," Rindt replied as if it were self-evident.

"Hey, he talks—!" Will started to say, but Andrew shot him a look that told him to shut up.

"We really don't need you. I thought we made that clear," Andrew said reasonably. "Your job is to look after the bones and report back to the cardinal. Anything else is out of your jurisdiction."

"You need not tell me my job, Dr. Shepard. There can be no harm in my accompanying you."

Andrew seized on that. "Well, as a matter of fact, Colonel, there could very well be. Some of these tests are extremely sensitive; a subject's brain waves can be disrupted by something as simple as there being too many people in the room, and if we don't get accurate readings . . ."

Rindt was listening, but with a faint air of condescension, his entire posture suggesting that he would not be moved. Out of the corner of his eye, Andrew saw a cab pull up and Giuliana get out. He was far more relieved than he'd care to admit. Maybe she could get her trained watchdog back on his leash.

"Sorry I'm late—" she began, joining them breathlessly. The absolute chill in the air, the defensive stances of the four men, told her something was wrong. "What is it?"

Briefly Andrew explained.

"We don't need him!" he hissed, practically in her ear. Somehow the two of them had managed to walk a few feet from the rest of the group, out of Rindt's earshot, Andrew hoped, as he held Giuliana by the elbow in a gesture that startled both of them. Realizing that he was taking liberties, disturbed by the feelings her proximity was arousing in him as much as by his own boldness, he released her. She did not back away. "Dr. Sabatini, please. We've been very indulgent with him so far, but he's out of line this time. I won't have Nicolao upset, and I won't have the baseline tests skewed by his constant poking around."

Giuliana exhaled thoughtfully, roughing up her luxuriant hair, deciding. Finally she nodded.

"I will deal with him!" she promised.

Whatever she said to Rindt, she said it in rapid-fire Italian that none of the other three could follow, and Rindt answered in kind. Giuliana's face was animated, Rindt's was a mask. Her words were voluminous, his succinct. But it was clear at the end of the exchange which of them had won. Without another word, Rindt turned on his heel so that none of them could see his face and strode quickly away.

Giuliana was breathing hard when she rejoined the three waiting men.

"He will no doubt—how do you say it?—'snitch' to the cardinal about me. But for now, at least, he has been reminded who is in charge of this mission."

Nicolao's medical examinations were comprehensive by any standard. By the time they were done the researchers had assembled a profile of a subject whose level of fitness was astonishing. Muscles were supple as silk at rest, solid as iron when contracted. Tendons and ligaments exhibited scars of healed-over injuries, but the team calculated them to possess at least twice the vitality of the average thirty-year-old. Even his blood was thicker and more potent, more oxygenated than any blood they'd seen since working with steer plasma in graduate school.

Then the moment arrived when the qualifying tests ended and the baseline tests began. The entire team focused on Nicolao's three-pound brain.

First, an electroencephalogram monitored electrical activity. The MRI snapped detailed images of his brain in wafer-thin layers. No surprises there. It had begun to shrink as a result of aging, but it was still larger than the brains of his contemporaries. And the tumor, nonmalignant but insidious, lay clearly defined, surgically inaccessible, but far enough away from the areas of the brain that they hoped the memory resurrection procedure would affect.

A SQUID (superconducting quantum interference device) captured magnetic field variations in Nicolao's brain as he responded to a series of visual and aural stimuli.

Impatient and curious even in his depressed emotional state, he asked to see the results of each test. He beamed with pride at the SQUID when he viewed his head in green lines of wire frame animation, each thought and reaction reflected by brightly colored directional lines moving with his unconscious and conscious thoughts.

Finally, there was the PET, or positron emissions tomography.

Andrew explained to Nicolao that this was the test that would be most useful to them, for it tested trace blood flow, a proxy for brain activity.

A lab technician injected a mildly radioactive solution into Nicolao's carotid artery.

"Nuclear stuff in my blood?" Nicolao growled.

"The numerals on your wristwatch are more radioactive than this, Nic," Will assured him.

"But why put it there when you want to see my brain?"

"Your blood will deliver it there," said the lab tech, sounding bored; he probably had to explain this to several dozen patients a day. "Now don't move, don't even swallow. We need you to remain absolutely still."

"How long will this nuclear stuff take to get there? Will I feel it?"

Will glanced over at the large color monitor.

"It's there already, Nic. Any time, Doc."

"Nicolao, I'm going to show you a series of simple images, like this triangle and this circle. I'll hold them up for you to see. We want you to try to memorize the shapes. We'll then slide you back into the unit, where the equipment can read your brain activity as you recall the sequence of shapes."

"Great! Fish I could remember, but those colored cutouts look like my grandson's toys. Baby stuff!"

Andrew didn't have much of a sense of humor by this stage and it showed. Nicolao sensed it and settled down.

"Fine, Doc. Do it."

Andrew first held up a triangle, then lowered it and raised a circle, then a square, a rectangle, a circle, an oval, and a triangle again.

Nicolao concentrated, trying to burn the sequence of shapes into his memory. The technician slid the tray on which he was lying eighteen inches back, so that his head was surrounded by a large doughnut-shaped detector.

"Okay, Nic, repeat the shapes back to me," Andrew said loudly enough for him to hear deep inside the humming machine.

Nicolao remembered haltingly: "Triangle, circle . . . rectangle, circle . . . circle . . . uh . . ."

As he tried to replay the scene of Andrew holding up the cutouts, white, orange, and yellow areas fluttered and glowed on the color monitor, a 3-D image of Nicolao's remembering. All the activity appeared in the right hemisphere of the brain.

"That ought to do it," said Will as he slid Nicolao out of the machine and helped him into the anteroom where his clothes were waiting for him.

Andrew remained glued to the monitor, examining the pools of blue amid shifting, molten fields of yellow. He turned inquiringly toward the technician, who was about to explain that only the department analyst could give him an accurate reading of the results. But Andrew was so desperate for the last indicator of Nicolao's baseline that the technician read his urgent look and gave in.

"His test is average, somewhat lower than mean," he said. "But the pattern is clearly identifiable."

"It's a good baseline, then?"

"As good as any, Doctor."

Nicolao reappeared, tucking in his shirt, and Andrew walked him across the UCSD campus, back to the Bio-Genera compound and the apartment behind the lab that they'd arranged for him. They needed to keep a close eye on him, for medical and scientific reasons. If and when "X" arrived, they would want to keep him, her, or it under strictly controlled observation.

12

AT 4:50 A.M., IN THE HALF-LIGHT OF PREDAWN, Andrew's mind roused more readily than did his sleep-numbed muscles and joints. Beyond reflected moonglow the wilderness posed, an ebony mass, the darkness around it velvet gray. Above the trees, stars flew east as his burning feet crashed again and again into the frost-hardened path. His weary limbs resisted as he jogged, but his will moved them beyond discomfort.

Why am I running? Why is fitness suddenly important? he wondered. *It sharpens the mind,* he told himself. *It builds energy.*

A loose stone shifted under his right foot as he pushed off, and his ankle folded unnaturally to the left, sending a sharp pain racing up his leg all the way to his brain, triggering a flood of adrenaline into his bloodstream. He kept his pace, denying the thought that he might have sprained something . . . or worse. Simultaneously, however, he checked the abused joint by testing it against a bend in the path. It felt strong. Good. Just a scare.

Builds energy—right. His lungs and joints screamed at every step. His throat burned, his face itched under a film of sweat. He craved water, coffee, air.

Outwardly, he seemed humorless and distracted. Inwardly, his spirits lifted with every fresh calculation as he visualized the injection later this morning.

A shadow emerged from the grayness ahead, a slender jogger in shorts and a hooded jacket cooling down, walking it off. She greeted him as he overtook her.

"*Buon Giorno*, Dottore Shepard."

Looking up, he recognized the dark eyes first. Then her face, more disarming now with her hair gathered back into a ponytail. *She runs!* Why hadn't he encountered her before?

"Good morning . . ." He slowed to a walk, paused to catch his breath. ". . . Dr. Sabatini."

"Fourteen hours a day in your laboratory is not enough to wear you out, I see," she teased him.

Bent over, hands on knees, he managed to gasp, "It's supposed to give you . . . more energy."

"That's what they say. I'm not so sure!" she smiled.

"Thank God . . . someone else who hates the running . . ."

"*Si*. I like the darkness, the *pace*."

"The pace?"

"Forgive me—the peace. But, I am interrupting your morning exercise?"

"Are you kidding?" Andrew laughed, finally recovering his wind. "Thanks for the break!" He found the pulse at his wrist, which, strangely, wasn't slowing the way it should. "Any excuse to stop," he grinned.

"*Bene*, then!" She began to walk again. He matched her pace; she didn't seem to mind.

"The sun is about to come up. The best view in California is here by the cliff," he suggested, happy to have regained his voice.

"I like California very much," she said, accompanying him without the slightest hesitation. "The ocean, the sun; it is like Italy, only newer."

"Do you miss it?" He guided her past a campsite where two hang-gliders were cooking breakfast over a wood fire. "Italy, I mean."

"*Si,* I always miss Italy, even when I am there."

The point of view intrigued him, and he said nothing. They sat facing the deep violet sea. Two hundred fifty feet below, waves thundered on Black's Beach, challenging half a dozen or so stalwart ocean swimmers who began to rouse from their sleeping bags.

Even without speaking, she compelled something within him. Her taut, voluptuous body, the precise bones of her face, her honeyed skin drew his eyes no matter how much he thought himself in control. When a breath of wind pressed around her, her body responded. Despite her recent exertion, she seemed poised and energetic; she wasn't even sweating. With their proximity now, he couldn't help noticing how ambivalent she seemed.

She sat straight, forcing her body to be strong, but her eyes focused distantly wherever she gazed, whether to the Pacific horizon or into his thoughts. Everything about her body communicated discipline, self-confidence, control. But the side of her Andrew now saw hinted at . . . what? Incompleteness? Need?

"I wish there were someplace I could feel that way about," Andrew said quietly after a brief interval. "Haven't found it yet."

"You don't feel this way about La Jolla?"

Andrew shook his head, trying to see what she was looking at. She was admiring the embrace of land and sea, watching the nude swimmers tiptoe with shoulders up around their ears into the raw surf.

"So beautiful." She laughed softly. "Are you a religious man, Andrew?"

"Not in any orthodox sense, but in my way."

"I have heard about California's unique spiritualism."

Andrew laughed. "Nothing like that. I'm a lapsed Catholic, actually. Classic case of the good son, altar boy, the whole nine yards. Science and experience outpaced the Church's dogma. And there were . . . other reasons."

Her eyes. She was listening to his silent turmoil. She had seen what he had come to believe only he saw. He wanted to acknowledge a fellow spirit, an equal.

"And you do not wish to speak about these . . . other things." It was not a question.

Andrew shook his head, let the opportunity pass. "What about you? The Vatican, the company of dry old men, is the last place I'd expect to find you."

"You expected a dried-up old woman," she suggested with a hint of humor. "I think I would have wandered also, given the opportunity to find my way on my own. But Italian parents work harder on daughters, even after they leave home for the city."

Her face, with its sensuous lips and flashing dark eyes,

brightened in the rising sunlight. He felt a jolt of recognition. He felt that he had met his own. And now gratitude for meeting her nearly overwhelmed his capacity for small talk.

She absently massaged her bare calf and countered each of his small moves with unconscious shifts and tilts of her own.

"Don't you ever have doubts?" he asked her suddenly.

"Don't you?" she countered. She understood what he meant. "Doesn't everyone have days when they ask themselves 'Am I doing the right thing?' "

Andrew smiled. "That's fair. But in your line of work, I wouldn't think you'd be allowed to doubt. What would your superiors—the cardinal, much less the pope—think if you did?"

"I don't think His Holiness is aware of my doubts," she said, carefully not mentioning Cosa. She wondered if Andrew was naïve, not to understand that Cosa was the kind of man to whom one did not offer what was not required. "But if he were, I am sure he would encourage me to find my way."

"Really? That's not the Church I remember."

Giuliana smiled. There was such an innocence to him, after all! "The rules of the Church have always changed, but the faith is what truly matters. If you are fortunate enough to have it, the rest of life is in the details."

"What if you lack faith?"

"Then life is harder. But I believe you have it. How can you work in science and not believe in something greater than yourself?"

"Life is hard enough without organized religion's balking at progress, its obsession for control," he argued.

"The Church is many things to many people," she countered. "To me it is a source of guidance and comfort. Like any family, it will have arguments, but it endures for the benefit of all. It allows me to use my skills for good purposes and forgives me my flaws. In return I support it and forgive its flaws."

Her command of such practical spirituality appealed to him. "Maybe you're right," he acknowledged. "As long as it works for you."

"But it does not work for you." Again, it was not a

question. She was watching him intently, her head tilted slightly, sensing he wished to change the subject. "Do you have a family?"

"Recently divorced." Andrew waved the words away, embarrassed he had let them slip. The phrase had escaped between thoughts like a cat bolting through a crack in the door.

Giuliana looked down at the beach. "I'm sorry."

The turn in the conversation made Andrew uneasy. He had lost control. "Listen, I didn't mean to keep you so long," he apologized, rising to walk.

"Will you join me for breakfast?" she asked.

"Sorry. I've got to do an errand in the village before we get started this morning. It's going to be a big day; won't have time later. Rain check?"

"*Scuzi*?"

"Rain check. Another time, maybe?"

"Oh!" she laughed, comprehending. "Certainly. Well, *addio,* Andrew." She held out her hand.

"I'll see you at the lab at ten." Andrew shook her hand briskly and immediately regretted it. He was behaving like a schoolboy. He had thought that all the years with Margaret had rid him of such swift enthusiasms. He turned and continued running south. He didn't want to; he wanted to stay and watch her walk away. Finally, he couldn't stand it any longer and turned to look back. She was walking purposefully across the seventeenth fairway toward the hotel. He turned away again just in case she happened to look back.

Little chance of that, he thought sadly.

For all her seeming self-confidence, Giuliana also felt awkward. She was drawn to Andrew's self-containment, his skill at solitude. She hadn't known what she was looking for, until now.

She spotted him running along the cliff's edge. His legs were long, stretching over two meters of ground with each stride, like a Greek messenger. Something stirred deep within her. Then she remembered the call, her obligatory daily call from Cosa. Just ten minutes! She broke into a run.

Back at the hotel, she compiled her notes and only

thought of Andrew once more before the phone rang at seven o'clock. Duty calling. Rome sounded across the miles.

If there had been in Giuliana's nature any possibility of coming to terms with the politics of her employer and his own arcane mission, Jurgen Rindt thought, toweling off after his own morning run, that possibility was irretrievably shattered when she established a personal connection with Andrew. It would make his own task that much more difficult.

Her "rebellion," if it could even be characterized as such, had begun gradually. Even before their public scene on the day Nicolao went to the university hospital for testing, she had grown less responsive to his commands. Before their departure from Rome he had briefed her, attempting to make it clear that, while she was nominally in charge of the overall assignment, in matters of security she was not to question him.

"There are dangers," he had cautioned her. "Dangers I may not have the luxury of explaining at the time they occur. When I tell you to respond in a certain way, you cannot question, you cannot debate. You must respond."

"You're making a melodrama, Rindt!" she had dismissed him at the time. And she had thrown his words back at him, mocking him, that sunlit morning outside the main entrance of BioGenera, in the presence of strangers, men she had known for a scant few days, yet trusted more than she trusted him. It was not acceptable.

Since then she had resisted him, subtly at first, pausing for a moment before diverting her attention to his comments, questioning his cautious attitude toward Andrew and Will. They had proved themselves many times over, had they not? she had demanded of him, tongue-lashing him in Italian within the hearing of the very individuals whose trustworthiness was his concern. In reaction, Rindt grew more alert, more sensitized to danger. There was too much he could not explain to her, the constant liability of someone in his dark business. But Giuliana Sabatini had changed since their arrival and was continuing to grow in a direction that made him wary.

That was why he had taken it upon himself to shadow her everywhere, so subtly that he was able to overhear parts of her conversation with Andrew on the clifftop this morning without her even knowing he had left the hotel. He would stretch himself as thin as necessary to be everywhere at once, silent, invisible, his instincts and his lethal skills honed and ready.

There is a bearskin on display in a museum in Bad Aussee, Austria. Stretched on a field of green felt behind thick museum glass, it measures nine feet. Visitors to the museum lower their voices when they approach the tall display case; children, without comprehending what they see at first, are drawn into the spell of the huge hide.

Occasionally when he is on leave from an assignment about which he can speak to no one but his confessor, the man who shot the bear visits the museum. He stands off to the side of the case and watches the stunned reactions of the visitors as they confront the great hide. Soon he remembers and experiences again what they can only imagine.

He recalls with painful clarity the size of the animal, rearing up to its full height with an almost human grunt of exertion to challenge him—the scars on the huge chest, the four-and-a-half-inch claws, the massive head and furious eyes, the stench and feral heat of it. He can hear its heavy breathing, feel its rancid breath on his face the instant before he pulls the trigger.

Who had been more frightened, he or the bear? It was the only time in his life he could remember feeling fear, and that made Rindt respect the bear. In the intervening years he had thought only good thoughts about the bear, great and noble thoughts, heart thoughts. He had not been alive until he killed the bear. From that day, he knew that no God could save him from another like himself.

Whatever admixture of genetic alchemy had produced Jurgen Rindt, he had been a stranger from birth.

Son of a Parisian French mother and an Austrian Swiss father, he had taken their constant screaming battles as the prototype for life. A Jesuit education had offered him a cool, intellectual sanctuary away from the fray and rendered him hungry for ever more knowledge. When he surpassed his teachers, the hunger remained. If the hunger to know, to understand the order of things, could be considered an emotion, it was the only emotion he possessed.

If there was a God, he did not answer. And if there was no order? Then order must be created. Before he was twenty, Jurgen Rindt had designated this as his task. Whatever disparate masters he served, it was in fact only the order their powers could command that commanded him.

Freeing himself from his Jesuit professors at a university in northern Italy, he roamed the back alleys of Europe. Frankfurt, Marseilles, Lisbon, Liverpool—all dismal, bloodstained places where a man either killed or was killed—became his proving ground, then his hunting ground. After completing his apprenticeship on the streets, he promoted himself into the army of France, which quickly promoted him into the beret of the specialist.

Again he surpassed his instructors, accepting ever more dangerous assignments, moving farther into darker realms, leaving fewer traces, fewer contacts who could be trusted.

The death of his superior in an argument on Ile Raiatea in the Society Islands left him with a price on his head, his days numbered. He had gone to ground in Portugal under another man's name when the retiring commander of the Vatican's Swiss Guard had somehow traced him. Impressed, Rindt decided to at least hear what the contact had to say before he killed him. Instead, he found himself persuaded, recruited, in command of the Vatican's secret army.

Vatican City was quiet, the pay generous, the benefits infinitely negotiable, including, in the name of his designation as "defender of the Defenders of the Faith," the salvation, if any was possible, of his immortal soul. It was heaven for a refugee from hell.

Andrew reviewed the mountains of test data one final time with Will, who had stayed in the lab through the night.

To his relief, Will confirmed once again that Nicolao was indeed the ideal candidate. All the tests indicated that both he and Andrew were as ready as they would ever be.

The next morning, Nicolao had an elaborate breakfast in the executive dining room with Andrew, Will, Delphine, and Giuliana, when she wasn't on the phone with the cardinal. Mike Gindman couldn't be there. He'd had to fly to New

York to calm the nerves of one of BioGenera's investors who'd heard rumors about the procedure and gotten the jitters. Gindman's disappointment had been palpable.

"I was in on the conception, you'd think I'd be able to be there for the delivery!" he'd grumbled. "Dammit, I was looking forward to this . . ."

Delphine had made soothing noises and put him on his plane. He'd have to settle for watching the video when he got back.

Only Rindt was conspicuously absent. He'd chosen to remain in the lab, keeping watch over the locked vault that contained the bones.

While Nicolao devoured a bloody-rare sixteen-ounce steak, six scrambled eggs, three servings of hash browns, four glasses of freshly squeezed grapefruit juice, and a pot of Colombian espresso, the others picked at their own breakfasts or just had coffee, pretending to a buoyant mood with cheerful teasing.

Andrew wondered if *Apollo 11*'s Armstrong, Collins, and Aldrin had had butterflies as they'd celebrated their last breakfast in the old world at Cape Kennedy that July morning in 1969. Did they know the world would be transformed by their footsteps in the dust of the moon's Tranquillity Base?

Delphine had offered to arrange for Nicolao's parish priest to hear his confession and bring him communion before the procedure began.

"Think I should hedge my bets, eh?" He'd thought about it for a moment before shaking his head. "Nah, it's too late now. I'm too far gone, lost too much. Besides, God knows how I feel. No point my trying to fool him . . ."

While Nicolao took a walk around the campus with Will and Delphine to settle his digestion, Andrew made ready in the lab. He had rehearsed the procedure at least a hundred times in his mind since dawn, visualizing the regenerated DNA flowing to Nicolao's brain, migrating into his native cells.

He would attempt the procedure first without weakening Nicolao's immune system with radiation. They would inject the material into Nicolao's bloodstream and wait, just in case there was some way that the foreign DNA could survive the attempts by his system to reject it. Perhaps there was some as-yet-unknown principle that would enable Nicolao's mind to welcome the new material and make it its own. It had worked with Niko. Wouldn't a human-to-human transfer be at least as compatible as a human-to-chimp one?

Failing that, they would take the more aggressive approach of temporarily destroying Nicolao's immune system with radiation. It was necessary with bone marrow transplants and most likely would be required with DNA injection. But given the nature of the growing tumor in Nic's brain, Andrew hoped it wouldn't be needed.

Showered and comfortable, Nicolao reappeared in the lab at precisely ten o'clock.

"Day's half over," he announced cheerfully, rubbing his rough hands together. "Fish don't bite any better for waiting. Let's go to work!"

The time for the injection had arrived. Quietly, without fanfare, Will helped Nicolao onto the examination table and started an IV in his arm. The old fisherman talked more than usual, though he actually said little. So many years at sea had developed in him a transparent self-control that masqueraded as confidence.

"Okay, Nic, I'm going to sedate you just enough to take the edge off," explained Andrew.

"Not too much," Nicolao objected. "I want to see it all."

"We don't expect anything dramatic. The sedative is a precaution, really. I don't know how long it will take for your system to absorb the injection. In the meantime, it might be a good idea for you to take a nap. You should be groggy after eating the breakfast you had!"

"Hah! In the old days, I could do a day's work on a meal like that!"

"We're videotaping the entire procedure so you can watch replays later." Will pointed to the camera staring down at them.

"I've heard 'bout guys like you, Dr. Austin!" Nicolao chuckled.

Giuliana appeared in the doorway. "Sorry I'm late! The cardinal telephoned again. He insisted on knowing every detail about our Nicolao's morning."

Her affection for Nicolao had been instantaneous, and he treated her like a favorite niece.

"How's my sweetheart?" he growled now as she touched his arm, took one of his big hands in both of hers. "The cardinal, he's your boss?"

"*Si.*"

"You tell 'im he's a lucky boss for me, eh?"

"*Si,* I will." Giuliana kissed the old man's calloused hand. As she turned away from him, she saw Andrew uncap a syringe, hold it up, and expel a few drops of clear fluid from its needle.

"What are you *doing*?" She looked around for confirmation of what she was seeing. Rindt was already on the phone to the Vatican. "You cannot give him the injection without speaking to Cardinal Cosa first!"

"No time," Andrew double-checked the dosage. "The culture is ready."

"You must wait, Andrew."

"Sorry," he said evenly, avoiding her eyes. "If we don't inject now, it'll be days before we get another opportunity."

She looked again at Rindt, who was simmering as he waited for his call to go through, then she looked back at Andrew and the syringe.

Andrew studied her for a moment and reached a decision. "Will, go fill another syringe," he said quietly but firmly.

Rindt relaxed a little when he saw Will cross the lab. Giuliana was immediately at his side.

"He must not do this, Will!" she breathed. "The cardinal must first grant his permission!"

"It's kind of pretty, isn't it?" Will observed cheerfully as the clear fluid refracted the light into a shimmering rainbow in the syringe.

"Please, Will!" She stayed at his elbow, determined. "Cosa will never allow—"

Will slipped around her and headed toward the examining table.

Andrew was just removing the needle from Nicolao's IV.

"Oh, my God!" Giuliana gasped. "Oh, my God, are you crazy?" she whispered, careful to turn away from Rindt. "You tricked me!"

"There was no time, Giuliana. It's done."

Rindt angrily snapped the phone shut, stalked over to the table, and snatched the empty syringe out of Andrew's hand.

"You are a fool, Dr. Shepard!"

Andrew shrugged as Will winked mischievously at Giuliana; he had already started the camcorder.

The room fell silent except for the soft whoosh of the air-conditioning and the muted *whirr* of the videotape turning steadily in its casing.

Nicolao shifted to ease a cramped back muscle and drifted off to sleep. That was the last thing he remembered. His head rolled lazily to one side.

He sniffled and everyone jumped.

Giuliana gasped, covering her mouth with one hand. Andrew reached for Nicolao's wrist. Will lunged for the crash cart. And Nicolao, startled by their reactions, groped in the air for something to hold on to. Giuliana leaned over him to touch his shoulder and calm him. He settled down and again there was quiet.

Eventually Nicolao fell asleep. His vital functions settled into the hallmark waves of healing slumber.

"Now," said Andrew, "we wait."

13 THE DRONE OF VOICES OVERLAPPED THE THUD OF hammer blows. Iron pierced his tortured limbs. Breathing was an agony, like fire. Wood smoke lined his nostrils. Flesh melted.

The muted crumple of burning marble subsumed, drowned out by chanting as his heart dried into dust. Rodents trod through his heart dust until they also returned to the soil. Shadows melted into the darkness.

The environment around him altered. Air became charged, oxygenated; breathing was easier. Light became organic, as natural as happiness. He was lighter, moving upward. Simple images became acute, significant—a piñon nut glistening in the light formed in his mind, an emerald pine needle cluster floating from its branch into a deep blue sky. The air was warm, almost hot, familiar.

I know this place!

His atoms spun, danced, accelerated to the speed of light, expanded outward to the sun, around it and back. He left himself and grew lighter still. He knew this dimension—so familiar, like pure energy—and passed through six coordinates comfortably, naturally.

He was expanding, coming apart in a free-form ballet, all sound and glory. He soared over alpine peaks, into a shimmering blue sea, down through the sea floor, through the Earth's mantle into its molten core and out the other side, out into space, into infinity and back.

The universe slowed and washed over him in waves. Gravity embraced him and he began to descend from where he had traveled so effortlessly before. He felt himself collapsing into his core, yet somehow felt denser, heavier, more than what he was.

Silence became noise, a roar that hurt his ears. Voices attempted to break through. He began to shiver violently. It was suddenly so cold! Then everything stopped.

The blood throbbing in his skull stilled. A soft whirring sound wound through his mind. His eyes darted under his lids, then paused. He awoke with a jolt, pulled from a nightmare . . .

"Nicolao?" Andrew called, a rescuer guiding the lost from a dark forest of unconsciousness. "Nicolao? How're you feeling? You're in the BioGenera lab and everything is fine. Nicolao?"

The man's eyelids twitched. Eyes darted left, then right, then rotated in a circle beneath the lids. The whites showed first, then dark pupils flashed before the eyelids shut tight again. Finally they opened and coaxed order from the brightness.

The man who returned Andrew's searching stare was clearly not the same man who had laid down on the table two hours earlier.

"Nico-lao?" repeated the man, scowling ferociously.

"It's Dr. Shepard, Nicolao. Are you all right?"

"Quod?"

"Nicolao?"

" *'Quod,'* " repeated Giuliana. "He's speaking Latin. *'Quod'* means 'what.' "

Andrew rubbed his jaw nervously. "Nicolao—?"

"Nico-lao?" the man repeated, his voice stronger, his faculties reassembling themselves.

"Nicolao, do you know where you are?"

"Nullus," he said, his voice a growl.

Andrew looked at Giuliana for a translation. She shook her head.

"He answered, 'No'? He speaks Latin, but he understands my question in English. How is that?" Andrew asked aloud, directing his inquiry as much to himself as to Giuliana.

"Perhaps he retains Nicolao's receptors . . ." began Giuliana, but she was cut off.

"Nicolao!" the man responded to the name again, outrage in his voice. *"Nullus—Pietro!"*

"Peter?" asked Giuliana.

The man nodded affirmatively and tapped his chest. "Peter!"

"Peter," Andrew repeated.

"Peter, *ita.* Peter," he smiled. "I Peter—eh, I am Peter." He fumbled with meaning and was surprised to hear himself speak another language.

"Peter?" Andrew leaned closer. "Can you understand me?"

He nodded. *"Ita."*

"I'm Andrew Shepard."

Peter stared.

"I'm your doctor."

"Doc-tor?"

"Medicus," Giuliana added in Latin.

"Medicus . . . doc-tor." Peter tested the sound on his tongue.

"Rofeh," Giuliana offered, trying the Hebrew word for "doctor" on a hunch.

Peter understood the word *rofeh.* As he nodded, he studied Giuliana—her uncovered hair, her extraordinary face. His expression shifted into disbelief.

"Medicus?" he asked her, jerking a thumb in Andrew's direction. *"Ita?"*

Giuliana laughed quietly, then turned serious again and nodded.

Peter looked Andrew over skeptically.

"I'm a scientist," explained Andrew defensively. He had no idea what Giuliana thought was funny, but he suspected he was the object of their joke.

"Scien-tist," repeated Peter and again looked to Giuliana for confirmation. "Scientist," he said again. He was gaining command of the language center in Nicolao's brain with startling speed. "Scientist. Eh, *medic—doctor*. A seeker of truth, eh?"

Giuliana and Andrew both brightened. "Yes."

Peter nodded and repeated: "*Medicus* Andrew Shepard." Then he looked inquiringly at Giuliana.

"Giuliana Sabatini, *etiam Medicus*," she said.

Peter raised his eyebrows, impressed. He was enjoying himself. He licked his lips, extended his large, calloused hand. "Peter, seeker of a drink. Water will do."

Will, who had been loitering in the background, out of Peter's range of vision, got a bottled water out of the refrigerator. Only Rindt remained where he was, against the wall behind Peter's head, calculatedly invisible.

Peter raised himself up on his elbows and looked around the lab, then swung his legs and sat up. What his vision encompassed, what his brain made of it in those scant few seconds, was anyone's guess. But when he made eye contact with Rindt, he paused. However strange he might find his surroundings and the people in them, this was a type of man he had known before.

Then he noticed the bottle Will had placed in his hand.

What must plastic look like to a man who's probably never even seen glass? Andrew found himself wondering. Like Giuliana, like Will, perhaps even like Rindt, he was holding his breath, wondering what their visitor would do next.

Peter held the bottle up to the light, gazing through it with a look of wonder. Seeing how it distorted each of their faces as he turned to look at them, he chuckled with an almost childlike delight. Then he remembered his thirst. He lowered the bottle to the level of his mouth, sniffed at its contents, shrugged, and drank it down in one pull, a few drops dribbling down his chin. When he finished, his face contorted sourly.

"It's like air. No taste!"

No one commented. Deciding that Will's strange garb designated him some kind of servant, Peter handed him the empty.

"Another," he demanded.

Will brought a second bottle. Peter dispatched it as quickly as the first, then sighed contentedly. He was still studying Andrew.

Andrew checked to make sure he didn't have peanut butter on his lab coat. Not seeing any, he looked to Giuliana for an explanation. She was also puzzled.

"Those aren't the clothes of a doctor, a seeker of truth!" Peter roared. "You look like a—a *cavillator*, a *scurra*! Ha, ha, ha!"

Giuliana looked at Andrew anew, as if trying to see him through Peter's eyes. Then her own eyes widened and she burst into laughter. She tried to control herself as Andrew stood there helpless and flushed, but it was no use.

"He says"—she gasped, tears running down her face— "you look more like a jester, a clown."

Her laughter got Peter started again. Will joined in, even Rindt might have smirked. Everyone was enjoying themselves, except Andrew.

Finally Peter swallowed his mirth and they all settled down. He straightened to test his body and luxuriated in it, looking down at his feet, raising up his hands to examine them. *"Dum spiro sper—"* he began. His face went white.

"What is it?" asked Andrew, alarmed. *"Quod?"*

Peter stared intently at his hands, turning them, inspecting them as if for the first time. "My . . ." He stiffened, afraid of his voice. "These aren't my hands!"

"Calm down, Peter; it's all right. I can explain—"

Peter grabbed Andrew's lab coat lapels in an iron grip and yanked, pulling him down to his face.

"What is happening to me, you Godless devil?" he hissed through clenched teeth. "And whose voice is . . . Who is speaking? *Where is my voice?*"

Will quickly injected a heavy dose of sedative directly into Peter's deltoid muscle; it would take too long to drip through the IV. Peter didn't even react to the sting of the hypodermic, but within seconds his eyes clouded over and rolled back tentatively in their sockets. His shoulders slumped. Andrew and Giuliana eased him back onto the table. His head settled onto the pillow and into a deep repose even while his hands kept their viselike grip on Andrew.

Andrew pried Peter's hands off his coat and placed them on the heaving chest.

It seemed apparent that Nicolao was no longer present in his body; someone else had taken his place. If that was true and this wasn't just some bizarre reaction to the treatment, then Andrew's ideas had been right up to this point. One person's characteristics had been transferred to another.

Whoever it was, his personality, his intellect were incredibly sharp. Now came the bigger challenge: positively identifying the new personality and coping with its disorientation. Andrew had succeeded more completely than he could have anticipated. The specimen, his "subject," was more than just a recovered memory speaking like a ghost through another man's body; he was fully human, with emotions and needs and questions.

"Jesus Christ!" Andrew muttered softly. How could he possibly have prepared himself and the others for this? They were now on an uncharted frontier, confronting a stranger.

Will tried to whistle but couldn't. His mouth had gone so dry he couldn't even spit.

"Did you see his eyes?" Giuliana blurted.

"That isn't Nicolao in there." Andrew spoke more to himself than to the others.

"This man is on fire!" Giuliana observed excitedly.

Andrew lifted Nicolao's right eyelid to check his corneal-retinal potential. He saw flashes in the eyes, darting and glancing. What was Nicolao seeing?

"Our visitor has arrived," Rindt said quietly into his cellular phone after the usual preliminaries. He listened for the anticipated question from the other end. "Can we be certain he is who he claims to be? Not as yet. I will keep you informed." Again he listened. "The Facilitator?" It was the agreed-upon code name for Mike Gindman. Between himself and his interlocutor, Rindt never used names. "He is inclined to work alone in his office, late into the night. . . . Yes, I thought you might find that useful."

He ended the conversation as abruptly as it had begun.

When Nicolao-Peter-X or whoever he was awoke the following morning, he was a different man, calmer but wary, on his guard, clearly out of place in the high-tech laboratory. They had moved him into the simply furnished apartment while he was still under sedation, but even there he found objects to marvel at. Will, who had crashed on a cot in the lab in case their patient woke during the night, found him fingering the acrylic blanket on his bed in the early-morning light, clearly intrigued.

"Such soft wool!" he remarked. "And it takes the dye well, I see. What animal does this come from?"

Will was spared having to explain how many little acrylics were needed to produce one blanket by Andrew's entrance.

At least their patient appeared to be comfortable with Andrew and Will. And Giuliana's arrival added a sparkle to his disposition.

He ate everything the executive chef brought down to his apartment and asked for more. This was a good sign. Appetite indicated health. Peter was healthy and then some, normal in every way. He had retained Nicolao's voracious appetite.

Except he wasn't Nicolao.

. For one thing, he was more curious. At the same time he was not at all contemplative. There radiated about him a force, an aura, an inborn urge to activity. He was strong, wholeheartedly and forcefully committed to whatever or whoever was the object of his attention.

Although he reverted to Latin when under stress or stumped for a particular phrase—Giuliana's Church Latin came in handy when this happened—his mind had somehow wired his language skills to Nicolao's and with some concentration, he could speak English, and do so without Nicolao's guttural accent.

Andrew enjoyed Peter's fascination with the technology and marveled that he adapted so readily to the extraordinary situation in which he suddenly found himself. As Will helped him dress in Nicolao's work shirt and jeans, Peter smiled at small miracles like buttons and zippers, chuckling as he had at the sight of the plastic water bottle. He walked with the team across the golf course to the medical school, taking in the sight of cars and buses and golf carts without comment, and he consented readily to the EEG, MRI, and SQUID tests and endured them without a hint of annoyance. On the contrary, he seemed to be enjoying himself. When the time came to take another positron emissions tomography reading to compare with Nicolao's baseline, he was like a schoolboy: cooperative, enthusiastic, and involved.

Giuliana had not objected to Rindt's presence this time. They took their places in the shadows behind the lab technician.

"I'm going to show you a series of simple images, like this triangle and this circle," Andrew explained. "I'll hold them up for you to see. You memorize the shapes. We'll then slide you back into the unit, where the equipment can read your brain activity as you remember the sequence of shapes."

Andrew was careful to repeat every detail of the test he had done with Nicolao, even going so far as to wear the same clothes he had worn that time. He wanted a precise comparison.

"Great!" Peter answered. "Fish I could remember, but these . . ."

Andrew's heart stopped. Those were the same words Nicolao had used. *Had all the positive signs so far been an aberration? Or was Nicolao's brain responding to the familiar stimulus with a familiar reaction?*

Andrew stared at Peter, just as he had seen himself do with Nicolao on the videotape. He didn't have to act. The experiment was going awry and he was worried.

"Fine, *Medicus*," Peter said calmly. "Do it."

Andrew showed him a triangle first, holding it still for a second, then lowered it. He raised a circle, a square, a rectangle, a circle, an oval, and a triangle again. "Subject X"— Peter's official designation as long as the lab technician was within earshot—watched calmly. When Andrew paused, X raised his eyebrows as if to say, "That's all?"

The technician then slid the tray on which he was lying eighteen inches back, so that the large doughnut-shaped detector encircled his head.

"Okay, repeat the shapes back to me," Andrew said loudly enough for X to hear above the scanner's hum.

Peter recalled them easily: "*Triangulum*, circle, square, rectangle, circle, oval, *triangulum*."

On the PET readout, white, orange, and yellow areas fluttered briefly, then settled into pure hues that glowed as Peter remembered.

Andrew had hoped the pattern would vary from Nicolao's test. It did, and significantly so; it was more direct, the yellows and oranges more intense. Peter's pattern was immensely more efficient. There were now also frequent blooms of deep red, indicating peak synaptic activity.

"*Bene*, Peter! *Verbatim at litteratim!*" Giuliana congratulated him.

Peter smiled contentedly.

"That'll do it," the technician said, just as before, as he pulled Peter out of the machine and helped him to the anteroom to change.

Andrew double-checked film from Nicolao's test against Peter's and didn't know whether to laugh or scream.

They had done it, whatever "it" was.

The technician returned to his control panel and studied the video image.

"Impressive. Either Mr. Soares has learned his lessons well or this is a superior memory at work," he said as he drew lines on the screen, marking the contrasting patterns. "He's got a much more efficient memory. Not photographic, just more adept. Whatever you guys are up to in that lab, it's working."

"Then you'd say that this mind is fit?" Andrew asked.

"Definitely. There's very little resemblance to Mr. Soares's original test. I can't believe it."

"Neither can I," grinned Andrew. It was too good to be true. "Neither can I!"

Sooner or later, Andrew knew, Peter would grow tired of the strange marvels of his new world and ask the more obvious questions, questions that would be difficult to answer.

He seemed to sense that the medical center was not the place to ask such things and waited until they were back at the lab, accosting Andrew while he was analyzing the test videotape. Peter watched silently for some moments as fluttering patterns of bright primary colors swelled and evaporated like clouds on the weather map of his psyche. Andrew scanned the video, leaning in closer to the screen for replays.

A series of glows flashed in eight separate areas of the cerebellum, then migrated to the center and merged to form one bright pool of cadmium-yellow light. Andrew rewound the tape again. The points of light flashed to life like newborn stars in different reaches of Nicolao/Peter's mental universe, then raced to the occipital lobe, where they formed a brilliant memory nova, collapsing and fading as the next memory process began. Andrew couldn't get over the power of this "new" mind compared to Nicolao's. Yet here it was in living color: the mystery of memory itself captured on videotape.

"Andrew?" Peter's voice interrupted Andrew's thoughts. He settled into the seat beside Andrew, contemplating the younger man solemnly from under his shaggy brows. Andrew turned away from the video image. *Here it comes!* he thought.

"Now, in my vain life I have seen everything . . ." Peter spoke matter-of-factly, confident that Andrew could follow him. "But this"—he gestured toward the screen, then himself—"this is a powerful thing you do with me, with my soul."

Andrew waited for him to complete the thought.

"So, I wonder: How is it you have performed this *miraculum*?"

Andrew had trusted that the answer would come to him when the time arrived. He waited for some inspiration and— nothing. He was a blank.

"You do not strike me as a man of any special faith," Peter observed with a disarming tilt of his head and an open sparkle in his eye. "So I ask you again: How did you do this miracle?"

"It's not a miracle."

"No? This is something you have done before?"

"Not with another human being, no. But it's not a miracle, just science. Good science. Highly advanced science, but not a miracle.''

''Oh.'' Peter seemed disappointed. ''Then perhaps you can explain this . . . science . . . in terms an old man can understand. An old man who is not as smart, not as educated as you.''

''Well, it involves DNA and the cel—''

''D-N-A?'' Peter rolled the letters on his tongue, evaluating them for some cabalistic significance but finding none. He frowned.

''Deoxyribonucleic acid,'' Andrew tried. This was not the way to do it. How would he explain it to a group of grade school kids? ''DNA is the—the formula—the recipe, let's say, for every living organism.''

''To make bread you need a recipe. To make a man, you need DNA,'' Peter suggested.

''Something like that.''

''Where is this DNA?''

''Inside you.''

Peter seemed to accept this. Unconsciously he felt the muscles of his chest and abdomen, as if searching. ''Where, exactly?''

''In your cells. In every cell in your body.''

'' 'Cells?' '' Peter said expectantly.

''Very small—so small you can't see them with the naked eye—complex units of protoplasm, usually with a nucleus, cytoplasm, and an enclosing membrane . . .''

Andrew's voice trailed off. Peter was listening earnestly, but it was clear from his expression that Andrew's explanation was flying way, way over his head.

'' 'Things seen and unseen . . . ' '' he murmured.

Andrew laughed. ''Well, in a way you're right. We can see genetic changes in subsequent generations of plants, animals, or man, adaptations to a changing world. Through systematic observation we develop theories. From theories we get principles. From principles, we get understanding.''

''Like debating the Torah.'' Peter's quick mind seized upon an analogy he could use. ''We learn the truth about the unseen God by arguing the Torah. Do that long enough, you realize that the force that makes us what we are—and better than we are—is a miracle.'' Andrew started to protest the word, but Peter did not give him the opportunity. "Again, I ask you: How did you perform *this* miracle?"

"It wasn't a miracle, it was science," Andrew insisted. "I took DNA from your bones and injected it—"

"My *bones*! Great God in heaven, man, that smacks of witchcraft! What right did you have to use my bones in your 'recipe' for this—this whatever it is?"

Andrew was taken aback, stunned by Peter's outburst, but before he could gather his thoughts to respond, the explosive side of Peter faded and was replaced by his charming, boyish curiosity.

"Where are they?" he demanded. "I want to see my bones."

"They're in the vault. You can see them when I've finished here."

"What did you do, rob my grave? How did you get them?"

"The Vatican lent them to us."

"The Vatican?"

"The headquarters of the Roman Catholic Church."

Peter digested this. "So this—Roman Catholic Church— had my bones and let you borrow them?"

Andrew nodded. This conversation was becoming increasingly bizarre. He tried to imagine it from Peter's point of view but couldn't.

"Let me get this straight," Peter was saying. "You took this—D-N-A—out of my bones, and did what with it?"

"Purified it and injected it into the bloodstream of a man named Nicolao Soares." Andrew tried to explain it as simply as possible. "A man whose mind was being destroyed by a tumor."

"A brave man," observed Peter, touching the body he inhabited with new reverence. "And where is Nicolao Soares's mind now?"

"We're not sure," Andrew answered honestly.

Peter held Andrew's eyes, waiting for him to elaborate. When no further explanation came, he inhaled deeply and struggled for control. When he spoke, his words were precise, his voice was commanding.

"You rob my grave for my 'D-N-A,' " he began slowly, his voice rising. "You rob Nicolao Soares for his body. God knows where his mind, his spirit are! You bring my vain being to life two thousand years from when I lay down to rest, and you don't see the work of a miracle in there somewhere?! *Are you out of your mind?*"

"But science made your memory resurrection possible," Andrew said doggedly.

"You keep saying that, but you still haven't told me how it works."

"I'm not quite sure."

" 'Not quite sure'?" Peter minced his words.

"All right: I flat out don't know."

"Then how can you insist it's only science?"

"*What else is there?*"

He hadn't meant it to sound like a plea, but there it was. Andrew wanted to argue that miracles were for children, emotional props for the ignorant, who didn't understand, couldn't see the cold, methodical beauty of scientific protocols, the cause-and-effect logic of an experiment, properly performed, achieving the expected results.

Was that why you were dancing around this very room the night Niko's consciousness became yours? he asked himself. *Is that why your heart was pounding when you saw the differences between Peter's PET test and Nicolao's, why you keep replaying that video again and again, as if you can't believe what you're seeing?*

He could see the video screen out of the corner of his eye, the image on pause, where he'd left it, midway into the bloom of another nova of thought in Peter's brain. His eyes met Peter's.

"What else is there?" Peter repeated Andrew's question, this time without mimicry. "Ask yourself this: Who or what created the D-N-A in all of us? Who or what created the inspiration in your sorry being to bring me back here? Not science, not your pathetic doctor's skills. You may choose to deny, but you know the answer. You call yourself a scientist, a seeker of truth? You study facts and look for proof? Well, what more proof do you need of the miraculous than me sitting here before you now?"

Andrew didn't respond. Something deep within him held him back from arguing with Peter, some dawning hope that Peter was right.

• • •

"I must report your success to His Eminence." Giuliana tried to sound casual.

"Not yet, Doctor. Please!" Andrew restrained his irritation, but he couldn't disguise it entirely. Addressing Giuliana so formally annoyed him; he was afraid of betraying his true feelings. "I admit that what we've seen looks very promising," he continued, trying to project his most reasonable tone, "but it could be just a fluke. It's too soon to tell."

"Clearly, Andrew, this man is not Nicolao Soares!"

"It could be anybody, any consciousness. It could be latent memories from Nicolao's childhood!"

"You're going to tell me Nicolao spoke both Latin and Hebrew in his childhood?" Giuliana was skeptical. "I agree it's too soon to make a positive identification, but I must tell my superiors something!"

"It's too early!"

"Maybe it's later than you think!" Her tone was clipped, almost a warning, if not a prophecy.

"That's a possibility," Andrew said reasonably, caught up in his own thought. "If my theories are right. If I have injected a latent consciousness into Nic Soares's DNA, it may be a perilously fragile effect. It could be a spark, transitory and useless."

"It could be a miracle, Andrew!"

"Listen, Giuliana, listen! Damage to the DNA in the human cells' mitochondria results in declines in energy production capacity. Once that happens, the decline is chronic, ultimately resulting in functional insufficiency."

Giuliana waved away the technical jargon with a particularly Roman gesture. "What are you saying exactly? That Nicolao—or Peter—might die?"

"Not a physical death; at least, I don't think so. But the spark of resurrected consciousness might die."

"Oh." She was suddenly subdued.

"Then again, it might not," Andrew tried to reassure her. "What I'm saying is that whoever this consciousness is may not be around long enough for us to study it. Nicolao's tissue may not have the endurance to sustain it."

Giuliana stared, unable to speak, her mind racing.

"Will you give me just a little more time?" Andrew asked quietly. She nodded—consenting, for now.

What the Mossad knew, it was safe to assume, its Muslim counterpart would soon learn also. Because the relics being held under such rigid security at BioGenera were on loan from the Vatican, the imams were immediately curious. Here was potential for reinterpreting the early history of Christianity, perhaps even for debunking the "myth" that Christ was God. The imams saw the obvious advantage at first.

But Islamic moderates argued for the significance of Christ as one of their own prophets. Perhaps there was danger in discrediting Christ, they suggested, for in so doing would they not also be questioning a basis of their own faith?

The secret world of Islam observed, but chose inaction, for the moment.

The secret world of the Central Intelligence Agency was typically less introspective. The disposition of the bones had been tracked almost from the moment Jurgen Rindt and his Haliburton attaché left the *Grotto Sacre* up to the present. A cumulative file originating with Religions Section/Vatican Subsection and—because of the sudden attentiveness of the Mossad—cross-referenced and distributed to Middle East Section, scrolled down computer monitors and into additional subsection files before being compressed into a one-page précis that ended up in the in box on the assistant director's desk.

"Let me get this straight," the assistant director said. "You're suggesting they're trying to resurrect Saint Peter. As in Saint Peter the Apostle, the biblical Saint Peter?"

"It's our considered opinion, yes, sir," the Vatican subsection chief said.

"Well, so what? Assuming it's even feasible, I somehow don't see it as a threat to national security."

"Superficially, no, sir. But, inasmuch as fundamentalist regimes bear watching regardless of which brand of fundamentalism they preach—"

"Since when did Christianity become a fundamentalist religion?" the director wanted to know.

"Not Christianity, sir." The section chief swallowed. He wasn't sure of his boss's religious persuasion, and he realized he could be on very thin ice here. "Just Catholicism—from the perspective of America's predominantly white Protestant leadership."

The director frowned. "I don't follow you."

The section chief held a file folder filled with statistics in his lap; he riffled some of the pages significantly. "Roughly nine out of ten of the world's Christians are Roman Catholics, sir. America, on the other hand, is still a Protestant-based republic. We in this country are often misled by our own numbers into believing that Protestant sects are demographically dominant, when in fact they account for only a minuscule minority worldwide. It's been batted around by some of our troubleshooting software that if the Catholic brass were to announce that they had one of their historical Big Guns on hand, so to speak, to give credence to their pronouncements on politics as well as religious issues—"

"Yes—?"

"Ever since the Founding Fathers, the Bible has been used to prove the 'alien' nature of Catholics, that when pushed, their loyalty would be to the pope in Rome, thus making them a threat to the American way of life."

The section chief was warming to his subject. "Those fears are still strong, sir. I quote the Reverend Lou Sheldon of the Traditional Values Coalition in 1993: 'We were here first. You don't take our shared common values and say they are biased and bigoted . . . we are the keepers of what is right and what is wrong.' " He looked significantly at the assistant director, who appeared to be unmoved. He began to explain: "If the man who was at the right hand of Jesus suddenly shows up in the Vatican and argues that the American way of life is wrong . . ."

A slight shift in the assistant director's posture meant his attention was flagging.

"Well, sir," the section chief concluded, closing the folder decisively, "we're not saying it's a definite, but we could be looking at something along the lines of what's been happening in fundamentalist Muslim countries in recent years.''

The assistant director was dog-earing one corner of the report absentmindedly.

''The Catholic Church hasn't been a political threat since Galileo's time,'' he said finally. ''Science has become this century's religion, and I agree that any new development in science bears watching. Which is why Genetics Subsection briefed me on the BioGenera thing two days before you guys did. I also have to admit that the thought of the Vatican in cahoots with a bunch of geneticists gives me an uneasy twinge. But in my observation, science and religion usually end up working at cross-purposes.''

He took the précis and slid it into his out box.

''I'll want updates,'' he said. ''But, in my judgment, this is not high priority at this point in time.''

14

PETER EMERGED FITFULLY FROM HIS MYSTERIOUS past. Sometimes irascible, often gentle, always self-possessed as he mastered the new world, he revealed a complex personality rich in appetites.

Overhearing Andrew telling Giuliana how close Orin Sharpton had come to scuttling the experiment before it even began, he flared: ''By doing right you put to silence the ignorance of fools! Judas, Sharpton . . . *semper idem*!''

Giuliana giggled.

''What?'' asked Andrew.

'' 'Judas, Sharpton . . . always the same person,' '' she translated.

Then, basking in the afterglow of an exceptionally good Cabernet from Gindman's private stock, he showed his contemplative side.

''If I were to begin the life journey again, my friends— oh, my!—that is what I do, eh? I open my eyes more,'' he reflected.

There had been entirely too much information for him to absorb at first, and for several days he could not tear himself away from the television screen in his small apartment. Will had introduced him to CNN's world news, and Peter became entranced. He couldn't turn away from the spectacle of human tragedy. He was also drawn to the Learning Channel and became engrossed in program after program, from documentaries about Rwanda's silverback gorillas, to home repair how-to (he asked Will to get him some silicone and spent an afternoon recaulking the tiles in his shower), to histories of the world's great civilizations, to mysteries of the Bible.

Certain vast blocks of knowledge he absorbed wholesale and without blinking, yet other seemingly minor data caused him to scowl and grow silent. That the Earth was round and was only one tiny speck in a vast universe did not surprise him. That human beings could still kill each other over differences of language, culture, religion did, but only just.

It hadn't occurred to Andrew or to anyone on the team that he wouldn't be as content as Nicolao had been to remain in his apartment, watching TV, taking his meals in the executive dining room or sometimes alone, submitting to Andrew's endless tests and questions, walking the grounds in the company of Delphine or Will with, of course, the ubiquitous Rindt a few paces behind.

He grew bolder in the days that followed, as if learning the ropes of a new vessel, growing more confident of his mastery. So, too, did Andrew as he probed the new psyche in his laboratory.

"Hypnosis?" Giuliana repeated.

"It's the only way," Andrew assured her.

"Only way to do what?"

"Verify Peter's true identity and differentiate any retentive Nicolao traits."

"Then you believe Peter is a separate personality," she observed.

"I believe memory resurrection works and that we have brought back the consciousness of someone named Peter. Let's leave it at that."

"*Bene,*" Giuliana smiled, content. Andrew wasn't ready to accept what she was coming to understand: That was Peter in there, perhaps Simon-Peter, the most famous of them all. She was scarcely ready to believe it herself. Besides, she was sworn to secrecy. No, she would take the experiment in small steps, learn the facts before making that leap to belief. "Hypnosis it is."

"It might help you to adjust," Andrew said, as he explained hypnosis to Peter.

Peter's inborn curiosity and trusting nature stood him in good stead. He consented.

Andrew had asked Dr. Lauren Griffiths to do the honors.

"Ordinarily I'd refuse," she informed him briskly as they made their way down the corridors to Peter's apartment. "It's a two-hour drive here, and I haven't had a private consult in—oh, goodness, longer than I'd care to admit. But there is the matter of confidentiality. We really don't want an outside therapist involved. And I must admit this case has me intrigued."

She had at least twenty years on him and he a good six inches on her, but Andrew found himself hustling to keep up with her in her sensible shoes.

"One question," she said. "He wishes to be addressed as 'Peter?' "

"That's his name," Andrew said defensively.

She nodded, making a mental note. "Lead on, Dr. Shepard. Just don't forget you have me here on sufferance. We do things my way."

"Yes, ma'am," Andrew managed before she breezed through his lab under full sail.

Peter glanced up from *Headline News* and sized her up from beneath his shaggy brows.

"Let me guess." He reached for the remote and shut the TV off. "Another doctor, no?"

"Lauren Griffiths," she said warmly, extending her hand. "I'm a psychologist, Peter."

"A speaker for the soul." Peter's mind translated the term literally as he gripped her hand briefly in his own. This custom of men and women touching each other so casually was one of those minor things he had difficulty with. "And you are here to speak for my soul?"

"To help your soul speak for itself," Lauren Griffiths suggested.

Peter nodded, not ready to believe quite yet but willing to cooperate.

Dr. Griffiths insisted that only Andrew and Giuliana be present. She had brought a tape of acoustic guitar music, having found that it distracted most patients from background noise that might disturb their concentration. It helped Peter to clarify, surrender. He soon slipped under the turbulent surface of consciousness into the muted currents of his inner mind.

"He's achieved a good trance level," Dr. Griffiths informed Andrew after a few moments. "You may ask your questions now."

"You have told us that your name is Peter," began Andrew.

"Mm-hmm. Petros, Petrus, Pe-ter," acknowledged Peter.

"Is that your real name?"

"Yes, now."

"What do you mean 'now'?"

"I was born Simon."

Andrew's face fell. This Peter personality was a phantom after all, maybe only one of several.

". . . Simon Bar Jona. My real name, it's Petros. Greek, eh, Pe-ter, as you call it," he explained. "Petrus in Latin."

"Why is Petros your real name?"

"Because that's the name He gave me."

"Who gave you?"

"My master."

"Master?"

"Mm-hmm . . ." Eyes still closed, Peter remembered proudly.

"What do you see right now?" Lauren Griffiths prompted.

"Petronilla . . . she's writing my letter . . ."

His voice took on a deep, resonant tone that none of them had heard him use before.

"This is now the second letter that I write to you, beloved, and in both of them I have aroused your sincere mind by way of reminder; that you should remember the predictions of the holy prophets and the commandment of the Lord and Savior through your apostles . . ."

"Who is Petronilla?"

"Meus venustus filia."

"His daughter?" asked Andrew.

"*Si*, his 'lovely daughter,' " Giuliana elaborated.

"Nicolao's daughter is Marie," Andrew recalled, unsure what to ask next.

"No, Petronilla!" Peter rumbled.

Andrew and Giuliana glanced quickly at one another.

"Listen to me!" Peter insisted. "I was arrested after the fire. I am in the Tullianum, a dead end for anyone unlucky enough to be imprisoned here. I am in the Hole."

"What hole?"

"The *cisterna* . . ."

Afraid to interrupt, they remained silent and waited.

"I am pushed through a small hole into darkness. I fall into dark water and have to fend for myself. . . . Minutes stretch into days, and days into interminable weeks. . . . Sunlight is just a memory . . .

"I learn to judge time by odor. . . . Night suppresses the putrefying death winds, and day cooks anew the human decay that surrounds the Tullianum. One morning, Petronilla appears, accompanied by a centurion.

" 'One hour,' the guard snaps, eager for the fresh air near the stairway. The stench where I am is unbearable.

"Petronilla is sobbing, . . . her trembling extinguishes the oil lamp in her hand. Gradually she calms herself and finds strength to give me news of my family. She has brought parchment, a chicken quill, and some ink. I have never taken to writing, avoiding the chore whenever someone is willing to write for me. I accept and write the encyclical. This more than anything else convinces her that I know I am near my end. She leans through the hole in the wall of the *cisterna*, strokes my hair, and hums softly . . .

"From Petros to the exiles of the Dispersion: Having purified your souls with the discipline of charity, give constant proof of your affection for each other, loving unaffectedly as brethren should, since you have all been born anew with an immortal, imperishable birth . . ."

He stopped and drifted. His eyes glistened. Andrew looked anxiously at Dr. Griffiths. She shook her head. No cause for alarm; this was normal.

". . . Since I know that the putting off of my body will be

soon," Peter went on, *"I will see to it that after my departure you may be able at any time to recall these things. You will do well to pay attention to this as to a lamp shining in a dark place, until the day dawns and the morning star rises in your hearts . . ."*

He drifted again.

Andrew noticed that Giuliana hung on every word. The color had drained from her face. She barely breathed.

"When I finish," Peter continued, his voice recovering its more familiar timbre, "I fold the letter twice, wrap Petronilla's hands around it and kiss her, first on her head, then her hands, finally on each cheek. Does she realize that I bless her with the sign of the cross? Maybe when she relives it later to her mother . . . I must be strong . . . for her.

"Before she leaves for the final time, she hugs me, she wants to take me with her when she walks out of this terrible place. 'I will always honor you, Father,' she says proudly as she looks at me one last time . . ."

No one spoke for a few moments.

"Why is Petronilla sure it's the last time she will see you, Peter?" Andrew prompted.

"She knows what they will do to me."

" 'They'?"

"Yes, the centurions."

Silence again. Andrew shifted and leaned forward.

"Peter—?"

"Ita?"

"What year is it?"

"Anno Domini . . . 64."

Giuliana gasped.

"There is a minuscule percentage of the population that cannot be hypnotized," Dr. Griffiths said as Andrew and Giuliana walked her out to the lobby. "But it's impossible to lie once under deep-trance hypnosis. That man is who he says he is."

St. Mary's Star-of-the-Sea welcomed the prodigal Andrew with the same fragrant embrace he remembered from boyhood. Not counting his wedding day, it had been that long since his last visit to a church. It had been Giuliana's idea for him to come with her.

"You've gone to Mass every Sunday since you've been here?" He was surprised, but wondered why he should be. She was Special Papal Liaison. Did he think she'd leave her religion in Rome?

"In the Vatican, I go to Mass every day. Sometimes twice a day." Her voice was neutral, matter-of-fact. Her eyes danced. She was testing him.

The walk down the Mexican clay–tiled aisle was shorter than he recalled, but when he genuflected, the cool-edged bite into his knee brought it all home. The varnished wood of the pew groaned as he sat in the second row, a slight shudder running the length of the fifty-year-old live oak boards and up his spine.

Why had he come here? To be with Giuliana? Or was he looking to prove something to himself, the same thing he'd argued with Peter—that it was science, not faith, that made the world go 'round?

As the church filled with worshipers, his eyes lifted involuntarily. He wondered why God would bother with such a small space when the universe offered so many other opportunities. He wondered, too, glancing sideways at Giuliana, what she thought of this garish example of American Catholicism, with its bright subtropical colors and gold leaf. Then, as the Mass began, Giuliana seemed to be transported somewhere else.

Andrew wished he could go with her.

The priest who said their Mass seemed to be trying to beat some previous speed record; he rattled off the prayers and invocations as if he were an auctioneer, and his sermon was so nondescript that Andrew couldn't even remember the topic. As Giuliana crossed herself following the final blessing and they found their way out into the great outdoors, he almost felt like apologizing.

Why? he wondered. *It's not my church. Hasn't been in decades. Why do I feel responsible?*

Giuliana seemed to read his mind. She touched his arm gently.

"Yes, I know. It was terrible. Worse even than last week's. I'm sorry to have inflicted it upon you."

"I—" Andrew flushed. He didn't know what to say. "Why do you bother, then?" he blurted before he could stop himself.

Giuliana shrugged, searching for the words. They had started to walk back to Andrew's car, but drifted out of the parking lot and onto the pleasant residential streets surrounding the church.

"It doesn't matter that they"—she gestured back toward the church behind them—"lack faith, I have it."

They walked in silence for a few more blocks, not touching, comfortable together. No one walked in California. Andrew had always thought it was a good measure of a couple's compatibility, their ability to walk together, to fit. He banished the thought as quickly as it had come.

"I should go back," he said, motioning toward the church, the parking lot, his car. "There are some more tests I wanted to run this afternoon . . ."

"Poor Peter!" Giuliana said with exaggerated pity. "Even God rested on the seventh day."

"Yes, but—"

Suddenly her arm was linked with his.

"Will is on duty today, is he not? He will page you if there's anything you need to know. Can't you let him run the tests and call him later? There's a little café, we passed it driving here. Surely they'll have a telephone . . ."

Andrew surrendered. It turned out to be a lovely afternoon.

"Nicolao's hysterical, maybe suicidal!" Will shouted, meeting Andrew and Giuliana in the foyer of the lab.

Andrew's beeper had gone off just as they were ordering dinner. An almost perfect day of driving up and down the coast, walking on the beach, making reservations at a restaurant Andrew knew only by reputation, had been abruptly ended. He secretly cursed himself for not being at the lab, as if he could have somehow foreseen what was happening.

They found Nicolao in his shower, weeping. Through his tears he alternately hummed an unfamiliar tune and chanted a litany of his children's and grandchildren's names. Only half aware of where he was, he didn't seem to care that the three were watching him. He was as removed from his usual inhibitions as a person could be and still function.

"He's been cursing himself for letting Marie and Anthony down. He keeps singing their names like an incantation." Will grimaced as he watched the tragic scene.

"Why haven't you sedated him?" demanded Andrew.

"I did. He dozed for a half hour, then this."

"Give me a hand." Andrew wrenched the water faucets off, stepped into the shower stall, and helped the old man out.

They toweled him off, wrapped him in a warm terry robe, and helped him back to bed. He leaned on the two younger men, his arms over their shoulders, staggering, a dead weight.

"What'd I do, what'd I do?" he kept repeating in the familiar guttural accent they hadn't heard since Peter's arrival. "It's all wrong . . . all wrong . . ."

He was childlike. He followed instructions and eventually stopped crying, but he was bewildered, his spirit broken, a shell of the man Andrew had grown to admire.

They sedated him again with a dose equal to half the injection Will had administered earlier.

"I think we'd better restrain him," Andrew decided, looking down on him on the bed.

"Aw, Doc!" Will protested, but Andrew was weighing the potential for violence in the kind of despair he'd just witnessed.

"Do it!" he ordered.

Nicolao drifted off quickly, though not before murmuring once more ". . . all wrong!"

Andrew called Lauren Griffiths and got her answering service. He told the operator it was urgent. When Griffiths herself called him back, he apologized for the lateness of the hour and related what had happened.

She sighed and responded, "I'm on my way."

While they waited for her, the three sat in the lab and discussed what to do in the event that Nicolao had returned permanently and Peter had gone the way of the consciousness that had once occupied those bone fragments.

"The procedure isn't holding," Will observed quietly, pouring coffee for the three of them. "Nicolao's consciousness is fighting it. Maybe if we increase the dosage . . .''

"Absolutely not!" Andrew was adamant. Nicolao's behavior frightened him; he refused to be responsible for evoking that kind of reaction from another human being ever again. He was not going to even discuss increasing the DNA memory resurrection dosage to bring Peter back.

Nicolao had agreed to that possibility in advance when he signed the contract with BioGenera, but Andrew now realized the limits of his commitment to the procedure. He had succeeded beyond his expectations already. No, he would analyze the data they'd collected so far and refine his technique for another try sometime later. But he would not endanger Nicolao any further.

In any event, this was not the time for debate. Most important right now was to save Nicolao's life. The science would take care of itself.

There had been a time when the Romans themselves elected the popes. Even now, centuries later, this gave them a proprietary interest in the man who ruled their Church. It was traditional for those who found themselves in the vicinity of the Apostolic Palace late at night on their way home to look to see if the light was on in the papal apartments. If the pope slept, the world was at peace. If his light burned long into the night, it could signify world crisis, a spiritual apocalypse. Then again, it might only mean his dinner had not agreed with him.

This night, the light in Luke John's bedroom had been extinguished at the usual early hour and remained unlit all night. Couples walking the cobbles arm in arm (she, perhaps, with her shoes in her hand) looked up at the darkened window and sighed contentedly before going on their way.

If the light went on in Cardinal Cosa's apartments in this hour before the sun came up, no one noticed.

On the far side of the world, the phone on Mike Gindman's polished desk rang softly. In the deserted penthouse, it sounded like an alarm.

"Gindman," he said, willing his pulse rate to slow down. He'd spent most of yesterday evening on a conference call, negotiating a three-way deal with clients in Tokyo and Shanghai, but he wasn't expecting any calls tonight. He'd

instructed Delphine before she left for the night to set her
phone to pick up interoffice and routine outside calls. Who
the hell was this, and how had they gotten his inside line?

When the voice on the other end identified itself, Gindman stopped asking questions. For the first several minutes,
all he did was listen.

"Your Eminence," he interjected finally, "right now you
know as much as I do. The memory resurrection procedure
has shown some preliminary success, but no conclusions can
be drawn as yet. It's my policy to leave my scientists alone
to do their jobs. When they have something substantive,
they'll report it to me. I assume the members of your team
do the same for you."

Again he listened while Cosa talked. The cardinal's English was ponderous but correct. That was why his choice
of this particular word caught Gindman off guard.

"A 'deal,' Your Eminence? Sir, I'll remind you that your
office has a formal contract with mine that sets out quite
specifically the terms and conditions of our agreement—"

Was it only an echo on the overseas line, or was it the
sense that this conversation was not going unheard that
made Gindman pause for breath, allowing Cosa to continue
his ever-so-persuasive argument uninterrupted?

"I see," was all Gindman said when Cosa himself finally
paused for breath. "Just one question, sir. Would I be out
of line in surmising that what you and I are discussing at
this moment may not necessarily be mentioned to your—
employer?"

The calm in Gindman's voice was deceptive. *Making an
end run around the pope!* he thought. He was, by his own
admission, not a religious man, but in terms of sheer historical longevity, the papacy had outlasted any secular re-
gime in human history. It was enough to make the short
hairs on the back of Mike Gindman's neck stand on end.
What Cosa said next didn't help.

"Mr. Gindman, His Holiness Pope Luke John is my nominal employer. But any pope is in essence a man. Man is
finite. He lives, he dies, he is replaced by another. But that
which he represents is as eternal as it is ever-changing. In
my experience change sometimes requires, shall we say, a
little push . . ."

The subliminal echo on the line seemed to grow stronger. Gindman hunched conspiratorially over the phone. What was the best way to use a user?

"A point of view that coincides with my own, Your Eminence," he conceded quietly. "What did you have in mind?"

"We'll wait and see what condition Nic's in when he comes out of sedation," Andrew explained his decision to Will and Giuliana. "Then I want Dr. Griffiths to give him a going-over and—"

A hair-raising howl sounded from Nicolao's apartment.

Will was closest and arrived first. Andrew tried to hold Giuliana back, but she pushed past him. None of them could believe what they saw.

Furniture was overturned; the sheets were torn off the bed and lay in a tangled heap on the floor. Blood was splattered on the bed, the walls, the drapes, the ceiling, and the shower was running full blast, staining the bathroom floor pink.

Something hurtled past them and—catlike, inhumanly strong—swung Nicolao bodily out of the shower, wrestling him onto the bed. Rindt. Nicolao was naked again, his wrists slashed, two deep lacerations that made his arms flail like pressurized hoses out of control, spraying blood into the air as he struggled with Rindt.

"Sedate him!" Rindt hissed between clenched teeth, his eyes boring into Andrew.

"But he's already had enough to kill him," Andrew shouted back, grabbing Nicolao's feet and holding them down.

How was he shaking off the sedative so fast? He was responding like a bull!

"Does this look like a dead man to you?" Rindt demanded. Nicolao's arms were slippery with spurting blood. He managed to swing one fist free and bring it crushing into Rindt's face. The blow would have staggered a normal man; Rindt barely flinched, then regained control, gripping Nicolao's wrists in spite of the blood and the old man's desperate strength.

"Another fifty milligrams, Will," Andrew ordered. There

was no time to consider what else to do. He stepped back—
let the colonel get blood all over himself.

Will hesitated but then did as he was instructed. It wasn't
the ideal solution, especially with this much blood loss, but
it was the only way to control the old man long enough to
stitch him up. Will got the shot into him, and they waited.

Nicolao grew tractable. Then dreamy. Once he tensed to
an upright position, eyes ablaze in a final throe against the
narcotic, then went limp and fell heavily onto the mattress.

Andrew moved in quickly to check his vital signs. Everyone else caught their breath. There wasn't even time to call
a med team over from the university; he'd have to do the
suturing himself. It had been years since—

He couldn't get a pulse. He could see Nicolao's skin turning livid, the veins in his powerful neck starting to collapse.

"Goddammit, code blue!" he shouted as he cleared Nicolao's mouth and began CPR. He straddled the old man
and punched his barrel chest, leaning into each blow with
all his weight. Will handed him a stethoscope, but Andrew
couldn't detect a heartbeat. Nicolao wasn't responding.

Will rolled in the emergency cart with the defibrillator
and charged the paddles. Andrew jumped down from the
bed and grabbed them.

"Clear!" He triggered a high-joule blast into Nicolao's
chest. Nicolao's body arched off the bed and then collapsed
onto the mattress.

Again Andrew listened for a heartbeat. Nothing. No
agonal breathing, not even a rattling exhalation of air dis-
lodged by the violent electrical current.

"Clear!"

Another electrical charge coursed through Nicolao's
stilled organs, forcing current to flow, imitating life but not
inspiring it to recur in the cells. Nicolao, and whoever else
had occupied his body for a time, were gone, departed.

The room fell silent. It was that peculiar quiet of the living, shocked when confronted by the suddenness of death
in their midst.

Andrew stood slope-shouldered, the image of defeat. An
uninvited memory of Anna's tiny lifeless body flashed in
front of him; he wanted to howl as Nicolao had in his own
despair. Giuliana knelt, crossed herself, and bowed her head

in prayer. Andrew imagined Nicolao's spirit leaving the bed, carried heavenward by Giuliana's respect and faith.

When he looked back at Nicolao, he was amazed to see Will also kneeling in the shadows. Andrew knew Will as a practical humanist; the thought that even he could ultimately rely on a higher faith made Andrew feel lacking. He respected Will's self-sufficiency, even envied it. To find out at this point that his assistant needed faith in something more made him feel suddenly vulnerable.

There was no time for this now.

"Will, let's get on it," Andrew said coldly. Together they cleaned up the body, closing the wrist wounds with pressure bandages, and prepared it for the morgue.

Far away in the penthouse, Mike Gindman was still on the phone with Cosa. He heard what sounded like some sort of commotion in the room where Cosa was—voices, perhaps another phone ringing.

"One moment . . ." the cardinal said, sounding distracted. Abruptly, he put Gindman on hold.

What the hell? Gindman thought. His immediate impulse was to hang up, let the cardinal call him back. Something made him remain on the line. After a small eternity, Cosa was with him again. Gindman caught the end of a phrase in breathless Italian, as if Cosa had not yet finished speaking to someone else. Someone actually in the room with him, or on another line?

"Forgive me, Mr. Gindman." Cosa seemed to be composing himself even as he spoke. "Apparently I have wasted your valuable time. There will be no need for us to reach a separate agreement after all. Your Subject X is dead . . ."

"*What?!*" Gindman jumped out of his chair, the urge to put Cosa on hold this time and dial Shepard's lab almost overwhelming him. Then he came to his senses. *Nice trick!* he thought. *Kudos to the cardinal; he almost had me fooled! How the hell can he know what's going on right under my nose? Next he'll tell me he was only kidding. It's a trick to throw me off balance, make me think he's omniscient. Big joke!*

He was about to say as much to Cosa, but the cardinal was still speaking.

". . . most unfortunate, Mr. Gindman. Obviously your Dr. Shepard's experiment was too much for the poor man's troubled mind, may he rest in peace! You will no doubt have many details to resolve in the next few days. For my part, I must break the news to His Holiness. When you are finished with your paperwork, you will of course provide me, as agreed, with meticulous detail as to the man's utterances, his behavior, everything, in the time he lived . . .''

"Your Eminence, just a goddam minute—"

"Forgive me, Mr. Gindman. I am saying an early Mass this morning and must be on my way. I shall pray for Mr. Soares's soul. *Addio.*"

Gindman hit the direct line for Shepard's lab. The phone rang unanswered until it was rerouted through the voice mail system. When he heard Andrew's recorded voice asking him to leave a message, Gindman slammed down the phone and headed for the lab.

It was Giuliana who met Lauren Griffiths in the darkened lobby this time. The two women sat long into the night, talking over in soft voices what had happened. Starlight shone in on them through the long windows. It was unnaturally quiet.

Andrew found himself at his desk finally. It had taken more than an hour to explain things to Mike Gindman's satisfaction.

"Jesus Christ!" was all Gindman kept saying. "Jesus Christ!"

The next step, with Will's help, was to clean up the blood. Their lab coats were saturated, and they'd tossed them in the disposal, but Andrew still kept finding random splashes on his pants, his shoes, soaked into one of his shirt cuffs.

He tried to enter the night's events in his file. Disconnected words were all he could manage. He shut off the recorder, let his hands fall uselessly to his lap, an ironic echo of the way Nicolao's hands had flopped in response to the violation of his wrist veins.

15

IT WAS ALMOST DAWN. GIULIANA HADN'T SLEPT. She continued to pray over the lifeless body for a few minutes more. She had never seen anyone die before. She couldn't remember any of the prayers associated with last rites, so she began to recite the rosary. "Our Father, who art in heaven . . ."

"You will do well to pay attention to this as a lamp . . ." a voice rumbled through the stillness.

Giuliana opened her eyes and looked around. There was no one else in the room. Then she saw Nicolao's lips moving.

". . . shining in a dark place, until the day dawns and the morning star rises in your hearts . . ."

The hair on Giuliana's arms stood on end. She was terrified. And mesmerized. Nicolao's chest rose and fell, his mouth moved to form the familiar words she now heard from the lips of the corpse.

"Dio mio!" she cried, scrambling to her feet in terror.

Andrew was there first, followed immediately by Will and Rindt.

"Andrew!" Giuliana whispered hoarsely. " 'The morning star rises in your heart . . .' " she repeated, but she could not go on.

Will and Andrew were too busy checking Nicolao's vital signs, confirming that he had spontaneously revived.

"Pulse 68 and regular, blood pressure 130 over 72, respiration 10 . . . lungs clear . . ." Will reported, pulling the stethoscope out of his ears and the blood pressure cuff off Nicolao's brawny arm, poking and prodding and shining lights in his eyes. "Color good, no cyanosis. Skin warm and dry to the touch, pupils respond normally . . ." He gawked at Andrew, exasperated. "It's like he's just been napping."

"He's back! Don't ask me how, but he's back!" exclaimed Andrew, not knowing what to do next.

Giuliana moved closer and recited verse from the New Testament: " 'Purify your soul with the discipline of charity . . .' "

She looked expectantly at Nicolao and waited, but he appeared to be dozing again.

" ' . . . and give constant proof of your affection for each other . . . ' " Again she waited. But still he slept.

A third time she picked up the reading: " ' . . . loving unaffectedly as brethren should, since you have all been born anew with an immortal, imperishable birth . . . ' "

". . . through the word of God who lives and abides forever . . ." Nicolao's lips moved and the voice jumped in where she had left off. "Yes, the mortal things are like grass . . ."

" ' . . . and all their glory . . . ' " Giuliana prompted, beginning to weep joyfully.

The corners of Nicolao's mouth lifted. ". . . like the bloom of grass." He opened his eyes and looked at Giuliana. The fire was back.

"Your Holiness—?" Giuliana knelt.

Whoever it was in Nicolao's body was momentarily confused but recovered and soon appeared to be relieved. He swung his legs onto the floor, flexed his shoulders, then looked at Giuliana in wonder.

"Greetings in Christ, my child. Why do you address me with such honor?"

"Because I represent your successor, Pope Luke John, 302nd inheritor of your scepter. You are Simon Peter?"

"I am."

"First pope of the Roman Catholic Church?"

"Catholic? I am a Jew!" he roared.

Giuliana looked up at Andrew, unsure how far to go in telling Simon Peter about himself, but he gestured for her to continue, encouraging her. He clearly was following her lead, eager to learn what she apparently already understood.

"Well, Your Holiness"—She sat on a chair beside Peter's bed—"those Jews who followed Jesus—"

" 'Followed' him?"

"*Si, assectators,* believed that . . ."

Giuliana faltered, looked nervously at Andrew. Was Peter ready for the realization that nearly two thousand years had passed, that the events of his life experiences were ancient history?

"Those who believed Christ's teachings and accepted him

as the Son of God came to be known as Christians. Later, in the second century anno Domini, Saint Ignatius of Antioch referred to the Christian Church as *catholicus,* or universal. Since then, it has come to be known as the Catholic Church. Roman Catholic because it is headquartered in Rome, Italy, and has been since you founded it.''

Peter thought about this for a moment. A faraway look entered his eyes as he remembered. One needn't know the Gospels to imagine what he saw in his gallery of recollections. Through his eyes, Giuliana could almost see the charismatic carpenter's son confronting a blind beggar along the dusty road to Jerusalem and curing him with a word and a touch.

''How many—er, what did you call them again? These men . . . after me?''

''Popes, Your Holiness. In Italy we call them *il Papa*— Father. Three hundred and one.''

Peter scratched his chin and rolled this news around in his mind for a few moments.

''Three hundred and two total, right?'' he asked.

Giuliana nodded.

''Just how long have I been . . .'' He waved his hand in a circle, searching for the right word. ''. . . away?''

Giuliana again looked to Andrew.

''Can you remember us? I'm Doctor Andrew Shepard. The scientist who brought you back?''

Until that moment, Peter's eyes had been only for Giuliana. Now he glanced around, as if for the first time, seeing sterile white walls and electric lights and strange machinery. He brushed Andrew's question away as if it were an insect.

''How long?'' he demanded.

Andrew looked at Will for encouragement, then Giuliana. By their expressions it was clear they were waiting for him to take the lead. He rubbed his forehead nervously as he decided that there was no sense in delaying the inevitable. They'd lost Peter once and might again soon.

''Let's see, you went to sleep in . . .'' Andrew temporized, looking to Giuliana for the year.

''A.D. 64,'' she supplied.

''That would be . . . almost two thousand years ago,'' Andrew said carefully. He watched the old man warily, expecting a violent reaction, but all he saw was Peter adding up the passage of that much time and accepting it.

" 'Went to sleep,' Doctor?" Peter looked skeptically at Andrew.

"Died," Andrew corrected himself.

"Better!" Peter acknowledged. "Better that we call it what it was."

"Petros, *per favore*," Giuliana hesitated, until she saw the kindness in his eyes. "How much do you remember? Tell us."

Peter gathered his thoughts. Then he sighed. "All right. I remember the fresh air when I was taken from the Tullianum, the walk to the Circus . . ."

"Circus?" asked Andrew.

"The Circus of Caligula and Nero. Outside the wall . . . They wanted to hang me on the cross like Christ. I fought that. It wasn't right. It would have been an insult to his memory."

"Fought? How?" asked Giuliana.

"One of these to a sentry's jaw," Peter held up a balled fist. "He went down like a fish into a basket." He laughed.

"Then there was a sword to my throat, but the one in charge told him to leave me alone. I didn't run away when I could have. He was a veteran and respected that.

" 'What's the problem, prisoner?' he asked me.

"I don't deserve to die as the master died, I said.

" 'None of us do,' he answered. 'But that is how it is for you.'

" 'Hang me head to ground, Sentry,' I asked him.

"He looked at me for a moment, then said, 'It's worse that way, you know. Much worse.'

"I didn't say anything. I didn't trust myself. He understood and it was done. He was right, it was worse than anything you can imagine." He closed his eyes to shut out the memory of the agony. "The last thing I remember is the way the air stilled and the world went . . ." Peter didn't finish.

He smiled tightly as he remembered his last moment on earth. "So that was almost two thousand years ago, then," he marveled, looking around the room again.

"That's right," Andrew answered, braced for the explosion when this new consciousness comprehended that he was resurrected after two millennia. But the explosion didn't come. Peter merely reached over and patted Giuliana's hand before he settled back into the bed, curling onto his side away from them, his head buried deep in the pillow.

Giuliana leaned forward and whispered, "Rest now."

"Hmmm," Peter agreed pleasantly. "Just a little rest. This body isn't what it used to be . . ." He drifted easily toward a deep sleep. *"Non sum qualis eram."*

" 'I am not the person I was,' " Giuliana translated.

"I'll say!" quipped Will.

The room was soon filled with quiet snores. Andrew dismissed Will.

"You get combat pay for the past two shifts," he said. "Take the rest of the day off."

"No argument!" Will yawned, staggering toward the door.

Andrew noticed Rindt, a shadow amid the shadows on the wall.

"Looks like you can start earning your keep." Andrew nodded toward the sleeping form. "Don't take your eyes off him for a second."

Rindt acknowledged this with a ghost of a smile.

Andrew took Giuliana's arm and guided her toward the door.

"We need to talk."

"You're really convinced this is the actual Peter, Saint Peter, aren't you?" Andrew asked Giuliana.

"Sì." She smiled.

"What makes you so sure?"

"You heard him. He recited parts of the First and Second Letters of Peter from memory. I don't know anyone, even a scholar, who can do this so exactly!"

"It's possible. Somebody else could know Saint Peter's writings, couldn't he?"

Giuliana shrugged reluctant agreement.

"Couldn't he?" Andrew wanted to hear her admit it.

"Possibly. A theologian, maybe. Even an actor who had taken the trouble to learn the lines. But a Portuguese-

American fisherman with a grade school education? It's not probable, Andrew.''

"Well, I can't afford to accept your belief on faith, you understand? I've got a random personality here in my lab, an unidentified personality. It might be Peter, it might not. Could be anyone.''

"You said this the last time, too. Before he—before he died!'' Giuliana flared. "What does it take to convince you that your own experiment has worked?''

Andrew clenched his jaw and didn't answer.

"Besides, that personality is not so random, Andrew.''

"What do you mean?''

Giuliana walked to the windows, fingertips raised to her lips in thought. She appeared to be trying to decide something.

"The bone fragments are from the Vatican. We know this, *si*?''

"*Si*. Yes.''

"The cardinal, he did not tell me which remains he obtained for this experiment, but he admitted they were from the *Grotto Sacre*. I know also that he had some heated confrontations with Monsignor Kleiman, a zealous protector of the relics. The cardinal, you see, has always had doubts that the bones in the niche are Peter's, though he will not go so far as to argue with the pope on this matter. Too many Church officials have accepted the pronouncements of Pius XII in spite of the way the excavations were mismanaged.''

"You've lost me,'' Andrew said frankly. How long had it been since he'd slept? "I'm afraid I don't follow Church politics all that closely.''

"Not politics, Andrew, archaeology,'' Giuliana corrected him. She took a deep breath. Could she give him an overview of the history of the relics without boring him to death?

"There is physical evidence to support the legend that Peter's remains were hidden in the Graffiti Wall by early Christians to save his body from the Roman pyre. Two thousand years, however, is a long time for any grave to remain undisturbed. Anything is possible. And most of the damage was in fact done in our own century.

"Excavation of the *Grotto Sacre* beneath the basilica of St. Peter's was begun during World War II. In December

1942 an excavator named Antonio Ferrua discovered bone fragments deep within the Graffiti Wall. It was late in the day, so he left them as he found them, with the intention of properly documenting and removing them the next day.

"At the time, Monsignor Kleiman was nominal overseer of the excavations, and he took his job too seriously. He had already been banished from the excavation site by the archaeologists for his persistent interference. Nevertheless, he took it upon himself to examine the excavations every night after the scientists had left. When he shone his flashlight into the crack in the excavated wall that night and saw the bones exposed, he was horrified. To leave the bones uncovered overnight was a sacrilege! He had a workman, a *sampietrini*, collect the bones in a wooden box and store it in an upstairs closet behind the Chapel of St. Columban. For reasons known only to himself, he also neglected to mention this to anyone.

"This incredible stupidity flawed the entire excavation project. Ten years passed before the bones were found in the chapel and it was determined that they were the same bones that had been taken from the Graffiti Wall. As a consequence, Dr. Anna Aldobrandi was especially meticulous in her examination of them, and it was another seventeen years before she would absolutely confirm their identification.

"The cardinal's secrecy about this, his assigning Jurgen Rindt to accompany me, his equivocation when I asked him directly, can only mean that he still has doubts. But even he cannot doubt this." Giuliana gestured toward the old man sleeping in the next room. "It all adds up to Peter."

"But it also helps that you want it to be Peter, doesn't it?" Andrew challenged her.

"*Si*, don't you?"

"Of course. But I can't afford the luxury of an emotional reaction. I've got to keep my objectivity."

"Isn't there another reason?" Now it was she who was challenging him. "Andrew, it's all right to admit you are afraid."

He wanted to be angry, wanted to argue, but she had seen into the heart of him. "All right, maybe I am afraid. Afraid of—of the *idea* of Saint Peter, afraid of having my faith tested. I mean, who am I to be part of a miracle? To be honest, I'm not sure I want to know.''

"It's a little late for that now, isn't it? You cannot un-invent the steam engine, unsplit the atom. You've performed the memory resurrection procedure; you must accept the consequences. You are already playing a role in history. You can't exit the stage now!''

"Why not?'' Andrew asked.

"Because the play isn't over! Because mankind must know what is possible, what is on the other side. And because Peter is here, with us, now. You cannot simply abandon him!''

"But Saint Peter? I'm not ready for this.''

Giuliana laughed, incredulous. Their situation was ridiculous. "None of us is ready. For him especially.'' She walked to the window, then back again quickly. "Besides, there is a chance that Dr. Aldobrandi was wrong. There's a chance it's not Peter at all!''

"How much of a chance? Giuliana—!'' he demanded when she did not answer. He was exhausted.

"A very small chance.''

Andrew nodded grimly. "That's what I thought.''

Giuliana thought for a moment. "I told you the first day I came here that I had contacts. Sources that even you do not have access to, who may be of help. Let me call one of them now.''

Andrew yawned. His head felt about ready to explode. "Can it wait until tomorrow? Peter's not going anywhere, and God knows, the rest of us could use some z's.''

Giuliana looked at him quizzically. " 'Z's'?''

"Why do I feel like I'm the only one left around here who speaks English?'' Andrew demanded rhetorically. "Z's. You know, sleep.''

Giuliana got it and laughed. Her laughter was like bells.

"Yes, I suppose it can wait until this afternoon. I will call Dr. Small from my hotel and arrange an appointment—''

"Dr. Small?'' Andrew echoed. "Not Phil Small.''

"Why, yes. Dr. Philip Small is chairman of forensic pathology.''

"—right down the road at the med school,'' Andrew finished for her. "Why didn't you tell me he was one of your contacts? With all the time we've spent back and forth at UCSD, running all those tests . . .''

"There was no need until now," Giuliana said practically. "But as one of the world's leading experts on ancient human remains, he may be of some assistance to us."

Andrew shook his head. The more she seemed to gain in self-confidence, the more he felt his own slipping.

"You amaze me!" he said. "I don't think I'm ready . . . for any of this."

"Oh, Andrew, you're ready for it! Was Moses ready for the burning bush? Was Peter ready to be crucified by Nero? Was I ready to die as a little girl of only seven?"

Andrew looked up, startled. *"What?"*

"There is a life after this one," she said with conviction as she came over to him and sat down. "Believe that!"

A calm settled over her, an unmistakable tranquillity. Andrew waited for her to continue, but she hesitated. Tentatively he took her hand, held it lightly in his own.

"I'm listening."

"I was terribly ill," she began. "My temperature was killing me. Meningitis, they would say later, but at the time no one knew. My mama could do nothing to help me. So Papa carried me twenty kilometers to the hospital at Tivoli.

"I was in and out of consciousness. Soon I went into septic shock . . ." Her English faltered. "The doctor, he try ice packs and drugs, but nothing worked. I hear the nurse say she can't detect my pulse. There is panic. It is a small village hospital and they are not prepared.

"Then, I am suddenly outside myself and the pain is gone. In the blink of an eye I am up high, near the ceiling, by the window looking down as the doctor tries a clumsy form of CPR. The nurse counts aloud as he pushes hard on my chest. I move closer to see my body better and realize that I never see myself from outside myself before. Suddenly I see myself from every angle . . .

"I think that the big doctor pushing so hard on my little body should hurt, but it does not.

"He continues this for some time. He seems to want me to live more than anything in the world. The doctor's and the nurses' thoughts reach out to me with such power! But it is no use. Finally, he stands back and swears. *'Maledizione! Peccato!'* He is so angry.

"I am flying, faster and faster, but with grace, you see? Where is the wind in my face? Blowing my hair, drying my eyes? I have no face, no hair, no eyes. I am a pure thought moving in the bright light, looking directly into it, drawn forward by—by what can only be described as love.

"There is a presence there with me, a wisdom of everything, not just about my short life but everything. It is a face, a force. So joyful and open and generous. I am drawn to this . . . spirit, as it is drawn to me. We are happy.

"Oh, it is so lovely, so much more meaningful than anything I have ever experienced! I want to stay there forever. There is no reason to go back. But then the presence makes it known to me that now that I have shared in that love, I should go back. I look down at myself lying there motionless and, without any warning, I am gasping for air, my head splitting apart, my body on fire. I am alive and I know that I will live."

Giuliana's arms rested limply in her lap. She had withdrawn her hand from Andrew's in her rapture, and he hadn't dared touch her again. Now he didn't even speak.

"There is nothing to fear in dying, Andrew. It is not painful. It is warm, complete acceptance, a panoramic awareness of all knowledge, an all-embracing love. These are the gifts that await us. I know that this moment and every other moment of my existence offers me an opportunity. I can embrace these blessings, or I can mark time. But I am accountable for the quality of my life. I will have to exist with the knowledge of what I do or fail to do for all of eternity. I must be true to myself and to others because each moment lives forever."

She couldn't know she had touched an open wound in Andrew. Her words resonated and found a harmony with his secret thoughts.

"I know that death is not the end," she continued. "It truly is only the beginning of another life so bountiful and exhilarating that by comparison these fleeting days on earth seem awkward, insignificant. Finally, I know we have a soul. Our bodies, these are only a temporary reflection of one reality in the universe.

"We are souls in motion." She smiled, her eyes welling up with joy. "We are souls. It taught me things, Andrew, grown-up things that help me even now. Life is hard. What comes after is easy. In that moment, I also discovered that I am a child of a force so knowing, all wise, all loving . . . it is all right to treasure the faith of my childhood, that is all that matters. We are all children.

"I have kept this experience locked away, but it is as real for me this moment as it was thirty-one years ago. Surely we have a memory for something more important than roses in December. I believe this. I know this. That is Saint Peter in there, I tell you."

Andrew's skepticism melted like frost against the authentic details of Giuliana's memory. She had experienced the mystery; he'd only heard about it. Giuliana had answered questions Andrew didn't know he was asking. Suddenly there were tears in his own eyes. He told her about Anna.

"And so you have been lost ever since!" she whispered finally when he was finished. "*Mi dispiace*. Now I understand."

She hadn't touched him once while he was speaking, the words pouring out of him in an unstoppable flood as he described his unadulterated joy in Anna's sheer existence, the bottomless void once she was gone. Had he and Margaret ever shared so much? Had he ever shared this much of himself with anyone? Now Giuliana leaned forward and touched his face with her cool hands, touched him to his soul.

"When people talk about what they believe in, I never know what to say," Andrew said. "If I had any faith when I was younger it was superficial, a belief in the trappings, nothing more. It burned away like fog once—once my daughter died. Now all I have left is my work, and even that's suddenly become more than I think I can handle."

Giuliana caressed his face, not knowing what to say, wishing she could take away his anguish with such a simple gesture. As she withdrew her hands he took them in his own and kissed her palms.

"Thank you for listening," he started to say. A sound from the room behind interrupted them.

"Hey there!" A booming voice called from the doorway. They looked up and saw Peter beaming at them, positively glowing with energy.

16

THEY WERE COMING TO KNOW PETER. HE WAS NOT a complicated man.

"Sometimes I think he chose me because I am so simple, eh? No accident that he named me *Petros,* rock. For my thick head, as much as to instruct me to be strong, to stand fast against what was to come. He knew, and wanted us to be prepared. And I think also it was one of his gentle jokes."

"Somehow we don't think of Jesus as someone who made jokes," Andrew remarked dryly.

"You did not know him as I did," Peter said, implying it was Andrew's loss.

It was Giuliana who spent the most time with him, hanging on his every word. She was fulfilling her responsibility to the cardinal, who still called her as often as a dozen times a day (and, she knew, spoke to Rindt almost as often), wanting to know every minute detail. But she was also drawn to this charismatic old man, as much by the strength of his personality as by his importance to the project, to history.

He readily discussed his background, spoke fondly of his birthplace.

"Bethsaida, a little village much like any other, though I was not to know this until I began to travel first with the master and later in my quest to do his bidding. Growing up there, I thought it the most wonderful place in the world. I suppose it is long gone now."

"We can find out," Will assured him. He had promised to initiate Peter into the mysteries of something called CD-ROM as soon as he could free up some time. "It may still be there. Things have a way of staying unchanged in the Middle East."

"The Middle East!" Peter tried it on his tongue. "How much more there is to know of the world than there was in my day!

"We were fishermen, common people. I received the same education as any Jewish boy of my time and station, how to read and write and recite my Torah. I was naturally good with figures, and became head of the Bethsaida fishing cooperative. Then the master found me, and changed my life."

A profile quickly emerged of an elemental human—energetic, forceful, committed, and extremely likable. He brought with him key survival skills, including healthy skepticism, humor, and an alert self-awareness that would hold him in good stead in the modern age. He was remarkably quick to notice inconsistent behavior toward him, and he reacted candidly.

"Not so different from Jerusalem or Rome, my friends!" he laughed as he devoured his and half of everyone else's dinner portions. "People don't change so much. In my time they were simpleminded, willing to take literally the things their leaders told them then. You still accept today. What I see on this television, these assurances that the right medicine, the right shampoo, the right leader, the right pair of jeans will give you a perfect life, is no different than the village fool in my day believing some magic potion will make him attractive to women, when what he really needs is to eat fewer onions and learn a trade and stop loitering about the well annoying other men's wives. Everyone wants easy answers, in your time as much as mine. It's not the people, only the things they desire, that change."

Flexibility came naturally to him. Peter never let expediency dictate his conduct, yet there was an innate wariness to him that Giuliana theorized had been learned by necessity during years in the midst of enemies. Blindingly quick to respond to danger, real or imagined, he never wasted movement. Possessing an unusually strong need for personal space, he couldn't endure prolonged physical contact with other bodies; it stole his control and made him vulnerable. If he was crowded into an elevator, he could not wait to be out and in a comfortable space again, though he never revealed any anger or showed his intentions; he simply moved away.

At first Peter disapproved of what Andrew and Giuliana had done in raising him from the dead. For the first two days after his awakening he had sunk into depression and intense inner turmoil, then he rebounded.

"I ask to understand this *magicus*," he explained after a time. "What purpose is in this? *Cui bono*? What good, and why me? Then I accept. It takes some time; I am old and stubborn. The answer is simple: God intends me to be here for a reason, and he has blessed you, Andrew, with miraculous powers."

"Extraordinary, yes," Giuliana said before Andrew could start to protest again. "But 'miraculous'?"

"*Ita*. Who am I to question what is? Neglect not the gift that is in thee, I say. Besides, I like it here. I want to see more. For now, there is only one thing I need to understand. What use do you intend to make of me now that I am here?"

It was the one question Andrew had most been hoping to avoid.

"We need to run a few more tests," he temporized, avoiding Peter's eyes. "Get you acclimated to your new surroundings first. Then we'll bring you upstairs and introduce you to our CEO, Mike Gindman, and we'll discuss future plans."

"Chief Executive Officer." Peter had already asked Giuliana what the initials meant. "It's quite a title. Almost as good as Messiah!"

And so it went. Andrew and Giuliana inquired, explained, described, listened, and evaluated. They grew close to Peter in the way strangers forge lifelong friendships during captive afternoons.

Will was also fascinated by Peter and got a big kick out of bringing him up to speed on modern technology. From the beginning Peter had asked for detailed explanations of everything from the syringes used to inject him to the complex machinery used to examine him. Again, his perception of what was to be expected in a world based upon a God whose intentions had been made clear to him through the words of his master, as opposed to what he found alien and strange, was surprising.

Television, for example, he accepted as a matter of course, channel surfing with great ease once the intricacies of the remote control had been explained to him.

"Fenestra!" he pronounced it. "Like a window into many worlds, one within the other. *Microcosmos.*"

When Will introduced him to the wonderful world of personal computing, he was beside himself.

"All the knowledge of mankind at one's fingertips! Even the great library at Alexandria is as nothing compared to this!"

"That'll hold him for a while, Doc," Will reported. "But this is one bird you're not going to keep caged for long."

"I know," was all Andrew managed to say.

Albert Brankowicz, Ph.D., specialist in biblical history, had been summoned to Washington for a meeting with the special assistant to the president. He didn't ask where the White House had gotten the information on the Vatican's involvement with a West Coast genetics lab. Something told him he was better off not knowing. He'd been asked for his expert opinion, and he would give it, in time to beat the traffic on the Beltway and make a five o'clock flight home.

"The New Testament contains only hearsay about the first, twelfth, thirty-second, and thirty-third years of an obscure Jewish ascetic who roamed a remote corner of the Roman Empire two thousand years ago." Brankowicz slipped into lecture mode easily; it was how he earned his livelihood. "These accounts were written by men of limited education and uneven literary skills decades after the events themselves took place. Yet the world's largest organized religion is based upon this erratic reportage. Almost one billion people live and die by what this young man and his band of outcasts supposedly did and said.

"The King James Version records approximately thirty thousand words attributed to this man-god. Yet everything that is *known* about Jesus Christ would fit into one paragraph, a short paragraph. We know more about the men who followed him than we do about Jesus."

"What about Saint Peter?" the special assistant asked with studied casualness.

"Peter is mentioned nearly two hundred times in nine out of the twenty-seven books of the New Testament. That's more than all the other Apostles combined. Is it only because Jesus chose him to lead the separatist movement after his death? Or was there something so compelling about the man himself that he almost seems to upstage Jesus? That's a debate that will continue long after you and I are dead."

"Conclusions, Dr. Brankowicz?" the special assistant asked. He had taken no notes, sat with his hands folded on his desk during the entire interview; Brankowicz wondered if this conversation was being taped. "Suppose Saint Peter were to walk the Earth today?"

Brankowicz weighed his answer before he spoke. "As a potential witness to the life of Jesus, he would present a very real and compelling challenge, both to the foundations of Christianity—and by implication to Judaism and Islam as well—and to a Western civilization predicated upon what we define as Judeo-Christian values."

"In other words, you're suggesting he'd make trouble."

Brankowicz laughed ironically. "I'm suggesting no such thing! *He* wouldn't necessarily be the problem. But he certainly wouldn't pass through the world unnoticed."

Deep in the windowless, soundproof, and what some Muslim extremists hoped would someday be tomblike confines of the Tzahal Milkhama Kheder, the war room of the Israeli Defence Forces, Brankowicz's Jewish counterpart briefed a phalanx of generals and political leaders on essentially the same topic.

"There is still debate about whether Jesus ever actually referred to himself as the Son of Man, or if this was a literary device inserted by later writers to 'prove' his messiahship. However, his calling of disciples and healing of the sick fit with the Elijah profile, supporting his claim to be a prophet at the end of time.

"He may only have been an opportunist, someone well read enough to live his life in fulfillment of prophecy, as so many other would-be messiahs did before and after him. What makes his message a threat to the State of Israel is his claim that the leaders of the restored Israel would not be hereditary, not the descendants of Abraham, but artisans and fisherman. Every attempt to keep us in exile for nearly two thousand years was based upon the havoc wrought by that message.

"Now we hear rumors that one of his followers is alive in our own century. These rumors do not even have to be true in order to encourage our enemies to once more strive to drive us into the sea.

"Impostor or reality, we must stop this man before he undoes all we have accomplished . . ."

One aspect of Peter's arrival that no one had foreseen was his difficulty in adjusting to the noise level of the twentieth century. His senses were assaulted by the gauntlet of modern machinery. Every new noise startled him. The annoying hum from Torrey Pines Road and nearby Interstate 5 never let up. Cars squealed and honked. Trucks backfired, ground gears, and coughed black diesel exhaust. Car stereos blared. Police cruisers and ambulances and fire trucks wailed every which way. At least ten times a day, the Amtrak commuter train rumbled by. Even the Pacific Ocean pounded on the beach like thunder; the Sea of Galilee in its worst moments had scarcely whispered.

Giuliana had found him a quiet spot to walk: the tenth green of the golf course just before it opened for the day. A noise penetrated the surrounding silence midway through his first morning walk. He cocked his head and listened.

"Quod?"

Giuliana pointed to a contrail threading the deepest blue sea of sky overhead. A gleam flickered at its tip. "An airplane, Your Holiness. *Aeroplano. Tero.*"

"A machine?" he asked in wonder. "What does it do?"

"People use it to travel quickly over great distances."

"Volo? Man can fly? How?"

"Something called aerodynamic lift." Giuliana shrugged, hoping he wouldn't ask her to explain further. He shook his head in wonder, watching the jet for several minutes, thoroughly intrigued.

Television sometimes lost its appeal for Peter. When it wasn't blaring disjointed conversations from around the world, radio commercials pitched long distance cellular telephone service, department store sales, and fast-food bargains. Giuliana often found Peter sitting in silence in his apartment, as if recuperating.

At other times he developed an explosive restlessness. Andrew could no longer confine him to his wing of the BioGenera campus, let alone the laboratory itself. Peter was like a wild animal who was expected to be grateful for his unnatural captivity after a rich, full life in the fenceless wilds.

"How much longer before I can speak to this Gindman?" he cornered Andrew and demanded one morning.

"Soon. He's out of town."

"When will he return?"

"End of the week or early next week." The delay annoyed Andrew as well, though he wouldn't say as much to Peter. Ever since Nicolao's suicide, Gindman seemed to be looking for excuses to be out of town, avoiding the project entirely, as if waiting for disaster to strike again. "As soon as he returns, I promise I'll introduce you to him."

Peter accepted this, temporarily. His predawn walks with Giuliana increased in distance and diversity; they helped him physically as well as mentally, but, most important, they allowed his natural ebullience and curiosity to take flight.

He asked about the wildlife in the Torrey pines beyond the fence, about the whales he saw breaching on the horizon as they migrated south to Mexico. He and Giuliana talked about civilization and faiths and governments. This expanded freedom worked so well that Andrew agreed to allow Peter to take walks by himself, on the condition that he check in hourly and always be back for their continuing research work, interviews, and debriefings. Peter cooperated in this honor system without complaint, never missing an opportunity to stretch his wings, and was always back safely and on time.

Besides, he knew Rindt was never more than a few steps away, watching his back.

Still, his restlessness grew. He would sweep into the outer wings, introducing himself with a laugh to this doctor, with a hearty wave to that assistant. He admired the uniforms of the security guards, asked them to show him how their

walkie-talkies worked; he once spent an entire afternoon discussing fertilizer with one of the groundskeepers. No one
was quite sure what to make of him, but he brightened the
atmosphere around him wherever he went. His abundant appetites revealed themselves in the smallest interactions, and
his buoyant spirit filled the halls of BioGenera. He embraced
his new life.

Once a week, a nurse from the medical center arrived to
check his blood pressure and confer with Will about his diet,
nutritional supplements, whether or not he should have a flu
shot. Watching her move about the room, aware of the friction of her stockings, her rounded bust, the enigma of white
on white, the flare of her hips, Peter was easily distracted.

He flirted with her. A veteran of the wards, the nurse was
immune to his enthusiasm. Giuliana caught him at it and
gave him a reproachful look. Peter was quick to defend himself.

"After all, the Song of Solomon says: 'How fair and how
pleasant art thou, O love, for delights!' "

"But what of Matthew, who said, 'Whosoever looketh on
a woman to lust after her hath committed adultery already
in his heart'?" Giuliana asked playfully.

"Who is Matthew?" Peter asked ingenuously.

Giuliana remembered that the Gospel of Matthew was
written long after Peter was martyred.

"One of your admirers," she quipped and walked back
into the lab.

" 'How fair and how pleasant art thou, dear woman'!"
Peter shouted after her.

A shiver tickled the back of Giuliana's neck, Peter's gaze
a lambent pressure on her hair, the small of her back, down
to her behind, where it lingered, to her thighs, calves, her
ankles. She wanted to turn around and see his expression
but decided instead to prolong the sensation. She kept walking across the lab in full view, knowing Peter was drinking
in her form.

She tried to imagine Cosa or Luke John or any of Peter's
spiritual descendants possessed of such a natural, healthy
attitude. She'd caught a glimpse of it on occasion from Monsignor Murphy, but even he repressed his appreciation to the

point of suffocation. How much more joyous might the world be if all men were as full of life as Peter?

His irrepressible curiosity continued to exercise itself. Andrew knew that the time would soon come when he would have to satisfy Peter's need for freedom. How he would accomplish this he hadn't a clue. Neither did Giuliana, who began to express concern about what Rindt might do if she couldn't control Peter's roamings.

Colonel Rindt updated the cardinal two or three times each day. Cosa had reduced the number of his calls to Giuliana, preferring for the moment to rely more on Rindt. Giuliana was simultaneously relieved and wary. Eventually, she knew, Cosa would want to interview this new consciousness personally. Would he settle for a teleconference or would he insist that Peter be brought to Rome? How long would he wait before he made some sort of move? Increasingly protective of Peter, Giuliana determined not to lose control of him to anyone else.

But Cosa was way ahead of her. He addressed his concerns directly to Rindt.

"I don't need problems, Colonel. I am relying on you to keep me informed and handle any contingencies."

"*Capisce*, Your Eminence."

Returning from a phone consult with Lauren Griffiths, who was still marveling at Peter's "reintegration," as she insisted upon calling it, Andrew and Giuliana found Peter charming a pretty technician in the cafeteria, drawing delighted laughter and blushing rebukes from the young woman.

Peter saw them and joined them. Andrew noticed that he walked with a limp.

"You all right, Peter?" he asked.

"Just sore joints."

"Joints?"

"My ankles. What else can an old man expect, eh?"

"Sore joints, I guess," Andrew laughed, masking his concern.

"No other joints are sore, Peter?" Giuliana asked, suddenly very interested.

"Oh, the usual stiffness. Our walks help me loosen up."

"But the ankles are sore in a different way?" Andrew tried not to sound too clinical.

"Like the devil!" Peter admitted.

"Romans sometimes cut a body from the cross... through the ankles," Giuliana thought aloud as soon as Peter was out of earshot.

"And Peter's subconscious could be transferring that memory into Nicolao's joints," added Andrew.

"And if the victim was strong and took too long to die, *crurifragium.*"

"*Crurifragium?*" repeated Andrew.

"Breaking of the *cruciarius*, the victim's legs," she explained. "To hasten death while still on the cross. If the victim couldn't straighten his legs, he couldn't pull himself upright to draw air into his lungs. Crucifixion is death by exhaustion and suffocation."

"I always assumed the victims bled to death," Andrew said, assessing Peter with new admiration.

Giuliana was shaking her head. "Dr. Small can explain more fully. Come on—we'll be late!"

Dr. Philip Small stood six and a half feet tall. Perhaps the juxtaposition of his height with his last name had given him his sense of irony; certainly his profession had honed it. As a dealer in death, usually violent death, a pathologist had to have an intact sense of humor. His lifelong study of ancient remains only served to reinforce his conviction that no animal but man was capable of such creative ways of killing.

"The only sure way to tie the bones to Peter would be the presence of some disease or deformity specifically known to have been suffered by him," he said, after Giuliana explained why they had come to him.

"By all accounts, eschatological and coincidental, Saint Peter was a bull of a man, free of disease and given to a loose temper," she said.

"So the legend of his cutting off the ear of the high priest's assistant in the Garden at Gethsemane is most likely true," Dr. Small suggested.

"It fits his personality perfectly," Giuliana agreed. "Besides, it's mentioned in the synoptic Gospels."

Andrew sat listening to the two of them, feeling like a fifth wheel. Sometimes it was a disadvantage to be a specialist; there was so much general knowledge he'd never had time to absorb.

"But, as far as you know, no mention of any physical deformity?" Philip Small persisted.

"Non," answered Giuliana.

"All right, then, let's assume the Roman practice of breaking the crucifixion victim's legs to hasten death," Dr. Small continued. "The Romans always crucified their victims just outside the city walls, usually on any natural elevation where they could be seen. This set a visible example for the citizenry and especially for the slaves and freedmen, while at the same time keeping the stench and potential disease at a safe distance. The only problem was that predators—wolves, vultures, and other scavengers—tended to feed on the remains after the victim was taken down from the cross. This is why the bodies were often also burned on a pyre, because there are rare recorded instances of survivors managing to crawl away from the predators and save themselves."

"My God!" Andrew said, visualizing it.

"What the Roman *quaternio* did when the victim was near death was to deliver a coup de grace that would hasten death. When the *cruciarius* had reached a severely weakened condition, the soldiers would break the person's legs with a powerful blow that hastened death in one of two ways: it deepened the level of the victim's traumatic shock, inducing unconsciousness and coma and virtually assuring death or, in the event the victim survived that, it would be impossible to straighten upright to obtain more oxygen.

"Remember, the *quaternios* had to keep a schedule to execute all criminals and political prisoners. They had it timed, based on the weight and age of the victim, to a matter of hours. A large-framed, heavy male, for instance, tended to succumb more quickly than a small, slender woman. Based on decades of experience, the soldiers were able to reduce the time of death to under three hours. That way they could start the pyre, burn up the day's work, and be back in the barracks by nightfall.

"I can lecture you on how the angle of the arms to the

vertical increased the number of pounds of pressure exerted on them." He swung his swivel chair, warming to his subject. "I can tell you how the evidence from the Shroud of Turin proves conclusively that the nails were not driven straight through the palms of the hands, but that they were in fact driven at an angle through the wrists. I can also tell you how this increased the intensity of the victim's pain. I can even tell you that not every victim was crucified in the manner we're familiar with from religious paintings; that the Romans in their creativity sometimes hung their victims upside down, or laid them out horizontally, even impaled them with stakes through the genitalia."

"Jesus!" Andrew thought he was going to be sick. He hadn't felt this nauseated since handling his first cadaver in premed. Philip Small laughed wryly and took pity on him.

"Sorry! I'm a bit of a zealot on the subject. But let's stick to the case at hand."

"Unfortunately, the sections of femur and tibia recovered from Peter's tomb were not complete," Giuliana said. "We cannot be certain whether or not they were subjected to *crurifragium . . .*"

Andrew listened to her in awe. It wasn't as if the horrors of the previous conversation didn't affect her; it was as if she had learned somehow to accept these things and to rise above them. How he envied her self-assurance!

". . . there is, however, something else that may negate the significance of whether or not *crurifragium* was performed," she went on, a finger to her lips in concentration. "According to the legend, as the *quaternio* prepared to crucify him, Peter asked if they would crucify him head down. He said he was unworthy to die in the same way as Christ. Not caring how he hung on the cross as long as the result was the same, the guards did as he asked.

"One theory is that the nails holding Peter's feet may have been jammed so tightly that the soldiers were unable to extract them once he was dead. It would have been easiest to cut down the body with an ax through the ankles."

Andrew winced. He remembered how Peter had hobbled out of the cafeteria and limped away.

"Were any foot bones found in the tomb?" Andrew asked, suddenly excited.

Giuliana shook her head. "No."

"I think you may have answered your own question," Philip Small suggested.

Andrew had Will supervise the afternoon session while he measured Peter's feet and went out and bought him a pair of high-tops.

"There goes the budget!" Will quipped, squinting at the price tag before tossing the shoes one at a time at Peter, who caught them easily. "Here you go, Michael Jordan; knock yourself out!"

Peter grinned. If he didn't get the reference, he would look it up on Netscape later. He laced up the shoes and pumped them up with their custom air cushion support, and he was transformed. The relief from pain showed immediately. Elated, he stood up and modeled, then went for a brisk walk to show them off.

The limp was gone.

And Andrew finally believed.

17 "IT'S GETTIN' TO BE TOO MUCH, DOC," WILL CONfided as he and Andrew watched Peter work the hallway and the grounds, poking his head into the labs to see what was going on, charming every woman from the youngest receptionist to the seventy-something nutritionist. "He's like a bull in a barn full of heifers. He'll kick over the traces any minute now."

"Can't let him off the grounds, Will. We'll lose him for sure. He doesn't know what kind of world it is out there."

"He's getting a fair idea," Will pointed out. "Now that you've outfitted his feet, you'll probably want to get his eyes checked too."

Andrew's response was a puzzled frown.

"With all the time he spends squinting at the boob tube and soaking up info off the Internet, he's going to end up needing bifocals," Will explained. "As for what it's doing to his brain . . . this morning he asked me if I thought the

Inquisition was a historic aberration or an integral part of current Church policy. Hell, son, my people were Methodists; how was I supposed to answer that?''

"I don't think even the pope could answer that one," Andrew remarked. "All right, Austin, what do you suggest we do with him? Give him the car keys and tell him to be home by midnight?"

Will scratched his head. "Well, maybe I missed something in the start-up phase, but what *were* we planning on doing with him? We'll have run every test there is to run by this time next week. What then?"

"That's for Gindman and the board to decide," Andrew said distractedly. He saw Will open his mouth to protest and cut him off. "With our input, of course. Besides, let's not forget the Vatican. Giuliana says eventually Cardinal Cosa will want to see 'the results of our experiment,' as she put it, as will the pope. Good thing Peter's so fixated on flying; she'll have no trouble at all getting him on a plane and taking him to Rome to show him off."

"Like a trained seal!" Will muttered.

Andrew eyed him narrowly. "You want off the case?" he asked after a long moment.

"Hell, no! I just don't want to see the old boy hurt, that's all.''

Peter solved the problem himself. He was more than an hour past his check-in time before Andrew realized he'd gone walkabout.

It wasn't the first time they'd lost him. Sometimes he was religiously punctual, checking in one minute before the hour like a dutiful child. Other times he was anywhere from a few minutes to half an hour late. On those occasions he would grin disarmingly.

"In my day we didn't drive ourselves mad with clocks and schedules; we lived from sun to sun. Perhaps we lived more fully than you. Let's say we start the next hour now, okay?"

Looking back on it, Andrew realized that none of this was random. At first Peter had strained at the short leash they'd put him on, pushed the envelope as far as he dared, until keeping up with him became a full-time occupation.

An hour didn't pass during which at some time Andrew or Giuliana or Will didn't look up from whatever they were doing and ask "Where's Peter?" He had conditioned them by his seeming carelessness and, like good lab rats, they'd responded to their conditioning.

"Perhaps you're more in need of my services than you care to admit, Dr. Austin," Rindt couldn't resist saying when Will came searching. "Left to your own devices, you would lose Peter in traffic. He is with Gindman."

"Shee-it!" Will didn't even bother with a snappy retort; he loped up the stairs three at a time. Breathless, he ground to a halt in front of Delphine's desk.

"Too late," she said, nodding toward Gindman's closed door.

"The two of them?" Will panted. "Alone?"

"Mm-hmm." Delphine seemed to be suppressing a smile; she busied herself with her filing. "Been at it for half an hour. They're having a grand time."

Will settled himself comfortably against Delphine's desk as if it were a hitching rail in the Yaak Valley. "You don't mind if I wait here for him, do you?"

Delphine motioned toward the seating area. "Suit yourself. Just don't expect me to entertain you. I've got work."

"Yes, ma'am!" Will retrieved a *Sports Illustrated* from the glass-topped coffee table just as a burst of male laughter sounded from behind the closed doors. "What the hell are they talking about in there?"

"Beats me," was Delphine's reply. "But apparently they plan to be in there a while. They've ordered sandwiches and beer."

"Sandwiches and beer," Will mouthed after her. "Did either of them say anything to you?"

"Oh, yes!" Delphine said brightly, a twinkle in her eye. "Mike ordered his usual tuna and Swiss from the Cheese Shop, and an Amstel Light. Peter said he'd have the same, only hold the Swiss."

"Very funny!" Will said off Delphine's tinkling laughter. There were footsteps on the stairs. Giuliana joined them.

"Have you seen—?" she started to say. They both simultaneously pointed at the doors. Giuliana assessed the situation, the fact that there was no other exit from Mike

Gindman's glass office than through this room. She sat down beside Will on one of the couches, leafing through a copy of *Mirabella*.

A half hour passed quietly, except for the occasional exuberance of the men inside, the muted electronic tones of the telephone, the crinkling of magazine pages. A delivery boy arrived with the sandwiches and went on his way, passing Andrew, who was coming up the stairs. Before he could even ask, all three gestured toward the closed doors.

"I don't believe it!" Andrew fumed, mostly at Will, but his anger included Giuliana. "I can't believe you just let him stroll on in there."

"He was already there by the time we arrived," Will offered.

"What're they up to?" Andrew asked irritably.

"Sandwiches, beer, and guy talk," Delphine answered as she clipped a letter to others in a file.

"Beer! Christ, Austin, where's your head? Alcohol might alter the MR effect on his brain function."

"I warned him, Doc," Will shrugged. "He just grinned and closed the door."

Andrew subsided into silence but refused to sit down. He paced from the seating area to the windows and back until even Delphine's patience was worn thin. Another half hour passed. Suddenly the door to Gindman's office burst open, and they all looked up like guilty children.

Peter was chuckling over some shared joke. He shook Gindman's hand heartily, slapping him on the back as if they'd known each other for years.

"Great talking to you, Mike! Let's do lunch again sometime."

"Anytime, my friend, anytime at all!" Gindman beamed, only then noticing the assemblage around Delphine's desk. "What are you all sitting around for? Is this what I pay you for? Get back to work!"

Will and Andrew took Peter in tow; Giuliana followed them down the stairs. Peter turned to blow a kiss at Delphine before Andrew homed in on him.

"You mind telling us what that was all about?"

"I figured it was time I introduced myself," Peter explained. "He's a great guy, Mike Gindman. We have a lot in common."

"I'll just bet!" Andrew muttered. "And exactly what did you find to talk about?"

"Marketing strategies!" Peter said gleefully and refused to say anything more.

"If you don't find something to keep him occupied," Will said now, "he'll tunnel out under the wall—hell, through the wall. I've seen that look before."

"We're waiting on the Vatican," Andrew explained. "We're partners on this thing, remember? We can't do anything or go anywhere until they decide what they want to do next. One minute they're calling Giuliana sixteen times a day wanting to know every word Peter's uttered since he got out of bed, whether he prefers red wine to white, briefs to boxers. Now they've gone silent. It's a mind game, like keeping us waiting on the relics when they could have said yes or no right away. So we wait."

"Nothing says you've got to wait here," Will said ingenuously. "Long as you and Giuliana have him in your custody, you're still fulfilling your part of the deal."

"Where are we going to take him that he won't get into trouble?"

"You haven't been out on your boat in a while. That front off Baja should be pushing some good air by one o'clock or so," Will suggested.

Andrew smiled absently, already feeling the wind on his face. His one indulgence was a sloop called *Kestrel* that he'd bought secondhand when he got his first raise at BioGenera. He'd dreamed of taking his wife and baby daughter sailing every weekend. At first Margaret said Anna was too young, it was too dangerous, she'd sunburn. Then Anna was gone and Margaret wanted to be alone. She had her therapist, Andrew had his boat.

Then Andrew was alone and, in his darkest moments, toyed with the idea of selling *Kestrel*. But some instinct told him it was at his darkest moments that he most needed the freedom of a boat.

For months now he'd paid the marina fees without thinking, paid a local kid to keep up the maintenance. When was the last time he'd taken her out, felt the swells beneath him? Longer ago than he cared to remember. Will was right. Peter wasn't the only one who needed to stretch.

"Fourteen to sixteen knots is my guess," Will was saying, watching Andrew grin.

"Cover me with Gindman?"

"Handled."

Mike Gindman found himself standing at the window, clenching and unclenching his fists, staring out over the golf course without seeing it. Good God, what had he gotten himself into?

The memory resurrection procedure had generated more documentation than any other single project since he'd taken over BioGenera, and Gindman prided himself on the fact that he'd not only read every word of it, he'd understood it. So why wasn't he prepared for the full impact of the outcome, the flesh-and-blood man who'd just monopolized an hour and a half of his busy life and made him love every minute of it?

I guess I didn't expect him to be so . . . real! Gindman thought. *Maybe I thought this ancient memory would just speak through Nic Soares's mouth like a ghost at a séance, then fade back to whatever netherworld it came from. I didn't expect him to stick around long enough to march in here like a doppelgänger, drink my beer, and ask me when I intend to "let him out of this fancy prison."*

Now Cosa wants me to turn him over directly to him on the q.t., without telling anyone—not the media, not even the pope. Why? So he can do what with him? Put him on display like the Indians Columbus brought back to Isabella? Put him on the rack and grill him, lock him in the dungeon if he doesn't like his answers? If Peter thinks this place is a prison . . .

Mike Gindman never had doubts, not about anything. He was having doubts now. The best way he knew to dispel doubt was to take action. He hit the intercom button.

"Delphine? We still getting nuisance calls from the media?"

He heard her laugh. "What you mean 'we,' Kemosabe?

I'm fielding six or seven calls a day, if that's your question. Inquiring minds want to know.''

"Uh-huh." Gindman made a decision. "Call in the usual suspects. I think we're overdue for a press conference.''

Peter appeared in the parking lot, dressed for adventure in khakis, a rugby shirt, a Billings Rodeo Days windbreaker, and a smile as wide as the Pacific. His fashion statement made Giuliana smile.

"I'm assuming you can swim?" Andrew asked him.

"Like a ballast stone!"

"But—"

"Not to worry! I've sailed all my life."

"All right, but you wear a life vest on my boat." He motioned Peter into the front seat of his car, secured his safety belt. When Giuliana slipped into the backseat, Peter looked surprised.

"You're coming also?"

"*Si.*"

"A woman out on the boat? Praise God, I love the twentieth century!"

He brightened even more when he saw *Kestrel* riding the harbor wake in her slip.

"That's a toy!" he laughed. "A stiff gust could snap her back! That's not a sailing boat, it's a . . . a . . ."

"Sloop," Andrew supplied. "And a lot tougher than one of your wooden scows, Peter. Climb aboard and see for yourself."

Peter stepped over the rail into the cockpit and shifted his weight back and forth. *Kestrel* rolled reluctantly, her mast drawing a sensual fifteen-degree arc in the clear blue, then efficiently righted herself.

"Good balance," Peter admitted. "But let's see how she likes those swells." He nodded toward the six-foot rollers outside the harbor.

"Hurry, Andrew," urged Giuliana as he consulted his mental checklist before casting off. "Hurry, before Rindt finds us!"

"Will can keep him busy."

"Don't ever underestimate Rindt. He will find us."

Andrew moved quickly. He didn't want Rindt to spoil his time alone with Peter and Giuliana. After making sure Giuliana was safely aboard, he untied the bow line and springer, leapt behind the helm, and started the engine. While the Volvo Penta diesel roused from the night chill, he stowed the stern line.

"Quickly, Andrew!" Giuliana said, pointing to the end of the dock. He looked and saw the rental car pull up and Colonel Rindt walking briskly toward them.

Andrew shifted into reverse, throttled the boat clear of the slip and into the channel, spinning the helm to starboard and shifting into forward. *Kestrel* responded by quickly slicing a bow wave. She had sniffed the wind and knew exactly what to do.

"Dottore Sabatini! Shepard!" Rindt's voice boomed across the water. Andrew ignored him. Feigning surprise, Giuliana waved. When he kept shouting, she held a cupped hand to her ear and shrugged.

Peter quickly learned the ropes of this strange new vessel with its multicolored lines and fancy sails. Before long, he had raised the main and genoa. Moving over sheets and around the emergency inflatable, his feet found clear deck amid the tangled order. His fingers gripped halyards and winch handles with a minimum of wasted effort. He became mystifyingly one with *Kestrel*, a timeless sprite from another dimension.

The last they saw of Rindt, he was standing rigidly on the dock, looking like something out of a gangster movie in his Italian-cut suit and mirror-polished shoes, his cell phone at his ear, no doubt calling Rome.

Peter was a natural. He adjusted sheets and lines before Andrew could ask. When the wind shifted, his wise hands reflexively slipped the genoa sheet and his eyes went to the telltales.

A steady twelve-knot breeze powered *Kestrel* north at a thrilling clip, almost as far as Del Mar. Giuliana curled up on the deck, her back against the cabin, raised her face to the sun, and luxuriated in the Southern California afternoon. The wind kept Andrew and Peter on their toes as they tacked north, working the boat to its maximum potential speed and forgetting the procedure, forgetting everything but the moment. They were three friends playing hooky, having a great time.

Soon, as happens so often at San Diego's latitude, the winds gave out. They lay becalmed some distance offshore, not minding at all.

Andrew went to the cooler for beer and soft drinks. By the time he emerged into the sunlight the other two were talking about religion again. It was either that or politics or history. Peter was insatiable.

"Nine hundred million Christians!" he marveled, checking the mainsail. "I have never heard such a big number. And a billion Muslims! What is this number, one billion?"

"A thousand millions," Andrew supplied absently.

They stared at him as if he were speaking in tongues. The two of them seemed sometimes to communicate on an almost telepathic wavelength. Andrew suppressed a twinge of jealousy.

"And how many Jews?" Peter ventured hopefully.

"About nineteen million," Giuliana said, almost apologetically.

"That's all?" Peter was crestfallen.

"That's all," Giuliana sympathized. "Your people's history since the Diaspora—suppression, pogroms, the Holocaust . . ." She gestured, unable to finish. "I'm sorry!"

Peter counted on his fingers, wrestling some arithmetic equation under control. Finally, he found his answer and looked at Giuliana in despair.

"Jews are outnumbered fifty-nine to one. They don't have a chance," he observed sadly.

"Maybe, maybe not," Giuliana smiled sympathetically. "Judaism has endured longer than Islam and under much more adverse conditions. Who can say?"

"All right, then, in terms of numbers, we have Islam, followed by Christianity, with Judaism somewhere out there," Peter gestured to the remote horizon. "Who else?"

"Hinduism with six hundred fifty million. Then Buddhism, three hundred seven million—"

"No kidding? Buddhism's still around?" asked Peter.

"You know of it?" Giuliana was surprised.

"Siddhartha Gautama was five hundred years before my time," Peter reminded her.

"But how did you know about him?" Giuliana asked.

"Bedouin camel traders, roaming mercenaries. Platitudes and common sense—I never thought it would last." He sighed, checked the lines and telltales one more time, then finally came to rest, lowering himself easily to the deck and opening a beer. "Who else, then? What we used to call 'pagan' religions—animism, the Roman pantheon, not to mention the Greeks."

Giuliana shook her head. "Animism, yes. Not so much anymore, but there are countless small pockets of secret tribal religions that we don't know about. Most were destroyed, along with their followers, during Europe's colonizing era."

"I've been reading up on that," Peter responded, a dangerous frown taking over his face. "How much blood has been shed in the name of religion? From Rome to the Crusades to the conquistadors, it seems to me that more have died of religion than of pestilence and flood!"

Andrew laughed out loud. "Hey, Peter, look at the bright side: You outlived Greece *and* Rome."

"True!" Peter laughed too, but not as heartily. "At least that's something."

"Why Rome, Peter?" asked Andrew. "Why would a good Jew go so far from his own, all the way to Imperial Rome?"

"It had Europe's oldest Jewish community. Oh, the arguments! A good Jew loves a good argument. My days there were exciting, what with the squabbles in the synagogues. Rome had twelve. I preached in all of them, the ghettos too. This fisherman found plentiful fish in Rome."

His eyes sparkled as he remembered those difficult, red-blooded days. "So it all led to something, eh?" he asked. "My work counted?"

"Your minor Jewish heresy became today's Christianity," Giuliana told him proudly.

" 'Heresy'? I was faithful to the law, to Jewish law!"

"*Si*, Peter. But weren't you radical in your preaching about the kingdom?"

"Radical? I suppose in the eyes of some."

"Jewish culture was—is—tribal," Giuliana suggested. "A man's status was dependent upon his descent, adherence to custom. So when you left your temple, your village, and your family to walk beside Jesus, what were they to think?"

Ancient regrets caused a shudder in Peter's bones. There had been such accusations—from the Pharisees, of course, who had the most to lose from the change he and his brethren were advocating—but confusion and acute distress on the faces of ordinary people as well. He could hear echoes of his relatives' jeers when he left his wife and family to go with the master, heard himself arguing that he was not abandoning them, merely extending his family to include all of his people. Had it been for this, this world he saw around him, filled with more controversy and strife than even his own contentious times? Pools gathered at the corners of his eyes as he listened to Giuliana.

"We never meant to cause such pain," he began. "It was meant to be a message of hope, of joy. People misunderstood."

"Change frightens," Giuliana tried to comfort him. "It is hard for people."

"I stayed close to the law. I respected the Sabbath, the compassionate slaughter of animals . . ." Peter rubbed his chin and looked west, thinking so hard that he didn't see anything. "It was Paul who was the radical. He would have nothing to do with the old ways. Maybe I was too old to change; I suppose it's possible. But I don't think so. I was there beside him! Paul wasn't. I know what Christ meant. And he didn't mean for us to replace one corruption with another!"

"Your differences with Paul have been long suspected." There was a fervor to Giuliana suddenly. Her whole body had gone taut, attentive; she was closer to absolute truth than she had been since her childhood "death."

"He meant well, and God knows he was sincere," Peter allowed as he squinted up at the telltales. "But he wasn't *there*.

"Chris-ti-an-ity." He tested the sound of it, the feel of it. "Maybe Paul was right about more things than I gave him credit for. But he was wrong in wanting to disavow the Scriptures; that was never Christ's intent. He did not condemn the Bible by his teaching, only the laws that the prophets and priests derived from it.''

He had sprung lightly to his feet, his movement barely stirring the boat. He leaned against the mast, gathering his thoughts.

''We meant to *simplify*!'' he said, his voice becoming somehow larger without becoming louder. ''To offer a simple message that anyone could understand. Instead, you tell me, these—these *nine hundred million* souls—have continued to divide and subdivide the message into—how many different sects?''

''Many,'' Giuliana supplied. ''By the fifteenth century—''

''Anno Domini,'' Peter said with her. Giuliana laughed.

''Anno Domini. The Catholic Church had become what you say—a corruption. Inflexible and corrupt. Some Christians attempted to do precisely what you and your brethren attempted—not to break down their Bible, the New Testament, but only the laws that the popes and bishops had constructed like so many fences around it. They split from state churches and splintered off into new movements. There are now Anglicans, Lutherans, Baptists, Mennonites, Presbyterians, Methodists, Mormons, Pentecostals, Unitarians, Jehovah's Witnesses, Seventh-Day Adventists . . .''

''And they all consider themselves followers of Christ?''

''*Si.*''

Peter was silent for a time, then thought aloud: ''So many beliefs, so many faiths. And all based upon this New Testament. And it isn't even the Bible.''

Giuliana was taken aback. ''It is to Christians!''

''But it is written like these tabloids that Will shows me!'' Peter protested. ''Only this morning I read about a large woman in Mississippi who gave birth to a two-headed donkey. The village idiot in Bethsaida would not believe this, yet you people do!''

''Some of us, anyway,'' Andrew chimed in, checking wind direction.

''This New Testament was written by men with an agenda. Dramatists, zealots, and eccentrics.''

''And the Old Testament was not?'' Giuliana challenged him.

''That was different,'' argued Peter. ''The Hebrew Bible

was written over a period of five hundred years, yet it reveals an almost miraculous consistency. It is history, but more.''

"History?'' Andrew echoed. "As in the earth was created in six days?''

"It was all people knew at the time!'' Peter roared. "Not everyone had the knowledge of science that you do, Dr. Andrew Shepard. Maybe two thousand years from now you will seem just as ignorant!''

"Hey, no offense!'' Andrew held up his hands to show he was out of his league and retiring from the fray. He would let Giuliana field it from here, while he busied himself checking the compass, readying *Kestrel* for when the wind did pick up again. It was a small boat; they couldn't fault him for eavesdropping.

"Afternoon, ladies, gentlemen,'' Mike Gindman began without preamble, standing easily behind a bank of microphones at the main entrance to the BioGenera compound, the company logo seeming to float in midair against the soaring glassed-in entryway, within easy camera pickup range just above his head. "Shall we get this over with?''

On the flagstone path before him, jostling for the best seats among the too-few folding chairs set out between pricey landscape shrubs, representatives of local and national media, and even a stringer for the Tokyo-based *Asahi Shimbun* who just happened to be in San Diego on vacation, were still struggling to set up. Camera crews picked their way among thick snakes of cable strung from sound trucks in the parking lot, trying to find the best angle against the midafternoon sun. Gindman had planned it that way.

"C'mon, Mike, cut us some slack, will ya?'' came the first protest, from the balding, heavyset senior man for the *Los Angeles Times*. "What're you hiding in there that you won't even let us in the front door?''

Gindman deliberately waited for the murmured consensus to subside, rubbing the side of his nose ruminatively.

"What am I hiding in there? Gosh, Harry, you seem to know a lot more about that than I do. My impression is there's nothing beyond those doors but a dedicated group of very well-paid scientists who are trying to get a day's work done. I let you people start roaming the halls, it's going to cut productivity by a factor of four. I'm not paying people to give interviews. Besides, we've got hot labs in there, handling very volatile viruses—on government contracts, before anyone here gets too excited. They're all listed in the prospectus you were given when you got here. But if one of you gets lost on the way to the men's room and releases the next Black Plague, you'll turn around and pin it on me. Can't have that.''

Their answer was a predictable nervous laughter. Gindman could bullshit with the best of them. He rarely said anything of substance, but he could somehow always be counted on to give them a juicy quote for the six o'clock news. They didn't know whether to love him or hate him.

"Okay,'' Gindman began. "Let's not waste each other's time. You're here because somebody you know told somebody they knew that BioGenera's in league with the Vatican to bring about the Second Coming—''

"That's a slight exaggeration, Mr. Gindman!'' a chirpy little blonde from one of the networks piped up. "What we heard was—''

Gindman held up an authoritative hand, and she stuttered to a halt, nervously fluffing her lacquered hair.

"Don't they teach format in journalism schools these days?'' he wondered rhetorically. "Oh, that's right, I keep forgetting; they're not journalism schools anymore, they're media arts centers. Even so, the procedure is this: First I make a statement, then I open it up to Q&A. Think you can remember that?''

18 "THE SCRIPTURE THAT SHAPED US CONTAINS DIScussion of life's most important issues and sincere debate about God's meaning,'' Peter argued. Andrew, busy with rigging now that the wind had finally picked up, thought of asking him to help but decided against it. "Matters that will be just as important to mankind in two thousand years or two hundred thousand.''

"True," Giuliana agreed. "And in contrast to the five hundred years it took to compose the Old Testament, the original books of the New Testament were written in a relatively brief period of time. Its importance is in its continuity with the testament you knew, but also in its two most important themes: the divinity of Christ and the Resurrection. It speaks to the central importance of faith."

"It is also disjointed and overly emphatic," Peter said dismissively.

"It is still unmatched for its expressive power, its drama, its illuminating insights into how to live!" Giuliana's voice rose. Suddenly she stopped. She could not believe she was arguing with a saint. And she was revealing too much of herself, her innermost feelings. "It is also the most widely read book in human history," she concluded reasonably.

Peter waited until he was sure she had finished.

"It's just so cheap, somehow. I expected better of those who came after Christ. This New Testament is all fables and letters and tales. The Gospels!" he growled. "Tell me, who are these men who wrote them? Who are Matthew, Mark, and Luke? I knew a man named John, but I recognize almost none of what he wrote."

"Wait a minute!" This stopped Andrew in his tracks. "They were Apostles like you, weren't they?" He looked from Peter to Giuliana. "They were followers of Jesus, who wrote down what he said and preserved it for history, right?"

"Like the earth was created in six days?" Peter reminded him. "You cannot have it both ways. Either the Bible is history, or it is not."

"We don't know much about the origination of the Gospels, the translations from the Greek, the adaptations and rewritings," Giuliana explained for the benefit of both men. "We know even less about the individuals who wrote them. As nearly as modern scholarship can judge, the Gospels were written between 70 and 110 A.D. But they are Christianity's only evidence about Jesus, his teaching, his Passion."

"That doesn't make any sense—" Andrew began, but Peter was even more outraged.

"Then that explains why I recognize neither these men

nor what they write about Jesus, or me, or anyone else who was there!''

"The Gospels were written long after you were dead."

"And with such authority! Neat trick."

"You don't recognize the events they describe?" Giuliana asked, visibly paled.

"Hardly. They're too neat, too calculated. Where is the passion? Where is the heat?" Peter roared.

"So they made up these stories?" blurted Giuliana.

"No, I don't mean that! As we became better teachers, we found that certain lines, sayings, even whole stories were effective in getting our message across to the people. So if it served Jesus' instructions to us, why not? Then those who followed adapted the stories to their purposes. Merchants do it. Lawyers do it. That must be what happened, why I recognize so little that is written in these 'Gospels.' ''

Giuliana appeared shocked. "Peter, I can understand how an evangelist would use Jesus' words to affirm his lesson. But don't you see? We live in times when it is difficult to trust. We have been lied to. We are cautious. If what you're telling us is that everything we know of Jesus is completely wrong—''

"These Gospels may not be true, but—''

"If they're not true, then they are lies!" blurted Giuliana. The very Gospels she had relied upon in her darkest hours had betrayed her trust.

Her vehemence startled Andrew. Giuliana doubted, too! This paradigm of Catholic virtue and achievement sitting across from him suffered the same dark fears that had plagued him, paralyzed his spirit.

They sailed silently for a time until they were distracted by a sudden explosion of the ocean surface. A dozen dolphins shattered the glass of the undisturbed water as they leapt glistening and whistling into the afternoon sunlight. Peter laughed with delight, clapping his leathery hands and mimicking the dolphins' cries. Andrew and Giuliana were so shocked by Peter's revelations, they couldn't share his joy. Soon the dolphins were a mile away and Peter's excitement ebbed. He sighed contentedly, breaking the silence.

"Why should you trust the Bible?" he repeated Giuliana's heartfelt question. "Indeed," he seemed to agree, *"why?"*

"With the new insights on first-century writings coming to us from Qumran," Giuliana observed, "some scholars now believe that Paul toned down the original writings, softened them to make them more palatable to the Roman authorities."

"Paul was a determined man, all right. He'd do whatever he felt necessary to do to keep the Word alive."

"But if the Gospels we know today are more like Hellenistic romances than the original Word . . . if Christianity is not so much about 'loving our enemies' as about an apocalyptic message of vanquishing our enemies, then we have it all wrong!"

"No, Giuliana. Jesus never spoke of the kingdom to come as an apocalypse."

"Are the Gospels that we know antithetical to the Gospels you knew?"

"They're different. They're not the Word as I knew it. Somebody's been in there 'improving' it. Take this 'Mark,' for example. Who is this guy? And from what I see, 'Matthew' and 'Luke' wrote their versions based upon what they learned from him."

"Most scholars consider Mark's Gospel to be the earliest and most authoritative."

"It is, eh?"

"*Sì*. It's attributed to 'John Mark,' a companion of Paul . . ."

"Paul never met Jesus, either," Peter interrupted irritably.

"I know. But some scholars believe he was also an associate of Peter's—of yours."

"An 'associate' of mine? Hah! Who says this?"

"Eusebius."

"When did this Eusebius—whoever he is—come to this conclusion?"

"Around 325 C.E."

"Common Era," Peter said automatically, calculating the span on his fingers. "Two hundred sixty years after me!"

Giuliana nodded. "Did you ever know a man named John Mark?"

"Yes," Peter said ironically. "He died under the wheel of a Roman chariot."

"Could he have written his Gospel based on stories you told him?"

"Not likely."

"Why not?"

"He was fourteen years old when he died."

"A brilliant boy, perhaps?"

"He was also blind, deaf, and mute. That's why he didn't see or hear the chariot coming." Peter paused, exasperated. He was coming to understand the impenetrable tangle of history. Men with purposes solely their own had written in his name, placed their interpretation on his lips! Perhaps he should have written a gospel of his own.

"Our subject is an elderly gentleman with a terminal illness who has volunteered for this experiment," Gindman said. They were finally getting down to the real questions.

"What's his name?" someone shouted.

"I'm sure if I tell you, you'll all give me your solemn oath not to show up on his family's doorstep asking a lot of questions they can't answer," Gindman replied dryly. "He's asked for confidentiality, and we're giving it to him."

"Can we talk to him?"

Gindman ignored that question entirely. "Next?"

"We understand he's undergone a complete personality change, that he's speaking in someone else's voice!" someone from the back of the crowd shouted.

"I understand they're running *The Exorcist* on late-night," Gindman snapped back. "Come on, boys and girls—what are we, spirit mediums?"

"May we speak to any of the scientists involved in the procedure?"

Gindman seemed to ponder that one, scratching his head thoughtfully. "Unfortunately, as luck would have it, they're all off the premises today. Sorry!"

Giuliana thought over everything Peter had revealed and sighed. "This is too much. You would not joke with us, would you?"

"I do not lie," he said seriously. "Ever. Lying killed a

part of me that night outside Caiaphas's gate. I denied Jesus. I won't lie again.''

"So many answers to the eternal questions: What is true?''

"You,'' Peter answered sincerely. "You are truth. You ask because you are evolving toward perfection, growing, discovering. You are becoming truth.''

They sailed on a port tack for several minutes in silence, listening to the breeze whisper through the rigging and their private thoughts.

"Jesus was a simple, direct man with a clear message. How could so many corrupt his goodness?'' Peter demanded finally, the anger rising again.

"Look to your time, Your Holiness,'' Giuliana urged him. "The Sadducees were temple worshipers. The Zealots, fervent nationalists. John the Baptist was a fanatic who espoused a new age. The Essenes were reactionary isolationists, and the Pharisees were somewhere in the middle. Then along came Jesus, who said how you lived your life was more important than adherence to the law.''

"Exactly! He tried to save us from such factionalism!'' Peter protested.

"The Holy Father must hear this!'' Giuliana said to no one in particular, just heaven and her own thoughts. "Directly! His Holiness might not like what he hears, but he is a good man. He is the pope, the only man capable of helping you. I warn you, however, if you meet him, you will change history.''

It was clear to her that Peter could provide testimony that would prove or disprove the traditions, the theories, the very foundations of the Bible. They had only begun to scratch the surface. What could he tell them of Lazarus, of the miracle of the loaves and fishes, of the Resurrection? Giuliana could barely contain her imagination.

Andrew, on the other hand, wouldn't allow himself to believe that Peter's presence would change anything. He forced himself to think only in terms of the biochemical marvel he had created.

"Don't give him any ideas!'' he said.

Kestrel rocked gently as the wind filled in and the southwest current strengthened. Shackles rang her hollow mast.

"Speak to the pope, eh?" Peter mused. "How far is Rome?"

"The other side of the world. About eighteen hours by plane."

The mention of planes made Peter smile. He squinted up at the cloudless sky and nodded. "I must do this thing, this *volo*."

"Mr. Gindman, what about the relics on loan from the Vatican?" the *Asahi* reporter wanted to know. "Aren't they in fact the bones of one of the early popes, possibly even those of a saint?"

"The Vatican can answer that far better than we can," Gindman told her. "We deliberately chose not to know the alleged identity of the relics in order not to contaminate the experiment with prior knowledge." He glanced at his watch. "One more question."

There was the predictable feeding frenzy, everyone shouting at once. Gindman let them shout; he would choose which question to answer.

"How long before you can give us more complete answers?" the network blonde shrilled, her voice somehow carrying above everyone else's.

"Not until the experiment has been concluded," Gindman said.

"And when will that be?" the blonde persisted. Gindman raised an eyebrow at her.

"That's two questions. Thank you!" He turned on his heel. Delphine was ready for him, holding the door as he strode through the lobby and back into his inner sanctum. Two very large security guards stood behind the glass, arms folded, eyes leveled at anyone foolish enough to even think of trying to come inside. The feeding frenzy was over for today. The sharks closed their notebooks and reluctantly began to swim away.

Adeodato Cardinal Cosa was not given to thinking in clichés. Yet, when the Lord worked in mysterious ways, what else was one to say save that the Lord worked in mysterious ways?

There was also the fact that God helps those who help

themselves. How fortuitous, Cosa thought, that he had Rindt to inform him of the facts surrounding the subject "Peter's" death and apparent resurrection within the walls of Bio-Genera. He had been able to use that information to negotiate with Gindman. It had been essential to demonstrate to Gindman the hierarchy of the Vatican, to explain that it was sometimes better to treat with the power *behind* the throne.

Gindman, Cosa mused. A Jewish name? The information Rindt had supplied him indicated that Gindman paid homage to no religion. Was that significant to Cosa's needs?

Cosa had made it clear to Gindman that, whatever transpired next, it was essential that Peter speak to him before he spoke to the pope. Surely this was reasonable. If Peter in fact came from another century, there would be subtleties, nuances of this modern society and its rituals that he would not understand. Who better than a lifelong courtier to explain them to him, to groom him for his audience with arguably the most influential man on earth? To, in other words, tell him what *not* to say to the leader of nine hundred million souls?

It was also vital, Cosa thought, that Luke John not learn of the subject's suicide. Despite Dr. Sabatini's meticulous reports, Cosa himself was still not clear on whether it was the saint Peter or the man Nicolao Soares who had slashed his own wrists and effectively died. To burden Luke John with such knowledge might provoke if not a crisis of faith in this simple man, at least a profound doubt about the efficacy of this procedure.

Cosa realized that he was approaching a crossroads where his career and his faith were about to intersect. The only question remaining was which vehicle would survive the collision.

He could promote Nicolao Soares as Peter and take the risk that he might be wrong. In that case his career would be ended. Or he could counsel caution to His Holiness and gamble that Nicolao was not Peter reincarnate. Odds favored this position. Nicolao was American, was he not, from the land of self-promoters?

At worst, he would demonstrate lack of faith. Granted, that would be a sin, but a common one. Worse would be proof of his lack of vision, his failure of imagination. Professionally speaking, that was mortal sin.

Adding it up, then: Getting it right in this case equated to minimizing risk. So that would be his strategy—unpleasant and a little humiliating, but more profitable in the long run.

Pope Luke John wanted to meet Peter. It was up to Cosa to stall him as long as possible.

"The scientists at BioGenera are still conducting tests, Holiness," Cosa told him now. "The man's continued good health is essential."

"I had hoped at least to speak with him by telephone before my trip to Africa," Luke John suggested.

Cosa responded with a gesture. "It may be possible to arrange that, Holiness. I will see what I can do."

"I have read Dr. Sabatini's reports." Luke John's eyes glowed with a quiet fervor. He had seemed more energetic to Cosa lately, as if he had shaken off some long-present torpor. "Do they include everything?"

"They contain every relevant word that the subject Peter has spoken to date," Cosa hedged. He had censored the reports beforehand, to eliminate all mention of the suicide.

"They would suggest, then, that our hopes have been realized, that this man is our saint."

"Perhaps, Your Holiness," admitted Cosa reluctantly. "But he may also be a bad seed, looking for fertile soil in which to grow. As always, I advise caution."

Pope Luke John weighed this. "I will wait, Adeodato. But not much longer."

Andrew, Giuliana, and Peter got back to the lab at sunset. The sight of the last of the television sound trucks pulling out of the parking lot set off little alarm bells in the back of Andrew's brain.

"Wonder what that was all about?" he mused aloud, rolling down his window as he approached the security booth. "Hey, Gus? What's going on? Did we make the six o'clock news?"

"Beats me, Doc. I heard one of those yokels talking about you people raising the dead in there." Gus jerked his thumb back toward the complex. "That mean I got to watch my back? What am I looking for—vampires, werewolves?"

"Just snakes!" Andrew muttered, driving through. He parted company with Giuliana and Peter in the lobby. "Catch you later," he said and headed straight for Gindman's office.

Gindman met him with a cold-eyed stare. "I wasn't aware that I needed your permission to hold a press conference, Shepard. Don't you have the roles reversed here? Or is it my turn to go downstairs and tell you how to run those Hood machines?"

He's way too defensive! thought Andrew. *What's he hiding?* But there was no graceful way to find out.

"I just wondered why I wasn't informed, that's all."

"If you hadn't gone AWOL—and taken a valuable piece of BioGenera property with you—you would have been informed." Gindman spoke evenly, before Andrew could protest. He nailed him. "Yes, he's our property. Subject X. We created him. And as long as he exists in his present form, BioGenera is responsible for him. You go off the grounds with him again, you ask permission first. Got that?"

Andrew's temper boiled, but he contained it. In a shouting match with Gindman, he would lose. There were other ways to play this game.

"Andrew? My God, what a coincidence! I was just going to call *you*. Guess we're still on the same wavelength, for some things anyway."

When had he first started thinking of Margaret's voice as strident? Andrew wondered. He'd called her at the station house and she was using her Cop Voice, but it was more than that. Still, he needed her help. There was no time for emotional reactions.

"Why were you going to call me?"

Margaret lowered her voice. "Well, I got a call from a friend at the Boston bureau of the FBI. He knew you worked for BioGenera and wondered how much I knew about what you were working on."

"Oh, great!" Visions of his personal profile flying around cyberspace in some FBI branch office gave Andrew chills.

"Exactly. I told him you and I had split, and you never talked about your work, and he seemed to accept that. But what is going on that would make the FBI pay attention?"

"Who's your friend?" Andrew wanted to know.

"He's credible," Margaret countered. Since when had they started keeping secrets from each other? "He wouldn't have called if it wasn't important. Anyway, a friend of his at N—at one of the other agencies—heard that the Vatican is cultivating something called the Votto Protocol."

She'd started to say NSA, as in National Security Agency, Andrew thought. Or was it the National Reconnaissance Commission? Yet another of those redundant government agencies created to mind the citizenry's business. They were all alphabet soup to him.

He realized he was only half-listening.

"The what?"

"The Votto Protocol. Spelled V-O-T-T-O."

Andrew's mind went absolutely blank. He had no frame of reference for what Margaret had just said. "Who—or what—is Votto?"

"I don't know. My contact doesn't either. Some diplomatic or political strategy is his agency's best guess. Anyway, they think it's related to whatever is going on at BioGenera."

Andrew didn't respond. What the hell could anyone know? That he had resurrected memory from Vatican relics? If the FBI in Boston suspected, how many others knew? Had Gindman's impromptu press conference helped or hindered? Panic began to rise in Andrew's chest; he quashed it.

"Andrew?"

"Yes?"

"Are you . . . is everything all right?"

"Sure. Of course. But what exactly did this guy say to you? Are you sure he asked specifically about BioGenera?" he asked.

"Yes. Guess he thought I might be able to tell him if there was anything to the rumors."

"Rumors?"

"Not rumors exactly. He wouldn't elaborate. Just hinted at the Votto thing. Some pretty smart people have picked up a scent that led them to me . . . to you. I don't know if what they're after has anything to do with your experiment, but experience tells me anytime a rumor, or whatever they've got about this Votto Protocol, travels this far through this many agencies, there's something to it. Thought you should know," Margaret said from the safe distance of her official voice. "And you didn't hear it from me."

"Understood," said Andrew. "Can you—I don't want you to jeopardize your position or anything—but if you hear anything else . . ."

"Sure. No problem."

A commotion rose at Margaret's end. Andrew heard a dispatcher's exchange with a distant unit, her lieutenant's gruff response, and some barking about an incident on I-15.

"I've got to go," Margaret said briskly. "But you should know that once an investigation like this gets started, once they get in . . . Ah, just a minute, Andrew . . ."

The line clicked off. He waited, expecting her to pick up again, but heard a dial tone instead. The connection was gone.

Andrew couldn't shake the uneasy feeling Margaret had left with him.

"The word 'Votto' mean anything to you, Peter?" he asked across the room.

"*Voto*? Let's see. It is 'veto' in Latin."

"No, V-O-T-T-O."

Peter shook his head no.

"What's Votto?" asked Will.

"Something to do with the Vatican. I don't know."

He went back to his levels and blood results and saw that Peter was holding his own in Nicolao's system, perhaps getting stronger. Nicolao's red blood cell count was rising and his antibodies were . . . decreasing? No, Andrew observed, not decreasing but simplifying. The most recent ones, which had evolved to respond to the increasingly complex viruses of recent times, were sloughing out of his bloodstream, leaving the sturdiest, oldest known cells.

"Come here, Will, look at this," he said, unable to trust his own reading of the charts and figures. "Nicolao's blood and immuno system . . ."

"They're metamorphosing, regressing," Will observed quietly. ". . . devolving . . . into an older configuration. Really old. And there's something else I want to show you."

Will pulled the films of Nicolao's tumor from his file. Some had been taken before the procedure, some only a few days ago.

"Here, here, and here." Will pointed out the growth indicators. Andrew studied them. "See it? The growth rate's slowed markedly since the procedure 'took.' It might be only a temporary effect. It might be completely coincidental, but . . ."

He let his voice trail off, unwilling even to speculate. He studied the blood cultures again.

"Older," Andrew said. "If these patterns continue, his immune system will be unlike anything we're familiar with. It's already beyond historical records. Serologists and immunologists have only speculated about the composition of blood and immuno systems from . . ."

"Two thousand years ago?"

They each turned and looked over at the man whose blood they were studying. He was lost in the pages of the Bible, utterly absorbed and shaking his head slowly, sadly.

19

DELPHINE'S MOUSE FINGER TAPPED AND SWERVED with lightning speed as she navigated menus on the World Wide Web. After downloading thirty-one new articles from various newsgroups and more than two hundred messages in her E-mail box, she went surfing on the Internet, looking for anything that might be useful to Gindman. If she also chose to share her findings with Andrew and Giuliana, her boss didn't need to know.

She stroked in search strings and read as reports streamed in from around the world. Genetics: Six hundred four papers, news articles, and press releases—the usual stuff. Genetic engineering: Amgen quarterly figures . . . Genentec's success in identifying seven more variants of the genetic marker for multiple sclerosis . . . Factor VIIIC . . . Senate debate over government regulation . . . a *TIME* cover article on the future of the species . . .

Memory: A *Journal of the American Medical Association* article about the results of a study demonstrating the positive effects of aging on memory . . . Sixteen new reports on Alzheimer's . . .

Good! she thought. *Not a whisper about BioGenera or memory resurrection.* Gindman's press conference had put out the brushfires, at least for now.

Vatican: A few articles about the pope's upcoming visit to Africa and three reviews of the newly released catechism . . . an announcement of a new online church for shut-ins . . . some correspondence between a student at the University of Chicago and a cleric in Tabriz . . .

Delphine stopped. Why would an Iranian cleric and a student from one of the world's most prestigious universities be corresponding about the Vatican? Probably just academic discussion, but it wouldn't hurt to check. She entered ''Religion.islam'' and opened the student's message file:

''. . . *my thesis concerns politicization of religion in the West . . . will churches merge with states to form Muslim-like theocracies to survive, or will the tribalization of ethnic subcultures refactionalize religious unity? . . .*''

Delphine clicked open the Muslim cleric's response:

"The answer to your search may be found in the Koran. If you need additional support for what I tell you, examine Votto. At least some within the Vatican believe the body and soul are best governed by the same ruler . . ."

A flick of the finger and the two messages emerged from her laser printer. She didn't know what Votto was or if it was significant, but she'd save it anyway.

The night was clear, gray, the pines green and vibrant in the drifting air. Andrew was losing control. Giuliana, too. Whenever they parted at the end of the day something of each remained. Each day a little more remained until they were more with each other than not.

Andrew hadn't allowed himself to consider the possibility of loving again. Maybe someday but not now. But Giuliana had broken through his defenses. He would find himself thinking about how she might laugh at something he found funny. He recalled her intoxicating scent, how the air changed polarity when she entered a room. He wondered how her olive skin would feel to his touch.

Their movement into one another's orbit was natural, planetary, inevitable. Caught in that momentum, they drew closer in ever-tightening circles of interest.

There were mountains of data to review and little time. While Will corralled the milling herd of stray figures, Andrew and Giuliana teamed for the analytical work. They categorized the incoming readings on Peter's physical and mental progress since the injection, then extrapolated small conclusions, trailing the key that would help them forecast Peter's future.

Unfortunately, his reemergence as a completely distinctive personality was so rapid and complete that they were pressed to keep pace with him. While thrilling, the work was exhausting. After a few hours they sat back and took time to eat the cold cashew chicken and egg rolls they'd ordered hours ago and lapsed into the drifting conversation of two people who were innately opposites.

"My family goes back centuries—to Bernini, my Aunt Lorenza says—but we don't really know for sure."

"Before long we'll be able to know the identity of our ancestors for certain."

"*Si?*"

"Sure, as a by-product of DNA profiling. It solves so many problems." Andrew swallowed the last of his egg roll.

"You're never far from science, are you?"

He nodded sheepishly, ashamed to be so narrow.

She considered first his words, then his silence, like a listening bird.

"My brain is like an out-of-control machine sometimes," he admitted. "It hums and buzzes, soars, then blunders into fog. Why? What is this beast, this three-pound monster for?"

"The mind loves the unknown, the mystery of it,'" Giuliana answered easily.

He imagined reaching out and touching her.

She rescued a strand of lettuce from the edge of her egg roll, sliding it delicately between her lips.

Andrew lost his thought. She was too much. Too sensual. Too smart. Too insightful. She seemed to radiate substance, humming like a high-tension wire.

Soon they drifted into more intimate conversation. It was effortless, natural.

"I was sick of feeling dirty at some point with every man, of lust in every face, every touch," Giuliana confided in him. "I immersed myself in the Church, removed myself from all the rest—from seeing men, from conversation in the piazza, the whirl. They were all certain I was a snob." Her eyes darted about the room, as if she were searching for her thoughts somewhere outside herself. "I wasn't, but fear looks like that sometimes. Why Margaret?" she asked.

"Because it was expected. In college we both felt like misfits. As a couple, it was easier for us to blend into a culture of couples. We disappeared easily enough. What I didn't expect was to lose myself and my feelings."

"When did you know it was over?"

He thought for a moment as he sat in the river of cool air from the window. "Certainly by the time Anna died. Maybe before. Maybe Anna was the only thing that held us together by then."

If he could walk across the floor and touch her, he would

be fully alive and in the world. But between them stretched dangerous frontiers. It was a world of complex and intersecting universes.

Facing Andrew, listening, Giuliana calmed to stillness.

It was at that precise moment that he fell in love with her. He was scared out of his skin by the thought of it, but there it was. He decided to keep it to himself. He didn't trust the words forming in his mind, after enduring the ruin of marriage for so long.

She wasn't troubled by his silence, by the ocean of awkwardness between them. It's the discipline of suffering, he thought, remembering her death as a child. She couldn't be reached by small concerns.

She continued looking at him. Then she looked away and began to gather up the remnants of their impromptu dinner, the greasy plastic and cardboard containers looking incongruous in her graceful hands.

He was lost. He knew it. He had already knit his soul to this woman.

The cardinal had not celebrated Mass this morning. He told himself he would fulfill his obligation later in the day. For the first time in thirty-seven years, he knew he would not.

He listened carefully as Rindt related Peter's colorful behavior over the past several days.

The mischief, the sailing and flirting, didn't particularly worry him. "Peter's passion for life undercuts the perception of him as a spirit, not to mention a saint," Cosa suggested.

"He is a man," agreed Rindt.

"As long as his actions defy his sainthood, we have little concern . . ." Cosa thought aloud.

"He doesn't claim to be a saint, Your Eminence."

"True. But humility reinforces saintliness."

"Your Eminence—" Rindt's words were clipped. It was not only the impersonal nature of the long-distance call but his need for precision, factuality, a need to cut through Cosa's woolgathering. "I believe this consciousness is in fact an ancient one. I am coming to believe it is Rome's first bishop. If it is, that is what you hoped for, *corretto*?"

"*Si,*" Cosa concurred.

"Yet you wish others to believe he is not who you hope he is."

"*Corretto*. Yet . . ." There was a brief pause. He had come dangerously close to revealing his game plan to his subordinate. "*Grazie*, Colonel; that will be all."

"*Prègo. Buona notte.*"

The cardinal returned the phone to its cradle. As he did so, he was distracted by a movement outside his open window.

It was a pigeon, stunning in its bright-red plumage. Such brilliance was common among Old World species, but it was unusual to find one in the city. Wings arched, it spiraled down to the piazza, landing among the ordinary browns and grays, and began to feed. A deep, rolling cooing sound filled the morning air as the others deferred to the flamboyant arrival and fell in behind it, giving it first peck at the scraps of food left over from last night. Cosa watched the milling flock merge into a semblance of direction and drift cloudlike across the piazza, feeding and cooing. Then, as if responding to some silent cue, the thousands lifted behind the red pigeon into Rome's bright morning and soared as one shadowy mass over the ancient wall.

With Gindman's okay this time, the threesome was back aboard *Kestrel*. One more day to play hooky before Andrew compiled his final report and Giuliana hers, and they reported to their respective superiors.

The land breeze had died, and there followed a brief stillness. The sea breeze arrived as a whisper, then built to a heaving wind and stirred the *Kestrel*'s mainsail. Her boom swung ponderously across the cockpit, over the heads of the three until the mainsheet snapped taut and halted the boom's arc. The vessel heeled and accelerated through the chop and spray.

Andrew was beginning to accept loss of control as his new state of being. His nerves were on full alert and his stomach rolled while his mind raced, but he realized that he couldn't go back to ignorance, not now.

Neither could Giuliana. She willingly looked into the dense and tangled undergrowth of her faith, probing the hollows for weeds amid the truths that had been handed down to her, exploring the shadows, comparing what she had learned from the nuns to what this eyewitness offered her.

She had to believe him. But what if his words made her beliefs meaningless?

"Jesus had never been to Jerusalem until that day," she began tentatively.

"The day before Shabbas, in the midst of Passover," Peter prompted her. "Never."

"Then why? Why on that day, at Passover of all times? He had to know, you all had to know, that Jerusalem was a tinderbox at the best of times—the tensions with the Romans, the priests in the temple intolerant and suspicious. And Passover, with so many thousands of visitors overflowing the city . . ."

Peter sensed her inner struggle and took her delicate fingers gently in his scarred hand. "Say what you mean to say. I won't be offended."

Giuliana took a deep breath. "There are some revisionist scholars who claim that Jesus chose the moment deliberately. That he had a plan to go into that dangerous place and light a match. That he was a revolutionary looking to start a revolution."

Peter selected his words carefully. "You—they—are looking at it from a modern point of view. As if he wanted a—a photo op, a PR opportunity. A chance to issue a sound bite for the evening news." If he heard Andrew suppress a laugh, he chose not to notice. "Jesus was a good man who spoke up when he saw evil, wherever he went. His speaking out in the temple was not without precedent. It was merely the one incident that got him the most attention."

"But why not go to Jerusalem at another time, a more normal time, when the city was not teeming with so many pressures?" Giuliana persisted.

Peter thought for a moment, intrigued by the question. "Why not ask why the sun rises in the morning, why dogs chase cats, why I am here now and not before? Jesus lit fires in the hearts of everyone he met. He was determined to meet more. So we went to Jerusalem."

He saw Giuliana shake her head, trying to understand, to accept. She could not escape her twentieth-century perspective. Peter tried a different approach.

"Part of what made Jesus so effective was his focus. 'There are reasons and there are results,' he used to say. He didn't have much patience for reasons. Either you did right or not. He didn't want to hear explanations for evil. 'Leave that to the corrupt, the thieves in the temple,' he said. 'Do right. Look upon every person you meet as holy and you will always do right.'

"He was a man of powerful beliefs, and powerful passions. That part of him has been lost down the centuries. I have been studying your 'Church history.' It amazes me, the image of Jesus you carry in your minds. Those religious paintings of a pale, soft-handed aesthete—he was a carpenter's son, a man who preached in the open air, tanned and robust, brimming with life! In this century you would make him 'accessible to the masses.' He is either a hippie—oh, yes, Will played songs from *Jesus Christ Superstar* for me—"

"You must have been horrified," Andrew chimed in.

"I laughed!" Peter contradicted him. "I laughed until I wept. And now your 'revisionist scholars' would make him a revolutionary, a Che Guevara. Why can't you see him as he was? The Pharisees never got it, and neither do you!"

"That's hardly fair!" Giuliana had found her voice at last. "It was two thousand years ago. And if, as you say, the Gospels are inaccurate, what else do we have to go on?"

Peter started to speak, then hesitated. She was not yet ready to hear what he had to say. If he had learned nothing else in two thousand years, he had at least learned to curb his impatience.

"Why Jerusalem, you ask me." He returned to the original question. "Why not? Jerusalem was the center of Judaism, and a good choice because the Jews there were so condescending and snobbish, not just to Gentiles but to other Jews as well! *Amé-Haaretz*, they called us—'people of the land'—implying that we were stupid. Whew, they were rude! Mean, canting, shrill snobs they were."

"You're saying, then, that Jesus saw Passover in Jerusalem as an opportunity, not a challenge?" Giuliana suggested. "More people, greater opportunity to speak his message, that's all?"

Peter nodded. "Now, me—I was worried. I never cared

for crowds, and we saw tens of thousands—all colors and tongues. But I followed him into those crowds because I had committed my final days to him. We knew the end was coming. Didn't really matter where we were, as long as we were with him.''

Giuliana absorbed this in silence for some moments. She drew her knees up, and rested her chin on them like a small child listening to a storyteller. Looking down on her from where he was checking the rigging, Andrew felt his heart lurch.

''Tell us about the temple incident,'' Giuliana asked Peter quietly. ''What really happened?''

''Did he cause a stir, you mean? *Ita*, he did that. Never saw him so worked up.'' Peter's eyes glowed with remembrance; he rubbed his calloused hands together, flexing his fingers as if reliving his master's anger. ''All those shysters in expensive clothes, doing the priests' bidding. The noise! I never took to animal sacrifice as it was, but then to profane the spirit of the place by shaming hardworking men into changing their shekels for temple coins to buy a lamb for slaughter within the temple walls. These people seldom had coin enough to buy meat for their families! And the bleating of the lambs, their terror, the death wails, the smells. . . . The priests had turned praise of the Almighty into humiliation and degradation of the weak.''

Peter scratched his beard and shook his head sadly.

''Did you help him?'' Giuliana asked softly.

Peter shook his head. ''Another regret. But he went off so fast; none of us could do anything but watch. He simply exploded. Suddenly tables and shekels were flying every which way. The whole business stopped, the hubbub died down. It was completely silent; even the animals stopped bleating. Everyone stood dumbfounded, watching. No one had ever done anything like this before. It was like he burst a giant boil festering within the temple, and all its poisons erupted into the light for everyone to see.''

''No one tried to stop you?'' Andrew wanted to know.

''They were stunned. We got out of there, walked to the outskirts of the city. He was so worked up that none of us could talk to him. But by the time we got away from the crowds, he had calmed down. He took us to the house of Lazarus.''

Giuliana sat up straight. The glow in her eyes matched that in Peter's.

"Yes, I will tell you of Lazarus," he promised her, pulling himself to his feet and stretching the kinks out of his old bones, heading for the ice chest where he got himself a beer, twisting the cap off effortlessly. "But first things first. All this talking is dry work.''

"Lazarus was an old friend, and he was dying. I say that knowing that we did not have the medical knowledge you have today. We arrived too late. Lazarus's sister, Martha—a strong woman—described his final moments. Jesus asked for and was granted permission to see his friend once more, to honor him.

"Two neighbor women had cleaned the body, applied expensive perfume that sweetened the air, and were wrapping the body when Jesus entered. The women stood aside to allow him close. He prayed silently beside the body. Then he reached over and touched the shrouded head, a final good-bye. We were turning to leave when the head jerked off the pillow, and then the whole body shuddered. We were all amazed, of course. Jesus shouted, 'Lazarus!' ''

"Then he was not already buried in a cave?" Andrew asked. "Wasn't he supposed to have been dead for three days, and then Jesus called out 'Lazarus, come forth' and he—''

Peter waved his words away like blowflies. "He was there in the bed, the body still warm, his limbs bound. How was he supposed to have walked out of a cave if he was tied hand and foot? Jesus had the presence of mind to take charge. 'Untie him,' he said. My brother Andrew rushed forward and helped the women untie the hands and feet.''

Giuliana leaned forward, all attention. "Did Jesus will Lazarus alive again?''

"What does it matter?''

"But the Gospels—''

"Never mind the Gospels! I was there, and that is what I saw!''

There was silence.

"The fire was back in him, I'll tell you that. Jesus was happy to spend an hour with his old friend, and then we left. He was calmer, but different."

"Different?" Giuliana repeated. "How do you mean?"

Peter shrugged. "Don't know if I can describe it. He seemed heavier, as if he knew he'd turned some corner. He hardly smiled again," he remembered quietly. "He was more intense, as if he were wrestling with something he knew he could not change."

Andrew fetched another beer, climbed across the cockpit, and settled back into his place beside the wheel. They'd devoured roast beef and tomato sandwiches for lunch and a light supper from a local gourmet deli awaited them in the ice chest; they would feast on cold lobster and pasta salad and raspberry sorbet before returning to shore with the setting sun. For now, they subsisted on words and thoughts and silences, sun and sea and wind. Andrew wished this moment could last forever.

"There's only one thing I've been wondering," he said as he propped his feet on the starboard winch drum.

"Hmm?" Peter answered without looking up from the water.

"You remember events in your life from two thousand years ago as if they happened yesterday."

"Mm-hmm. As far as I'm concerned, they did. There was no time—is no time, for me—between then and now."

"You mean you remember nothing of what happened in the interim, in between—"

"—of your time at the right hand of God?" Giuliana finished for him. Somehow she had moved to sit closer to him, not touching, but beside him.

Peter turned around to face them. His expression was serious. He took two gulps of beer. "No. I've thought about it and I sense I was—restless—with spiritual perfection. You know, it's glorious to be free of doubt. To *know*. It's a luminous isolation, but isolation nonetheless. I missed the struggle; I wanted to remember what it is like to guess, to suspect instead of forever knowing."

"Most of us would give anything to be freed of our uncertainty!" Andrew's voice was plaintive; he wished he could be free of the doubt that ate at him constantly. But

Giuliana touched Peter's arm. She understood.

"I can still feel the stench of the Tullianum at the back of my throat." Peter's voice had gone hoarse. "Rome's midday breeze pausing just as I blacked out on the cross. Next thing I knew, someone set me on that gurney in your laboratory."

Andrew and Giuliana waited. Peter looked at them openly.

"I know that is where my soul has been. But not for the life of me can I recall it."

"You feel sure that you were with Jesus?" asked Giuliana.

"As sure as I know I am here with you now."

"Did he ever speak of heaven?"

Peter studied the horizon. Now, perhaps, Giuliana was ready to begin to understand what he had to tell her.

"He never spoke of heaven as a place, as a parallel universe. His revelation was of a new awareness, a new life. He didn't distinguish between earth and heaven, or now and tomorrow. His kingdom—heaven as you are calling it—is in the future, yes. But it is also with us here and now."

"You must have had moments of doubt," Giuliana suggested.

Peter made a disgusted noise. "Absolutely! I pestered him with questions all the time. That much, at least, the Gospels got right."

"When did you know the truth?" she pressed him.

"That last night at the feast of the Pasch. He spoke with such authority." Peter grimaced as he relived the pain. " 'Love one another,' he said." He paused; the right words were eluding him. "It wasn't anything new. He'd preached love in villages and in the fields and on hilltops. But that night his tone was unmistakable. You'd have had to be deaf, dumb, and blind to have missed his meaning: This is the end."

"That's the part I don't understand . . ." Andrew began.

"He believed the world as we knew it would end with his death. That he was dying in order to lead us into a better world," Peter said simply. "That is the nature of messiah."

"But if he was wrong about that"—Peter gave Andrew

an amused look—"I mean, the world hasn't ended. We're still here."

Peter shook his head pityingly. "And so he was 'wrong.' And the world was not created in six days, and God is not an old man with a beard, and heaven is not a place. And perhaps someday the Big Bang will be 'wrong' too. These are details, Little Brother. They are not what matters."

Stung, Andrew subsided into silence. Giuliana gave him a sideways look and, subtly, reached for his hand and interlaced her fingers with his.

The sun tipped toward the horizon. Peter was lost in his own thoughts.

"I asked him, 'Lord, where are you going?' He said, 'Where I am going you cannot follow me. But you will follow me later.'

"Not wanting to react too quickly—I always made trouble for myself with him when I spoke too quickly—I thought over what he said. I thought: This can't be. I—we— are supposed to accompany him into the kingdom of God, away from our enemies who even now surround us, waiting outside the doors of the house like hungry lions for a chance to kill us and lap up our blood.

"Finally I said, 'Lord, why can't I follow you right now? I will lay down my life for you.'

"He continued chewing the bitter herbs dipped in wine. Without looking at me he repeated, 'You will lay down your life for me?' Then he shook his head sadly. 'By cockcrow,' he said, 'you will disown me three times.' "

Tears welled up in Peter's large hooded eyes.

"You see, he knew my heart. That was when I knew that Jesus was the Messiah."

A freshening wind thundered in the mainsail. Peter reached for the sheets and his muscles tightened with the familiar sensation. Andrew nodded to himself as he spun the wheel to port. It was as if they had been sailing together their entire lives. The *Kestrel* shuddered and began to move at a comfortable angle to the wind, south toward Port Loma. A little longer, into the curve of the harbor, the labyrinth of masts and yards, and northeast toward home. As the sensuous distraction of sailing the *Kestrel* ebbed, the disturbing pressure of questions returned.

"Peter?" Andrew's voice was low as they worked side by side, securing the rigging, moving in synch. His questions seemed so childlike compared to Giuliana's spiritual comprehension. "Why do so many of us feel lost, disconnected from our own souls? You talk about our 'true spirit state.' What if this, this life here and now, is our only true state?"

"It is not," Peter said emphatically. "I tell you this because I know. For you, for now, it must be a matter of trust, of faith."

Andrew shook his head, rejecting it. "Don't tell me that. It's not good enough. If there is a spirit world, why can't we remember it? Wouldn't it make us better people if we could?"

Peter pulled the last knot taut and sighed thoughtfully. "I'm not sure, but I think our forgetfulness is a blessing. If we remembered the glorious perfection of the spirit state, we might live in utter distraction from the mission for which we exist in this life. Because each of us does have a mission, Andrew. The only real tragedy is that so many of us never recognize that, or don't live long enough to act on what we know. But we are not being denied by this forgetfulness. Rather, we're being protected so we can accomplish our spirit goals.

"It's too bad we don't carry over our memory of conflict," he mused. "Today's ideological conflicts are not so different from those of my day. Caesar vied with Caiaphas, Caiaphas with Jesus, everyone with everyone else for the possession of men's souls then, also. Caesar and Caiaphas forced their codes on others just as your dictators do, and like your dictators, they were successful for a time."

" 'Render unto Caesar . . . ' " mused Andrew.

"A man's body can be enslaved, but his mind and soul fly free. He will always find his own truth." Peter's eyes blazed with certainty. "The life within is more powerful than any army. Ultimately, the meek strike back. It is a fact."

The wind had brought a drop in temperature; Giuliana

had gone below to get a sweatshirt, catching only the end of this conversation.

"If so many believed that Jesus was the Christ, why didn't they defy Caiaphas, strike back at the Romans?" she asked.

"Jesus was a little-known evangelist, a little-known *rural* evangelist." Peter hauled in his fishing lines the old way, hand over hand. "A nobody. *Amé-Haaretz*, with dung between his toes as far as Caiaphas and his lot were concerned. We Apostles were even more obscure. No one took us seriously, especially not Roman historians. The empire was spectacle all around them, with naval battles staged on artificial lakes of wine for the amusement of idle citizens. *Wine*, while Palestinians and Samaritans were starving! The arrest and dispatch of a carpenter's aberrant son was a trifle. Who cared?"

"But your contemporaries must have understood his importance," Andrew reasoned. "If they were willing to give their lives for the man, wouldn't they have made notes, described him in letters?"

"Why?" Peter grinned, amused at Andrew's assumption. "He promised to return. Most of us believed that meant straightaway. We were going to pass into the kingdom of God. Compared to that great prospect, scribbling notes hardly mattered."

"What about historical documentation, a diary or journal?" asked Giuliana. "You said yourself you wished you'd written your own gospel."

"I say that now, with two thousand years' hindsight, but at the time?" Peter shook his head. "History was about to end."

He peered into the depths of the water for a long moment, as if seeking some truth in the disappearing fathoms of sunlight.

"I would like to talk with him," he said at last.

"Jesus?" Andrew asked.

"No, Luke John. This 'inheritor of my scepter,' as you call him." He looked at Giuliana expectantly, as if it were a minor matter to be arranged.

"Certainly, Peter. So would I."

"Then let's."

"Meet with him, with His Holiness?" Giuliana had misinterpreted Peter's casual tone as idle chat; she hadn't realized that he was seriously suggesting meeting the pope.

Peter nodded. "Why not?"

"No reason I can think of. Formal arrangements will have to be made, of course, and in view of his upcoming travels it may prove difficult, but—"

"Tell me, Giuliana," As before, he took the tips of her fingers in his hand, avuncular, encouraging. "Does he talk much about God?"

"I—I'm not sure what you mean."

Peter paused to find the words. "What is it he's after, this Parnell, this Luke John? For the life of me I don't know why he chose that name. Is he concerned with amassing numbers of souls? Or is he working for the benefit of mankind?"

Giuliana considered it for a moment, then ventured: "Both, I'd say. Yes, both."

Peter waited.

"If he favors one or the other"—Giuliana weighed her words carefully—"I'd say that he prefers souls to bodies."

"A missionary, then."

"I suppose that's true," Giuliana agreed, a little surprised at the simplicity of it. She hadn't viewed Parnell objectively since—well, since before she could remember.

"You will arrange it?"

"I'll see what I can do."

"Good!" Peter gave her fingers a little squeeze before releasing them.

Would it be possible to bring Peter and Luke John together directly, without having to go through Cardinal Cosa first? She would consider the logistics later, when she had absorbed the full significance of it. A casual chat between two old men of a spiritual bent or a meeting of minds that could change history? She must find out what Peter intended. What questions did he have for Pope Luke John? And what answers? Would Cosa listen to her? Would he care about Peter the way she had come to care for this guileless man? Would Luke John hear Peter's ancient heart and timeless spirit? She shivered.

"If heaven is not a place, but here and now . . ." She

distracted herself with a more personal and immediate concern. Peter turned his eyes away from the setting sun to give her his full attention. "Then what of purgatory? I somehow . . . I have never been able to accept the idea of hell, of a loving God who could condemn any of his children to eternal torment . . . but we are so imperfect, even the best of us. There must be some purifying process, something to prepare us for selflessness, for love . . ."

"Idem," was Peter's ready response. "The same. Like pure spirit—'heaven'—purgatory is here, now."

"But—" Giuliana objected.

Peter looked at her deeply, his voice carrying easily through the hissing bow wave and creaking rigging, unheard by Andrew yet clarion to Giuliana.

"You are suffering in your heart as you strive to love as you were meant to love." Giuliana started. "You are suffering on your journey to becoming your finest, best self. You are now in purgatory."

20

ANDREW WILLINGLY LEAPT INTO THE ABYSS, NOT knowing how to slow his descent, not even intending to try.

He saw to it that he and Giuliana spent more time with each other, away from the lab. What better excuse than to play the good host, showing her San Diego's best views, pocket gardens, and historical sights? Here they were in a garden of stone, final resting place for the anonymous pioneers of Old California Mexico. If these people had spirits and those spirits were now in some state of luminous isolation, as Peter called it, they couldn't be happier than he was here among the mortal wrecks with this woman.

For her part, Giuliana was aware of everything at the interstices of her world and Andrew's—the spring of the sod beneath her feet, his attentive motions. She wanted to tell him, to give him an unequivocal sign of how she felt. She sat on a stone bench and caressed one of the grave markers, tracing the letters of the name with warm fingers against cold marble.

"They are dead. But you and I, Andrew, we are alive!" she whispered with the strange excitement in her voice that he'd come to anticipate in recent days.

Andrew reached down and grasped her small waist, lifting her to her feet. She was weightless.

Delphine was out for a late lunch. Mike Gindman would swear he neither heard nor saw anything before Jurgen Rindt was suddenly there, standing less than a foot from his desk. Ordinarily Gindman had nerves of steel. On this occasion, he jumped out of his skin.

"Don't you ever knock?" he said lightly, hoping his voice didn't give him away. "What can I do you for?"

"I have spoken to His Eminence Cardinal Cosa," Rindt said evenly. "You will prepare Peter to travel to Rome. Arrangements have already been made. Dr. Sabatini and I will accompany him."

"How soon?"

"Now."

"I'm not sure Dr. Shepard has finished running tests. Maybe you should check with him first."

"Dr. Shepard is of no consequence. Dr. Shepard is not even on the premises. Neither is Dr. Sabatini." Rindt didn't elaborate; he didn't need to. "It is now three P.M. You will see to it that Peter is ready to board a six P.M. flight tomorrow evening."

"I'll see what I can—" Gindman started to say, but Rindt was already gone.

Given a choice between anger and fear, Mike Gindman would opt for anger anytime. Who the hell did this guy think he was? He'd get Peter ready, all right; that was part of the deal. But no one dictated terms to him. Peter would be ready when he said so, 6:00 P.M. flights be damned.

He found himself calculating how long it would take Rindt, Giuliana, and Peter to reach Rome, and wondering why it nagged at him. Hadn't he seen something on the news about the pope leaving for Dakar this morning? These overseas junkets took two weeks or more, and the pope was an elderly man; he would need at least a week to rest after such an arduous journey.

Now why, Gindman wondered, would Cosa want Peter to arrive in Rome when the pope was out of town?

Nobody pays you for wondering, he warned himself. He would wait until Delphine returned from lunch, then tell her to relay the news to Shepard.

He closed the door of her suite and she quietly vanished into the bathroom. The drapes were closed; a soft light reached under the door and cast its spell on the darkened room. He busied himself with setting out glasses and some wine from the courtesy bar, noticed a small unopened box of Italian confections and set them out too.

The light beneath the door died. He sat down on the bed while his eyes adjusted to the darkness, willing himself to relax, to make no sudden moves. She appeared in the shadows. The fleeing sun slipped through the drapes and found her outline. A dusky ray illuminated her figure, softening it like candlelight.

She had taken off her jacket and shoes. Her bare feet moved soundlessly across the thick carpet, the light dress flowing against bare legs, her delicate hands easy at her sides. She moved confidently, sure of herself.

As they looked at one another in silence, he drank her in.

Giuliana spoke first. "This will be my fondest remembrance."

"Mine is you moving to me . . ."

They spoke in circles, instinctively making smaller and smaller revolutions until they found their starting point.

"I've been so afraid of losing myself to a man. I've suppressed my feelings, hidden them for so long, preserved them, holding out for heaven. You know, Italian men are so romantic, but they think only they know what is best for a woman. I've always known what is best for me."

Giuliana came to where Andrew was sitting and took his hands. He rose to face her.

The afternoon held its breath.

"You are so beautiful."

"Beauty doesn't mean much, you know." She leaned back to look at him.

He didn't answer. He tried to memorize everything about her: the gold flecks in her left iris, the creaminess of her cheek, the sweetness of her breath.

"I've had only a few lovers. During my time of loneliness, while I waited . . ." She looked away. ". . . for you."

"Giuliana . . ."

"They took, but I don't think I ever gave to them. They just . . ." She waved her hand to complete her thought with uniquely Tuscan grace.

Andrew felt himself levitate.

"Now," She bit her lip and gazed steadily up at him, "I want to open myself to exploration, to reveal myself . . . to you."

Andrew wrapped his arms tighter around her. They shifted for a better purchase of each other's warmth, found the right hollows to fit into.

"So here we are . . ." he began.

". . . with these feelings."

"You found them . . . I forgot I had them, now I can't lock them away anymore." He spoke softly. "Nothing can rival the pleasure I feel being near you. I haven't loved in so long . . . I could love you, Giuliana."

His voice carried like an *adagio*. Her pulse quickened; she forgot to breathe.

Reaching for the box of candy, she broke the seal, extracted a wafer-thin sweet and rested it on his tongue. It evaporated, leaving a fragrant mist. He'd never tasted anything so fragile and transitory. Just as he absorbed the experience of its suggestion, like an emotion, it was gone. What is it?"

"*Violetta petalo*. A sugared violet petal."

"Mmmmm."

"It will help you understand me and my feelings, perhaps."

"Like a little miracle."

"*Si. Miracolo.*"

She caressed him, then fell deeper into his warmth. An involuntary moan of pleasure filled the space between them.

"It's settled, then," she sighed.

"Are you frightened?" asked Andrew, hearing comfort in his words even as he fought a fear he'd never known.

"Not anymore." She surprised him again. She listened to him beyond the words, beyond the static of mixed signals.

The telephone rang, its rattle harsh and foreign.

Giuliana moved to it reflexively, before she was aware of her reaction. When she realized that she had broken Andrew's embrace for what would surely be Cardinal Cosa, she hesitated, unsure whether to answer. It rang twice more while she considered.

The mood was broken. She was still superstitious enough to believe in divine intervention, so she lifted the receiver, immediately regretting her surrender to guilt.

"*Si?* Yes, Delphine, he is here. One moment."

She handed the telephone to Andrew, who listened for a few moments. Giuliana watched the anger cloud his face.

"Listen, you tell him . . . No, I'm not taking it out on you, I—all right. I'll be there." He hung up.

"What is it?" Giuliana returned to his arms.

"Gindman. He wants to see me. Now. How the hell did he know?"

"He is your Cosa; he knows," she murmured, slipping one hand into his shirt, trying to recapture the intimacy, her lips lightly brushing his ear. "I worry, Andrew, for you and me."

"I have to go," he said. "Tonight . . ." He pulled her closer.

She held his hands to her lips, suddenly awkward, needing more than she could control. "I want you too much!" she murmured. He kissed her. "No, if you kiss me . . ."

She leaned back and bit her lip again. Her nearness intensified his heat, the sight of her breasts rising and falling within her dress ignited his passion. Her hand drifted through space like silk on heavy air and she moaned soundlessly. The awkwardness was gone—no words, no mixed signals. Just agreement in a sensual code of understanding to postpone the inevitable.

"Watch yourself, Doctor," Gindman warned Andrew, storming into the lab, stark determination in his voice.

"Since when am I under a curfew here?" Andrew shot back. Gindman must be really fired up to come down here, to Andrew's turf, instead of summoning Andrew to the inner sanctum. Something had changed in the few hours he'd been gone, something Andrew couldn't put his finger on. "My private life is my own business."

"The hell it is!" grumbled Gindman. "When your actions jeopardize BioGenera business, they become my business. I personally don't care who you screw in your free time, as long as you don't screw BioGenera in the process. I'm not talking about her, I'm talking about Rindt. Stop playing games with him. He may be a pain in the ass, but he's the pope's pain in the ass. Until we've got memory resurrection on the market and paying for all this, we treat him with as much respect as we would Christ. Got it?"

"He's over the line, Mike," Andrew objected. "He's everywhere. He's suffocating me, Giuliana, and, worst of all, Peter."

"He's doing his job. Besides, as if his boss weren't reason enough, in case you haven't noticed, he's one scary guy. You're not in a position to piss him off."

"I can't worry about that."

"Oh, of course you can't! You're feeling immortal right now, like a teenager, but take a hint, Doctor: You are mortal and you're headed for a fall. And your genius? Only theory until I made it real. You're expendable. The minute you get in the way of the contract BioGenera has with the Vatican, you're out of here."

Andrew looked plainly at him. Whatever his recent self-confidence had gained him, he realized that it had just met a superior power.

"How long will it take you to brief Peter for a trip to Rome?" Gindman's entire attitude softened when he asked this.

Aha, Andrew thought. *So that's what this is really all about. Cosa's yanked his chain, and he's taking it out on me.*

"I need a week," he stalled.

"You've got three days," Gindman said and stalked out of the lab.

Giuliana surrendered to Peter's enthusiasm and agreed to join him in a glass of Cabernet Sauvignon over a late lunch.

"Andrew would disapprove, you know. He's concerned it might affect your brain function."

"I hope a little at least!" Peter grinned. Then he grew serious for a moment before the twinkle in his eye reasserted itself. It was long enough for Giuliana to see what he was doing.

"*In vino veritas*, I see." She smiled sadly.

He recognized her inner chaos. She was too exhausted to pretend. She opened her heart to him. "Jesus forbade divorce, did he not?"

"What he objected to was the man who disposed of his wife when she offended him. Remember the times. A Jew could set his wife aside merely by speaking the words 'I divorce you.' The Romans screwed anything that moved, especially each other's wives. Jesus preached tolerance, forgiveness. He emphasized the potential of the marriage relationship, the chance for two people to develop trust and commitment. If those who came after him sometimes bent his words to their own uses . . ." Peter dismissed them.

"Jesus challenged disposable principles."

"Yes. The soul is not disposable. Guide your life by what is best for the soul. The Creator understands that we have a responsibility to do what is clearly right and moral for two suffering people to save themselves. People sometimes marry for the wrong reasons. Sometimes life, small tragedies, change them so they are no longer the same people they were when they were young and hopeful. They try to honor their promises, but sometimes it's impossible. Jesus doesn't turn away from them for divorcing. I am quite sure of this. He knows what is in their hearts."

"And in mine, I hope!" Giuliana sighed, desire welling up in her eyes.

"And in yours," confirmed Peter.

"But the Church tells us it is wrong."

"The Church has its place, but it has to earn that place in your life. Look, priests and popes are between you and the Creator. The Creator has more compassion for you than all those disciples who wrote the Bible." Peter savored another sip of the red wine. "Where is it written, Giuliana, that we must surrender our mind, our soul to anyone but God?"

"But the Church represents God. The pope represents God!" Her voice rose in frustration.

"The pope represents the pope."

"Who then speaks for God?"

Peter smiled. "Listen."

"To what? I don't hear anything."

"Keep listening, child. You'll hear God."

She began to understand what Peter was telling her. It was so simple, so bold, so contrary to what she had been taught. Yet there was resonance to his urging. He spoke the original message, the inspiration for what she had learned, before time and human interference had obscured it.

"The souls in heaven never look back, Giuliana. Listen to your heart!" Peter smiled. "Heaven will follow."

Andrew was sincere in his concern for Margaret, but he had to strain for courtesy. He had grown more distant; it was no longer possible to disguise his discomfort. Living under the same roof with her even temporarily, coexisting, had been awkward at best, impossible since Giuliana.

The beach house was almost finished. Some rooms were still swathed in drop cloths, he didn't think he'd ever be free of wood shavings and plaster dust, but at least the water had been turned back on and the bedroom and kitchen were accessible. They'd both be more comfortable once he was out of here.

"I'm sorry, Margaret." He picked up the last box of his belongings. "I still love you."

She felt a chill, shrugged it away.

"It's not enough," she heard herself say without a trace of the bitterness she felt.

Normally the *New York Daily News* is no more newsworthy than any other newspaper. But this morning one of its overworked reporters had scooped the legitimate press.

A front-page picture of the brass Florentine statue of Saint Peter in the basilica, the one with his right foot rubbed smooth by superstitious pilgrims, appeared under the oversized headline: SAINT PETER IN CALIFORNIA CLINIC!

Inset lower on the page, a grainy, computer-enhanced surveillance photo showed Peter laughing with a nurse. It was

Peter, all right, captured through the windows just outside his laboratory suite. Gindman guessed it had been taken from the seventeenth green with a powerful lens.

"Goddammit!" he roared.

Delphine appeared and put the morning edition of *USA Today* on his desk. He saw the same photo, this one with an attempt at controversy: FISHING BOAT CAPTAIN OR PRODIGAL PRINCE?

Gindman scanned the articles to learn how much they knew and was relieved when each story proved to be only unconfirmed rumors circulating among employees at the secretive BioGenera research compound.

"Dammit," he growled. "Who's the neglected asshole so desperate for self-importance he's got to try to scuttle the best thing we've ever done?"

They both read the article, searching for clues. As Gindman read, he relaxed a little. "Could be worse, I suppose . . ."

"It is." Delphine pointed to a passage halfway down the page:

"According to reliable sources, the experiment has been extraordinarily successful. The resurrected memory is that of a biblical personality, probably Saint Peter, although no one on the scientific team will confirm this except the subject, who talks freely about his 'friend' Jesus."

"Christ, that does it!" Gindman slumped back in his chair. "Now we'll have every kook and loon in the Western Hemisphere waiting on our doorstep for a miracle."

"The PR people are sending over a crisis management brief with the text of an announcement they recommend you make later this morning," Delphine said.

"Another press conference?"

Delphine nodded. "Only this time you can't get away with smoke and mirrors."

She'd hoped to get a smile out of him at least, but Gindman only looked grimmer. "Dammit, is Hill and Curtis at least going to send somebody down here to fill me in?"

She nodded again. "Okumuri is on the way with his team. And . . ." The intercom buzzed and she answered it.

"No calls," growled Gindman.

"Oh, yes, he'll take it here. Just a moment." She put the

caller on hold and handed him the receiver. "It's Jeremy Hill, from London."

Gindman brusquely grabbed the phone. He was angry, but personal attention from the top was his style, so she knew he was secretly mollified.

"Jerry? Talk to me!" he spat into the receiver. "Mm-hm. Good. At nine-thirty." He checked his watch. "What about your people? Check it out. I want to choke this leak off before it can screw things up any worse than they already are. Fine. You do that."

"I'm doing a satellite interview at nine-thirty," he said to Delphine as he replaced the receiver.

Delphine frowned. "Doesn't that make the rumors look true?"

"Hill says it's the best way to nip this thing. Stonewalling doesn't work anymore."

"You're not going to tell them the truth, are you?" Delphine was incredulous.

"No, no. We claim BioGenera proprietary interests, intellectual property, and all that, say we only wish we were that successful with such an exciting experiment. But this is science, not science fiction, thanks for the national air time." He smiled, waving as if to the network news producers.

Delphine laughed, but just a little. She wasn't convinced yet that making Mike Gindman available to the media wasn't too great a risk.

Another secretary from down the hall entered with the *Wall Street Journal*. Delphine took it from her.

"Read it to me," Gindman ordered.

" 'High on the sleepy cliffs of La Jolla, California, BioGenera CEO Mike Gindman is smiling. Why? Because he has boosted his company's stock by twelve percent in just three weeks. Does he know something we don't? Does BioGenera hold the key to the next era in bioengineering? Or has Gindman simply outflanked investor skepticism with a showman's mastery over the media?

" 'Are science and history about to be made? Or is BioGenera behind the leak to inflate stock values on the eve of its annual report?' "

Delphine glanced at her boss, looking for a hint. But he was wearing his poker face. There wasn't a sparkle or a twitch to hint at what he was thinking. She smiled when she realized that she might never know the answer to the reporter's question.

Andrew, Peter, Giuliana, and Will watched Mike Gindman's performance on the small television at Will's desk. It was over quickly. Gindman's implacable calm and leadership made the reporters look trivial. He was totally focused, helpful, and as earnest-seeming as one of the boys.

"As I'm sure you understand, ladies and gentlemen, the specifics of BioGenera research, such as the identity of donors or recipients, must be kept strictly confidential. That's only fair to the good people who work so hard to find ways to better our lives, wouldn't you say?" He turned the question around with the innocent expression of an altar boy.

"You can't be serious!" a reporter wailed from the back of the room. "This is the story of the century, of the millennium, for chrissakes! How can you possibly expect to keep that from us?"

Gindman didn't answer. He didn't have to. He knew that by swearing before the audience of millions the reporter had hung himself and his profession on the gallows of public opinion. Frustration had gotten the better of him. Everyone in the room knew it.

"He's very good, isn't he?" Peter said as he watched Gindman leave the podium. The others laughed.

Cardinal Cosa's face and neck turned scarlet as he stared at the television screen in his office. The scene switched back to CNN's Atlanta studio, where news anchor Bobbie Batista segued smoothly into a story about the pope's upcoming trip to Africa. It was almost verbatim the release Cosa had approved just ninety minutes earlier, his counter to the *Daily News* fiasco. He muted the volume and stared, transfixed by this sudden loss of control over the project. His right hand squeezed the crucifix that hung from his neck. The knuckles turned bone white. Blood spurted between two of his fingers and flowed across pale, bloodless skin, unheeded.

The crisis was over. News teams would remain camped on BioGenera's front steps, trying to sniff out a story, until further notice, but that was Gindman's problem. Andrew and Giuliana orbited into the darkness of her suite at the Torrey Pines Grande. Anticipation of being discovered stimulated them beyond the familiar constraints of conscience. Their need for each other was too great to deny any longer.

Andrew stripped down to his jeans and waited by the window, backlit by the glow of late-afternoon sun from behind the heavy drapes.

Giuliana emerged from the bathroom wearing a curve of wine-dark silk, her deep chestnut hair brushed and radiant. Andrew memorized every flash and refraction, every mystery in her eyes, on her neck, her skin, the currents of light on the shimmering gown. Hanging from her bare shoulders by polished strands, silk flowed over hips, streamed and then fell into shadow.

He was unable to move. He wanted this moment to last for eternity. Here was the missing half of his heart. Here was his life's salvation.

The phone rang. It might have been thunder, but it went unheard. Giuliana unbuckled his belt and lowered his jeans to the floor. Her eyes traveled upward. Then she lowered his shorts, memorizing his every detail. Without touching him, she stood and nodded, motioning him to sit on the bed.

He had to restrain himself from reaching out to her, to expose the breasts that distended the silk and swelled the light.

"I don't care about Cosa . . ." she said quietly.

It was clear she wanted him to wait, to match her fragile violence. As her finger prompted a thin strand off her shoulder, she surrendered to his eyes, reading his every thought.

"I don't care about Rindt . . ." Slowly she revealed a creamy breast and was visibly pleased when Andrew's mouth parted with anticipation, his pupils glowed like blue pearls as they caressed her. She felt her nipples straining, then noticed Andrew hardening.

"I don't care about Jes—" But here she stopped; she couldn't say his name, even now.

Revealing her other breast the same way, she had never felt so excited. It frightened her. Averting her eyes, she eased her gown whispering to the carpet.

"Andrew . . ."

He couldn't answer. The sound of his own voice would be ruinous. It would betray him.

"... I want you to know of my longing for you."

"Tell me."

Her breath swelled from parted lips as her gaze fell down his chest, riding the eddies of her passion. She reached out to grasp her dream before he disappeared or she awoke. But she wouldn't allow herself to touch him.

"... of my *desiderio*?"

"Yes," he answered hoarsely. *"Si."*

He reached for her tousled hair, attempted to capture moonlight in his hand. But, like Giuliana, he didn't trust himself. His hand traced the intricate currents where gravity pulled at the light. It fell and drew a line in the scented air less than a thought from her tawny skin, down, along and around her curves. She shivered lightly at his restraint and fought another wave of desire to touch him.

"I ... confess."

"Giuliana—!" He shuddered.

"Shhhhhh," she whispered. "Let me tell you."

Barely audible, his breath warmed her shoulder, then melted into a quiet groan.

"Tell me."

"My desire ... is for you ... and *il piacere* ... the fulfillment you will give to me ... a river ... surging onto my shores, wave after wave ... just ... feeling your power ... inside me. I ... I will give you ... I will open to you and hold you ... as you fill me ...."

"Giuliana. I—"

"Shhhhh. Listen. I want to caress you slowly ... to lead you away from this earth ... to make you erupt, no ... *detonare*, but *adagio* ... ohhhhh, *cos' lentamente*. I want to strain your heart till it bursts with a need that only I can satisfy ... I want to make you die so you can live, so you only want to live with me ... in me."

She kissed him, hundreds of kisses as she brought him back from the death he had been dying. She murmured and whispered and laughed, each sound a new facet of the love they were defining for themselves. It had not occurred to him that he could fill her with a need or wonder as great as what he felt.

Their breathing quickened. Moving with Giuliana's rhythms, he complemented her, guiding, manipulating, urging. Giuliana fought with all her strength to slow her motion. She desperately wanted to satisfy the need to feel Andrew probing her, filling her emptiness, making her a part of him.

Ultimately, she could not hold back, and she surrendered as naturally and forcefully as in a dream. This urged him on to find more strength than he was aware he possessed. To find her rhythm. To multiply it until she was swept away in his arms.

One storm passed and another came without warning. They held each other in the intervals to recover strength. Then they began again, he hovering over every part of her body, his breath glancing on her every fantasy, his whispers beatifying her. She knelt over him, sharing her garden's secrets, visions of what he had always dreamt but never believed could be his. He whispered his absolute and eternal need for her.

"I want to give you everything," she murmured, sliding back to take him. He, so swelled and powerful now, needed to probe beyond to her secret embrace. But she pressed with both hands on his chest, instructing him to remain still; she wanted to take him this time. Without looking away from his eyes, she lowered herself and took all of him into her.

Then she held his entire length in a powerful grip while she teased him. He thought he would explode if he didn't thrust his hips to experience her completely again. But her need to prolong this orgasm was clear.

Without losing her grip she slid up the length of his shaft and stopped suddenly, just when he anticipated relief. Then she lurched and drew all of him back inside her and stopped. She kept both of them on the razor edge of ecstasy in this way for an eternity, until they each knew simultaneously that they couldn't bear the delay. Gasps replaced whispers and she ascended, arching skyward, shuddering with cries to Andrew, to another world. Resurrected, alive.

In the hush of her darkened suite, in the certain rhythm of their hearts and breathing and caresses, she heard something she'd never heard before, yet knew was herself. She listened and heeded the urgings from within and made heated, passionate, uninhibited love with Andrew, this other half of her eternal self.

Two souls reunited in one body. In their exaltation they came to oneness, however fleeting. And for that moment at least they appeased the accumulated rages of their daily separateness.

They became one. That oneness, born of melded dreams and fears, fused their ancient seeker-selves into a single generous spirit. Sense echoes joined with complete acceptance and need and unquestioning love. Her spirit knew his and his hers. They had taken separate journeys to this moment, but now they had found one another and were again complete.

They made love all afternoon, trying to catch up on all the years that had been denied them. It was futile and they knew it, but still they tried frantically to melt into one another.

Later, Andrew reluctantly dressed and, hovering over her, caressed her cheek with his fingertips, kissed her lightly, and again. He had to leave, for a meeting with Gindman. The world beyond this room, beyond Giuliana, seemed suddenly trivial.

Giuliana remained in the bed and drifted languorously in the afterglow, listening to the surf, basking in the warmth of Andrew's lingering presence, his scent on her skin. She felt she was glowing. Making love to him gave her an inner richness and excitement that was new to her.

She lay there, content for the first time in her life. A familiar presence began to grow within her, a spirit from long ago. It believed in fairy tales. It saw wonder in the smallest details. The princess was reborn. She drifted in the scented sea of love and enjoyed the way her body ached for Andrew already. She imagined what he would be doing to her right now, how she would encourage him with her hips, her words, and how he would respond with his strength. She imagined the future together with him.

The telephone rang. She let it ring three times, and answered it this time.

"*Dottore*, His Eminence is recalling you," Monsignor Murphy announced abruptly.

"Recalling me? That's absurd!" cried Giuliana. "There

is so much yet to be done. Why does he wish to recall me?''

''What can I say to you? It's his opinion that the scientists at BioGenera have had custody of—of what belongs to us— long enough. He's also heard things and he's concerned.''

'' 'Heard things'? What has he heard?''

''You know I couldn't tell you if I knew,'' Murphy tem- porized. ''I can say that His Eminence made his decision shortly after speaking with Colonel Rindt this morning.''

Basta! she thought, stopping it from leaving her lips at the last moment. She had forgotten about Rindt. That was a mistake. He was a professional fly on the wall, after all. She knew this, and still she had allowed herself to forget about him.

''Put His Eminence on the line, *Monsignore*.''

''He's not available just now,'' Murphy hedged.

''Put—him—on!'' Giuliana repeated with an imperious- ness that surprised them both.

''*Dottore,* I can't do that.''

''*Monsignore*, this is between the cardinal and me. I will speak with him, now.''

Murphy put her on hold. Vatican Radio sounded on the line, a blessing from His Holiness on the Feast of Pentecost. Giuliana prayed silently for the Holy Spirit to give her strength, to contain her gathering rage.

''Dottore Sabatini,'' the cardinal greeted her evenly, braced for a confrontation.

''*Buon Giorno*, Your Eminence.'' Giuliana stood straight, trying to draw in more oxygen and regain control of her nerves. ''This is not the time for me to return to the Vati- can,'' she said immediately, not giving Cosa time to play his courtiers' games.

''Oh? *Percé*?''

''The procedure is succeeding, as you know. I think it would be unwise to disrupt it at this time. Peter trusts me. To introduce someone new at this point might disturb him.''

''I appreciate that, my dear.'' Cosa chose familiarity in an attempt to throw her off balance. ''And I am not mini- mizing the work you have done thus far. I was especially pleased with your restraint when Peter provided clues to his identity that Dr. Shepard wasn't suited to identify. That was wise.''

"*Grazie*, Your Eminence. But you need not worry about Dr. Shepard. Within his own field he is quite capable, and he takes his responsibility to the Church quite seriously."

Cosa's silence was calculated. Giuliana resisted the urge to say too much.

"I am satisfied that he considers the interests of Nicolao Soares and now Peter as his first priority, followed closely by his obligations to the Church," she added. "He is a professional. This is his moment, I think, his mission. We are fortunate to have him."

She *was* talking too much. She bit her lip, hoping the cardinal couldn't see through her enthusiasm.

"*Si*, that is good. And what about you, my child?"

How much did he know? Giuliana wondered. How much had Rindt told him? She resisted the urge to pull the sheet off the bed, to cover herself against some superstitious belief that he could see her, could somehow know what she had just done.

"I? I am fine, *grazie*, Your Eminence." She didn't give an inch. She'd watched Cosa manipulate the uninitiated too many times to be taken in.

"That pleases me," Cosa said with what sounded like genuine warmth. "You will forgive my somewhat obsessive concern, but it is just that our interests are so significant. Any possibility of your losing your professional perspective. Well, I know you wouldn't jeopardize a project so vital to the Church."

She realized that he knew about Andrew. While her reports to Rome described the scientific protocols in painstaking detail, Rindt's were no doubt more sensational reading. Had Rindt tapped her room? There was no underestimating his enthusiasm for his work.

"Your Eminence, if you feel you must recall me, I will need at least a week to break the news to Peter, to tie up all the loose ends—" she began, but Cosa wasn't listening.

"You are such a lovely woman and the Lord has asked so much of you. Surely, you must have temptations." Cosa's voice trailed off delicately.

"I don't know what you mean, Your Eminence."

"I'm sure you do, my dear. I also have chosen a difficult

life. But the Church is quite clear about certain human failings.''

"Failings?''

"Of the flesh. Of the heart. You were given this responsibility because of your strength and purity, my dear. The Church is relying on you.''

"Your Eminence, the Church is my first priority. I know precisely why I am here. But at no time do I recall having taken a vow of celibacy.''

This time Cosa's silence was the silence of surprise.

"That is of course a matter for your own conscience, my child,'' he said at last. "I will pray for you.''

"*Grazie*, Your Eminence,'' Giuliana said, deliberately keeping the irony out of her voice.

She replaced the receiver, reviewing the conversation in her mind. Cosa had been bluffing! He had no intention of recalling her; he simply wanted to impress her with his power, his omniscience.

Only God is omniscient! Giuliana reminded herself. She stood very still on the carpet, naked, thoughtful, and searched the darkened room for any telltale signs of Rindt's work.

21 PETER WATCHED THE BBC NEWS EACH MORNING BEfore beginning "work'' with Andrew, Will, and Giuliana. It came off the satellite between 6:00 and 7:00 A.M., after his shower and before breakfast, well timed to satisfy his innate curiosity about the world as he dressed.

This morning's news featured the usual scenes of refugees in Africa and Eastern Europe, another body being carried away on a stretcher in Gaza, and sound bites from Parliament. He enjoyed the spirited debate among the ministers and lords. It reminded him of his arguments in the temples. But the juxtaposition of this often silly bickering with the reality of a world of bloodshed, disease, and starvation disturbed him as profoundly in this life as it had in the previous one.

He had not been brought here by accident. There was a reason, something he and he alone could do. He just needed to discover what it was.

An image of the papal miter over a crossed scepter and key appeared beside a commentator who was criticizing Pope Luke John's latest tactics in his fight against abortion. Scenes intercut between the pope's blessing from his apartment window and his sermon to a crowd of four hundred thousand on his current African tour, from wartime scenes of Buchenwald concentration camp to a photo of Kurt Waldheim.

"Against all odds, the Vatican today surpassed Pope John Paul's affront to survivors of Nazi concentration camps when it awarded a papal knighthood to ex-Nazi trooper Kurt Waldheim . . ."

The scene switched to familiar images of Islamic terrorist attacks and their mangled victims.

"This time, the Holy See has opened negotiations with terrorist regimes in Iran and Libya to gain support for its fight against birth control in the Third World. These Faustian dealings by the Vatican threaten the credibility of the world's leading faith, as well as the souls of Christians who are already reeling from unprecedented assaults on their faith from within and without . . ."

. . . and back to scenes of abortion protesters in St. Petersburg, Florida, alternating with footage of Pope Luke John blessing children and Americans worshiping in Iowa.

Peter's face darkened and his eyes welled up. He couldn't believe what he was seeing. The seas on which his barque was required by God to sail had been stormy in his day, yes. But nothing could have prepared him for the hatred and evil fury in the pictures that flashed on his television screen.

His successor had chosen to treat with killers in order to gain support for a position that was unrealistic at best, unnecessarily cruel at worst. What was happening to God's children?

And what could he do about it?

• • •

Andrew had shown her another universe of possibilities, Giuliana realized, a galaxy in which together they were the sun and everything else was just following blindly in their gravitational pull.

How can something so good be wrong?

Andrew had given her a gift of unprecedented joy and fear. She saw now that her life had been barren, without meaning, lived for an ambiguous future, paying dues, investing a lifetime for a reward to come. Then he brought her doubt.

Can there be eternal consequences to fragile temporal emotions?

"The souls in heaven never look back," Peter said to her.

But heaven wasn't a place, it was a state of grace. She had never felt more blessed than when she was in Andrew's arms.

"Listen to your heart, heaven will follow," Peter said.

Hadn't her heart and her conscience always protected her before? The Church had cultivated her conscience. Maybe Rome was fallible. Only by coming to terms with her most deeply held convictions, only by identifying the commitment to which she could attach her fate could she hope for peace. Happiness would have to grow from that decision, regardless of its rightness or wrongness.

This is the essence of life, she thought, *the gradual accrual of questions over answers, doubt over certainty, humility over pride.* The Church had anesthetized her senses, numbed her God-given emotions. She had experienced the wounds that strengthened others only from a distance. She could see through the eyes of saints, but not those of sinners.

Until Andrew.

Wisdom was coming at an unendurable pace. For as long as she could remember, the Church had illuminated her secret moral compass. Its needle pointed reliably true north when she was lost in indecision. Had she only been following as a lamb, without taking responsibility for her fate?

After an interminable night of this turmoil, she grew resentful—of Andrew, of the Church, of her myopic past. She was exhausted, looking for any excuse to rid herself of the pain. When she arrived at the lab, she was dressed in a high-collared blouse and loose-fitting slacks. Perhaps such attire could render her asexual, give her immunity.

"What's wrong?" asked Andrew. It was more the expression on her face than what she was wearing that gave her away.

She was sullen and distant. "Nothing!" she said without looking at him.

Andrew was bewildered. He, too, had had a rough night. Between his own self-recriminations and Peter's snoring, he'd gotten about fifteen minutes of sleep.

"Can I take you to breakfast?"

"No!" she snapped, "I need to be alone."

"Why?"

"I don't know. I—I need to think." Giuliana fell into the nearest chair.

He started to go to her, but stopped and fought a rising panic. Her sudden change of heart disoriented him. Like a caged animal, he reacted first with rage.

"Goddammit, Giuliana! Talk to me. We love each other!"

"Maybe we were wrong," she said with infuriating calm, attempting to appeal to his controlled side.

How can the only perfect moment in my life be wrong? he wanted to ask. "Not me. I know what I want; I know what's right. The answer to both of those is you."

She looked around, afraid. Of what? That Peter might overhear? Of the laboratory itself, the sense that emotions did not belong in this place of cold science?

"Andrew," she said as softly as she could manage, hearing herself speaking again, the way the dying go on talking after you're sure they're dead. "Sometimes . . . sometimes you think you're one person, then you discover you're someone else."

"What the hell is that supposed to mean?" he demanded.

She didn't respond. He stared out the window at the ocean, struggling to regain his composure. Before he could say anything else, Giuliana spoke.

"Andrew, please—!" she said haltingly. Tears burned in her eyes and splashed down her cheeks as she tried to reach out, to build a bridge to the only man she had ever loved. "It's just that I have never been so confused. I am terrified.

Such feelings cannot be ignored." She wept silently.

He crouched before her and took her hands. She seemed to have aged since he turned to the window; weeping consumes more energy than any other human act. Andrew wanted more than anything to take the reasons for her tears away from her, take them on himself.

She smiled faintly when she saw his expression, that look of still waters she had come to love more than life. His quiet became a quiet they would share.

"Don't try to ignore your feelings, Giuliana. But try to come to terms with them. You're feeling guilt; that's understandable. Nothing the Church taught you prepared you for this—for me," he finished awkwardly, more than a little amazed at his own ego.

"This . . . we . . . are impossible. You know this?" She turned away and curled up in the chair, leaned her head on one hand and seemed to fall asleep.

Andrew unburdened his heart in soft whispers, just loudly enough to carry into her subconscious.

"I love you as no one else ever will . . ."

"Andrew . . ." she murmured at last, and took his head into her arms, swaying gently in cadence with his sobs, soothing him. Neither knew how long they stayed like that, rocking away the pain of paradise lost, leaving fulfillment behind. Again she moaned as her river of tears cut a canyon in their lives, a chasm across which he could not reach her.

Peter held the chimp Niko in his arms. If he stood at a certain angle to the window, he could see the gaggle of reporters gathered at the front entrance of the compound without their seeing him.

Fools! he thought. *Has no one thought to watch the other entrances? A man could slide out the service entrance behind the cafeteria, slip through a hole in the golf course fence, and be gone before they had their minicams rolling.*

Niko stirred, stretched against Peter's grip, and sighed. Idly Peter scratched his head.

"It puzzles you, doesn't it?" he asked the creature, not expecting an answer. "Well, how do you think I feel?"

Curious as always, Peter had asked Andrew in detail about the early stages of the experiment and had subsequently been "introduced" to Niko who, to all appearances, still retained Andrew's consciousness.

"No way of knowing how long the effects of the procedure will last?" Peter had asked, seeing his own fate mirrored in Niko's.

Andrew had shaken his head. "Extrapolating, I'd say that if the effect is temporary, it would be affected by the life span of the individual holding the consciousness. If a chimp's lifetime is, say, forty years—"

"—and a man's three score and ten," Peter said.

"We're doing better than that these days, at least in the industrialized world," Andrew pointed out.

"Ah, yes, the 'industrialized world.' As opposed to that so-named Third World, where your current pope would have people breed until they die, like animals."

He's not my pope! Andrew wanted to say, but he was too exhausted for debate. "Let's say, then, that my memory in Niko's mind lasts a year—"

"Then mine in Nic Soares would last twice that," Peter suggested.

"Again, it's all conjecture. On pure conjecture, I'd say you'll be here in Nic Soares's body as long as my consciousness stays with Niko, maybe for a lifetime. I'm sorry."

Peter frowned. "What are you sorry for? For giving me a chance to feel the salt spray on my face again? Perhaps a chance to finish unfinished business? Though I must say I've lost my knack as a fisherman. Two trips out and not a single bite . . ." he mused.

"I've been playing God."

"Now you are afraid."

"Now that it's too late? Yes, I guess I am. I've had . . . a lot of regrets these past few days."

Peter knew he wasn't speaking only about the procedure. He scratched Niko's head one final time and put him back in his cage.

"Andrew," he said passionately, "believe this if you don't believe another thing I tell you: *This* is your chance! Live deeply, without regret. There's no fear of dying, no fear of death there nearer the bone. Don't save anything for later. Don't play it safe. And don't worry about getting hurt, because the more you spend what's in your heart, the more interest it earns, until it comes back to you a hundred times a hundred thousand. This is your time.''

His words made Andrew's heart ache so badly that he imagined it tearing in his chest.

"You're a good man, Andrew," Peter's voice brought him back. "And you've done a great service. I have been brought here for a reason, and I will do what I must. It may not necessarily be what either Gindman or Cosa has in mind."

Will had reported finding Peter going through Nic Soares's papers recently, studying his driver's license and his passport, paying particular attention to travel commercials on TV. He'd even asked Will to show him how credit cards worked, and cash machines. Andrew wasn't surprised.

"Peter, whatever your plan is, it could be dangerous. It's a very different world out there from the one you knew."

"Is it? And who says I have a plan?"

"Whatever you do could affect untold lives."

"As I have done before. As you have, by bringing me here. Doing the right thing is never easy, Andrew. I've never been so sure of myself that I didn't think twice."

"You might be discovered, caught before you accomplish your mission, and disappear without a trace. I don't approve of suicide."

"Who said anything about a mission?" Peter demanded. "Besides, I have an obligation to Nic Soares to look after this body of his. Whatever you think I am doing, it is not suicide. I am merely taking an opportunity to review my life, and perhaps do a little good along the way."

"It's not just you I'm worried about, my friend. It scares the hell out of me."

"That's why the less you know, the better." Peter winked. But Andrew didn't share his lighthearted attitude. Peter grew serious again. "Ask yourself this: Are you so sure that turning me over to this Cardinal Cosa is the best possible thing? What if I refuse to go? I'm an autonomous human being, a free soul. You do not own me; no one does. I answer to no one but my Creator.

"With all respect, Andrew, what are you afraid of? What's the worst that can happen to you, eh? I'm the one in danger of being kidnapped, maybe even silenced. All you have to worry about is losing your specimen, your proof that your ideas are right.''

''There's more to it than that—''

''Besides, my God, that's nothing. I've watched as men, women young and old, little children were burned for their beliefs—for *believing*!''

Peter's voice took on an elegiac tone, ''I remember a girl, not quite a woman, burned terribly, hairless and purple. She had escaped the cross in the Circus and was fleeing. Her skin had broken and clung to her in patches, her flesh and the tatters of her clothing indistinguishable, fluttering as she moved . . .''

''What had she done?'' asked Andrew, suppressing a shudder.

Peter looked sadly at Andrew, pitying him for his lack of understanding. ''She was a Jew, like me, a minority in Rome, where the majority were so afraid that they invented new forms of agony to amuse themselves. It was all right to torture the minority. They couldn't retaliate and it distracted the Roman's mind from his own spiritual emptiness.

''She was drinking at a fountain, drinking water like it was air. Apparently she'd escaped one of the crosses and was wandering the backstreets. She was so far gone she was euphoric, not conscious of anything around her. I tried to get her attention but she would not look up from the water. When a squad of soldiers marched through a nearby intersection she looked up, not out of fear but drawn to the noise. Her eyes were bright red, so red her eyelids glowed.

''She got sick to her stomach there beside the fountain, then staggered away and started to run in awkward strides. I followed her, wanting to help. She ran into a wall and collapsed like coals, rolling her head and looking back to where I had been. She kept rolling her head trying to find me. When I got to her side it was just in time to see her eyes flash brighter, almost white, and then fade to black. She was gone, driven to a better place by intolerance, her agony ended.

''The methods used today are a—how do you say it?—a 'walk in the park' by comparison.'' He pantomimed a handgun with his massive right hand, cocking his thumb and then firing, "Bang, you're born!" he grinned.

Andrew laughed nervously.

"If either of us wanted a safe life, we'd be in other lines of work, would we not? And we would never have met."

"What a shame that would've been." Andrew grinned.

Peter cheered him on. "What binds us is a miracle, so let's enjoy it! How do you change things for the better? Not in safety. The timid, the weak, the lambs of the world benefit from what we do. They need our courage."

"I'd like to believe that," Andrew said, allowing himself to fall under Peter's powerful spell.

"Take it from me: You're doing something important. Now you must allow me to do the same."

"If—when—you do decide to go, I'll need to know where you are at all times," Andrew insisted.

Peter smiled ingenuously. "I'll try to keep that in mind."

Andrew left him sitting alone.

Later in the day, at the hour when light travels up walls, Rindt sensed a calm in Peter. Now that the cardinal had summoned his charge back to Rome, Rindt was more watchful than ever.

"Got a coin, Colonel?"

Rindt reached into his pocket and tossed him a 500-lire coin, a slender Roman maiden embossed on one side, a piazza on the other.

Peter held it up. "Let's flip. Heads—this statuesque lady here—there is a God in heaven. Tails—the piazza—this is it. Nothing beyond this life."

"All right," agreed Rindt.

"Now, you have everything to gain and nothing to lose by betting on this lady—God. You wager one puny existence. No, not even that. You stake the way you decide to live that life against the ultimate win—an eternity of bliss. If you win, the lady comes up—God exists and you've won it all."

"Do it."

Peter tossed the coin. Both men watched it flash through the slanting light and land on Peter's calloused palm. He slapped it onto the back of his other hand, looked and grinned.

Rindt laughed. It was the first time Peter had ever seen the man laugh spontaneously.

"What if I had chosen not to play?" he asked Peter.

"You don't have a choice. You're in the game already." Peter grinned, pleased with himself.

"Blaise Pascal made that argument three hundred fifty years ago," Rindt smiled.

"Who was this Pascal?"

"A French philosopher."

"And what if I told you I made the argument more than a thousand years before Pascal? Who, then, is more original?"

Rindt nodded his appreciation.

"But you don't agree with the argument, the bet?"

"I am a pragmatist who doesn't gamble." Rindt moved from the light and left the room.

Unable to sleep, Peter dressed and went out into the night. As he neared the guard shack, he heard voices. Gus was being chatted up by a sweet young thing from one of the cable stations and he was enjoying every minute of it.

"Seriously?" Peter heard her burble. "You were at Anzio? Gosh, I think my grandfather was at Anzio. You don't look nearly that old!"

"Well, you know what they say," Gus's words were slurred; he'd had more to drink than usual before coming on duty, "you're only as old as you feel."

His cracked laugh was lost in whatever the reporter said next. Instinctively, Peter hovered in the shadows, listening.

". . . love to help you, sweetheart," he heard Gus say finally. "But they'd have my butt in a sling if I let you get by me, even to go to the ladies' room."

Peter took that moment to step into the open. "Evening, Gus!" he called out heartily.

Gus squinted until he recognized him. "Hey, Nic! How's it going, buddy? Out to get some air?"

"Yeah. Walls're closing in on me!" Peter hunched his shoulders, simulating claustrophobia.

"Know the feeling. Watch out for muggers up in them

hills!'' Gus called as Peter waved and moved on his way. ''Who, him?'' Peter heard him say to the girl, his raspy voice carrying on the cool air. ''Some old guy named Nic the docs are working on. That's all I know . . . What's that? Saint Peter—*him*? Nah! Don't tell me you believe that malarkey? I thought that was just to boost the ratings.''

For hours he wandered the clifftop hiking trails seeking inner peace, but he couldn't find it. Even the antics of nocturnal creatures were lost on him. He was a mortal, flawed by his very existence. He knew that he was being hunted by blackhearted men who wanted his miracle for themselves. It was only a matter of time before a tyrant cause found and silenced him.

He had seen it before, in the moon-shadowed Garden of Olives, a man younger than himself shouldering the terrible burden of his imminent agony at the hands of cowards. A good man, gentle and true-speaking, a man seemingly unfit for heroism. A man, like himself.

And just as on that night when, across the small valley, temple torches profaned the stars, BioGenera's blue fluorescents flickered in the distance, high squares of light challenging the laws of sunrise and sunset. It too was a temple of human conceit.

So much had changed. And nothing had changed. He laughed bitterly at himself for thinking differently. What did he expect, miracles? So here he was back on his tired, calloused feet again. Frightened for his life, as Christ must have been. Dreading the suffering to come, as Christ had been. Yet he knew he was obligated to submit to what had been placed before him.

He would leave immediately. He would revisit the old places. Just a few days. Then he would submit to his fate . . .

Peter was gone. Andrew knew it immediately upon entering the lab. Even in his distracted state, he knew.

Will's ear tilted to the receiver propped on his raised shoulder. ''Let me know if he stops by your area, okay?'' he said, seeing Andrew and waving halfheartedly. ''Thanks, Delphine.''

''What happened?''

''Jesus, you look terrible.''

"Never mind that!" Andrew dismissed Will's concern. He didn't have the energy to deal with it. Peter was his priority. "Where is he?"

Will lifted a handwritten note from his desk and read:

" 'I am going away for a while. This chance may not come again and I cannot let it pass. I am sorry if this causes you trouble, but you understand. *Praestat sero quam nunquam. Paete.* Don't worry. I will take care of Nicolao's body and return it to you after I am done. Do not follow me. Peter.' "

He handed the note over to Andrew, who read it himself as if willing the words to change.

"Most of his gear's still in his room," Will continued. "Just his usual clothes and a change are gone. And Nic's wallet, passport, ATM card."

"He didn't say anything?" Andrew's mind kept scouring for hints. "Let something slip in the past few days?"

Will shook his head.

"No telltale signs? No unusual high spirits? Anything specific that could have set him off?"

Will shook his head again. "Nothing."

Andrew wasn't surprised. He already knew the answers to his questions. He was just stalling for time, time to adjust, to formulate a plan. Now he had to put himself in Peter's place. Where would he go? He was Andrew's responsibility; he would have to follow him. He focused on the problem in the air before him as if it were a three-dimensional puzzle. He worked the edges:

Step One: Read Peter's mind, determine where he would go and why.

Step Two: Cover your trail. Vault your essential notes and burn the rest. Identify every known contact Peter has had since his "rebirth." No, farther back than that: since Nicolao first checked in at the lab. Andrew charted his map of responsibility in a rush of clarity. He knew he had to find not only the small solutions but how they were meant to fit together. He needed to know the purpose.

"Doc?" Will was holding out the phone to him. "It's Delphine."

"Andrew, Mr. Gindman needs to see you. Can you come up right away? It's important."

"But—" Did Gindman know? Could he keep Peter's disappearance from him if he didn't? Andrew was flying blind.

"It's not a request. I'm sorry."

"I'm on my way." Andrew handed the receiver back to Will. He was going to have to deal with Gindman eventually anyway.

Delphine's chair was vacant. There was no one on the penthouse floor, no human sound except Rachmaninoff—the BBC on Gindman's shortwave. Andrew peered through the doorway. Gindman, hands clasped behind his head, motioned him to a chair on the far side of his desk. No preliminaries. Down to cases.

"Dammit, Shepard, I warned you." There was no anger in Gindman's words, only cold disappointment, the tone of a teacher whose brightest student had failed him. "Delphine's making the rounds, polling the regulars. Her network's better than mine—more diverse, at any rate."

"I see," Andrew said. He didn't know what else to say. Part of him wanted to bolt—not to run away but to run after Peter, stop whatever was about to happen.

"I know it's still early," Gindman went on, as if he were talking to himself. "That's part of the problem."

Andrew raised his eyebrows. "I'm sorry?"

"The obvious is never apparent at first. Learned that in G2." Gindman seemed to be in that peculiarly helpless position where everything that could be done was being done by dedicated, professional people and there wasn't a damn thing for him to do but hurry up and wait. "It's like losing anything, I suppose. Till you stumble back across it, you never know."

His rambling put Andrew off balance. He didn't know what was expected of him. Simple companionship during the wait? Active engagement in some sort of free-form brainstorming? "What do you want me to do?" he asked.

"You tell me!" Fury crept back into Gindman's voice. "I've got NIH, the world media, even the Vatican waiting on my every word. What am I supposed to say? 'The scientist running the experiment let him slip through his fingers'?" He stood, the chair flying out from under him in his haste. "What do I do? Abort? Apologize? Act natural and pretend we've only temporarily misplaced him? What? Suggestions welcome.''

By now he was at the window, watching Titleists soar over the seventeenth fairway.

''How the hell did he get past Rindt, that's what I want to know!'' Again Gindman was talking not to Andrew but to himself. ''Getting past the media hounds I can see. And we let him have the run of the grounds. I've questioned all the security staff. Had to let Gus go. Sonofabitch was drunk, and not for the first time.''

He ran his hands through his close-cropped hair, swung his fists impotently at his sides, changed gears.

''Peter told me things. Things no one who wasn't there could possibly know. And to think I let Cosa believe I'd cut a deal with him.''

''You *what*—?'' This news rocked Andrew almost as much as Peter's note.

''Spare me your righteous indignation!'' Gindman rounded on him. ''This was a business deal, remember? Cosa wanted me to deliver Peter to him while the pope was in Africa. I didn't say yes or no. I just said it in a way he thought meant yes.''

He sighed and seemed to surrender, but then straightened as if to breathe new courage into himself. ''I believe that is Saint Peter. God help us, Shepard, because whoever is trying to get to him isn't going to stop. Ask too many questions and you end up . . .''

He was staring out the window again, his hands motionless but still clenched into fists.

''You and I are on the hook with this Cosa.'' Gindman's voice lost its ruminative quality. Back to business. ''Me for reneging on a deal, you for letting a miracle escape from your grasp. I don't like it. You wanted to make a miracle. Well, you've done it. Now how're you going to protect it?

''Rindt thinks you're hiding him.'' He turned to make sure Andrew was taking that in, in all its meanings. ''I don't, but that doesn't help.'' He turned back to the ocean and resumed quietly, almost inaudibly. ''Find him, Shepard. You're the best friend he has in this world. You've got to find him before they do. Understand?''

''Of course,'' answered Andrew, surprising himself by his

ready audacity. It didn't take long to decide that Mike Gindman had advised him to break the rules.

"Go." The voice came from the glass, the greenery, and the ocean beyond. Gindman didn't look at him again. He just granted Andrew permission to become a renegade.

22

HE WOULD FOLLOW, REGARDLESS OF PERSONAL risk, to protect Peter from the soldiers of profit and religion and politics who claimed to know what was best for him. Someone like Orin Sharpton would dissect Peter down to his DNA, copyrighting his tissue samples and selling them for the good of science. Parts of Peter would be flung to the far corners of the world in formaldehyde and slide smears. The two-thousand-year-old man's earthly remains would be studied until there was no more person behind the specimen, no soul behind the nuclei.

As for Cardinal Cosa, Peter's memory had become a threat, Nic Soares's body the vehicle to carry it out. That thought was even more chilling. Andrew made haste.

In the final minutes before rushing to the airport, he swept through the lab, preparing it for his absence. He hid vital data and backed up computer files. The rest he destroyed. Everything that revealed his procedure was eliminated. Even random notes and reminders were shredded. He systematically removed every clue that might enable others to reconstruct his technique. He was nearly finished when Giuliana appeared in the doorway.

"I thought you would be gone by now."

His heart pounded, but he wouldn't let her see it.

"I'm on my way," he said.

"Bene."

He knew she meant she was relieved for Peter's sake, that Andrew was moving to find him. But part of him misunderstood on purpose. He couldn't stop himself. The wound was still fresh. Giuliana and pain were one.

She ignored his reaction. "Rindt is nowhere. I think Peter is in danger, great danger."

"Rindt?" Andrew leapt at the thought, grateful for her insight. "You think he'd . . ."

"Rindt is only the bullet. Someone else is pulling the trigger. I'm not sure they haven't pulled it already." She looked around at the open drawers and shredded notes for the first time.

"Cardinal Cosa." Andrew put the pieces of her metaphor together. The lag in his comprehension made his surprise that much more unguarded. "Giuliana, what the hell is going on? You expect me to believe that Cosa would take out a contract on Peter, kill one of the Church's own? That's crazy!" The frustration of the last two days boiled over at last. He tried to keep the lid on his emotions, but knew he was losing the battle even as his words rushed out of him. "And you—you work for Cosa. You consented to this!"

"I work for the Church!" She glared at him, matching his anger. "Grow up, Andrew. Listen to me! You have been lucky. You Americans are only now confronting reality. Italy lost its innocence with the Cæsars!"

Her anger caught him off guard. She was so certain of herself. The heat of her exasperation seared from six feet away. He turned back to his computer files to get his balance.

"Maybe it's just Cosa," he offered evenly, hoping to stem the escalating violence between them. They weren't really shouting about Cosa or Peter; he knew that.

"It doesn't matter." Giuliana managed to control the edge in her voice. "It's all the same to Peter."

The phone rang and Andrew ignored it. Will picked it up in the outer office.

"Hey, Doc—?"

Before he could say anything more, Andrew grabbed the extension and growled impatiently: "Shepard!"

Whoever was on the other end got his immediate attention. His expression went from recognition to alarm to disbelief.

"Margaret, slow down! Tell me exactly what happened." Listening to her with one ear, he was simultaneously aware of a dialogue between Will and Giuliana in the next room. He tried unsuccessfully to block it out, clamping one hand over his other ear. "He what? Tried to run you down—

while you were in uniform? Are you sure it wasn't just some
drunk?"

"—and it never occurred to you he might use all the
information you gave him to effect his escape?" Giuliana
was railing at Will.

"Hell, he's a curious guy!" Will defended himself. "Besides, I was the one who warned you all from the beginning
that he was going to jump the fence, but who listens to me?"

"Hold it down in there!" Andrew shouted. The two continued to argue, but quietly.

"Margaret, listen, did you get a plate number, at least a
make on the car? 'Late-model import, probably a
rental' . . ." Andrew found himself scribbling this on a Post-
it. "Yes, I realize it was still dark at that hour. I'm not
blaming you; I was just hoping. . . . Yes, I can. I'll stop by
on my way to the airport."

He put the receiver down and went to talk to Giuliana.

"What I can't figure is how he guessed Nic's PIN number
to access the cash machine," Will was saying. "Because
he's not using the plastic. The old fox knows we can report
them stolen and have the credit card companies put a trace
on them."

His voice trickled to silence when he saw Andrew's ominous expression.

"What can you tell me about something called the Votto
Protocol?" Andrew asked Giuliana quietly.

The color drained from her face and she seemed suddenly
fragile, weak. "Why do you ask?"

"Margaret mentioned it to me a couple of weeks ago.
Someone tried to run her down last night as she was helping
a couple stalled on the highway. Whoever it was aimed for
her. She jumped over the guardrail; they got away. I don't
think it's a coincidence."

"*Madonna!*" whispered Giuliana as she sank into a chair.
"*Madonna . . .*"

"Cardinal Votto was a powerful man, *duce conservatore,*
the leader of the theological commission during Vatican II,"
Giuliana explained. "Do you remember Vatican II?"

Andrew nodded. "In the early sixties. Changed the Mass
to English, took nuns out of habits . . ."

"*Si,* those are the changes most people see. But it was much more. You see, even thirty years ago, pluralism challenged the Holy See's control over its teaching. Converts came into the Church and brought diverse influences with them. Social standards also changed. Drugs entered the mainstream. Corrupt governments were exposed and damaged the people's trust. The Church grew more authoritarian, defensive. But the cat was out of the bag, as you Americans say. Reform had taken root. How could a person be betrayed by his own government and not become distrustful of all authority?

"The popes who followed John XXIII tried to stifle debate by equating the papacy with divine revelation. But it was Cardinal Votto who presented an argument, first proposed in the forties by John Courtney Murray, an American Jesuit, that compared traditional Catholic teaching with the American Constitution. His conclusion was that to follow the ideal Catholic scenario to its logical end, the Catholic Church alone should enjoy the support of the government and alone have the freedom to spread its teachings."

"Like the Shiites in Iran," Will suggested.

"Or the Holy Roman Empire," Giuliana added. "There are innumerable historical precedents. Votto's analysis went on to identify the corollary that when and if Catholics achieved a political majority in America, they would be obliged to restrict the liberty of other churches. This is not so outrageous as you might think. It happened in Spain."

Andrew couldn't tell from Giuliana's expression how she felt about what she was describing.

"When Vatican II opened, it became clear that the worldwide climate of sincere doubt was more powerful than Votto's kind of thinking. Debate raged for years, and the council moved toward openness. But the old ways were not vanquished. While Cardinal Votto may have retreated, he did not give up."

"The Votto Protocol," guessed Andrew.

"*Si.* It was Votto's plan to regain the Church's traditional autocracy."

"Even to the extent of attempted murder?" Andrew's voice rose in disbelief.

" 'By any means necessary,' " Will remarked.

"*Si*, it is possible. Margaret's accident can have no other explanation. We inside the Vatican have all lived with the awareness that old warriors who long for the days of absolute Church authority are around us, working beside us, praying beside us. But one never knows who they are. And if the opportunity arose, would they betray me and others to re-create an autocratic Church?"

"Like old fascists waiting for history to turn their way again," Will thought aloud.

An involuntary shiver shook Giuliana.

"The pope too?" Andrew asked. Giuliana had to think about it.

"*Non*, I do not think so," she said finally. "He would have 'blown his cover,' so to speak, tried to implement Votto's policies by now."

Andrew squeezed the diskette in his fist so hard that the plastic cracked. "*Cosa*, then. And however many others he has in his pocket. He has to be smarter than this."

"He's not an intellect, Andrew. He's not a tower of virtue but of ambition. He believes he is right, that it is his duty to pursue this course."

"How well do you really know him?"

Giuliana sighed wearily. "No . . . *affatto*, I'm afraid. Not at all. No one truly knows Cosa.

"Where is Peter's note?" she asked at last. "May I see it? '*Praestat sero quam nunquam,*' " she read aloud. Her expression was grave.

"What does it mean?"

" 'Better late than never.' He goes to Rome, I think, but—"

"So do I." Andrew looked at his watch. He had to pack. And he'd promised Margaret he'd stop by before he went to the airport. "I've got a noon flight to London, then—"

"But, Andrew, not right away. The pope is still in Africa, remember. Peter would know this. He would also know that Rindt is looking for him."

Andrew sat on the edge of Will's desk; it was as close as he dared get to her.

"Then where?"

•   •   •

When the housekeeper at the archbishop's residence in Los Angeles answered the door, she recognized the compact man standing before her. She didn't know his name, but she knew his type. They always arrived without notice, preempted the archbishop's schedule for brief minutes, then evaporated into the misty netherworld between God and politics on some vital errand.

This one wasn't like the others. He wore his dark European-cut suit as if it were designed for him, which it was. He was smoother. Almost priestly. This one is dangerous, the housekeeper decided.

"Come in," she said formally and held the heavy door for him.

His perfunctory smile didn't extend to his eyes.

"His Eminence is upstairs. I'll let him know you're here."

"I won't have to disturb His Eminence today, thank you. I only have to use the telephone."

Rindt's tone hinted at practiced control. He followed her to the study behind the towering pocket doors halfway down the main hall and dialed his office in Rome to check for recent dispatches. Receiving none, he hung up and dialed another, longer number. Zero-one-one, country code three-nine, city code six, and a proprietary number that scrambled his voice in a random digital pattern, routed his call back out of the country, through several blind exchanges, then finally into the Vatican, where it rang Cardinal Cosa's private line.

"Is the line secure, Your Eminence?"

"Of course it is," Cosa responded edgily. He still distrusted the equipment, and double-checked the LCD readout. It reassured him with an "Active" message. Without missing a beat, he interrogated Rindt. "You have found Peter?"

"I arrived too late to catch his flight."

"His flight? How could he have gotten away?"

Rindt normally didn't tolerate emotions. The cardinal's agitated tone concerned him. Ordinarily he knew His Eminence to be very cool in such a situation. If Cosa was worried, then that added to Rindt's concerns. Going on instinct, he ignored Cosa's need for reassurance and kept to the business of the moment. He would stay alert to Cosa's moods, however. If the team's leader lost his nerve, the team was vulnerable.

"By taking the *Concorde* to Paris and connecting through Tel Aviv, I can be in Jerusalem ninety minutes before him," Rindt was explaining.

"Jerusalem? How do you know he is going to Jerusalem?" the cardinal wondered.

"Call it a strong likelihood."

"Colonel, there is no time for mistakes."

"I am aware of that." He detested Cosa's second-guessing.

"*Bene,* then. As long as you understand his importance. What is your plan?"

"To keep him in sight. Those are my instructions, no?"

Cardinal Cosa bit his lip. This was where his future intersected with his faith. It had been inevitable; he'd known that. He had sensed that Rindt would call with such a situation sooner or later, so he wasn't surprised, merely ambivalent. Was he going to stay true to his career of power gathering, or would he obey his Church's commandments and leave the rest to God?

He believed in God, but now in the bright light of Peter's existence he saw that he lacked faith in the structures to which he had dedicated his life, the single most significant requirement for salvation, according to the Church. He himself had taught it to thousands. And, until today, he had believed it.

Bide your time, an inner voice urged. Play it safe. Another opportunity will present itself.

Mai, another voice countered, taunting him. Never!

He wasn't completely without faith. The first voice attested to that. But it was sufficiently lacking to favor the other voice, to hedge his bet with temporal power. Now, when he was confronted with what was most likely his unique moment, his time of critical significance as a human, he had to choose.

Now.

"I have new instructions," Cosa began.

With Will's help on the computer, Giuliana traced a rough map of Peter's life, highlighting each stop.

"Bethsaida to Galilee to Jerusalem, a brief stay in Cæsarea, on to Antioch in Syria, and finally to Rome," she explained with the sureness of her scholarship. "According to Acts 3 and 4, he and John were arrested in Jerusalem by the Sadducees in A.D. 30 for proclaiming Christ's resurrection. Then there is a reference in Acts 10:1 through 11:18 to his teaching in the house of a Roman centurion named Cornelius in Cæsarea, along the Mediterranean coast in northern Samaria. That was in A.D. 35.

"In A.D. 38 both Acts 9:26–30 and Galatians 1:21 place him in Jerusalem. Again in A.D. 49, he is still in Jerusalem, but he moved on to Antioch in that same year. Finally, in A.D. 64 there is his letter from Rome before his crucifixion, to the Christians in Asia Minor.

"Jerusalem to Rome, approximately twenty-three hundred kilometers or fourteen-hundred-plus miles, a significant journey by any standard but especially daunting during those times of slow voyages and even slower overland treks. But Peter's was a long and very rich life, and he was driven by a cause.

"If I understand Peter correctly, he will use the time before Luke John returns to the Vatican in making a pilgrimage. It is perfectly natural for him to want to visit places that had special meaning for him, old haunts, old battlefields." Giuliana surrendered the computer to Will and went to gather her jacket and her briefcase from Andrew's office. "I have already made arrangements to fly to Jerusalem and backtrack to Bethsaida."

"The hell you will!" Andrew's anger rose in his throat again as he stormed after her. "You're going to stay put right here. I won't have you flying off on a wild goose chase."

"And who are you to dictate to me?" Giuliana matched her anger to his. "You do not own me. I do not need your protection!"

"That's not what I'm talking about! Someone's got to stay here and answer to Cosa when he calls." Andrew spoke softly now, intensely, all but whispering. "And you know he'll call. How will you explain the fact that you've gone kiting off to Israel without getting his permission? God knows, he's had you watched every step of the way so far.

Rindt's the only one of his operatives you know about for sure. You'd not only put yourself in jeopardy—"

Giuliana dismissed the thought. "You read too many spy novels!—" she began.

"—you could lead him straight to Peter," Andrew finished.

Her hands flew to her face. "I hadn't even thought of that!" she said in horror.

"That's what you've got me for." Andrew managed a faint smile. "You sit tight here, hold the fort. Convince Cosa that everything's cool, that Peter's still in the country. He's headed straight for Rome; I know it. He speaks Latin, he can pick up Italian fast. He can go to ground there, hide out, wait for the pope to get back.

"Yes, he will end up in Rome eventually. But first he will go home."

Andrew shook his head. "I won't take the chance of going to Israel on a hunch." He almost succeeded in softening his tone. "I'll call you from Rome."

He left her standing there. Giuliana blinked back tears. Moments later she watched from the window as he strode across the parking lot, a man with a mission. She raised one hand and touched it to the glass in tentative farewell, but Andrew didn't look back.

The Porsche's powerful whine climbed to harmonize with the beating wind as Andrew tried to make up time. He had stopped at the beach house to pack, amazed to realize, as if for the first time, that his suitcase bore no colorful decals or Customs stickers, not even a check-in tag fluttering from the handle to commemorate his last flight. Where had he gone? Some scientific conference in some chain hotel in some forgotten city he'd never had time to see, locked in to a series of lectures and readings, seeing the same faces, eating the same meals, having the same conversations, watching HBO until sleep overtook him in a strange bed in a barren room. Why had it seemed so normal at the time? Why did it seem so pathetic now?

His was a life of paper and computer files, a life of the mind, a life that when it was gone would leave no trace of its vitality, no clues to its passions. He thought of the life

Peter had led, the life he was leading now—on the run, racing against time and other people's agendas—and he envied the grand old man.

He knocked on the back door of the house that had once been his own. Margaret's footsteps sounded on the kitchen's wooden floorboards; she let him in without a word.

"You need to disappear for a while," he told her. "Until this blows over."

"But I'm on duty—"

"Listen to me. You have to hide. Take some leave time; you've got enough saved up. Not for long, just until I can find Peter."

"I suppose I could go up to—"

Andrew motioned her to silence. "Don't tell me where you're going. Just go."

She didn't say anything. Then her voice came back, quieter this time. "All right. And, Andrew—?"

He looked at her expectantly. She shook her head.

"Nothing. Just— Be careful?"

"I will."

Spring's last rain had swelled the Jordan River, freshened the Sea of Galilee, and restored life to the melancholy air of winter. Then it moved into time, a memory to be cherished by farmers and merchants and schoolchildren of the surrounding towns during the approaching hot, dry days of the Syrian summer.

Fertile scents stirred the air and dispelled the staleness of winter. March? Could it be that time again? A gust of wind intruded into Peter's reminiscences and he lost his wife and family in the mists of time. Again.

A dizzying rush of regret swept over him. Why had he returned to Bethsaida? What could he hope to find that needed to be found? The years here had been hard—good, but hard.

Like so much about this part of the world, Peter remembered, life was a craft of scale, a skill learned in cooperation with other cultures in a compact space. Even the lake, only sixty-four miles square, was a disputed object. Fed by waters from the Jordan, it was Yam Kinneret to the Jews, Bahr

Tabariya to the Arabs; Rome's descendants had known it as the Sea of Tiberias.

Little had changed from the ancient memories of his family's oral history two thousand years earlier, except perhaps the pace of pollution brought on by technology, fertilizers, and war. The fragile desert still suffered under the stress of so many cultures' attempting to claim it for their own.

Below him, down the bank from the road where he stood, a two-lane snaked between timeless structures. A shed, a café, some low-slung hovels, a phone booth, an inn, a shop or two, then nothing for half a mile, and then a cooperative's meager herd of goats. Stone buildings, tin roofs, white smoke drifting from stone chimneys. This was Bethsaida. Like scores of other towns in northern Israel.

He walked the short distance down to the hotel. Everywhere he looked, he had a sense of knowing that sight before. Maybe it was the time after first light, before the sun showed itself over the far hills. The village was still asleep.

So much time had passed. A new community of tight-knit families had labored to create livelihoods from the desert sea, just as he and his contemporaries had. In his time he had known only hard work and the narrowness of the law. His people had little ambition for stories of other cultures, other priorities.

These new residents lived in a bigger world, however. They were well versed in the conveniences of the twentieth century, courtesy of American movies on evening television.

He knocked loudly on the door of a small boardinghouse. His pounding echoed down the vacant cobbled street. He remembered the hour. A dog barked in response but didn't bother to come over and investigate him.

"*Ken?*" A voice sounded from above. "What?"

Peter stepped back out onto the street and looked up to see a man wiping sleep from his eyes.

"I know it's early, my friend." Peter spoke quietly so as not to wake others. "But I've been traveling all night. Could I get some coffee and breakfast? I need a bed, too."

"Breakfast isn't until eight; seven o'clock in the fishing season. This isn't fishing season."

"I need to eat. Can I check in?"

"*Ach,* all right! You look harmless enough. There's coffee in the high cupboard. And fix whatever you like from the refrigerator.'' The man started to disappear back into the semidarkness of his bedroom.

"The door?'' Peter called up to him.

The innkeeper's head poked back out into the morning air just long enough for him to say, "It's open.''

Before Peter could thank him, the innkeeper was back inside and probably back to his dreams.

He made some strong coffee and drank it from a small cup as he surveyed the terrain that sloped down to the sea.

Some sea! Peter chuckled as he compared it to what he had seen in La Jolla. *This is a puddle compared to the great Pacific Ocean!*

"You found the coffee. Good.'' The innkeeper's voice sounded from behind him. Peter turned to see a short, frayed man in baggy pants and flip-flops shuffle into the kitchen. "My wife will be down to make you some breakfast.''

"Thank you.''

"American?''

"No, I'm from around he—''

The innkeeper looked more closely at him.

"Yes, America,'' he corrected himself. "But I have known Bethsaida.''

"Forgive me, sir, but you don't look that old!'' The man laughed a little and stared openly at Peter, now curious at the joke.

"Oh, I'm older than you think, my friend.''

"I swear some of you archaeologists are strange. Must be the fact that you're on your hands and knees all day, underground with no one to talk to but old bones, eh?''

"Excuse me?''

"Bethsaida! The excavations!'' The old man pointed out the window to the south.

Peter looked but saw nothing.

Now the innkeeper became irritated. He was being mocked by this scientist from America. But the stranger's humor was so odd and his own nature so generous that he decided to give the American the benefit of one more doubt. He walked quickly through the front door out onto the porch and pointed forcefully to a small encampment on the desert surface about halfway to the shoreline.

Peter saw a ribbon of smoke rising from a work tent near several mounds of freshly dug earth and the skeleton of a brick wall rising from a broad, shallow pit. There were three or four reedy figures in wide-brimmed hats huddled around the base of one end of the wall.

Peter suddenly realized that this village, junction, hamlet—whatever the residents called it—was at least a mile north of where he remembered his home to be. The realization that it was not only a forgotten settlement, an archaeological curiosity, shook him. He felt very much alone.

The innkeeper saw Peter's face go pale and empty. This village was his home and that of his father before him. And he recognized in Peter's face the unmistakable look of a man seeing his home. He didn't try to make sense out of Peter's obvious affection for Bethsaida. He simply found common ground with another native of this remote wilderness.

"I tell you what, I will have the woman make you a breakfast to take with you," he offered. "I'll show you to your room, you can put your things down, and then you can go to the excavations."

Peter nodded gratefully. He didn't trust himself to speak. Seeing his home's gravesite had moved him close to tears.

The walk down the hill to his village was quick. The footpath that had known countless goats and their goatherds had been ancient when as a boy he'd walked it into the hills for day adventures. Now the path was timeless, a permanent feature in a permanent land.

As the excavations opened themselves to him, he saw that the archaeologists were resurrecting the back wall of the cooperative shed where he and his neighbors had built fishing boats, repaired nets, and stored the tools of their trade.

Fifty yards to the left huddled a knot of young graduate students, engaged in peeling back the layers of history that had enshrouded the first level of his next-door neighbor Arom's house. They meticulously recorded every fragment of Arom's family's most pedestrian castoffs: two brass buttons, half a handle from an amphora, the remains of a man's leather sandal, a woman's broken comb. They were photographing a new layer of earth that was recently revealed. One young man scoured the surface for the smallest detail, calling out "F-7: ceramic fragment—plain," and so on. Another noted the find with a detailed inscription in her journal.

He wondered what they would find in his house. He wondered if they would find his house, if anything of its blunt utilitarian construction remained after twenty centuries.

The young man in Arom's kitchen rose to stretch his cramping back muscles before moving on to F-8. As he did, he noticed Peter watching.

"Boker tov!" he called cheerfully. Peter suspected he wasn't a native Jew. The lad's blond hair looked more like what Peter had seen on the hang-gliders above Black's Beach. And his accent was distinctively Southern Californian. His innocent bemusement in even the simplest phrase in Hebrew gave him away.

"Good morning!" called Peter.

The young woman looked up at the sound of Peter's English.

"California?" she asked.

"La Jolla, sort of," Peter answered with a smile.

"Cool!" observed the young man.

"Really," added the woman. "It's been centuries since we've heard a voice from home."

"Centuries, eh?" Peter laughed.

"Okay, two months," grinned the young man.

"A long time to be away from home," Peter sympathized. "So what do you think?" he asked, nodding toward Arom's kitchen.

"It's quite a find. Hard to believe it's gone unnoticed in a place that's been more or less continuously inhabited since before Christ's time," the young man said, bending back down to his work.

"Bethsaida was never a very popular place," Peter observed wistfully.

"You think it's actually Bethsaida?" the girl asked. Her colleague looked up to hear the answer.

"Yes."

"How can you be sure?" the young man asked. "What's your background?"

"There's so little information. And so far no discovery that's conclusive," the girl added.

"It's Bethsaida. Trust me," Peter assured her with a wink.

They nodded tolerantly, even a little condescendingly. Peter stopped talking and contented himself with a walk around the pit, remembering as they worked.

As he turned the corner into the open area behind his house, the area he shared with Arom's family, he remembered a scene often repeated on late-summer nights when they were boys. His bedroom window faced Arom's across the courtyard. One or the other would signal through the starlit night with an oil lamp, a stick with a scrap of cloth tied to it, or whatever else was handy. Then they would talk in hushed whispers about their futures, about the great mysteries, about how they might get to steer the boat tomorrow. Those were wonderful times. Those years between childhood and young adulthood were unique for their magical blend of growth and discovery.

Arom owned something that no one in Bethsaida had ever seen before. He had inherited a massive hunter's longbow and a quiver filled with half a dozen brass-tipped close-grained dogwood arrows from an uncle who had traveled as far as the Caucasus, bringing back exciting stories of the horse-mounted hunters along the Black Sea. The bow was two feet taller than Arom himself, but he was certain that he would someday grow into a brave adventurer who would trek into the distant mountains and slay a deer, that rarest of delicacies in the desert. He would call his father's house his own and add to it, making it an adventurer's retreat.

"Find any arrows? A hunter's bow?" Peter asked quietly, to keep the memory from overwhelming him. Arom had been a young man of twenty, a new husband with a baby on the way, when he'd gone overboard during a sudden storm on the sea and drowned. His bride's wails had blended with his mother's, resounding across the courtyard for days. So long ago, and yet in Peter's mind, not long at all.

"Bow and arrows?" the young man repeated without looking up. "No. Not much chance of that in this part of the world. These people fished. There was no game to hunt for at least a hundred miles," he explained patiently, his skepticism of this elderly tourist growing by the minute.

"Oh, I see," Peter responded simply.

He had so admired the bow and those fine brass-tipped arrows that Arom would occasionally bring them out into the courtyard. Peter delighted in testing his strength against the powerful yew bow. Neither boy could bend even the tips until they were both into their teens. By then they had taken on so much responsibility that there was no time for adventure, and the dream of the deer became a metaphor for what might have been.

Then Peter had met the man who walked on water and multiplied the loaves and fishes before his eyes. The carpenter's son touched an even deeper place in Peter's soul than the fine bow and arrow had. The boyhood dreams were soon lost in the dust of the life that he left behind in Bethsaida along with his wife and daughter, his boat, his nets, and his memories of Arom.

A sharp pain lanced his heart when he recalled the hurt and anger he had forced upon his wife and small daughter . . . before they came to understand his new faith and supported his conviction, before Petronilla journeyed with cousins to be with him in Rome. Oh, the fury that filled their house for so many days! He felt sorry to this moment for his rending of the family's secure life on the banks of the Sea of Galilee. It had been hell making that decision, an agony he wouldn't wish on any man, walking away from what was expected of him to join the Nazarene.

"Metal . . . brass, I'd say." The young man's voice broke excitedly into Peter's reverie. "Yep, brass arrow point. Looks like it still has some wood preserved inside! F-10."

"Brass arrow point." The young woman repeated what she'd heard as she wrote it down, displaying the discipline for which her profession was noted. But then she dropped the journal and ran to her colleague and studied the arrowhead.

After some thrilled speculations about what it might mean, they suddenly stopped talking, looked at one another in silence, and then above to the rim of the pit where Peter was standing. Carefully he stepped down into the pit and now crouched beside them, studying the arrow tip. He smiled knowingly and decided that it would be all right to tell them that the wood inside was dogwood.

"Dogwood," repeated the young man.

"Mm-hm. Pretty advanced for the time, wouldn't you say?"

"Unheard of is more like it."

"Until now," Peter observed.

"Until now," echoed the young graduate student.

"Are you convinced this is Bethsaida now?" laughed Peter.

"I want to believe it. But this arrowhead doesn't prove anything, not really."

"Oh, Tommy, for God's sake—!" the young woman interjected.

"It does to me. But then again, I already knew." Peter beamed. "Welcome to Bethsaida, my friends!"

He climbed back up to ground level and walked around to the far side of what had been Arom's house, looked back once more at his own, and continued down to the shore.

There he relived the storm that had overtaken them one day while Jesus slept and then subsided as suddenly as he awakened. He remembered trying to walk on water like his master . . . and nearly drowning. He remembered the miracle of the loaves and fishes that had transformed skeptics into believers not too far from this place. It all came to life as readily as if it had just happened.

After several hours of indulging his memories and gauging his sentiments against the realities of the place, he satisfied himself that there was nothing left for him here. No clue to why he should have returned. He saw only hardship in the faces of the fishermen, the sharp wind, and the bleating of the goats on the near hills. He felt vaguely ashamed of himself for his self-indulgence in coming here.

He had nearly two weeks to kill. Luke John's African tour ended the day after tomorrow with a spectacular outdoor Mass at a soccer stadium, a media event with a cast of hundreds of thousands and million-dollar video sales later. Then it was back to Rome, followed by a week's rest at Lago di Garda, his reclusive summer retreat. Yes, Peter had studied the man this well, to know what he would do next. When Luke John returned to Rome again following his vacation, Peter would meet him there. But he had time yet.

He decided he would go to Jerusalem, to prepare himself, to make certain he had not overlooked any clue to his mission. He must retrace the journey of his life. He would hitch a ride to Capernaum, his home for many years and the base of Christ's three-year ministry. Then he would take the ferry south across the western arm of the incomparable subtropical lake to Tiberias and continue by car south to Jerusalem. Perhaps there would be clues for him in the Old City.

Since the pre-Roman era, Bethsaida had seen strangers in every size, shape, and color. Lately, it was mostly just a trickle of pilgrim day-trippers looking for Peter's birthplace. They were universally disappointed when they saw the ordinariness of the small, undistinguished village. So they left after an hour, usually sooner, piling back into their automobiles and raising a quick cloud of road dust as they sped west to more promising sites. The archaeological team was unusual in the eyes of the locals. It had come two months ago and stayed.

When Jurgen Rindt appeared, it was evident to everyone that he was not a pilgrim. And when he asked around about the elderly stranger, people were tight-lipped. They might not have gotten to know Peter well, but he had been a friendly sort.

"A lot of folks stop by, look around, and leave," the blond archaeologist answered after looking up at Rindt. He decided he didn't like the man and went back to his work.

"After a while we stop noticing people," added the young woman, without looking up from her notes. She'd seen Rindt coming from a distance and resented the interruption. They'd made substantial progress after finding the arrow tips. That, together with Peter's assurance that they had found Bethsaida, gave them new enthusiasm.

Rindt stood stock-still, watching, waiting for them to grow uncomfortable enough to offer more information. He sensed that Peter had been here. After several minutes in which the young couple offered no more openings, he turned and left.

He presented himself at the innkeeper's front door. The innkeeper, reluctant at first, finally admitted that a man of Peter's description had just checked out.

"Where was he going?"

"I do not know," the harried man answered honestly. "He didn't say."

Rindt put a twenty-dollar bill on the counter, knowing that American dollars were highly desirable to hoteliers and restaurateurs, for despite recent down fluctuations in value against the new shekel, they were still a relative constant in the vulnerable economies of the Middle East.

"Did he leave a forwarding address?" he inquired smoothly. "A phone number?"

The old man flashed his willingness to cooperate in a business deal and laughed. "No, sir. No. This is not Tel Aviv. My guests do not carry cellular phones and Italian briefcases!"

"What did he do while he was here?" Rindt asked.

"Oh, he walked the beach. Stood for hours staring out at the water, watched the archaeologists and the tourists. Some of the people thought he was a little—well, you can imagine! Me? I think he was a little homesick."

"Homesick," Rindt repeated, prompting him.

The old innkeeper shrugged. "What can I tell you?"

"Apparently nothing." Rindt made for the door with a perfunctory nod.

From the shadows of the staircase where he waited, listening, Peter breathed a silent blessing on the innkeeper for saving his life. He would wait a day or two for his trail to cool before moving on to Jerusalem. He had not lived more than thirty years after the master's death without learning certain survival skills.

The graduate students looked up at the sound of Rindt's car as it sped up the embankment and down the dusty road to the west and veered expertly around a lumbering tour bus bringing the day's quota of tourists.

"Rush hour!" observed the woman.

Her partner in the pit chuckled and continued the task at hand, brushing away fine sand from the deerskin-wrapped handle of what appeared to be a magnificent longbow.

23

AS THE TOUR BUS TOOK THE TURNOFF FROM THE paved road onto the dirt path scored with tire tracks and slanting down toward the excavation, it raised a cloud of choking yellow dust. The two young archaeologists, used to this daily ritual, slipped their bandannas up over their mouths and noses while they waited for the dust to settle. Their eyes simultaneously traveled to the longbow.

"Uh-oh!" the young woman said. Their elation had been cut short by the tourists' arrival; now they had to conceal their new discovery against the chance that anyone from the bus might recognize it for what it was. Some of the greatest discoveries since Olduvai had been contaminated that way.

The young man began to kick all the dirt he'd brushed away from the bow back into place, erasing half an hour's work in seconds.

"Later!" he remarked grimly. His companion sighed, thinking of all that work to be redone. Then they both lowered their bandannas and put on their best company smiles. "It's show time, folks!"

Watching as the tourists filed off the bus, Peter smiled. The impatience of youth! Within weeks these kids would be headlines, their find unheard of for this time and place. Within months they would be in the eye of the newest archaeological controversy, fielding accusations that they had planted the bow from another dig. Their vindication a year from now would assure them both long and distinguished careers. Yet all they could think about now was the extra work.

The tour guide's voice distracted him. Clearly he was not speaking Hebrew, but Peter had expected English as a second choice, since so many tourists were American. Yet as he caught the mention of his own name—"Pietro"—he realized that the man, clearly a native Israeli, was struggling along in Italian.

Perfect! Peter thought. *If I listen to him I can learn the differences between the Latin I spoke and the language of today's Rome!* He sidled closer, grateful that he had chosen a plain white shirt this morning instead of the loud Hawaiian one. While the group was mostly single women and the occasional couple, they were middle-aged to elderly, dressed with Continental good taste, and he could blend right in.

It didn't take him long to realize that the tour guide's Italian was no better than his own.

"... and is believe here is where San Pietro is born ..."

There were murmurs from the group, as if they had been enduring this butchery of their language all day. A tall woman with salt-and-pepper hair was urged forward by the others.

"Percè?" she demanded of them. "Why me? Why must I always be the one to speak for everyone else?"

"Because you speak better English than any of us, Nula. Go on!"

"Aspet, give me a minute!" she whispered irritably, then turned to the tour guide, who, realizing no one was listening, had mercifully stopped wrestling with the language. "Excuse me," the woman named Nula said sweetly, her plain face warmed by the most genuine smile. "But you do speak English?"

"Fluently, *signora,*" the guide assured her, wiping perspiration from his moon face and looking greatly relieved.

"Excellent! Then you will speak to me in English, and I will translate for the others, okay?"

The guide grinned. "Okay!"

And so it went. The woman's voice was so easy on the ear, her ability to switch between languages so fluid, that Peter found himself learning Italian from her almost as readily as he had learned English simply by having it preprogrammed in his borrowed brain. He also found he enjoyed looking at her.

She was very tall, strong-boned and natural-looking, not a trace of makeup on her honest face, dressed in a neutral-colored shirtdress and serious walking shoes. Not pretty; she had never been pretty, but the years had softened features too stark for a young woman, rendering her handsome in middle age. This was a woman who had grown up in the country, unafraid of hard work, uncorrupted by her years of living and working in the big city. A woman who said what was on her mind. There was sadness in her dark eyes, the sadness of too many hopes and dreams set aside because the needs of others always took precedence over her own. A woman who would bend without breaking.

Suddenly she was standing beside him.

"I despise incompetence!" she announced, charitably out of earshot of their guide, who was leading the rest of the group, like a flock of sheep, up the hill to the inn for refreshments. "Where do they find these people? If you cannot speak the language, don't volunteer for the job!"

"You sound as if you travel a great deal," Peter offered.

She shook her head. "This is my very first trip abroad. I wanted to see the holy places. Obviously a mistake to come with a group, but a woman alone . . ." Her voice trailed off. Then, as if realizing she was drawing too much attention to herself, she put on a smile. "You see, I do this sort of thing myself, at home."

"This sort of—?" Peter was lost. Was it that he was listening to too many voices in his own head, particularly the voice of another strong-minded woman he had known, had argued with on this very spot, two thousand years ago, before embracing his small daughter and going to follow the master? Yes, his wife had been strong of mind and strong of voice, but nothing like this woman at all.

Nula's voice brought him back to the present. "Yes. I am a tour guide in Rome, in the Vatican."

"Are you?" Peter asked with great interest. Someone once said coincidence is only God trying to hide his footprints. "I've always wanted to see the Vatican."

"Well, then, you must," Nula said, as if it were decided. "When you sign for the tour, ask for me. My name is Nula. Nula Gatti."

"Peter," he said in turn. "Peter Soares."

They shook hands. Her hands were extraordinary—long-fingered, strong, the nails cut square and unadorned—her handshake as firm as a man's.

The others were all up the hill by now, in the relative coolness of the inn. Even the two young archaeologists had faded off for a siesta as the sun reached high noon. Only these two lingered, oblivious to the heat, shadowed by a third, who was more shadow than man.

• • •

Jurgen Rindt lurked behind an outcropping of bare rock, concealed from both the road and the inn by a series of small hillocks and a fortuitous twist in the goat path. He had left the car a kilometer up the road and walked back, his instincts telling him, regardless of the innkeeper's lies, that Peter had not returned to Jerusalem.

What more perfect venue for his task than the Palestinian countryside? He wouldn't even need the silencer here in these hills, where weapons fire was commonplace and death from gunshot wounds invariably attributed to terrorists. Peter and the woman were strolling beside the tour bus, giving him several options, from sighting Peter in the crosshairs for a direct shot in the back of the skull to the easy shot to the petrol tank, the spectacular detonation and conflagration, which would create enough confusion in its wake to give him ample time to escape.

The only problem was that the woman refused to get out of the way. Every time Peter's grizzled head passed across Rindt's gun sight, so did hers. With that Italianate need for proximity—the one thing Rindt, with his Germanic need for maximum personal space, had found most difficult to countenance in adapting to his role at the Vatican—she stayed as close to Peter as she could within the bounds of propriety, denying Rindt the clear shot he required.

Whatever else Rindt was, he was a professional, precise killer and a logical one. He didn't always ask his clients' reasons, but he required that there be reasons.

He would not kill Nula Gatti just because she got in his way.

Even with no one to see him, Rindt betrayed no emotion as he slid the safety back onto his customized Glock—slowly, silently, knowing how any metallic sound would echo in these hills—and concealed it in the shoulder holster beneath his jacket. Meticulously he brushed the yellow desert dust from his dark trousers and moved silently to a different vantage point. Once the busload of tourists was gone, he would seek his next opportunity.

A superstitious chill raised goose bumps on Peter's arms despite the heat; he hoped Nula wouldn't notice. Years of eluding Nero's spies had honed his senses; he knew when he was being watched. He did not need to see Rindt to know that he was here. Perhaps it would be better to forgo Jerusalem and head directly for Rome.

He realized Nula had asked him a question and was waiting expectantly for an answer.

"I'm sorry?"

"I asked if you were Sephardic," Nula repeated. "Soares does not sound like a Jewish name, unless your people originated in Spain—and you do have that look. Forgive me; I'm being rude. What must you think of me? Here we have barely met, and I'm asking you such questions—!"

Peter laughed, his laughter loud, defiant, echoing off the hills. Let Rindt hear.

"I don't think you're rude at all. I think you're . . . charming. And very perceptive. What makes you so certain I'm a Jew?"

Nula looked embarrassed. "Just a guess. A feeling. You're very genuine, not like most of the Americans I meet."

He took her elbow and led her around to the other side of the bus, where a sliver of shade remained; they took shelter there. If Rindt had had a clear view of them before, he would not now. They could hear the others coming back from the inn, scuffling down the goat path, all talking at once.

"Your group will be leaving soon," Peter suggested. "Maybe I should take a hike, hm? Disappear before tongues start wagging."

"We're just talking; there's no harm in that." A slight dew of perspiration had formed on her upper lip; she dabbed at it with a fine linen handkerchief retrieved from her purse. "Let them gossip! Old hens. They have nothing better to do."

From his new position, Rindt watched Peter place the tour bus between them and smiled his appreciation of a worthy opponent. He could still see the two pairs of feet—the woman's and Peter's—standing near the bus's right front tire. If Peter's should suddenly disappear, Rindt would go into action. He watched as the rest of the tourists straggled back onto the bus, saw it start up and begin the laborious climb back up to the paved road, raising a bigger cloud of dust than it had with its arrival.

Even before the dust had entirely settled, Peter was gone. Perplexed, Rindt scanned the vicinity, his better-than-20/20 vision examining every rock and clump of brush. He had hardly expected Peter to stand out in the open waving to the bus as it departed, but a man his age couldn't move that quickly. Rindt had assumed he would head back to the inn, or follow the bus up to the road. On an outside chance, he might have asked the driver to let him ride the few hundred feet to the road itself, save him the trek up the dirt path, but Rindt knew these Sabra entrepreneurs to be sticklers for official procedure. No tour ticket, no admission to the bus. Was Peter that persuasive?

The bus paused as if to catch its breath at the top of the rise, then swung onto the road. Rindt watched. It hadn't stopped long enough to open the doors, and no one had stepped out. Was Peter still on the bus, his generosity with American dollars perhaps convincing the driver to take him as far as town?

Allowing himself a moment of pure rage, Rindt moved off at double time. Even if he jogged back to his car, would he be able to overtake the tour bus before it blended into a herd of its fellows amid the cabs and cars and pedestrians and handcarts in the crowded streets of Tel Aviv?

Watching Rindt sprint for the highway, Peter chuckled, rubbing his calloused hands together in quiet glee. There were more goat paths through these hills than hairs on the back of a man's hand, more caves and secret places for a young boy to hide in, or an old man to take refuge in, than Rindt or his kind would ever know. Stretching the years out of his spine, hearing the bones crack, Peter thanked Nic Soares once more for keeping this body in such excellent shape, and set off the way he had come, back to Tel Aviv.

"Your Eminence?" Giuliana groped for her travel alarm and frowned in disbelief. "It's after two A.M."

"Is it?" Cosa seemed genuinely surprised. "Forgive me, my dear. An old man gets confused by the sunlight streaming through his window and forgets that it is not the same time everywhere in God's creation.''

Giuliana sat up in bed, now fully awake. She was not taken in by Cosa's ingenuousness. Cosa forgot nothing. He had deliberately called her in the middle of the night to make certain she was still here, and alone.

Or perhaps, she thought, he really is losing it. Losing control—of the procedure, of Peter, of all his plots and plans. She could almost pity him. Yet she remained on the alert.

''What is it that you want, Eminence?'' she asked cautiously.

''Reassurance, my dear. Reassurance that you are still there, in San Diego, still working with Dr. Shepard to locate our brother Peter before some harm comes to him. Our times must seem so strange to him; he is like a lamb among wolves.''

Giuliana continued to frown in the darkness, pulling the covers up around her shoulders against a sudden chill. There was a plaintiveness to Cosa's voice that alarmed her. If it was genuine, he was losing it, and that made him unpredictable, dangerous. Then again, it could be a performance worthy of the Palme d'Or at Cannes.

''Eminence, I assure you, Peter is no lamb. He can take care of himself, wherever he has gone.''

''And you have no thoughts about that, my dear?'' Cosa prompted, some of the old canniness returning to his tone.

''Who can say?'' Giuliana temporized. ''Perhaps he only needed some space, as the Americans say. A chance to walk out under the sky and listen to the wind in the trees, to stretch his wings. I know he felt very confined here. He may return tomorrow or the next day. That is why I thought it best to remain, in spite of your summoning me back to Rome.''

If he felt she had second-guessed him, Cosa gave no indication.

''That is probably the wisest course for now, my dear. And Dr. Shepard? Where is he now?''

''One would assume he is home in bed, Your Eminence!'' Giuliana replied sharply, as if the question offended her.

There was a silence on the line before Cosa said: ''Forgive me, Giuliana. The question was inappropriate. Where else would he be? If you would not mind, I will call you again in a few days, *si*?''

"*Si*, of course.''

"Only next time, I will check the clock first, eh?''

Giuliana replaced the receiver against the sound of Cosa's self-deprecating laughter, the most unsettling sound she had ever heard. For a long moment she listened to the darkness tick around her. Then a secret smile stole over her lips, and she hugged herself in silent satisfaction. She had thrown Cosa off the trail, buying time, she hoped, for Andrew and Peter both. With a clear conscience she lay back on the pillow and, for the first time in weeks, slept like a baby.

The low-slung oblong of native red sandstone that is the main building of Ben Gurion International Airport is in neither Tel Aviv nor Jerusalem, but the little town of Lod, a twenty-minute drive from the former, thirty minutes from the latter. Taxis are available from either city around the clock; there is also bus service provided by El Al, the official airline of Israel, which runs from six in the morning until ten at night. Most departees prefer to take a *sherut*, a taxi that can accommodate as many as seven people.

Passengers leaving Israel are required to pay an airport tax of a few shekels and then, in this land where rain is a rarity, walk outside the terminal in order to get to their plane. Those carrying European or American passports are passed through Customs with a minimum of fuss, unless they are of Arab ancestry. These unfortunates are lumped in with their brethren from Arabic countries, and it may take hours for Customs officials to examine every item in their luggage to complete satisfaction.

At the ticket counter this busy afternoon, a quiet difference of opinion was taking place.

"I'm sorry, sir,'' a doe-eyed Sabra with the name "Darya'' printed in English and Hebrew on her El Al name tag told the American Nicolao Soares sincerely. "That flight is completely booked. I cannot switch your ticket from tomorrow's flight to today's, not even on standby.''

"Every single seat is taken?'' Peter wondered aloud. "I wouldn't mind standing.''

Darya studied him to see if he was joking. "I'm sorry, sir. There's really nothing I can do. You'll have to come back tomorrow. Now, if you'll kindly step aside so I can serve those waiting behind you . . ."

Tomorrow may be too late! Peter wanted to tell her. The hair on the back of his neck told him Rindt was nearby, if not already in the terminal. Peter might succeed in concealing himself in Jerusalem overnight, but he would still have to return here tomorrow to get on the flight he had booked the day he arrived. Not only would he be an easy target for Rindt but, unless Rindt's aim was dead-on in such crowded quarters, so would anyone else who got in the colonel's way.

He would not have that on his conscience. He hadn't felt so hemmed in since that night at Caiaphas's gate.

Lost in thought, Peter moved through the crowd, the colorful clothing and babble of tongues reminding him all too acutely of that day in the temple. As he wandered aimlessly, one voice began to distinguish itself from the masses. Loud, abrasive, speaking American English with a trace of an Eastern European accent, it bore into Peter's consciousness like water dripping on stone.

"*Nu*, am I asking so much? Eight years I've worked for these people, since my wife, God rest her, passed away. 'Here, Morris, take this to Beijing. Here, Morris, this is a rush to Berlin.' Beijing—! By a week I missed Tiananmen Square; who knew but maybe they were going to start shooting Americans too? And since when was a Jew ever comfortable in Berlin, even with the Wall down? Worse, in fact, because East Germans are bigger anti-Semites than the West; trust me on this. Every hot spot in the world I been to, delivering packages for these people.

"Do I ever ask what I'm delivering, it's so urgent? Do I ever complain? So why now, when I ask for one extra day in Jerusalem, do I get *tsoris* from these people? 'One extra day,' I ask them. 'There was a disturbance in the Old City—Arab kids throwing rocks, a bomb threat, who knows?—but I didn't get to the Wailing Wall. One more day to say Kaddish at the Wall,' I ask them. 'Can't you find someone else, this package is so urgent?' 'We don't have anybody else,' they tell me. So, tag, I'm it! How do I get so lucky?"

Curious in spite of his predicament, Peter followed the

voice to its source, an obese and sweating man about his own age in a yellow guayabera shirt and thick bifocals, Dockers slung low enough to accommodate his ample belly, a legal-sized parcel about five inches thick, sealed in bubble wrap and then in Tyvek and labeled profusely, clutched possessively in both hands.

Not surprisingly, there was an empty seat to the complainer's left. Peter ducked into it. The annoyed-looking woman to the man's right, the unwilling auditor of his long-winded monologue, suddenly remembered an urgent errand at the duty-free shop and hurried away. Delighted to discover a fresh audience, the man beamed at Peter.

"*Boker tov!* You're waiting for the flight to Rome?"

Peter made a noncommittal gesture. "I was hoping to get on standby, but . . ."

"We've all got our troubles!" The man released one side of the package from his grip and offered a thick-fingered hand. "Morris Steinberg, Brooklyn, New York."

"Nic Soares, San Diego, California. I couldn't help overhearing your difficulties. How did you get into such a predicament?"

"I'm a courier," Morris explained, ever so happy to tell his story again. "Usually it's a wonderful deal. You hook up with corporations that need packages delivered person-to-person around the world. The company pays for everything—airfare, hotels, cab fare; you even get a meal allowance. Sometimes it's in and out in one day, but more often than not you wait around for a return package. You can spend up to two weeks in a place that way. A chance to see the world. I've been to London, Buenos Aires, Hong Kong, just about everywhere in the Caribbean; you'd be amazed."

"It sounds fascinating," Peter concurred. He had seen the telltale movement of shadow against shadow in his peripheral vision. Rindt was here. Rindt, who as Special Papal Liaison had diplomatic immunity from such inconveniences as metal detectors and Customs searches, who could come and go as he pleased. Sitting down, Peter was less visible, but he knew Rindt would find him eventually, by sense of smell if need be. "How did you get involved in such a thing?"

"Something my daughter suggested," Morris explained, looking suddenly morose. "To keep me out of her hair once my wife died. It all happened so fast! I'd just retired; Shirley and I were going to do nothing but travel—is that an irony?—when a shadow turns up on her mammogram. Two years later—surgery, radiation, chemotherapy, nothing helped. My beautiful lady, my sweetheart, was gone."

His grating voice had gone soft, and there were tears in it. He dabbed at his eyes beneath the thick glasses, found a packet of Kleenex in his shirt pocket, blew his nose noisily.

"I'm very sorry for you, my friend," Peter said sincerely. Rindt was scanning the Departures schedule without attempting to conceal himself. He wanted Peter to know he was here. Beside Peter, Morris Steinberg had gotten control of his grief.

"You sound like a man who knows from his own experience. You're also a widower?"

Peter nodded.

"You never really get over it, do you? We always expect to go first. And the way Shirley went, wasting away to skin and bone . . . I had to steel myself to go to the hospital every day, so she wouldn't see in my eyes how terrible she looked . . ."

"She's at peace now," Peter told him. Rindt turned away from the Departures schedule, scanning the crowd yet again, deliberately placing himself so that he could be seen from everywhere in the terminal.

He wants me to panic, Peter thought. *He'd like me to flee, to prolong the chase.*

"You say that with such confidence, Nic." Morris sounded almost angry. "How the hell do you know?"

Catlike, Rindt moved toward the line at the ticket counter. When he reached Darya, he flashed an identification of some sort and immediately earned her complete cooperation.

Bang, you're born! Peter thought, and gave his full attention to Morris Steinberg.

"Don't you? Listen to her, Morris. After forty years together, don't you still hear Shirley in your heart? What is she saying to you?"

In the din of Ben Gurion Airport, Morris grew very quiet. Suddenly he laughed.

"She's saying 'Morris, enough! Stop whining and get on with your life!' She had a friend, Judith; they went to Julia Richmond High School together. Judith's a teacher, retired. Thirty-seven years with the New York City Public Schools; this is a tough lady! Widowed since forever. Do you know, Shirley was trying to match me up with her? Judith would come sit with her in the hospital, but as soon as I walked in she'd leave, like she was shy or something. Shirley would whisper to me, 'Morris, look after Judith when I'm gone.' At the funeral, my daughter tells me she told Judith the same thing! Wasting away to sixty-five pounds, the pain so bad even morphine wasn't helping, and she's playing match-maker, God love her!"

Morris's eyes welled up again, this time with joy. "You're right, Nic. God would have to love such a beautiful lady, would have to give her peace after such suffering. Maybe I should take her advice, give Judith a call when I get back to Brooklyn." He sighed. "I just wish I had one more day, to go to the Wailing Wall!"

Peter's ticket was in his hand. He held it out to Morris.

"What's this?"

"Tomorrow's flight to Rome. I'll trade you. I've had a sudden change of plans, have to be there by tonight. It's rather urgent. And I'll deliver your package for you."

Morris looked dubious. "I don't know. It's not that I don't trust you, but if you don't know Rome, you could get awfully lost."

"My friend, I did business in Rome for over fifteen years. Know it like the back of my hand. Give me your daughter's telephone number and I'll call her the minute I've made the delivery. Trust me."

Morris thought for a minute longer, then decided.

"A *mitzvah* for you, a *mitzvah* for me." He pulled out his ticket and they made the swap. He scribbled his daughter's number on the outside of the folder. "I can't thank you enough. You're a lifesaver! If you're ever in Brooklyn— . . ."

"I'll be sure to look you up."

Darya blanked the screen where the passenger list had scrolled by under Rindt's scrutiny.

"Mr. Soares has a seat on tomorrow's flight to Rome,

Colonel. Arrives DaVinci Airport at 2300 hours. I hope that's helpful.''

"Very helpful, thank you,'' Rindt replied, and turned to leave, though not quickly enough to see a rugged, gray-haired man hand his ticket to the flight attendant who had just announced the departure of Flight 87 to Rome.

"*Boker tov,* Mr. Steinberg. Did you enjoy your stay in Israel?''

"Very much,'' Peter replied. "It was like coming home.''

He would not relax entirely until he had watched the attendants seal the door and heard the increase in engine noise that would be his final assurance that he was about to be airborne while Jurgen Rindt was still on the ground. Still, Peter thought as he settled himself in his aisle seat and fastened the lap belt, he could get used to this flying business.

He had been among the first to board. Now he observed as the cabin filled with passengers, most of them Italian. He listened avidly, once again absorbing as much of the language as he could. To his amazement, he heard a familiar voice.

"Oh, I don't believe it! Such a small world! Why didn't you tell me you were going to Rome this very evening?''

"I wanted to surprise you,'' Peter replied, concealing his own surprise. He rose to greet her, careful not to bump his head on the overhead compartment. "Where are you sitting, Nula?''

She showed him her boarding pass. "Right next to you, apparently.''

"He is coming to Rome at last.'' Rindt spat out the words in his irritation. "In fact, he is most likely there already.''

He had waited twenty-four hours, returning to Ben Gurion only to hear the flight attendant address an overweight American in thick glasses and a loud Hawaiian shirt as "Mr. Soares.'' Cosa didn't need to know this. Rindt would not give Cosa the opportunity to lecture him about letting Peter get away not once but twice.

"Coming home, then?'' asked Cosa. "And he does not know that His Holiness is still at Lago di Garda.''

"He makes our work easier, no?'' Rindt was confident

of Cosa's general intent but blind, as usual, to the specifics until he needed to know. That was how he, not Cosa, insisted it should be.

"*Bene*. He will wish to meet his successor. Excellent!" observed the cardinal.

"After all this, you *want* him to meet His Holiness, Your Eminence?"

"Of course not, Rindt. The pontiff is on holiday for another four days. That buys some time, but not much. We must make certain they do not meet. Here, then, is what you must do . . ."

Here, high in the Apennines, he could pretend that he wasn't the pope, could enjoy simple pleasures like other men.

In the center of the deep lake, a mile from the nearest shore, Stephen Parnell felt closer to God. Even the high altar in the Basilica San Pietro couldn't bring him closer to the saints than this small boat on this sprawling mountain lake. He looked around the still-dark coastline and imagined others waking to this paradise, finding peace in its remoteness.

The lake's glassy surface reflected gray light. He noticed the glow of the approaching sun over the far peak just as a pike snapped and rippled the stillness. *A big one*, he thought. Didn't he see the generous breakfast awaiting him at the end of his line? He heard a small cough drift across the morning from miles away. Another life, a mortal universe pursuing its fate.

The surface of the lake erupted in a small geyser four hundred meters to his left. When he turned to look, he saw only the splash made by a leaping fish. The thought occurred to Luke John that maybe the fish was reaching for heaven, trying to break the bonds of its existence below for the light and color above, even as, perhaps, the angels watched the surface of our universe and noticed when a human spirit penetrated their sphere.

You're getting fatuous in your old age, boyo! Parnell chided himself. *Spinning spiritual metaphors out of the simplicity of God's natural world. Enjoy it for what it is!*

He didn't really want to catch a fish. He just wanted to anticipate the catch, the thrill of the connection. He offered a silent prayer of thanks for the moment. The sun answered by peering above the far ridge and painting the opposite wall of the Alpine valley with broad strokes of golden light. *So beautiful, this place*, he thought. *So rare these times.*

He reeled in his line and laughed when he saw the hook picked clean of its bait. After wedging the pole securely under the bench, he took one last appreciative look around the lake. Then, placing one hand on the outboard engine's casing, he gripped the cord with the other and yanked firmly to start the engine. It coughed and sputtered encouragement but failed to turn over.

Getting too soft, thought the pope. He stood, braced his left foot on the transom, and gripped the cord handle with both hands this time. Leaning into it with all the strength in his aging body, he yanked sharply. The engine sparked to life and began to develop a satisfying throaty whine. As he turned to sit down, the sky flashed orange.

A loud explosion ripped the atmosphere and sucked the air from his lungs. Before he could find a handhold, the boat lifted high and the stern vanished in a hail of splinters. He saw only foaming dark lake water beneath him.

Gasping, he flew toward the darkness. Before he could comprehend, shock waves coursed through his body. He hit the water and sank into the frigid blackness.

24

PETER THREADED PAST THE ROTUND, MISTY-HAIRED curator of the ancient prison, into the damp chill of the underground chamber. The Tullianum, where he had suffered his final days, was now a shrine. A *sacellum*! The presence of the San Pietro in Carcere chapel, built in 1598 over the subterranean cell, couldn't comfort him. This place had been a dead end for state enemies two thousand years ago and it still smelled of despair.

Stepping down, Peter entered a small adamantine room with a high, arched stone-block ceiling. He looked up and saw the familiar imprint of the square opening in the dome. Once the orifice through which buckets were lowered to retrieve water from the cistern, it had been bricked in by his jailers. Even sunlight, the simplest blessing in a condemned prisoner's ebbing life, was locked away. There was no mercy at the Mamertine prison.

Busts of Paul and himself gazed fiercely over the room from a niche perched above the altar. Peter found the sculptor's impression of him intriguing. Had he looked anything like that? Turning, he was confronted by a large panel, a roster in blood and lampblack of the most prominent victims imprisoned here.

He couldn't read the odd Italian, but his memory of Latin and Greek helped him decipher some of the phrases. His and Paul's names appeared first on a long list of Romans and non-Roman "guests" of the Tullianum. All had been executed by the sentries, four under Nero, another under Severo, four under Decio, and so on. He hadn't known these men and women, yet his heart broke for them.

Continuing down, he picked out a word here and there. At the bottom, he recognized the command "*Silenzio.*" Checking his pocket dictionary, he slowly deciphered the rest: "Your footsteps honor in silence the terrible, glorious echoes of twenty-five centuries of history."

To his left was a depression in the stone wall behind a heavy iron grate. Above the grate was a carved inscription that read: "In this stone Peter was pushed by the sentries and the miracle remains."

Was this where the Hole had been? Or did his skull make this dent in the stone? He could hear Petronilla's sobs, hear himself trying to comfort her. Shuddering as he recalled his torment here, the worst punishment was his confinement in the dark, followed closely by his exit through the *cloaca maxima*.

Below the depression in the stone wall, stairs descended through the floor into what had been his prison cell. Down he went into the dank, semicircular dungeon twelve feet across and six feet high. Once confined in the dim space, he wanted to flee, but he was determined to confront his memory. The massive walls leaned inward, compounding the claustrophobic hopelessness of the place. Dripping water sounded from somewhere deep in the granite, it was impossible to know where. A small stone ledge rose from the floor around a spring that had once fed groundwater into the chamber. The stones under his feet had been worn down by millions of pilgrims over the centuries. Yet he still recognized them. His feet had memorized the small terrain centuries ago—its precise slope, its protrusions of uneven blocks and familiar seams.

The walls glistened in the faint light. To his left was the rough stone pillar to which he had been chained. Its sheer banality wounded him more deeply than anything else he had seen. Bending down to touch the post in the floor, he thought of the countless innocents who had despaired beside this scar in the stone. How much blood had drained into this depression and commingled with the dust of the dead?

"Peter?"

Turning, he saw Giuliana.

"Wha—!"

"It *is* you!" she exclaimed, at once furious and relieved.

Peter raised himself from the floor, and smiled at her incongruous beauty. She was a flower in this desolate, sunless place.

"Leave. You should not be here," he tried to stop her before she started in on him.

But she wasn't listening.

"How could you do this?" she seethed. "Don't you realize how much danger there is in what you're doing?"

"*St!*" hissed Peter as her voice rose. "Danger!? What in God's name will happen when Cosa discovers you have come after me? Who knows you're here?"

"No one. I couldn't just sit in La Jolla waiting for the cardinal to call. Not while you and Andrew were out here with Rindt closing in! You are in danger, Peter." Her concern overwhelmed her anger.

"I know. Now you, too. You mean Rindt."

"*Si, penso così.* I think so."

Peter chuckled. "I know so. He followed me to Bethsaida, then to Jerusalem." He waved away Giuliana's distress. "It's only here in Rome that I've managed to elude him. He must know I am here. I can't imagine why he hasn't followed this far."

"He will. Or if not he, then those who work for him. They could be anywhere." She gestured at the claustrophobic walls.

"As they were two thousand years ago. But am I to leave off what I'm doing out of fear? No, not this time. I must do what I must do!"

As she realized what he was saying, Giuliana was startled into momentary silence.

"What? What are you here to do, Peter?" she asked.

"Something is wrong," he said, frowning at the uneven stones of the floor. "I believe I am here to fix it. The only way I know to do that is to speak to this pope. But what words am I to say, when I of all the ones the master chose always had the greatest struggle to find the words . . ." He beamed at her suddenly. "The master is testing me. One of his little jokes. Andrew says he cannot imagine Jesus having a sense of humor. If he only knew—!

"I must find the words. I must fix what's wrong." He took her hands. "That's all I know. As for you, you have to trust me and let me go."

"Where?" Giuliana cried. "Where are you staying, how will I know where to find you? If anything were to happen to you. . . . You must tell me where to find you."

Peter lifted her chin and looked into her eyes.

"And if I did, would you be able to keep that knowledge from Rindt? Or Andrew?"

Giuliana looked away at last. "No," she said softly.

"Thank you for your courage. You will see me again. I promise."

He was moving away from her. Giuliana touched his arm. "In this life?"

Peter gave her a wink and turned to leave.

"I'm serious, Your Holiness. Where can I find you? And when?"

Peter thought for a moment and looked up the stairs to see if anyone was listening. He returned to Giuliana and whispered, "At the place of my greatest triumph." With that he turned and was up the stairs before she realized what he meant.

"When, Peter?" Her voice echoed between the oppressive stone walls. "When do I meet you?"

Peter didn't hear her. The place he had known so intimately in his final terror held intense power over him still, and it was getting to him. He couldn't intellectualize it. He rushed up to the chapel, glanced again at the litany of martyrs, and climbed up the next flight of stairs into the sunlight, where he paused for air.

After walking for several blocks, he sat down heavily on a bench on the Palatine hill overlooking the city. The hills opened expectantly in the direct sunlight. What did Rome expect of him?

It has always been this way, he thought. Strife behind every door, fear hardening every heart. In his time it had been the Pharisees, the Sadducees, and the Romans. Who now? There was no end to the fear. Nothing had changed. If Jesus were to appear again, he would be arrested and tried again. Those who believed themselves to be faithful would kill him. Again.

How was he to end it?

He leaned back and lifted his face to the sun. *How?*

The cab skidded to a stop before the sun-bleached San Pietro in Carcere on Via dei Fori Imperiali; the driver twisted around and impatiently thrust his hand out. Andrew dropped twenty thousand lire into his palm and escaped to the sidewalk.

He had roamed these streets for nearly two weeks, running up BioGenera's expense account, feeling more and more the fool. Maybe Giuliana was right and Peter wasn't here. Maybe he'd gone to Israel after all and Rindt had found him, arranged some sort of "accident." He could leave the body in the desert where it would never be found. No one would ever know.

The pope was due back in town today; if Peter didn't turn up soon Andrew would have to leave. He called Delphine every couple of days, and she'd told him Gindman was about at the end of his tether. Andrew tried explaining that he was employing his best scientific method, retracing the steps of Peter's life, roving his old haunts. Delphine had been impressed. Gindman hadn't.

Looking around at the skeletal remains of Imperial Rome, vigilant for Peter's aggressive gait and gray-white hair, Andrew saw only dark Romans, blond tourists, and merchants.

Nearby, along a walkway to the chapel, an English-language plaque identified this area as the crossroads of the ancient world, the place where Rome's conquering armies returned to victory celebrations that lasted for days. Despite his anxiety about finding Peter, the significance of this place distracted him. He imagined Peter, condemned and hopeless, forced to march down this cobbled street in a humiliating final struggle to his death. There was more to what he was feeling than mere imagination; it was the same spark he always felt on the verge of an insight, a breakthrough to the next level in an experiment. "Intuition" was not a word a scientist ought to use lightly. A hunch, then. Something was about to happen.

Andrew found the stairs that led from the street into the Mamertine and hurried down them, feeling instantly hemmed in. Seeing the panels of martyrs, the altar, and the dented stone with the iron bars over it didn't help. He barely glanced at the busts of Peter and Paul in his haste. He knew he was close.

The familiar click of her heels registered first. When he looked up, there she was before him, brow furrowed in concentration. Just then she looked up too. She started to brighten, then froze, wearing a Mona Lisa expression of guarded affection.

Andrew read her thoughts and cursed himself for whatever it was he'd done to hurt her. He wanted to resign his life and start again with a new identity. But Giuliana had a different goal. She needed to save Peter, for reasons even more urgent than Andrew's. So he stood there in the ancient dungeon, off balance and unsure, waiting for her to speak first.

He was close enough to touch her yet a lifetime away. She didn't trust herself, so she waited for a hint in his expression. He was hardened by travel, rumpled by fatigue, his emotions anonymous, like bird scratches in sand.

Seeing him like this, after two weeks of separation from him, two weeks during which she'd endured stampeding doubts and self-recrimination, should have been easier, but it was more difficult. She loved him for making her feel whole again. She hated him for making her so dependent upon him for happiness.

"I called your hotel last night," he said. "They told me

you weren't answering. I couldn't imagine where you'd be. Couldn't imagine—''

"That I'd follow you here? It was time, Andrew. Peter is here."

He couldn't help laughing. "You sound so damned confident! Just because you work for the Vatican doesn't mean you've got some inside track—"

"He is here, Andrew. I just spoke to him."

"You just—" The information rocked Andrew. "Just now, here." Giuliana nodded. "And you let him go?!"

She gestured helplessly. "How could I not, Andrew? Who are we to say what's right or wrong? He has a mission here. We can only let him fulfill it."

"I—oh, damn it! *Damn* it!"

Andrew wanted to shout, wanted to smash something. Every cell in his being resisted what she was saying, even as he wanted to believe she was right, that she had some insight, some perspective he couldn't see. Was that faith?

He believed in Giuliana, believed in her as he believed in life. Let that be his faith, for now.

"I hope you're right," was all he said. "God, I hope you're right!"

"Mike's not going to like your letting Peter go," Delphine observed plainly. Andrew had taken the responsibility on himself without mentioning Giuliana.

"He doesn't have to know," he suggested. "Not for a while yet."

"Frankly, Andrew, I don't know how long I can keep him in the dark, but I'll do my best."

"Thanks," Andrew said sincerely. "I knew I could count on you."

"Giuliana's with you, isn't she?" Delphine asked after a long moment.

"How'd you know?"

"I didn't. It was just a guess. A hope, actually," she added in a whisper.

The line was quiet. Andrew was embarrassed . . . and grateful.

"I'll make everything right, Delphine. Trust me."

"I hope you know what you're doing. There's going to be hell to pay when you get back."

"I'll take my chances."

He hung up the phone in the lobby of the hotel, went to the lounge, ordered drinks, and waited for Giuliana while she checked in with Monsignor Murphy. He tried to relax, but it was useless. Pretense was more exhausting than surrender to fear, so he paced and made a bad show of himself. He felt as if he was holding on to the edge of a cliff with one hand while it crumbled under his increasingly desperate grasp.

If he'd known what he was setting in motion, would he have been so confident? However this turned out, would he ever be confident again?

"I am certain that His Eminence is wanting to speak with you, Dottore Sabatini." Monsignor Murphy was stalling again. "Can't you please hold the line?"

What a thankless job, thought Giuliana, *to always be on the verge of a lie, without actually telling the lie!* Did Murphy have ulcers? Would he someday?

"No, *Monsignore*, really. I am very close to finding Peter. There is no time to—"

Cardinal Cosa picked up the extension, oozing ominous charm. "*Buon giorno*, my dear. Have you found him?"

"Your Eminence, I think it is only a matter of time before I do. I have, after all, only arrived in Rome. A few days—"

"How much time, exactly?"

"I cannot say, of course," she answered truthfully, grateful now that Peter had refused to tell her where he was staying. "Peter is a clever man."

"One would expect no less. Perhaps you can use some assistance?" the cardinal offered. "Colonel Rindt has also returned to Rome. In fact, he is probably not far from you at this moment." The cardinal's tone had acquired a self-satisfied lilt that frightened her.

"Has he any news for us?" she asked, trying to hold her ground.

"For us?" Cosa repeated and paused, letting her feeble presumption hang by a thread in the silence. "No. He thought Peter would go to Jerusalem, then reconsidered and is now in Rome.''

I can just imagine! Giuliana thought. Peter had mentioned Rindt's ''following'' him from Jerusalem to Rome. How much had he not told her?

''Interesting that he should consider Jerusalem. That was clever. I am impressed with Colonel Rindt's initiative. But apparently he did not find Peter in Israel, or he would not now be in Rome.''

She waited for Cosa's reaction to that, but there was none.

''You have come to know Peter very well, have you not, my dear?'' he asked her at last. Now it was Giuliana's turn to respond with silence. ''I am confident you will find him.

''I understand that Dottore Shepard is also in Rome.'' He switched tacks so suddenly that she was unprepared to respond. ''It occurs to me that you might pursue your search together. Join forces, as it were. Have you encountered each other?''

''Dottore Shepard left San Diego nearly two weeks before I did,'' Giuliana temporized. ''I assume he is conducting his search alone.'' It was not a complete lie, she thought.

''Giuliana?''

''Yes, Your Eminence?''

''I have faith in your judgment. I know that you are under stress, and I worry for you. Do I make myself clear?''

''Clear, Your Eminence?''

He might as well be holding a gun to her head. Or the keys to heaven. She wasn't going to fall for it this time. She knew the keeper of the keys personally. He had taught her to believe in a force beyond the Church. She had found faith—in Andrew, in Peter, in herself. She might never see Peter again, she might never again have Andrew as her own, but she knew she could live with herself. The cardinal couldn't frighten her now.

''*Si,* Your Eminence. I understand. You have nothing to fear in this important matter.'' She sounded appropriately deferential. Let him be satisfied with the illusion of control.

''*Bene*, I thought so. I must go now. His Holiness awaits,'' he added unnecessarily. ''God bless you, child.''

The line clicked off and Giuliana sat for a few minutes reminding herself of her newfound strength of spirit. She had used up a great deal of it dealing with Cosa. Andrew was waiting for her in the lounge. She would need a little bit more.

Andrew waited until she'd seated herself in an overstuffed leather chair before he sat. They made idle conversation until they ran out of words, then stared at each other uneasily across the barren no-man's-land they had created between them. It was Giuliana who crossed the open space.

"Andrew, what I want to say . . ." she began with a strength she didn't really feel. "I'm sorry about the way we ended. I don't have any claim on you . . ."

"Yes, you do."

She knew what he meant. He was fighting the impossible.

"You're married to your Church," he continued, recognizing her dilemma, reluctant to look her in the eye. Then, without preamble, he was arguing for her claim. "But you're not a nun. You're not bound by celibacy. Loving me doesn't violate your vow."

"It isn't that simple!" she corrected him. "I thought it was at first, but—" She couldn't finish.

"But what?" he asked quietly.

"I hurt. I have never felt so alone. I don't want to feel this way!"

"Don't you think I hurt, too? I was beginning to think it was my fate. Then I fell in love with you. You're all I can think about, all I want to think about. Peter needs me; he needs us. But I don't think I'm any good to anyone, not without you. I'm lost without you, Giuliana."

She came over to him. "Hold me!" she said so softly that he nearly didn't hear her. "Just hold me, Andrew, please?"

She melted into his body and immediately felt better as her polarity matched his.

"You're a lot of trouble," she whispered past his ear. "Maybe too much trouble for one lifetime!"

"Me?" he laughed. "I've got everything that's supposed to matter on the line for you, for whatever this is we have."

"I'm worth it," she assured him. "Not easy, but worth it."

He laughed again and held her tighter.

"Peter's near the end of his search," she whispered. "I'm certain of it. Let's give him the time he wants, alone. This is my city, my *Roma*. I want to share it with you."

As they were leaving, someone turned up the volume on the television in the corner of the lounge, causing them both to turn and look. While a breathless Italian voice-over urgently recounted facts of the breaking news story, scenes of floating debris (parts of a small boat, thought Andrew) washing up onto the shore played across the screen. The Chyron title in the upper left corner of the screen identified the lake as Lago di Garda.

"Madonna!" Giuliana gasped and pressed her hands to her face.

"What is it? What's he saying?"

The scene cut to file videotape of a recent papal audience depicting Pope Luke John blessing a little girl. The girl's mother wept openly and wiped her eyes with a handkerchief as her child respectfully answered the pontiff's questions. The scene then cut back to the debris and widened to show the reporter gesturing toward the middle of the lake and explaining in agitated tones to viewers. His Italian was rushed and emphatic. Images of several cardinals arriving at the Apostolic Palace were followed by a scene of Cardinal Cosa welcoming them into a high-ceilinged, gilded hall and disappearing behind tall doors framed by Swiss Guards.

"What's happening?" Andrew asked again.

"Oh my God, Andrew! The pope! He was nearly killed in a boating accident in the north," she explained. Her face was pale with the news. "He's alive, but it's a miracle from the sound of it. He is in hospital here."

"Cosa didn't mention it when you talked with him?"

"No," Giuliana said. "No, he did not. In fact, he made a point of telling me he was on his way to a meeting with His Holiness before he rang off."

They stared unblinking at one another, thinking.

"Well, now, isn't that interesting?" Andrew asked wryly. Giuliana was too stunned to speak.

"Let's get out of here." Andrew took her arm. "We've got to find Peter."

"That may be dangerous, Andrew."

"I can handle it. What choice do we have?"

"Not dangerous for us. For Peter."

Andrew recognized her meaning. He was off balance again, a student of danger. Back in San Diego it had been he who warned her of the dangers to Peter; here their roles were reversed. "Right. He needs time. He may be safer without us near him."

"Let's give him until morning," she suggested, comfortable with leadership for the moment.

"The pope. What about the pope?"

"It is better we stay away until we understand what is happening. He is safer without us too near right now, I think."

Andrew knew she was right and nodded, consenting to follow her lead. "So what do we do now?"

She threaded her arm under Andrew's, drew herself close to him, and led the way to the Metro.

25 NOT COUNTING THOSE THREE YEARS BETWEEN GAL-ilee and Golgotha, Rome was where Peter felt he had accomplished the most. There were milestones for him here. Like distant friends, a natural confidence developed between him and the eternal city as they got reacquainted. He carried his secret through the narrow streets, oblivious to the standard tours of ruins and temples, intent on the real Rome. And Rome opened itself to his memories.

He walked at a furious pace, matching his zest for the glory days against the youthful reflexes of Roman drivers. He passed the Coliseum while most of the tour buses stopped there; its construction hadn't begun until eight years after his death and it held no interest for him. He continued down the Via dei Cerchi past the Circus Maximus, another structure that came after him, on through the Piazza Numa Pompilio, down the Via di Porta San Sebastiano, through the gate of the same name, and out onto the Via Appia Antica.

Outside the old city wall he climbed a short rise to a cluster of overgrown markers. There among the untended limestone he knelt and paid his respects to his friend and "Apostle to the Gentiles," Paul. There were no plaques, no signposts. All he had to guide him was his memory of that afternoon, of Paul's stubborn dignity before his death, of the muted thud of an ax blade into wood.

He strode by the worn entrances of a hundred churches, passing one for the promise of the next. Then one old sanctuary caught his imagination. Gray and blanketed in soot outside, its interior was polished and stone cool. Twenty great columns with Doric capitals formed a vast nave and channeled his line of sight to a tomb with sculptures of Moses and Rachel and Leah standing defiantly behind a low iron rail. Up front, preserved in a splendid gold chest with clear glass sides were—he stepped closer to be sure—yes, inside, hanging like funereal drapery, were the rusted chains that had bound his wrists and feet during his imprisonment in the Mamertine.

He checked for a plaque that would explain. *San Pietro in Vincoli*. Saint Peter in Chains.

The pavement underneath his footsteps featured stunning squares and circles of porphyry, marble, and granite. Minute cracks spanned the majority of members crosswise. Fitted with tender mastery, they revealed character in a thousand ways, testifying to the roughshod passage of troubled centuries. Although they were meticulously kept, there were rivulets of fine amber moss in the crevices between them where winter rains migrated patiently under the floors.

When a sprawling cataract of golden sunlight found the high altar, a motion beside the tabernacle attracted his eye. He moved closer and detected the lazy movement of a fluffy tail. A saffron-eyed tabby, nestled between a taper's brass base and the tabernacle, extended her paw as if to wave. She yawned widely, studiously, her dignified stare holding Peter, who smiled contentedly for the first time since arriving in this ancient city.

He knelt and offered a brief prayer while the tabby watched him, her contented purr reverberating throughout the chapel. With a nod to her, he rose and left.

•   •   •

Outside, he rested in a small piazza while he weighed what to do next. He had ventured near the Apostolic Palace, where all the guidebooks indicated the pope appeared on the balcony weekly to bless the gathered crowds, only to find the crowd sparse and abuzz with rumors. He hadn't risked drawing attention to himself by asking questions; it was clear enough that His Holiness would not make his appearance that day, and Peter had moved on.

Luke John was no longer a young man. *Well, neither am I!* thought Peter with an inward chuckle. Was he ill? The word *l'ospedale* had wafted through the crowd more than once. Had Peter come all this way for nothing? No. There was a reason. He could wait—another week or more if necessary—to discover it.

He skimmed through the guidebook. He couldn't remember all the alleys he'd walked in his work here, all the estates. Even if he could, he'd never be able to find those places now. They lay buried under two thousand years of history's detritus, hidden beneath Rome's new roads and buildings.

The Trevi Fountain: "A coin tossed into the fountain ensures your return to Rome," advised the guidebook.

I know a better way, Peter thought.

"Piazza San Pietro," read the travel guide. "When Pope Sixtus V had the obelisk moved to its present location in 1586, he ordered that the golden ball at its tip, which the ancients believed contained the ashes of Julius Caesar, be replaced with a cross. Today, that large iron cross can be seen over the rooftops of all Rome. The iron cross houses a splinter of the True Cross . . ."

Peter closed the guidebook, returned it to the camera bag he'd risked charging on Nic Soares's MasterCard. He was no longer worried that a charge authorization could be used to trace his whereabouts. Rindt was near, he could feel it in his bones. It was time to cut short his wandering and head directly to the Vatican, perhaps for no other reason than to draw Rindt's fire, to expose him and whoever stood behind him for what they were. Had he been granted a new life only to die a martyr's death a second time? Well, why not? If that was what it took to get the job done.

• • • •

Ghosts of the Renaissance crowded Peter from every side. He followed the wide blue arrows on the floor down an infinite hall, through the Chiaramonti and Lapidary Galleries, lingered in the library with its exquisite collection of medieval manuscripts under glass, the legacy of the popes. Impressive, surely, but how did it serve the hungry child, the lost and lonely of this world? Trying to reserve judgment, to curb his chronic impatience, Peter moved on.

In the Sistine Chapel, he stood alone amid the buffeting waves of tourists, unconsciously turning on his once painful feet, awestruck and exhilarated in spite of himself. The events depicted on the ceiling bore little resemblance to the world Peter had known. Bartholomew had been slimmer and more common-looking than Botticelli's depiction in the "Last Supper" fresco. Paludano's resurrected Christ would have embarrassed Jesus. And Fra Diamante's Christ would draw amused stares from the Apostles.

Jonah's beatific plea to heaven upon his escape from the whale's mouth lifted Peter's attention, as it was meant to, to Michelangelo's magnificent scenes from the Old Testament. They sprawled in stunningly restored color from west to east across the ceiling sixty-six feet above, fifteen frescoes spanning 8,070 square feet, all created by Michelangelo's own hand. Peter's jaw slackened as he recognized key events from his childhood studies: the division of day from night, the creation of the heavens, the division of land formations, the creation of Adam and Eve, the Fall, Abraham's sacrifice, the Flood, David and Goliath. The icons of his time had not just survived, they had endured. Could he flatter himself that his preaching the old stories so long ago helped preserve them into Michelangelo's colorful century?

In an adjacent hall, he came upon Caravaggio's *Crucifixion of Saint Peter* and froze in midstep.

The look in the condemned "Peter's" eye as he registered his left hand being nailed to the *patibulum* shocked him. He felt a sharp sympathetic pain in his hand and flexed it quickly to assure himself of his distance from the nightmare.

One of the *quaternia* crouched under the base of the crucifix, hoisting the massive load of Peter and the cross. Another leaned into a rope to help raise it.

Peter's expression showed equal parts pain and concern

for the details of his martyrdom. He had a sense of dual perspective in which he marveled at a vision of the original scene fifteen hundred years before the work of art was created *and* admired it as a four-hundred-year-old masterpiece. How many others had secretly experienced such a time-shifted encounter?

A familiar voice, a woman's voice, passionate and forthright, traveled over the heads of a nearby knot of brightly dressed tourists to his unguarded ear. Like notes in a familiar concerto, her Italian was easy on the ear and connected with something deep within him. The voice of the tour guide nourished her listeners. Yes, they moved where she guided them and looked at what she described—the gilded Throne of Saint Peter in the apse, the *putti* frolicking in a gold-leaf sunburst—but her voice did more than that. It enticed. It seduced the listener into total attention, engaged the mind and transported it beyond simple interest to understanding, to meaning. Peter recognized the voice and appreciated its power.

A round woman to his left asked about the significance of the hundreds of bees depicted on Bernini's *baldacchino*. Bees were incorporated in the Barberini family's coat of arms, and Urban VIII, who commissioned the *baldacchino*, had been a Barberini. Peter knew this from the guidebooks, but apparently the woman didn't. Her mincing German accent was distracting enough to cause the others to turn and look at her, including the tour guide. Once again, Peter saw the woman behind the voice. It was Nula Gatti.

At the same moment she saw him, and her expression opened instantly into a broad, unguarded smile. They had both enjoyed their flight to Rome together, the intimacy of those captive hours. Peter had made her laugh, and she had returned the favor by helping him forget about Rindt and Nic Soares and his precarious presence in this new world. Now she brightened and tried to concentrate on the stout fräulein's question, but she was distracted by Peter, who grinned and waved discreetly.

As light cascaded from windows high in Michelangelo's incomparable dome and illuminated the papal altar, Nula made certain that her charges understood the dimensions of the human achievement of Basilica San Pietro.

"This church hosts fifty thousand worshipers, and on the holiest days, another quarter of a million faithful in the piazza out front . . ."

Like the pilgrims, Peter paused to imagine this great place filled with teeming masses of the faithful.

Suddenly a strident wail, like the sound of a snared rabbit, sounded from the center of the nave. Peter and the rest of the group turned toward the source of the commotion to see a monsignor ordering an attendant to remove a lame, bedraggled beggar. The beggar seemed not to comprehend what was happening to him as the attendant took his arm and pulled him toward the doors.

The tour group parted and Peter turned just in time to see Nula sweep past him. Instantly she was between the young attendant and his older prisoner, protesting loudly.

"Non, Monsignore! Non, signore! Non!" she insisted. The monsignor had already waddled off; Nula concentrated her efforts on the attendant. *"E mio fratello!"* she explained.

"May I help?" Peter interrupted.

The attendant held up his hand officiously. *"Non,* this is not your concern, *Signore."* He lifted the frail man bodily and continued to hustle him toward the door over Nula's protests.

Peter followed and grasped the attendant's arm in his iron grip. The young man stopped in his tracks.

"Why do you expel this pilgrim?" Peter demanded.

"Because he is crippled!" blurted Nula. She spun around, her dark eyes flashing, her salt-and-pepper hair flying madly.

"Because the monsignor has requested it," answered the attendant, confident that that was sufficient reason.

Nula's group and others had begun to gather in a wide circle around them in the center of the main nave. The monsignor reappeared and demanded an explanation for the commotion. Peter judged from the harsh expression on his face that he was accustomed to intimidating the humbler pilgrims who visited this place, his place.

"Why have you stopped, boy?" he demanded of the first attendant, gesturing to two more for assistance. "Keep moving, keep moving along. Get him out of here, now!"

"Scusi, Monsignore . . ." Peter tried out his rudimentary

Italian. "But is this not God's house, for all God's children?"

"My brother came to make his confession," Nula explained. The frail man shifted his weight to relieve the pain in his shorter, lame leg.

"He is not appropriately dressed, Signora Gatti!" snapped the monsignor.

"This man is dressed as well as he is able to be dressed, Monsignor," Peter pointed out patiently. He wanted to seize the monsignor and shake the pomposity out of him, but he restrained his rage. "Did Jesus turn away the beggar, or the misshapen leper? Can you do what Jesus himself would not do?" He glared at the officious monsignor. "You do this *ante Christum*?" His tone rose; he was genuinely puzzled.

Although only a few of the observers could understand what was being said, the lines in the conflict were clearly drawn. The monsignor flushed a deep scarlet and, looking around at the innocent expressions on the faces of the faithful, saw his predicament. He softened into resignation and then flashed irritably: "Very well, *Signore*. He is your responsibility."

Peter didn't know what that meant precisely, but he was willing to accept any terms that would allow the beggar to practice his faith.

"*Grazie, Monsignore!*" Peter waved amiably as he helped Nula's crippled brother west across the marble floor, walking slowly to accommodate the man's awkward gait.

"*Grazie, Pietro!*" Nula thanked him as she smoothed her hair, then her jumper. "*Grazie tante.*"

"By doing right you put to silence the ignorance of foolish men," Peter mused.

"From your lips!" Nula attempted a smile, but she was still incensed, the increase in adrenaline making her awkward and self-conscious; she completed the thought by pointing heavenward. "*Eco,* I could have handled that attendant, you know."

"I have no doubt!" Peter laughed.

She looked cautiously at him, gauging his laughter at her expense.

"This is Mafeo," she offered perfunctorily.

"You have a talented and attractive sister, Mafeo," Peter

observed. Mafeo, who understood no English, looked up at Peter with a contorted yet distinctly quizzical expression.

"He is not really my brother, you know," Nula confessed.

"No?" Peter searched Mafeo's features for some similarity to Nula's and could find none. "You lied, then?"

"Lied?" Nula was taken aback. "*Non,* I do not like to lie. I prefer to call it *una buga innocente.* A white lie."

"Sometimes it saves more trouble than the truth," Peter acknowledged with a grin. He was enjoying her way with such practical skills; it reminded him of another time in this city.

She looked up and smiled when she realized he understood her. "Mafeo, he is my uncle."

"Your uncle. I see." Peter nodded his acceptance.

Nula sighed. "All right, he's not really my uncle. But he is from my village. There my family and the neighbors looked after him. Somehow he made it to Roma and now he is my *zingaro zio.* My—how do you say it?—my 'gypsy uncle.' "

Mafeo heard the term and laughed out loud, showing stained and broken teeth. Peter began to realize his infirmity was not only physical. Behind the unshaven face and bewildered eyes lay the mind of a child.

"I see," Peter said gently.

"Do you?" Nula stopped walking and looked at him sincerely. "Do you really?"

She looked at him more closely to see if he was just being kind. No, he was listening, really listening, with the full attention of his hooded gaze, with the very inclination of his shoulders, his confident stillness. The sense of connection she had felt in the Israeli desert returned. She didn't recognize it at first, but she instinctively felt more welcome, less judged in his presence. She pushed a lock of shining gray and black hair behind her ear, threaded her arm through his and walked—no, strolled—with him toward the *confessio.*

Peter had seen couples strolling this way in the piazzas. *This is nice,* he thought. *Yes, this is good.*

When they reached the papal altar, Mafeo bent his knee to genuflect, slipped, and fell to the marble floor like a marionette. No sooner had Peter helped him back to his feet than Mafeo crossed himself and then pushed south toward the Cappella Della Colonna, where he managed after some effort to kneel before the small altar. There he prayed to an ancient painting of the Virgin on a column from the old basilica. Then he moved to the Altar of the Cripple and offered another prayer.

As Mafeo performed his personal stations, Nula pointed out the nearby tombs and statues to Peter, who listened to her descriptions with interest. From time to time he glanced into the darker reaches of this ornately shadowed place, watching and listening. Neither his five senses nor his sixth sense warned him of danger. Yet.

Next the three of them went to the south transept, where Mafeo entered one of the magnificently carved wooden confessionals situated along the curved wall. Peter and Nula settled in a pew to wait.

Peter watched as pilgrims washed up on the shore of the south transept to leave something of themselves behind before the tide washed them back out into the currents of society. He noted the little signs on the confessionals indicating the language of each priest hearing confessions—Español, Italiano, Deutsch, Mandarin, Inglese, Français—as well as his hours of operation. The confessionals had a permanent look about them, crafted of rare hardwoods, deeply oiled, burnished by countless sinners' knees. A faint stream of whispers in several languages emanated from the boxes as faithful Catholics unburdened themselves. Peter considered trying this for himself, but balked. God knew his thoughts; he didn't need an intermediary to talk with his Creator.

Human sound surrounded him like the sound of surf. Eastern Europeans said their rosaries half aloud, lips in fervent motion, an audible murmur filling the cool air between the marble walls. Clerics and nuns paced the polished floors with measured steps, reading their breviaries and meditating. Academics read and took copious notes. Everyone was engrossed. Was Peter the only one who had no particular sense of being calmed or nourished here amid all this ritual?

Beside him, Nula knelt with her eyes closed and prayed silently. Peter could not help but remember what had been here, a swamp beneath the shadow of the pagan obelisk where mosquitoes swarmed the dead and dying for easy sustenance from bound and lifeless limbs, the place where he and countless others had passed from agony into light. There was no plaque commemorating this. Peter knew he was near the site of his death, but so much was different. The buildings, the piazzas, the monuments, the "new" centuries-old trees, even the dimension of the Vatican hillside were transformed.

"Nula?" he whispered after she had crossed herself and sat down again, a look of serenity on her handsome face. "Is it possible to locate the exact spot where Saint Peter was crucified?"

Nula studied him for a moment. "It's very important to you, isn't it?"

"Very."

She did not ask why. She simply took the guidebook he offered her and turned to the illustration of the structures of Imperial Rome superimposed over present-day Vatican City.

"The Circus of Caligula and Nero," she enumerated them, indicating them with one long finger. "The Heliopolis Obelisk, which was moved from the Circus by Pope Sixtus V in 1586 to where it stands now in the center of the piazza."

"And where was it originally?" Peter asked. Nula pointed. "Then the site of Peter's crucifixion was just outside the basilica. Not far from where we're sitting now."

"Yes." Nula was staring at him intently. "I did not realize you knew so much. Are you a historian? When we met in Bethsaida, you told me you were a retired fisherman."

"Oh, I am," Peter assured her. "But a historian? No. Only a student."

"A student of many things," Nula said, giving him back the guidebook. His rough hand brushed her fingertips inadvertently.

Mafeo's confession was taking a long time. Peter and Nula could hear snatches of his slow speech as the priest questioned him in patient Italian. What "sins" could such a simple man have to confess? Peter wondered. The hum from the row of confessionals seemed to grow louder. Peter looked around him at the lines of faithful of all ages and races waiting for their opportunity to confess their sins to another human being.

The rattle of coins into a devotional box caught his ear. He turned to see an elderly woman in a dark suit lighting a votive candle, the flame reflected in her moist eyes. A crinkle of stiff paper drew his attention to an overfed couple stuffing fresh krona into another devotional box and greedily lighting candles.

The crinkling of dollars, francs, lire, pounds, deutsche marks, yen, and a hundred other currencies vied with the clink of silver dollars hitting piles of pence and nickels and loonies. Soon the clinking and rattling seemed to drown out the sound of human voices; all Peter could hear was the exchange of money for indulgences, of sins for absolution, the ringing up of sums on theological cash registers, the counting of commerce like trade in the bazaar.

Peter shifted in his seat, unable to sit still. All of this was occurring in the name of the master, in his own name! All around him the meek and powerless were neglecting their personal relationship with God for public ritual, abdicating personal responsibility, placing their souls in the control of the priests, paying the temple. The mission for which he had left his family, suffered for so many decades in poverty and mortal danger, sacrificed his life, had become—this!

At last he understood the master's rage that day in the temple.

Suddenly he was on his feet and flying toward the nearest confessional, the one with the sign that read Français. He pulled open the wooden doors to expose the priest inside, head bowed, with two fingers to his brow, listening.

"Stop this, man!" Peter demanded.

He pulled back the curtain to his left and was met by a startled young man, mouth agape, eyes wide, flushing scarlet.

"God hears your thoughts, son," Peter said not unkindly, but barely able to restrain his irritation. "You don't need to repeat them to this man!"

Frozen in her pew, Nula watched, horrified. *Who was this man, what was he doing? He was a maniac!*

Pilgrims stopped in their tracks, transfixed and uncomprehending. Two attendants near the papal altar had spun around at the shouting and were still trying to determine the nature of the disturbance when Peter flung open the doors of the Inglese confessional. A kind-faced man with snowy hair and an even whiter collar gasped and shielded his eyes from the sunlight and Peter's wrath.

"You interrupt this woman's relationship with her Creator, priest!" Peter shouted, building to his full fury. His eyes glowed with rage. When he turned to the woman making her confession he softened, but only a little.

"Go home! Tell your husband your fears. This priest cannot help you!"

The woman's face quivered then melted into realization as she looked into Peter's face. The worst day of her life suddenly opened around her and the universe swallowed up all her worst days, days spoiled by shame and guilt. She began to sense the rebirth of true belief. It was irrational, but there it was, flourishing in the heat of Peter's searing anger. Something within her snapped, and she was reborn. She would kneel before no man. She got to her feet and hurried away.

Half a dozen attendants were now rushing toward the chapel in the south transept. Pilgrims and tourists began to flow toward the commotion, drawn by Peter's thundering baritone, emptying from the scores of small chapels throughout the massive basilica.

Oblivious to anything but the minor tyrannies transpiring in the confessionals around him, Peter marched from one to the next, releasing fears and guilts and captive souls like animals from a zoo.

Nula had shaken off her amazement and rushed to the altar rail, where Mafeo was saying his penance. She intended to leave as quickly as she could with him in tow. Yet something stopped her. Peter's voice boomed in the great soaring spaces between the travertine stone walls and marble arches, building in intensity as it ricocheted off the Renaissance masterpieces, yet it calmed her heart as if it were the gentlest private assurance from her own personal angel. Private wounds from the past, only partially healed within her, were salved by his strength. She slowed her escape, then stopped. Instead of fleeing the chaos, she moved closer to it.

Peter continued to open all of the confessionals one by one. They stood empty, open to the light and air as priests and penitents alike experienced various reactions. Some visibly lightened as if a great burden had been lifted from them. Others merely shook their heads and walked away, distancing themselves from this mad man. Still others smiled openly, or began to weep.

The attendants had summoned a monsignor by now, not the fat, officious one who had given Mafeo a hard time but a frail, graying elderly man greatly distressed by what he saw.

"This is a profanity, a sacrilege!" he shrieked, motioning to the attendants to evict the troublemaker. But Peter kept eluding them, still speaking but no longer shouting, for the basilica had become as quiet as a tomb. Only the monsignor felt he had to shout, yet shouting did him no good, for Peter's voice carried like truth and freedom to every ear. Rushing after Peter from confessional to confessional, waving his hands helplessly, the monsignor was more sheep than shepherd.

By now six Swiss Guards had appeared, the click of their boots foreign and ugly on the marble floor of the nave. Never before had they been called into the church itself except for formal occasions.

It was clear to the soldiers that the monsignor was the only one threatening the peace of this place, but they were sworn to obey, and they moved to surround the powerfully built old man who continued speaking, his voice carrying easily throughout the basilica.

"Give yourself away. Even the thought of giving is a blessing with the power to affect others. . . . Reexamine all you have been told, dismiss whatever insults God's presence in your soul."

The priests who had remained, the penitents and pilgrims, listened intently. That the presence of the Guards offended them was apparent in their facial expressions. Though no one moved to defend Peter, it was clear that they might at any moment. Sergente Meola, the only ranking member of the Guard present, sensed this and wisely decided not to restrain Peter. Instead, he ordered his men to close ranks around Peter and guide him toward the doors.

"Listen to that voice within you!" Peter cried as he allowed the Guards to lead him away. "You will hear God in your most private thoughts!"

Nula elbowed her way through the crowd with Mafeo in her wake; she half noticed that Mafeo didn't seem unbalanced by the pushing and shoving, but she didn't have time to pay closer attention. Peter needed her.

One man in the crowd, a Roman from the looks of his formal blazer worn casually open, pulled a notepad from his pocket and wrote down Peter's words, looking quickly around and making further notes on the scene. He moved closer to Peter and the Guards and identified himself as a columnist with the Roman newspaper *La Repubblica*. *"Scuzi, signore*—your name, please?"

"Peter, my friend," Peter replied, unruffled by all the attention.

"Peter? Signore Peter who? Your last name, *per favore*?"

Peter paused and considered the journalist thoughtfully. Was this the time to shed his anonymity and announce his presence? Once he claimed his identity, he wouldn't have a moment's peace. No, he decided, it wasn't yet time to confront the world with the truth. But he would make a gift of his identity to this man, this soul with a purpose of his own. Although that purpose was not apparent to Peter at the moment, he knew that it was imminent.

"Peter. Just Peter. You will know who I am when Rome understands why I have come. Tell your readers that I am a simple person. Like you, Gianfranco, I am just a soul trying to do the right thing when confronted by so much that is wrong."

As the most respected print journalist in all of Italy, Gianfranco Fini had preserved his own anonymity, outside of a limited circle of acquaintances, for decades. He didn't ask this stranger with the American accent how he knew his name. It didn't seem important. He simply wrote down Peter's words in the shorthand that was indecipherable to others but internationally renowned for its accuracy. When he had written down Peter's words and checked them, he glanced up again just in time to see Peter smile amiably and, escorted by the colorful Swiss Guard through the oversized doorway, melt into the light of the afternoon.

Fini decided at that moment that he would publish the evidence he had collected of the until-now unproven campaign of political corruption in the south of Italy. It would mean that the life of respect and influence he had come to enjoy would end. It meant that he would risk everything for the simple principle of right and wrong. But he would do it. And while he was at it, why not give this Peter a few column inches in the spotlight on *La Repubblica*'s editorial page?

Outside, Sergente Meola leaned closer to Peter and said in heavily accented English: "*Signore*, you stay out of trouble, *per favore*?" He cleared his throat, tried to look stern, turned on his heel, and ordered his men to march away.

Smart vecchietto—old codger, thought Meola, as he returned to his post. *Nothing safer than a crowd, especially with the media at hand.* He scanned the milling thousands as he marched. *What is this all about?* One of his friends on the night watch told him he'd seen Colonel Rindt leave the Palace at 3 A.M. *Is the Colonel somehow involved?*

Peter glanced back toward the basilica; Nula and Mafeo were headed toward him. Mafeo crossed himself and smiled, revealing his mouthful of neglected, rotting teeth. It was the brightest light Peter had seen here.

"*Grazie, Signore,*" Mafeo said quietly, his speech murky but intelligible. Had Nula coached him in what to say? "You good man to, ah, *il relitto* like me."

" 'A wreck like me'," Nula translated.

"These bodies are wrecks, Mafeo, aren't they? Miraculous, yes, but nothing compared to the divine within us, eh?" Peter answered, noticing that Mafeo moved with greater ease, less uncontrollable shaking and flailing.

Mafeo seemed taller as they made the long walk down the steps, and his stride became increasingly natural. He began to weep.

"God bless you, Signore Peter!" Mafeo sobbed. He took Peter's hand and held it to his lips, then his forehead for a moment before letting go.

"Bless you, Peter," Nula said as she too squeezed his hand.

Peter was puzzled by their outpouring of affection but happy for them.

"I would like to stay, but I must see Mafeo safely home," she explained.

"We will meet again soon?" he smiled.

Nula held his eyes for an extra moment and nodded. She turned reluctantly away and accompanied her gypsy uncle down the steps into the idling crowds in the vast piazza. Mafeo moved like a man who loved his life, radiating good-will toward every stranger. Peter watched them both until they disappeared into the crush on the Via della Conciliazione. Then he joined the flow of Rome's contagious good-will himself.

Romans were digesting large lunches, lovers were weaving dreams in the afterglow, angels were likely also seduced by the city's civilized pace. Whereas Jews in the Palatine synchronized their threescore years with the law, Romans pursued their allotted time in a joyous race against the eternal, loving each moment, preserving it in their memories without regret and then courting the next. The calm, suspected Peter, was only the outward symptom of men and women distracted by their passions.

Just down the Via Mascherino on Borgo Pio, Peter settled at a table in the courtyard of the Ristorante Marcello to catch his breath and settle his raging heart. What had come over him? It was the temple all over again. But he couldn't help it, he told himself. The corruption of the master's intention had been too much.

He ordered a liter of Pellegrino, drank the entire bottle, and ordered another. He wondered if it was any more likely that he could quench his thirst in this Roman heat than he could accept what the Church, his Church, had become.

Seeing the Heliopolis obelisk towering over the neighborhood rooftops, he made a mental note to look for its original site as Nula explained it. *Not now, it's too dangerous,* he thought as he envisioned Rindt shadowing the basilica. He grinned and sighed as sunlight warmed his face and a slight breeze cooled his limbs. *Tomorrow.*

26

STEPHEN PARNELL WAS IN THE HABIT OF RISING BEfore daybreak to be alone with the world, at least for half an hour before the day started and the world was too much with him. The explosion on Lago di Garda had taken that peace away. He had faith that time would heal the violence in his thoughts. For now, however, all he could do was lie awake in the predawn and try to meditate.

He was remarkably intact, considering the force of the blast, his age, and the plunge into frigid waters. He'd suffered no more than a singed patch at the back of his head, friar's style, and a nasty cold. His vision still flared a bit in low light, but his personal physician assured him that was only a minor irritation to the optic nerve. It too would heal in a few days.

Were it not for the fact that a boy out delivering fresh eggs and the morning newspaper in his family's skiff had witnessed his plunge, it could have been worse. The boy's name was Marcelino. Stephen Parnell promised himself he would remember that name in his prayers from now on.

Marcelino had heard the blast and followed the sound, motoring into the flotsam, cutting his engine and leaping into the water to save the stranger, then took him directly to his parents' house on the south shore. Gio and Lucia Caioti welcomed the shivering elderly stranger in the sodden Aran sweater into their small house, gave him dry clothes to wear, hot food and brandy, and warmed him by their fire. Marcelino left to finish his deliveries; when he returned Stephen was deeply, mercifully asleep in a chair by the fieldstone fireplace. Marcelino helped his father carry the surprisingly frail old man to his own bed.

When he awoke, they ate again and shared stories. Gio said boats had caught fire four times before on the lake in his lifetime. Signore Stefano was lucky; all the others had perished. Stephen described the blast, and they said they'd heard it from three kilometers' distance. Strange. What, in a small outboard motor, could have caused such a concussion? But he was all right now; that was what mattered.

Stephen hadn't told them who he was, only that he was vacationing from Rome. They had been to Rome once, the Caiotis told him, and they enjoyed sharing their memories with him.

An aide announced Cardinal Cosa, and the door to the papal apartment swung open with a whoosh.

"Ah! *Buon giorno*, Your Holiness, *buon giorno*!" exclaimed Cosa when he saw the pope awake. "You look better this morning, refreshed!"

"I feel better, Adeodato, thank you."

"*Bene. Molto bene*. You are also smiling, Your Holiness. It is good to see you happy after such an ordeal. May I ask what it is you were thinking about?"

"The blessed Caioti family, and how generous and trusting they were. True Christians. And the best food I have ever eaten! I may have been born Irish, but I'll die Italian!"

"You chose to keep your identity from them," Cosa observed. His Holiness had been forthright in providing the details of his ordeal. "May I ask why?"

"I'm not sure. Perhaps it is too many years in Rome. Our times, don't you know."

"You feared discovery?"

"No, no. On the contrary, I feared their mistaking the office for the man. I enjoyed being one of them, just an anonymous fisherman. It was a good feeling."

"Well, thank God you are back with us, safe and sound. One does not wish to contemplate what might have happened if you had been seriously hurt, or worse . . ."

"Well, I wasn't," Stephen Parnell said. The conversation was making him uneasy. "I'm here and I'm still pope."

"Indeed you are, Your Holiness," Cosa replied warily. What had prompted Luke John to state the obvious? "Indeed."

"Now, speaking of popes, what can you tell me about Peter?"

"We are still searching, Your Holiness. So far he has eluded us. But we will find him, I am certain."

"The sooner, the better, Adeodato. The sooner, the better. One does not wish to contemplate what might happen to him, a man out of his time, in this callous world we live in.''

Cosa gauged Luke John's commitment to Peter and found it stronger than before. He also wondered if the pontiff was consciously mimicking his choice of words. He said nothing.

"Arcanum arcanorum," the pope said quietly. " 'Secret of secrets,' Adeodato. He can tell us. If we can persuade him to confide in us, we will know the unknowable!''

"You are convinced he is authentic then, Your Holiness.''

"Dr. Sabatini is convinced. Her reports veritably glow! I must meet him, look into his eyes, speak directly to him to be certain, of course. But I am ready to be convinced.''

Cosa had not expected Luke John to be released from the hospital as soon as he was, nor had he expected him to immediately demand to see all the reports on the BioGenera experiment. Cosa had had to consent; to do anything else would have aroused suspicion in a man whose recent brush with death could only have honed his instincts, made him more aware. Cosa had been caught off guard. That seemed to be happening with increasing frequency.

"And if he is, Holiness? If he truly is Saint Peter, then what?''

"With his word as eyewitness, we can answer for certain all the details that have puzzled scholars for centuries, offer proof to the skeptics, reinforce the faith of the simple man. Then the faith is reborn.''

"And if he is not who he says he is?''

The pope looked at Cosa closely, then turned away, back to his thoughts. In truth, he had no answer.

Peter watched tourists swimming against the tide of local custom, attempting to browse at the counters of shops and galleries that were closed for the afternoon rest. Gradually they adapted and retreated to fountains or trattorias to wait for the tide to turn their way again.

A familiar form passed through his line of sight. No longer in a proper tour guide suit, she was now dressed in light cottons that drifted in the ebbing heat. She moved with an energy absent in others around her, powerfully, as if the day had not yet taken its toll from her. When she turned Peter recognized her. It was as if he had known Nula Gatti from the beginning of time.

He stood and called out to her.

She paused in the thick Roman air. Her direct gaze took him into its confidence.

"Peter. How nice!" She brightened and approached him. Her English faltered in a nervousness that she only partly succeeded in concealing. Confident in her professional capacity, she was shy in private. "I hope I find you here!"

They shook hands, old friends by now. Peter offered her a place at his table in the shade. "Come. Sit with me." Her heart responded to him before her mind. She accepted.

"Coffee? Mineral water? Tea?"

She laughed at his enthusiasm; he was so open and honest. *"Acqua minerale, grazie."*

"Waiter—?" Peter lifted his voice to a man who seemed oblivious to their presence. "Waiter!" he repeated more forcefully.

"Acqua minerale, per favore," Nula ordered briskly. The waiter scurried and she turned back to Peter. "You do not lightly suffer fools," she observed.

Peter laughed. "It's that obvious?"

"From the very beginning," Nula said with mock seriousness. "It takes a temper to know one. I knew you had one even in Bethsaida, though I never expected what you did in the basilica today!" She touched Peter's arm for emphasis. He was shaking his head.

"I cannot imagine you with a temper."

"Then you don't know me very well."

"You are a lot like my wife, then. Emotional. Jewish women and Italian women, they're not so different," Peter offered.

For all their hours of conversation, in Bethsaida, on the plane, it was the first time he'd mentioned his wife. Nula tried to feel grateful that he'd told her so soon, before she let her feelings develop any further.

"I still cannot get over your being Jewish," she said, avoiding the topic that was really on her mind. "Such an interest in the Vatican . . . I would have thought . . ." She shrugged.

"You thought I must be a Christian."

She nodded knowingly. "Your wife did not come to Israel. Is she meeting you here in Rome?"

"My wife is dead," Peter said quietly.

Nula covered her mouth with her hand. "I'm so sorry!" she said though, strangely, the emotion she was feeling was anything but sorrow. "I . . . forgive me. Sometimes I do not know when to change the subject." She took a deep breath, tried to find a safer topic. "*Lei di dov'e?* Where are you from? You said America, I know, but—"

"California."

"I knew it! You are so bold and confident! I love that about Americans!"

"Yes, well, I'm not so confident these days."

"*Percè no?* Why not?"

"So much has changed."

"Rome changed? No. You have been here before?"

"Yes. A long time ago." He was saying too much. There was something about this woman that made him want to keep talking, reveal everything. He couldn't help himself. "I used to know my way around."

"During the war, perhaps?" Nula gauged his age and what might bring an American from California to her part of the world. "There were many American GIs stationed here in Rome, as well as near my . . . village—how do you say it?—my 'hometown.' I was born after the war, but I have been told . . ."

Peter's prolonged silence told her that it was time to change the subject once again. "Well, perhaps I can be of some service to you. Tell me what I can do to make you feel at home in Rome."

"You can tell me about this pope and when I may see him," Peter said with sudden enthusiasm.

Nula responded confidently. Here she was on familiar ground.

"What can I tell you about Pope Luke John? He was elderly when the College of Cardinals chose him, and the office has made him even older. But I think he is not so old as the world believes."

"No?"

"*Non.* The Irish are always young, even when they're old.

Anyway, he sees himself as a shepherd bringing the faithful back into the fold of traditional Christian values.''

Peter settled his elbows on the table like a judge considering new evidence. Nula found herself studying the way the dark hair curled on his muscled forearms. She felt like a schoolgirl.

"This pleases some and frightens others," she continued seriously, warming to her subject as much as to her auditor. "To Europeans and most North Americans, as I understand it, the pope's arguments have as much impact as anyone else's—no more, no less. It is only in the poor countries where people are superstitious and frightened that he is still heard with awe."

"I see." Peter rubbed his chin thoughtfully. For some reason Nula could not fathom, this information seemed to make him profoundly sad.

"As for Stephen Parnell the man, he has suffered Ireland's troubles. He lost his elder brother when he was nine years old, his mother and her two youngest ones after that. During the war, as a young priest, he wrote an essay about the parallels between occupation by Nazis and the British occupation in Northern Ireland." Peter's eyebrows rose as he absorbed this information. "He pointed out the fact that in both cases priests, college *professores*, social leaders, all disappeared. Survival became the only religion. No matter whether one cooperates, bribes his oppressors or defies them, the result is the same. Stephen Parnell lost everything, *tutto*. And his universe is turned, ah, *capovolto*, ah . . .''

"Upside down?"

"*Si.* Upside down." She gestured with her hand. "The wicked prosper while the good are persecuted. There can be only two responses: despair or faith. Stephen Parnell clung to faith. He does not become a Provo, like his brothers. He becomes a priest."

"An interesting choice," Peter said thoughtfully. "How was his essay received?"

Nula shook her head. "Not well. His bishop—how do you say it?—reprimanded him. The young priest became an older priest. He became *prudente,* cautious. Some say too conservative. 'Sold out,' I think Americans say."

"If you can't lick 'em, join 'em," Peter remarked. Where

had that come from? Something Will had said? Nula gave him a bemused look. "He became the very thing he was fighting against," he explained. "It's one way of looking at it. What do you think, Nula?"

The question surprised her. Most of the men she had known didn't ask her opinion on serious matters. The man she had married at eighteen used to shout at her that she wasn't entitled to an opinion, especially when he'd been drinking. Five years into their marriage he'd been run down by a motorbike. She'd barely thought of him since.

Now she shrugged. "Who knows what is in a man's heart? Maybe he's only frightened."

" 'Judge not, that ye be not judged,' " Peter smiled at her fondly. "When may I see him?" he asked innocently.

"The pope? In a quarter hour, on the balcony."

The crowd surged into the piazza like waves into a tidal pool, washing up against the stone resistance of the Swiss Guards and then back again, seeking equilibrium. In a short time the waters calmed, a Sargasso sea of the faithful. Peter and Nula waited in the tidal sway under the balcony.

When Luke John emerged into the waning sunlight, the faithful crossed themselves and listened intently. Peter understood their longing but decided he didn't approve of their adoration. No man warranted such idolatry.

Luke John's blessings disintegrated as they descended through the thick heat waves. His words glanced off stone surfaces at all angles and fell in muffled echoes on straining ears. Peter understood the Latin, the familiar *In nomine patri, et fili, et spiritu sancti* . . . The other languages, however, even the English, sounded like sleep-talking to him.

Then the pontiff was gone. Luke John, Peter's successor, bishop of the Church, disappeared behind the massive stone walls of the Apostolic Palace like a conjurer's doll. Peter felt cheated.

"So many people," he remarked. "They look like they expect miracles."

"*Si.* I think many hope for *miracolo*," answered Nula.

"So many looking for answers from a little man in bright finery, satisfied with so little!" He replayed the scene, turning it over and considering it. "Why do they place the responsibility for their own salvation in another man's hands?''

''We are weak. We can only be strong for so long, then we must surrender,'' Nula suggested as they walked slowly past the basilica.

A figure in black caught Peter's attention. It was Colonel Rindt. He was walking the edge of the crowd, squinting into the masses. Peter turned away before Rindt could see him and guided Nula out of the piazza. She had glanced at her watch and touched Peter's arm again in that way of hers.

''*Scuzi,* Peter, but I must go. My mother expects me. I always stop in after work to see if she needs anything. She will worry if I am late.''

''I could go along.''

''You are kind, but my mother, she is old and lives alone. Too much time to think. She might get the wrong idea.''

''Nula, you are a grown woman!'' he protested. He thought such antiquated notions had died out in his own time.

''You have much to learn, Peter.''

''And so little time. Stay a little longer.''

''The basilica is open for another hour,'' Nula protested. The more she wanted to stay with him, the more it seemed necessary to object. ''You should see the *Grotto Sacre*, the papal tombs.''

''I can see these things tomorrow, yes?''

''*Si.*''

''Then it's settled. I'll come with you.''

Nula threw up her hands helplessly and surrendered. They ran like a couple of youngsters to catch the Number 63 bus, laughing breathlessly as they threw themselves into the last two available seats. Before he knew it, Peter had integrated back into Roman life. Whatever was going to happen would happen at its own pace. It felt right. That was enough for now.

Late that night, when the day's emotions were spent and Romans lay deep in the empire of exhausted sleep, an ecstatic Giuliana lured Andrew out of the apartment onto her balcony.

Andrew laid out a blanket at the edge of a moon shadow

and slipped Giuliana's nightgown off her shoulders. Giuliana's fever rose at the sight of his muscled shoulders creating rippling shadows in the cool light. Without a sound they found the familiar rhythm. Afterward, their words came easily and honestly.

"There were things that I didn't want to know," confessed Andrew. "Things I was afraid of, until I met you."

"What things?"

"What I was capable of," he tried, detesting every syllable that betrayed him. "How trivial and unimportant my work could become. How much power I had to create misery. How much I could love, and how much I needed."

"Andrew . . ."

". . . how much life I was missing . . ."

"I know, I know . . ."

"You gave me a reason to face the truth . . . about myself."

She lifted her eyes. "I?"

"Yes, you." He kissed her.

She laughed ironically. "Andrew, you have described how I have been feeling. I was safe before you. I was comfortable in my ignorance, untroubled by the dangerous feelings that you ignited in me . . . safe. Believe me, I feel these things also."

"You do?"

"Of course." She looked away into the piazza, also searching for words. "I needed. But what? I had God, I had my work. A man? Pleasure? That's what made me awkward, lack of pleasure. Lack of being loved and the power that comes with love's luxury. We have a lot to learn, Andrew, so much to understand."

First light ignited the colors of the flowers on the ledge and the exhausted pair, who had slept curled and tangled on the balcony, roused themselves enough to move to the warmth of the bed.

Before long, the harsh ring of the telephone shattered the peaceful silence. The world rushed into the apartment.

Giuliana didn't move from his arms. Andrew reached reflexively to answer, not caring that he couldn't speak Italian.

"Don't answer it," she said quietly. *"Buona notizia sonni fino a mezzogiorno."*

Andrew didn't care what she said; the music of her voice was enough.

" 'Good news sleeps 'til noon,' " she translated anyway.

Sometime later, having risen to the surface of sleep, she saw that Andrew was gone. The shuttered bedroom had acquired the familiar muted rush of quiet, of morning alone. He must be changed, also, she thought. He didn't awaken easily, yet he had slipped silently out of her awareness, leaving a note beside the clock to tell her he was off into the dawn for coffee, in search of breakfast for the two of them.

She sat up in bed, pulled the sheet around her, and sat gazing into the middle distance. The familiar silence had seemed to shift for an instant, and she turned her head to listen.

Nothing.

The door of the apartment at the end of the hall closed. Footsteps sounded past her door and down the marble stairs. A Vespa whined past, followed by a young man's voice excitedly recounting last night. She visualized his girlfriend with her arms around his middle, head on his shoulder, listening, remembering, enjoying the sound of his voice in the wind.

Rindt watched from the darkness in the corner. From where he was, Giuliana reminded him of the creatures he had hunted—the still glint of watchfulness, senses alert, limbs not yet tensed for flight, not ready to believe in danger.

He moved along the wall in darkness. A distant smile moved across her expression. She twisted out of the bed to her feet and, naked, stepped lightly into the bathroom. The door closed, opened; she reappeared. She reached for a summer robe on the bed, distractedly tying it about her waist as she went into the kitchen. Rindt heard the refrigerator, water poured into a glass, and her returning steps.

"Where is he?" he asked calmly.

His voice could have been the concussive blast of a bomb for the effect it had on the unsuspecting Giuliana. The glass flew out of her hand and shattered against the shutters. She screamed and whirled away from him, reaching for a brass candleholder on the dresser.

Rindt recognized the momentary advantage and, despite his affection for her, used it. Sidestepping the wide arc of the candleholder, he grabbed Giuliana's arms and threw her against the wall.

"Scream again and I will kill you," he said dispassionately.

Giuliana gulped for breath, her eyes as wide as a deer's. She nodded wildly to indicate she understood him, even if she couldn't speak.

"I have been following you and Dr. Shepard for too long," he said evenly. "I believed you would take me to him. But you are too busy with each other. Still . . ." He pressed her into the unyielding coolness of the wall. ". . . I think you know where he is."

"I . . . I don't! I don't know where he is!" She tried to be controlled and threatening. The result was a hoarse squeak.

"Don't lie to me, *Dottore*. I don't have time!"

"I'm not lying. I don't know where he is!"

Rindt struck a glancing blow to the right side of her face.

"Don't toy with me, Giuliana. You're not good enough. I've let you string me along because I needed you, for the time being anyway. But ultimately you're incidental. Shepard also."

"What do you want, Rindt?"

"Peter." Rindt released his grip. "Just Peter."

"What for?" The flimsy robe had come untied; she couldn't make her hands stop shaking long enough to tie it, but clasped it about her instead.

"I don't have the luxury of answering questions like that, *Dottore*, any more than you have asking them."

"Who are you working for?" she asked, realizing now that the shadows of danger had a form, an origin. "Is it Cosa? Or someone else?"

Suddenly she was thrown violently across the room onto her bed. "Listen! That inquiring nature of yours is your worst enemy right now." He shook her again. "Do you understand?"

She changed the subject. "Memory resurrection—"

"It doesn't matter if memory resurrection works or doesn't work."

"It works. And it can help—"

"It doesn't matter! It doesn't matter whether your Dr. Shepard is a genius or not. None of that matters!"

"*Madonna!* Who are you? Who do you really work for?"

"Aren't you listening? It doesn't make any difference!"

"What are you going to do?"

Rindt laughed bitterly. He almost began to explain, but then stopped himself.

"You can't be serious." Giuliana read his intention in his face. A strange calm came over her. "Too many people know about him. Peter is a fact! Andrew will . . ."

"I can handle Shepard. He's a lamb, an innocent. But you—you know things. And you have faith. You are a liability, *Dottore*. A beautiful liability, but a liability nonetheless. Liabilities must be eliminated."

He opened the shutters, then the doors to the balcony and peered over the balcony railing. "Today is trash day, isn't it? I'll make you a deal. If you're still alive when Rome's valiant *spazzaturaio* call here, you can live."

He was on her and forcing her to the railing before she could register what was happening. As the reality of what he was doing hit her, she began to kick, viciously scratching and screaming. She was an uncontrolled nova of rage.

His hand covered her mouth and silenced her screams, but he had more difficulty with her clawing hands and pummeling legs and feet. One kick found his groin and she was sure it would cripple him, but he only inhaled slightly and continued calmly, methodically dragging her to the railing.

"*What the hell—?!*" Andrew's voice broke through her terror. For a nanosecond everything stopped as Rindt realized his predicament and bolted for the door, ramming Andrew against the dresser with one shoulder before Andrew could even attempt to stop him.

Giuliana stumbled back from the balcony railing, as far into the bedroom and safety as she could get. Andrew returned from his rush out into the hall—as if he could possibly have overtaken Rindt—and gathered her into his arms. She clung to him, pressing her forehead against his shoulder, her breath coming in ragged gasps and gradually slowing. They both stared disbelieving at the open door, at their ruined breakfast strewn across the floor. They touched each other's faces in wonder, grateful to be alive. Finally, after wrapping Giuliana in a blanket, Andrew went to the balcony and looked below for any sign of Rindt.

Their dark attacker was nowhere to be seen. He had vanished into Rome's light, as he had come.

27 ANDREW STEPPED BACK FROM THE TOWERING OBElisk and shook his head respectfully.

"This is where Peter was crucified?" he asked Giuliana.

"This is the place of Peter's greatest triumph," she echoed Peter's last words to her in the Tullianum. "Well, not precisely, but this obelisk is probably the last thing he saw when he was crucified and he can't know that it has been moved since his time."

"Where was it originally?"

"Over there." She pointed to an area a hundred fifty yards southwest, "to the left of the Arch of the Bells in Nero's Circus. Pope Sixtus V moved it here in 1586."

Andrew envisioned the operation that must have been required to move the massive monument and whistled softly. "Let's go check the original site," he suggested. "Peter would remember where he died, wouldn't he?"

"I don't know. So much has changed since Peter's time here."

There were fewer tourists near the Arch of the Bells, so it would be easier to spot Peter if he was there. They looked but didn't see him.

"Wait, I see him—there!" Giuliana grasped Andrew's arm and pointed to a man standing near a plaque, with his head bowed. They began running toward him.

Peter was lost in memories, his jaw muscles flexing tensely. The site where he had been martyred was now crowded over with buildings constructed under Michelangelo's genius eye. But neither time nor the addition of newer structures could alter the fact that this place outside the basilica wall was the site of his most important moment, his Golgotha.

He heard the chants of condemned spirits, their shrieks, the audible ascent of hope in their death rattles as they won their ultimate victory in the Circus. Beads of sweat glistened on his face.

"Pain doesn't make you stronger. It just hurts," Peter said by way of greeting.

"Let's get out of the open. Somewhere less public," suggested Andrew gently, the events in Giuliana's apartment earlier this morning still fresh in his mind.

"This is the safest place in Rome," Peter answered. "Trust me."

"We read about your scene in the basilica. What were you thinking?" asked Giuliana.

"I wasn't thinking. I was feeling."

"Do you mind?" Andrew snapped. His eyes hadn't stopped searching for Rindt since they found Peter. "Let's get out of here!"

They filled Peter in on what had happened as they walked swiftly down a narrow backstreet, alert for signs of Rindt or his subordinates. Giuliana's perfume trailed faintly amid the scent of freshly washed streets and the aromas of garlic and bread. Andrew watched the roll of her hips as she walked ahead and felt a renewed desire for her. Between Giuliana's effect on him and Rome's intoxicating influence, he was immune to fear. Beside him, Peter noticed and smiled faintly. Some things, the good, human things, never changed.

They turned into a small restaurant and took a table where they had a clear view of the street but could not be easily seen.

"The more I see of this new world of yours, the more I conclude that it is not so different from mine," said Peter, after a sip of espresso.

"What do you mean?" Andrew asked.

Peter glanced at Giuliana, who understood his meaning, then explained to Andrew: "The powerful have their reasons. Those reasons are as real to them as our motivations are to us. That hasn't changed."

"But the Church, your Church . . . It's impossible!" Andrew's voice rose in frustration.

" 'My Church'! *Certum est quia impossibile est*," Peter said, unconsciously echoing Giuliana. " 'It is certain because it is impossible.' "

"Andrew . . ." Giuliana put her hand over Andrew's and squeezed. "You must understand. I, we, don't want it to be this way. But men like Rindt are part of the Church, work inside or outside it, always. Perhaps the early popes deliberately recruited them. 'Better the enemy you know than the enemy you don't know.' But to deny them is lunacy."

"All right, forgive me my naïveté," Andrew said wryly. "What now?"

"I must speak with Stephen Parnell," Peter said decisively.

"*Si,* you must," agreed Giuliana. "But, *attesa,* Peter, wait. It's not so easily done. No one sees His Holiness except with the permission of Cosa. And we must not alert Cosa."

"Maybe I could get his attention during one of his public appearances," Peter offered.

"Unless . . ." Giuliana said quietly to herself, but then shook her head, unable to finish the thought.

Peter ordered three more espressos and seemed to enjoy the mischief of planning how to get past thousands of faithful pilgrims, the Swiss Guards, Cardinal Cosa, and Rindt. He began to sketch the layout of Piazza San Pietro, the Apostolic Palace, and the two entrances along the Via di Porta Angelica on the back of a table napkin. Andrew joined in, intrigued by the impossibility of the challenge.

"You know something, my friend?" Peter leaned in, beaming. "Despite Rindt, the danger, I have never felt so alive!"

"I was beginning to think I was crazy!" Andrew grinned, the recognition of Peter's meaning shining in his expression. "I wouldn't want to be anywhere else."

"Good! Because I need to do this."

"It could be risky."

"I know. I'm not sure I can bear suffering again at the hands of men. On the flight here, once I eluded Rindt, I thought maybe I should live down to the world's expectations. At least man would not have to suffer another two thousand years of chaos. If I try and fail, that is what will happen. If I fail . . .''

"If you fail, Cosa could be the next pope," Andrew voiced the apprehension they shared. "On the other hand, if you succeed, Luke John can help you bring some joy into the world, some light. You could—"

"*Allere flammam.*" Peter smiled warmly, then translated for Andrew: "Feed the flame."

They both looked toward Giuliana, to see if she agreed.

She was gone.

"Is Rindt with you?" Cosa's voice leapt from the receiver as Giuliana sidestepped the crush of pedestrians at the entrance to the Ufficio Postal near the Piazza Barberini.

"*Non*, Your Eminence, not since America," she lied.

"Where are you now, child?"

She hesitated. What she had in mind constituted a risk greater than any she could have imagined taking. Cosa's power seemed infinite, but Imperial Rome's legacy of fatalistic intrigue had been passed down through the centuries and flowed within her. Did she trust herself to outmaneuver the cardinal? Not really, but she had to try for Peter's sake. Could she protect Peter? Peter had taught her that the safest path is sometimes the one that leads directly to the heart of danger. She had to trust the cardinal's faith over the fears she guessed were guiding him now.

She ignored his question and rushed the words, fearful of being outwitted or losing her nerve. "Your Eminence, I have a favor to ask of you."

There was a short silence as Cosa absorbed the significance of her rebellion. "What is it?"

The crowds seemed to part for the three as they walked across the piazza to the famous Bronze Door leading to Constantine's Portico and into the Vatican Palaces. Andrew wasn't really surprised when Giuliana told them where she was taking them, but it was happening so fast! She had proven herself a resourceful partner many times, but this was extraordinary. The pope was going to meet with them right now!

A ranking Swiss Guard snapped to attention as they approached the stairs leading to the Door and escorted them past another Guard on the threshold, who also stiffened crisply as they passed. From the Bronze Door they were led far into the palace of Sixtus V, down soaring Renaissance halls, through glittering Baroque chambers and finally into the Sala Clementina, the antechamber of the pontifical offices.

They were still taking in the magnificent mural on the vaulted ceiling when the door behind them opened again and Cardinal Cosa made his entrance, ponderous and resplendent in his ruby robes, trailed closely by his personal carrion bird, the dark and compact Rindt.

Andrew was certain he knew Cosa or, more accurately, Cosa's type—clean-shaven and soft, wrinkles artfully drawn on his face, everything about him as polished as the art that surrounded them. Refined yet deprecating, sensitive yet brittle as armor, he was an impresario of power, a veteran of dual strategies: the coldhearted logic of terror in the field, gracious reason at the negotiator's table. Andrew judged that he was a stranger to no twist, contradiction, or flattery. The cardinal glided toward them forcefully, heavy with cheer and fatherly concern. Andrew didn't believe for a minute that Cosa felt either emotion.

"Ah! *Buona Sera*, Dottore Sabatini!" Cosa welcomed Giuliana, the proud *padrone* greeting his favored *protégé*. He extended his hand. Giuliana did not move to kiss his ring but only smiled crisply, a charitable affront, masterfully duplicitous.

"His Holiness—?" she prompted.

The cardinal ignored her and moved his attention to Andrew, playing the courtier, buying time. "Dottore Shepard, is it not?"

Giuliana would not be ignored. "You swore to me that His Holiness would be here," she said evenly. There was steel in her voice.

The cardinal glanced at her with more than mild annoyance, clearly displeased with her impertinence, and then flashed a smile again at Andrew. This was too much for her. Giuliana reached for the cardinal's arm to command his attention, her voice rising. "Where is—?"

She felt her wrist suddenly bent unnaturally backward and forced to her side. It all happened so quickly, so definitively that Andrew was caught off guard. He moved between Giuliana and Rindt and, taking his cue from Giuliana, repeated her question.

"Where is the pope?" he asked, surprised at the calm in his voice.

The awkwardness of the moment passed quickly. Cosa moved transparently beyond it as if it had not occurred. "Dottore Shepard." He shook Andrew's hand perfunctorily. "And"—he studied Peter closely—"this must be—?"

"Peter," said Peter simply, studying the man before him. "Who are you? And, for the third time, where is Stephen Parnell?"

Rindt intuitively rescued his patron from the humiliation of having to introduce himself. "His Eminence Adeodato Cardinal Cosa."

" 'His Eminence'?" Peter could not keep the irony out of his voice.

Cosa nodded politely; expectantly, thought Andrew. Peter's response was indifference. No man was greater than another to him. He stood with his arms folded, waiting for the obfuscation to end.

"Well, then!" Cosa said with forced brightness, as if everything was as it should be. "I want to thank you, Dottore Sabatini, for bringing our friend here."

He grasped Peter's elbow lightly and gestured him away from the group toward a set of gilded double doors. Cautiously, Peter allowed himself to be moved. Simultaneously, Rindt grabbed Andrew and Giuliana in his iron grip, crushing flesh into bone even as he graciously "invited" them to a nearby office.

"Surely, you will be more comfortable there while His Eminence interviews Peter," he suggested.

Andrew and Giuliana both resisted. Peter jerked his arm free of the cardinal's touch.

"Is something wrong, my friend?" Cosa asked. "I only want to speak with you privately, to get to know you a little better. It is not every day that we are blessed with such rare company."

"I have nothing to say to you sub rosa, Adeodato. Anything we have to discuss can be shared with my good friends Andrew and Giuliana.''

The cardinal flushed a little but recovered quickly. ''*Si*, I would prefer that myself, my friend. You see, there are certain protocols where His Holiness is concerned—''

''His Holiness,'' Peter repeated.

''His Holiness Pope Luke John, of course,'' Cosa offered helpfully, if a bit condescendingly. ''The Holy Father?''

''Our Holy Father is here, is he?'' Peter looked around, his dark features brightening.

''In the next room, of course,'' answered Cosa, thinking he understood. Then he took Peter's meaning and fell silent. Was Peter toying with him? ''Of course our Holy Father isn't here. That is—''

Peter watched and waited while the cardinal calculated. A door opened quietly, and a soft voice interrupted.

''Doctor Shepard, I'm presuming?''

Pope Luke John stood in the doorway, eyebrows arched. Sizing up the scene, he stepped over to Andrew without waiting for Cosa to perform the formalities.

''Yes, Your Holiness.'' Andrew extended his free right hand and bowed his head. It seemed appropriate at the moment.

When the pope gave Rindt a hard look, the colonel released his grip on Andrew and Giuliana and moved quietly behind Cosa.

''It is good to see you again, Dottore Sabatini,'' the pope smiled warmly. ''Are your parents well?''

''They are well, Your Holiness.'' Giuliana bowed and kissed his ring. ''I will tell them you asked.''

Luke John nodded and moved to Peter, where he stood facing him, hands folded meditatively at his chest. Despite their being approximately the same age, Peter overwhelmed Luke John's frail presence with raw vitality and robust physical power.

Cosa forgot to breathe as he watched the two men encounter each other. Whether Nicolao was Peter didn't matter so much to him as whether Stephen Parnell believed Nicolao was Peter. The result for the Church and Cosa was the same.

Without ceremony, Luke John simply motioned Peter,

Giuliana, and Andrew inside. Cardinal Cosa followed, but the pope held up his hand.

"*Grazie*, Adeodato," he smiled and closed the door, leaving Cosa standing alone before it.

Once safely inside, Andrew cleared his throat nervously. The full impact of where he was and whom he was with had begun to affect him.

"Your Holiness? Dr. Sabatini and I could wait somewhere else so you and Peter can speak privately . . ."

The pope's eyebrows arched formally. Andrew guessed that he wasn't yet convinced that Nicolao was Peter. *He'll know soon enough,* mused Andrew.

Luke John accepted the suggestion at last and gestured toward a side door. "Please feel free to enjoy any of my volumes, *per favore*. I think you, Dr. Shepard, will especially appreciate Gregor Mendel's original journal from the 1865 experiments in Brünn."

Andrew and Giuliana followed his gesture and stepped into another *sala* with soaring Baroque ceilings and hundreds of leather-bound manuscripts organized in neat rows on deeply polished bookshelves. Shafts of light thundered through high windows that opened onto a blindingly bright view to the east, over the gardens.

Luke John paused to collect his thoughts before turning to face his guest. He wasn't going to give this visitor anything, he had decided; Peter or Nicolao or whoever he was would have to earn his trust.

Father, grant me the open heart to accept your purpose, he thought. *I pray that this man is who he claims to be, your servant, Peter. Grant me the faith to see the truth if he is, and the courage to go on if he is not.*

When he turned around he saw Peter standing in the center of the great room watching him with interest.

"I am Luke John," Parnell smiled amiably as he crossed to Peter.

"Luke John," Peter repeated as he shook Stephen's hand firmly.

"Pope Luke John."

"Yes, I know. *Shalom,* Stephen 'Luke John' Parnell."

Luke John evaluated his guest. The streets of Belfast were

suddenly very much with him, and he felt the need for caution.

"You've got to be kidding!" Peter said bluntly, eyeing the pope's gleaming white cassock, beaded belt, and embroidered cuffs.

"I'm sorry?" Luke John's expression froze as his mind raced for a response to this unaccustomed behavior.

"Look at yourself!" Peter explained. "This—this costume!"

Luke John looked himself over quickly.

"I don't mean to be rude, it's just that—who wouldn't be suspicious of a man in such finery? A peacock needs to impress the peahen, surely, but who are you trying to impress? Listen to me, Stephen Parnell," Peter leaned close and whispered confidentially. "Clothes should never speak louder than the man, especially in our line. It's a rule, or it ought to be!"

Listen to how he speaks to me in this way! To hear him, he holds life's secrets in his hand! Luke John didn't know whether to be offended or inspired. Then he caught himself smiling. *At last, someone who doesn't flatter, scrape, and bow.*

Whether the man before him was a saint or a sham, Parnell realized he appreciated Peter's honesty, envied his confidence. For the moment, at least, he wouldn't worry about the rest. His cynicism began to melt away.

Peter had gone to the window and was inspecting the piazza five stories below. Stephen wanted to believe that this was indeed Peter, the powerfully built old man with backbone and an apparent willingness to use it, the rock upon which Catholicism was built. This man had the well-used body of a hard life: weathered face, coarse white stubble, a full head of white hair, a deep barrel chest that rose and fell forcefully as he breathed. His shoulders were thick as ocean swells, his limbs swelled with red-blooded muscles, his hands were plated with calluses. It was a body that had pushed against forces larger than itself. How much of that was Nic Soares, how much the soul of Peter animating him from within?

Under unruly white curls, wide dark eyes took in one of the world's most esteemed views with open curiosity. A hoarse whisper blended with feet on stone, bells, distant echoes, and the continuous hum of the Via della Conciliazione. Peter surveyed the surrounding hills, the position of the sun, and the red granite obelisk, getting his bearings in an environment at once strange and familiar. His hands gripped the ledge like a ship's rail.

Stephen looked at his own soft white hands and then hid them in his waistband. He cleared his throat. "Thank you for coming."

Peter didn't take his eyes off the obelisk. "Caligula and Nero had better taste than Romans gave them credit for," he said without looking away from his memories. "Vaticanus wasn't much, but the Church has made it the equal of the Capitoline and the Forum. Remarkable."

Parnell joined Peter at the window. "A fitting legacy," he answered quietly, looking to see what held Peter's interest. It was the Heliopolis Obelisk.

A tear fell from Peter's right eye and made its way down his cheek.

Luke John looked away. A man's tears were private. He excused himself by making a show of fussing with the coffee service.

"*Caffe*? And a glass of juice from the Vatican's own orange trees, perhaps?"

"You don't believe I am who I say I am," Peter said matter-of-factly.

Luke John turned so quickly that black coffee washed over the rim of the cup and onto the polished parquet.

"That's wise of you, Stephen. In your place I would reserve belief, too."

"I want to believe."

Peter stretched and inhaled deeply. "You're not a trusting man. It's in your writing. Yes, I've read your writing," he said off Parnell's surprised look. "I have prepared for this meeting carefully. You are at heart a skeptic, for all your show of orthodoxy. You don't necessarily believe those who came before you."

"It's my nature, a burden as much as a skill. It's that obvious?"

"No, not really. But I also used to doubt, and I recognized your need to know," Peter reassured him and settled into an armchair, his hands clasped easily behind his head. "Now, what can I tell you?"

Again Luke John took note of Peter's presumption and decided that a forceful fake was at least more entertaining than a reticent reality. This man's brashness appealed to the Irish in him, he supposed. He felt himself relax with Nic, or Peter, or whoever the man was, in a way he hadn't felt comfortable with his fellow man in a long, long time.

"I understand you say you're here from a time long ago. Two thousand years."

"I died here in the year 64. You'll have to trust me on that," answered Peter.

"And you are in fact Peter? Saint Peter?"

"I am Peter, yes. It's for another to say whether I am a saint."

"Well, Peter, you can understand my—our—curiosity about you. There are some who may not believe you are who you say you are."

"And you, Stephen Parnell?"

"I don't know." The pope laughed politely. "Can you tell me something that would prove it?"

"Probably not. It's the human condition to deny, to doubt rather than to examine."

"I'm examining."

"Yes, you are. Congratulations. But you ask the impossible and I don't perform miracles."

"All right, then, assuming you are who you say you are . . ." Parnell hesitated, looked at the floor, gathered his thoughts before saying in a measured voice: "Tell me about Jesus, about your time with him."

"Where shall I begin?" Peter seemed to ask himself as much as he asked Parnell. "That walking on the water was pretty convincing, wasn't it? Jesus came out of the sun itself, out of our hearts. He seemed to emerge from the space between thoughts. You know how sometimes when you are working hard your mind slips into a gap between thoughts? That's what it was like when he arrived that day on the shore. Something deep within me instantly welcomed him. The best part of me knew he was life itself. I felt as if all my life I had been preparing to meet him. I had never known it until then.

"He came at a good time. My head was full of a hard life's business. My heart was full of anger, dark and bitter at times, near to violence. Something I think you understand from your own life's experience, Stephen Parnell. It seemed to me that God had made a covenant with his people, but the leaders of Judea had perverted it."

Stephen smiled wryly. "Some of our detractors accuse the Church of the same thing today."

"How do you answer?"

Luke John avoided the question. "What do you think of our Church?" He gestured expansively with a generous sweep of his arm. "Are you pleased with how your work turned out?"

Peter dismissed all of the Vatican's splendor with a wave of his hand. "Do you know what I see? I see too many believers using their faith as an excuse. They choose their Christ or Yahweh or Buddha or Allah or whatever name they call God by, figure they've found the answer, and stop questioning, stop their search for truth.

"Today's Christians condemn anything that is disagreeable, deeming it sinful. Oh, I know, so do Jews, Muslims, Buddhists, whoever, but that does not make it just. And you support this injustice, Stephen Parnell! You don't mean to be judgmental. You think you're protecting the true faith, but you're only protecting your *image* of faith, your self-image as faithful. You're not helping our flock; you're telling them that it's all right to avoid the real work . . . *within* themselves!"

Peter's tone was friendly despite his criticism. He was a man unafraid of offending, comfortable with unvarnished truth, and he expected the same of his listener. But Luke John, for his part, was stunned. He was pope, after all, and accustomed to a certain measure of deference. Frontal assaults on the papacy, and on him personally, were the norm in the press, but he expected greater civility in personal meetings. Long removed from the rough-and-tumble of street discourse, the harsh rhetoric of everyday argument, Stephen Parnell had grown as soft as his hands; he was unprepared for such raw confrontation.

He paused, swallowed his pride, and waded into the deep issues.

"Can you tell me about those final days with Jesus in Jerusalem?"

"What do you want to know?"

Luke John thought for a moment. Where to begin? "Did you hear Jesus tell Pilate that he was King of the Jews?"

"No."

"Did he claim to be the Messiah?"

"Messiah?" Peter laughed. "No, Stephen. The idea of a warrior slaying his enemies in a great battle wasn't realistic. Understandable, considering the long suffering of the Jewish people, but not realistic. And we Jews are nothing if not realistic.

"We were wrong to place responsibility for our salvation in the hands of a fabled warrior. He made me see that. Anyway, by then he had given us the power of speaking truth. That's all, truth. He didn't come at a subject from the political, the 'religious,' the social point of view. He spoke from the inside out about the heart, the spirit, our attitude, our actions."

Luke John nodded slowly, absorbing this.

"What else?" Peter asked, a twinkle in his eye. Clearly he was enjoying himself.

"The crucifixion. Did it happen as our tradition tells us it happened?"

However painful it was for him to relive these moments, Peter knew he must offer Parnell definitive proof. He took a deep breath.

"Jesus was half dead already by the time he arrived at Golgotha. If flogging didn't kill a man, it took him years to find his feet again. By the time we saw him he was a shadow of the friend and master who had been arrested in the garden the night before—pale, shaking, and in shock. But he was still in that body. I saw him in the way he looked into the faces of the soldiers."

Luke John was listening intently. "Did the thief on his left really repent right there and then?"

"Yes, he did. It was very moving," Peter remembered. "But it was the quiet one on Christ's right," he corrected the pope.

Luke John turned scarlet.

"Nice try, Stephen," Peter grinned.

A smile brightened Luke John's red face. He was relieved. It wasn't much of a test, but he hadn't needed much. Something in him told him that God was speaking.

Andrew had taken the pope's suggestion and examined the Mendel journal, lifting it down reverently from the shelf, turning its yellowed pages with the care that such a volume deserved. Fascinated at first by the sketches, picking out a word here and there from Mendel's Latin and spidery handwriting, he eventually found his attention beginning to wander.

Giuliana, for whom these splendors held a certain familiarity, had touched none of the rare volumes, contenting herself with contemplating the view out the window. Sunlight bathed her delicate features. She felt Andrew's eyes on her and shifted her attention.

"What?" she asked him softly.

"What do you suppose they're talking about in there?" He nodded toward the door through which the two old men had disappeared. Had it been less than an hour?

Giuliana smiled. "The past, as old men always do. But a very different past than most old men have known. Then, I think, the future."

"The future of the Church, you mean?"

She shook her head slightly. "The Church is only the beginning. I was thinking of the future of the world."

28

"HOW DID YOU FEEL WHEN YOU SAW JESUS HELPless up there on the cross?" Luke John poured Peter some coffee at last, busying himself with everyday details as if to somehow distance them both from the horrors they discussed. "The need to help him must have been overwhelming."

"It was. I knew he could save himself. And I think he was tempted a few times. That's what was so impressive about him: he chose to become the enemy of those bitter people. The crowd hated him because his bloody, bruised, pathetic presence was an insult to their arrogance. He was the image of their own vulnerability. They were looking into a mirror and seeing their own ends. It enraged them.''

If he was not there, in fact, he believes he was there, thought Luke John as he listened. Perhaps it was Peter's plain way of speaking that penetrated his defenses. He could feel the distance between them shrinking. He was moving toward acceptance, unable to resist Peter's simple honesty.

"At about midday, when the sun was high, the heavens suddenly went dark.'' Peter's voice took on a deeper resonance. "This had never happened before. Now, I had seen many skies at sea, but never a complete absence of light like this terrible afternoon night. Many panicked and hid in their houses. But Mary and the rest of us stayed as close as the guards allowed.

"Then, after about—I don't know—three hours, Jesus lifted his eyes and cried: *'Eli, Eli, lema sabachthani! Eli!!'* He struggled mightily to draw air into his burning lungs. When he swallowed, pitiful noises sounded from his chest. He reached for air, using all his strength to straighten so he might swallow one more breath of the cool, dark air.'' Peter was breathing harder; Luke John noted the change. "The pause between breaths grew quieter and longer until each gasp came as a surprise. It seemed inhuman to stand by and watch him suffer so. I wanted to seize one of the soldiers' swords and run him through myself. Finally he didn't straighten again. We stared, all of us holding our breath, secretly praying that God would spare him any more agony.''

Peter swallowed some coffee to clear his throat; he no longer tasted it. He sat quietly, remembering. Luke John barely breathed.

"One of the soldiers, a young man from the south, pale with displeasure—probably his first crucifixion—checked the body and told his commander that the 'King of the Jews' was finished. The other soldiers checked the bodies on either side of Jesus and determined that they, too, were dead. The *quaternia* prepared to leave . . .''

"Wait! They left him on the cross?'' The pope leaned forward, incredulous. Any pretense of intellectual distance had fallen away by now.

Peter shrugged. "They were going to. That's what they usually did. But the commander saw us watching, staying close, and he began to curse. He knew we'd never leave the body of Christ for the dogs."

"As we understand it, a wealthy believer petitioned Pilate for Jesus' body . . ."

"Joseph of Arimathaea," Peter supplied. "Actually, he bribed the commander of the *quaternia* the equivalent of three months' wages, and the commander made up some story about his being short of crosses with all the criminals needing to be executed after Passover. Pilate accepted his story."

"Then you helped bury the body in Joseph of Arimathaea's cave."

"Yes. We cleaned his broken body, anointed it, and wrapped it in a length of pure white cloth that Mary had bought at great expense in the bazaar."

Luke John remembered something about the "length of white cloth" in the Shroud of Turin forensic report. The experts had concluded that the cloth was of high quality and would have been expensive by the standards of fourth-decade Jerusalem.

"We would have stayed with him all night if the soldiers hadn't come by and ordered us out of the necropolis. We rolled the great stone closed over the tomb and returned to the house. We collapsed, half dead ourselves. Sleep eluded us for most of the night but, one by one, our bodies overruled our emotions and we slept. For two days we slept. Whenever I woke up, Mary made me eat, which only put me back to sleep. It was two days before I could see straight or think clearly."

Both men fell silent.

"We sometimes forget that you were human beings like ourselves, capable of suffering such overwhelming grief," Stephen Parnell said at last. "I suppose we expect you to be supermen, larger than life."

"We were men, Stephen. Just men."

"Perhaps it is not so terrible," Cosa mused, staring at the closed door every time he passed it in his pacing. Rindt, as motionless as his employer was restive, watched him with growing disgust. "What could happen, after all? They will talk, His Holiness's faith will be renewed, life will go on. Alternatively, if this Peter reveals anything that contradicts His Holiness's beliefs, he will not be believed. Popes with far less faith have made extraordinary changes in the Church, popes with far more have passed through history as ciphers. Luke John's legacy has been one of caution, of conservatism. That will not change."

He looked to Rindt for comment. Rindt shrugged.

"And what do you think, Colonel?"

"I'm not paid to think. If I were, I'd say you were talking aloud to convince yourself. We have no idea what they're discussing in there; it could be anything from the fate of the world to the intricacies of fly-fishing. Until they have finished, this"—his gesture indicated the two of them and their waiting—"is wasted effort. I despise wasted effort."

Cosa eyed him narrowly. Insubordination from Giuliana was one thing, but Rindt was another matter.

"Very well, then, Colonel. Don't allow me to waste any more of your effort! I will not remind you that it is as a result of your carelessness that we are both in this position. Go. Take a walk in the piazza, enjoy the sunshine. Do whatever it is you do when you're not in my employ. I will contact you when I need you."

Rindt acknowledged his dismissal with the slightest movement of his head. *And you will need me!* his silence said.

"I do want to believe," Luke John said.

"Of course." Peter approached him. "A dialectic maybe?" He grinned and winked.

The pope laughed. "Let's see now, where shall we begin?"

He looked down into the piazza and caught sight of the diminutive Gobba, the humpbacked saint of the piazza, a local woman who had adopted the Vatican pigeons. Dressed in layers of dusty cotton prints with a faded blue-and-silver scarf pulled loosely over her hair and tied neatly under her fuzzy wrinkled chin, she shuffled painfully over the cobbles, lips in motion.

She was a fixture, as much a part of the landscape as the

pigeons. When he first became pope, Luke John had watched for her appearance daily, in all weathers, wondering about her. Where had she come from? Was there anyone to look after her? What permutations of personal tragedy or faulty biochemistry had made her this way? He'd thought of speaking to her, inviting her into the Apostolic Palace, asking if there was anything he could do for her. He had mentioned this in passing to some officious cardinal or other—had it been Cosa?—who had rigorously dissuaded him. How would it look, after all? He'd forgotten her until this moment.

He had seen so much suffering in his tours through the horn of Africa, the desolate refugee camps of Bosnia, the iniquitous ghettos of South America. Had he accomplished anything on those arduous journeys beyond the ritual gesture, the photo op, the occasional local riot and subsequent government crackdown, and his own near-prostrating exhaustion? He had journeyed around the globe, yet neglected the tragedy below his own window.

"Tell me, Peter, would I be right to leave the Church if I thought I could be a more effective servant outside the ritual of Catholicism?" he asked, his voice grave despite his attempt to keep a light tone.

"Why not take the Church with you on your journey?" Peter suggested. "Abandon the ritual, try something new?"

"The Second Vatican Council attempted to do precisely that—"

"Mere cosmetics!" Peter dismissed it. "It didn't do enough."

"—Yet there are those who have been trying to undo Vatican II's accomplishments ever since," Luke John concluded.

"Including you?" Peter asked incisively. Luke John did not reply. "You're troubled, Stephen," he added more gently. "Who in your situation would not be?"

"Sometimes I feel there is an unbridgeable chasm between me and . . ." Luke John looked down at the Gobba, who was shaking the last crumbs from her sack. ". . . her."

"We're not so different, you and me. I doubted. You doubt. Use it. When you're fighting within yourself, you're worth something. There comes a point, my friend, where the real and the imagined, past and future, heaven and earth, sin and grace, cease to be seen as contradictions.''

"You're not the firebrand I expected," observed Stephen.

"Don't remind me. I'm an old man."

Luke John chuckled.

"We're two servants of the same master. Looks to me as if you're working toward the same goals, but in your own way. Am I right?"

Stephen's face lifted. "I hope so. But you demanded 'common humanity' of the faithful. Surely 'common humanity' is the one thing we cannot have today. Not if we are to prepare adequately for the future. Surely you understand how different conditions on earth are now?"

Peter looked at the pope in silence. From his expression it was impossible to know whether Peter was saddened or angry. His next words filled the large room.

"Nothing has changed. Armies still roam the world. Tyrants accumulate power only to lose it all to younger tyrants. Peasants toil to fill their stomachs, often having no more to nourish their children than faith. Still, his message endures."

"Is mankind finding its way toward God?"

"You study these things. I should ask you."

"But it's your perspective I'm after. Please, Peter. I need answers only you can provide."

"Man has advanced all right, beyond the stars. But the Greeks pondered the same questions you ask me, didn't they? I see no evolution in your morality. For every child you're photographed with, patting its head while its mother weeps with joy, another child starves and its mother weeps with despair because men like you tell her there is no recourse but to bring children into this world that she cannot feed."

"Religion answers the yearning to know our purpose on earth!" the pope protested, stung. Would Peter have him take on the responsibility for all mankind?

What else have I done, he thought, *in assuming this role, this office?*

"Religion answers questions with theory. From what I see, the questions remain unanswered."

"What would you have me do? Adapt to the changes in the faith? Or resist them?"

"I cannot answer this."

"Why not?"

"You must discover this for yourself. Think, Stephen. Most of what you teach has nothing to do with what I know. The papal aristocracy? I remember community. Excommunication? I remember forgiveness. Subordination of women? I remember honor, respect, and equality."

"Peter, Peter, the world is more complex. So are the problems."

"No faith can be positive when it becomes more important than the individual's relationship with God."

"If our Church is not to teach, then what is our mission?"

"To learn," Peter said forcefully, as he rose and stepped to the window.

Early-morning shadows stretched across the fairways and greens beyond the penthouse windows. Before her workday officially began, Delphine took a few minutes to download the night's messages. Then she returned to her research. Her mouse finger flew in staccato bursts, guiding her back to www.religion.islam.edu. There were 1,867 messages in a new submenu titled "False Prophets." She scanned the message headers and immediately the words "Votto" and "Peter" began appearing frequently:

. . . Imam, could this be the prophet you warned us about?

. . . If this is true, then who will be the next to return from the grave?

. . . Science, after all, is Godly. What is born of Islam belongs forever to Islam, is this not so?

. . . resurrection from a test tube? If this is possible, then Allah permits it . . .

. . . May Allah guide us to the truth.

. . . May he protect us from liars.

. . . If death is indeed the penalty for conversion to another religion—which Peter did in converting from Judaism to Christianity—then how can anyone claim that Islam is tolerant?

. . . Only those born Muslims who turn away from Islam are guilty of apostasy, and therefore condemned to death. Peter cannot be condemned for the accident of his birth.

Observe his choices. Judge him by his actions. I believe that he is like us, a seeker of truth . . .

Delphine typed a quick note:

Dear Andrew,

Here is a sampling of what's being discussed on the Internet. Our friend is the subject of some scary dialogues.

Forces are in motion, Doc. Prophets are always targets.

Be careful. Stay safe.

L,
Delphine

As an afterthought, she checked the "Return Receipt Requested" option. After several days without hearing from Andrew or Giuliana, she was beginning to worry. This way she'd at least know if he was still alive and downloading his e-mail.

If he could get to a computer. If he remembered to turn on his beeper. Life was full of uncertainties.

"Stephen Parnell, God offers everyone a choice between truth and lies, between love and hatred. Take which you want, but you can never have both."

"Live by the truth? That's all?"

"That's all."

"But what is truth?"

"It's all in here." Peter tapped his heart, then his temple. "And here. You may have to dig through all the verbiage that has been piled on top of it, all the lies and falsehoods written in the name of 'religion,' but—"

"Lies? In the Bible?"

"Lies."

"Interpretations, yes, Peter. But *lies*?"

"If it's not true, then it's a lie."

"A white lie here and there by well-meaning believers—"

"Stephen Parnell, two millennia of blood and perversion of simple truth! Based upon the whims of who knows how many writers with who knows how many purposes! How can you countenance that?" Peter paced in lengthening strides, his voice building until it boomed and rattled. "I don't blame the early evangelists. I fault the organizers, the administrators, the theological entrepreneurs who pillage history!" Silverware applauded as he pounded the table for emphasis. "Why, if Jesus were to walk into this piazza today, he'd be arrested again."

"Here? Who would arrest our Lord?"

"Your bishops. Perhaps even you, Stephen Parnell. You would try to discredit him."

"I?"

"Just as in my time, most of those who would accuse him would believe they were protecting the faithful from an impostor. To know a person's spirit, you need only see his or her brand of intolerance. A person's faith is seen best in what they judge, what they condemn, their intolerance. Your church, Stephen Parnell, is historically consistent only in its intolerance."

"Our church is intolerant of evil, yes," Luke John defended himself. "Of extremists who offend human dignity and the faith—"

"Human dignity? What dignity is there in a child's destitution while you and your bishops live as opulently as the Cæsars? As for extremists, what would you call the Islamic fundamentalists with whom your office has so recently had dealings? Or shall we speak of old wars and Jew-killers? Pilate, Waldheim, . . . *semper idem.*"

"It is our responsibility to defend the faith against that which defies the canons!" Luke John said with a trace of an ancient stubbornness. He felt cornered, and he didn't like it. He was on his feet, physically and spiritually dwarfed by Peter's presence, but determined to face him down.

"Who wrote these canons?"

"Saints, scholars, fathers of the Church. And all in support of Christ's own instructions."

Peter approached him until they stood toe to toe. He grasped Luke John's shoulders. "Who told you Christ's instructions?"

"Why, the writers of the . . ." Luke John paused, embarrassed. ". . . Gospels."

He staggered then; only Peter's grip on his shoulders held him upright. Peter could feel the old man's unsteady heartbeat. A blind man could have sensed his sudden agony. Peter gently helped him back into his chair, where Luke John briefly buried his face in his hands.

At last he inhaled deeply, but couldn't will himself upright again. When he lifted his head, he looked older, his face gray, his eyes lit by the red hell from which he was slowly returning.

"I have devoted my life to defending the Bible, preaching what those committees of men wrote," he whispered. "Now you're telling me none of it has any meaning."

"Not at all," Peter corrected him. "It's a good start, but the lessons of the Bible are only that—a start. A child has fables in his storybook to help him grow up. A person has Bible stories to help him grow into his true spirit self. Once there, each of us must find our own path to true awareness."

"You're advising a reinterpretation of two thousand years of theological development," Stephen suggested.

"You have a responsibility to right what is in error," Peter answered without any particular emphasis.

"I am afraid." Stephen rose and began to walk to regain some control. After a few steps, he paused in the middle of the elaborate floor, facing nothing, just standing, suspended.

"Don't be afraid," Peter reassured him. "You know best. Remember this: You have the power to make each moment count. Live each hour consciously, gratefully, generously. Give something to every person and every creature you meet. It doesn't have to be much: Wish them good health or a bit of joy that day. Look them in the eye and feel their concerns for a moment; give to them your undivided attention. Better yet, share the humility of your own spirit. That's right, *humility*. Understanding grows from humility of spirit, from learning, not from the conceit of knowledge. Give that which you most desire for yourself to another person. Do this every hour, every minute, and you will accumulate incalculable wealth. Your soul will not be able to hold all the joy you will feel!

"You ask me 'who is God.' God is within you right now, just as God has always been within your heart and mind and every cell of your being. You ask how to get closer to God.

I tell you, it is simple, but you make simple things complicated. Listen to the best part of you—that is God speaking to you. Do not trust perfect people who tell you they know the one true way to God. Question any dogma invented by a human being. And, if you do nothing else, stop drowning out God's voice in the humble and meek with laws and dogma and judgment!''

Stephen lightened. It was true, one needed to fall, to fail, to die before he could be reborn into his new life. He was desperate to know. His mind raced, ticking off a lifetime's questions. It was as if Peter had reached inside him and touched his guarded heart. This new peace made him generous. He wanted to rush out into the piazza and embrace the world.

An attendant entered, bowing and smiling and puttering about. As he removed the coffee service, replacing it with a tray of fruit and cheeses, the incongruity of the scene struck Stephen Parnell as it hadn't since he was first consecrated bishop thirty years earlier. Then it was the contrast between the boy who'd grown up with bent spoons and chipped crockery and the prince of the Church with his retinue of servants. Now it was the irony of a man who dared to preach poverty of spirit while living in a palace. Stephen didn't even have to look at Peter to know what he was thinking.

When the attendant finally took his leave, the pope breathed a sigh of relief. Then he glanced at the headline in the morning *La Repubblica*, which had been set on the tray for His Holiness's later perusal. He'd thought he'd been visited with enough shocks for one day. He was wrong.

The headline PETER CLEANS HOUSE appeared atop Gianfranco Fini's column. Luke John read the brief column quickly; it was only four short paragraphs. He instantly recognized the paraphrase of Matthew's Gospel in the opening:

> *. . . went into the temple of God, and cast out all them that sold indulgences, and threw open the doors that hid the absolution exchangers, and the seats of them that sold peace of mind to the faithful . . .*

What is this, then? Luke John wondered. He read on:

*He was not wild-eyed or mad. He was a man who was
"trying to do the right thing when confronted by so
much that is wrong," he said. Not a soul in the great
St. Peter's basilica—not a single layperson or cleric—
was unaffected by his rage. This mysterious stranger
transformed all who were present with his magnificent
passion. Afterward, all of us remained where we were,
reluctant to break the enchantment. An elderly* signora
*nearby, her rosary still hanging from her fingers,
looked into the great dome and whispered, "Grazie,
mio Dio. You have spoken and I have heard you."*

*The man told me his name was Peter. When I asked
him for his last name, he answered: "You will know
who I am when Rome understands why I have come."*

Whoever you are, welcome to Roma, Pietro!

The smile melted from Luke John's expression. Why
hadn't he been told? *This man who has within a single hour
moved me to despair, then returned me to a more vigorous
faith, was responsible for upsetting the faithful in the basilica yesterday? How could this have happened and I not
know about it?*

He scented intrigue. How many such matters were kept
from him? How was he to lead if he was kept isolated from
those he would lead?

A more urgent realization occurred to him: All of Christian history turned on that Friday morning in the temple two
thousand years ago. Could history be turning again here in
his own house? He glanced quickly at Peter. Was he man
or spirit, skilled confidence artist or messenger of God?
Luke John suddenly had new compassion for the priests in
the temple—not for their brutality but for their doubt when
confronted by Jesus. Why couldn't they see that he was the
Son of God? Because he looked ordinary and human—like
Peter?

Mio Dio! Luke John whispered to himself and turned
away. His head was swimming! What to do?

He breathed deeply, first one breath, then another, and
felt himself begin to calm down. He remembered his own
favorite sermon, which he had given in more than sixty-two
languages over the years. It ended with the assurance to his

listeners that "... God is within each of us."

All at once Peter's meaning sank in and Stephen Parnell comprehended: God did not arrive with archangels and fanfares of heavenly trumpets. He arrived in a fellow human being. All one had to do to know God was to be attentive to the divinity within each person.

So simple, Stephen thought. *And yet—and yet . . .*

Nula Gatti decided to walk home that afternoon. Usually after a day of leading her tourist charges around the basilica she was glad to take the bus, grateful to be off her feet. But today she had the energy of a young girl. As she crossed the piazza, pressing a coin into the outstretched hand of the humpbacked crone in the head scarf who thanked her with a mumbled prayer as she always did, she felt like skipping.

Yes, she could admit it: She was in love. She and Peter had exchanged no promises and, for all the words they had shared, he was as mysterious to her as he had been the first moment she saw him. Yet she would love this man for the rest of her life, and with that love came trust.

Last night she'd asked him to join her when she got off work today. They could have dinner together, she suggested, perhaps take a walk or go to the cinema, nothing more elaborate than that. He had told her he had something important to do and did not know when he would be back.

"Is it dangerous?" was all she asked.

"I can't say for certain," he had answered honestly, and Nula accepted without question. If it happened that she never saw him again, her feelings would not change.

"Andrew?"

"Mm?"

Afternoon shadows had long ago stolen the direct light from the windows of the pope's private library. The lovers sat in two adjoining chairs, their hands bridging the space between, fingers interlaced, each lost in thought. He raised his eyebrows at her inquiry; she smiled fondly, squeezed his hand.

"Nothing. Nothing at all!"

• • •

"Peter, I must know. Tell me about that morning."

"After three days, the shock of what happened had worn off," Peter said. His tone was conversational. He and Luke John were old friends, discussing the fate of the world as old men have done since the beginning of time. "We were changed. We understood that the world would be shaped by the way we lived, by the choices we made. If we were courageous, then we would cultivate courage in others. If we hid from the dangers, intolerance would prevail. Our choices would create the world in which we lived, good or bad. This is still true. Then, on the third day something happened. What, I'm still not sure.

"We visited the cave on Sunday morning. Mary Magdalene came to get me. She couldn't sleep for her grief, so she visited the tomb before dawn, before she was to meet the other women and visit the cave. She discovered the tomb open, and a man—an angel, she insisted—was waiting for her. The burial linen and a bandage from Christ's head lay there where his body had rested. Mary came to get me and John. We went back with her, and when John saw the great stone rolled aside he got nervous. I was too excited to worry; I went inside and discovered three more 'angels' there. But no sign of Christ. Just the burial cloth."

"What did you think?"

"To be honest, I thought the Romans had had second thoughts and taken the body back. Then I noticed that the soldiers guarding the necropolis were acting strangely, as if they were embarrassed by something they had seen, or only thought they'd seen, something they didn't understand. None of their usual arrogance. They didn't act like victors; they seemed vanquished and confused.

"Then I thought, *Peter, you're a fool. Christ said he would return, and instead of waiting for him, you slept!*"

"What convinced you that the man who came to you three days later was Christ?"

Peter laughed. "It was he. You do not mistake the most important person in your life!"

"How can you be sure?" Luke John persisted, aware of how skeptical he must sound.

"I am certain of nothing but the heart's affections. I loved life. I loved who he was, who he made me. My heart knew that the man I saw before me was Christ.''

"This is important, you realize," Luke John spoke emphatically. "The Resurrection presents the most challenging article of Christian faith."

Peter sighed. "Then as now, people heard only what they wanted to hear, and that was the story of Christ's defeat of death. Once word got out that we had a secret weapon that could conquer *death,* everyone wanted to join. The rest was just detail for them.

"If I hadn't repeated the story of Christ's death and Resurrection, there would be no Roman Catholic Church today. You're a scholar, man; you're aware that every pagan religion has its death-and-resurrection myth. The people I preached to were peasants and freedmen, largely unlettered; they thought we'd invented something. If I had merely shared Jesus' wisdom and simple advice, he and I would have been forgotten in the mists of time."

"But is it true? *Did Christ rise from the dead?*" Luke John was trembling all over, his voice a plea.

"It doesn't matter." Peter's voice was even. Luke John stared at him—stricken, wordless. "It's like asking if God can create a stone so heavy he himself can't lift it. It's a child's argument, an insult to the intelligence that God gave us."

He strode to the window and stood there, arms folded across his powerful chest, eyebrows drawn down in concentration. Was it possible even now that this thickheaded Irishman did not understand him? In his time he had converted thousands with a single sermon. All he had to do now was convince one man. He turned back to Stephen Parnell, fire in his eyes.

"The details of Jesus' life are fascinating, Stephen, and I can regale you with them from now until the end of time, but they don't define, confirm, or deny this thing you call Christianity. I tell you what is important, the *only* thing that is important: recognizing the powerful and transforming spirit within you, me, and every other creature. *That* is what Jesus stood for. It is time to stop judging others and start loving—ourselves, each other, and our common potential for sanctity in this life and what follows."

Stephen Parnell joined Peter at the window. The movements below were suddenly personal. The flapping of wings held intense fascination for him. Every pilgrim's individual life story became important to him. All of creation was alive and growing in every creature, every individual. The weave of spirits in the undulating vista became a rich tapestry. With the look of a man who has decided to risk everything, Stephen asked, "Peter, who is God?"

Peter brightened. "Listen to that presence in the center of your being. Listen very carefully. And when you hear a voice speak to you, answer it. Prayer is not a one-way street. God likes good conversation as much as you. So answer that voice. You'll discover God within, Stephen. When you do, you will have the answer to your question and you will no longer ask 'Who is God?' We are God together."

The pope absorbed Peter's words and gazed at the milling crowds of the faithful below. Suddenly he was on his knees before Peter. "Peter, will you join me on my radio broadcast Saturday?"

"Get up, man; you're embarrassing both of us!"

"I want the world to hear your message."

"I will if you'll get off your knees." Peter saw himself in Stephen's expression. He could feel the moonlight on his face that night on the Mount of Olives, the sweetness in the bark and stones, the shadow of tragedy in the air. "Yes, Stephen. Of course. Now, get up!"

He helped Parnell to his feet, noticing that the old man needed assistance. At last Peter knew why he had returned here: To answer Stephen Parnell's desperate question, to provide the answer that could save humankind.

When the doors opened at last, Andrew and Giuliana saw a man who had aged years in the last several hours. They exchanged wondering glances: What could Peter have told Pope Luke John that would so dramatically burden such a kind man?

29

RINDT WAS ONLY FIVE BLOCKS AWAY FROM CAR-
dinal Cosa's office, but his call from a public
phone was routed more than eighteen thousand
miles in its ciphered trajectory to his superior. Cosa would
complain about the added expense, but Rindt was a committed professional.

The connection switched—a harsh static, another ring cut
short, a distant solenoid hammered home in an outdated
switching closet, then a barely discernible shift in the static.

Losing control of Peter was bad, Rindt thought. Having
to hold Cosa's hand was worse. He cracked his knuckles
one by one as he waited. Finally he heard the familiar ring-
ring, ring-ring.

"*Buon giorno, L'ufficio* Cardinal Cosa." Monsignor Murphy's familiar Irish-accented Italian sounded on the line.

Rindt did not bother identifying himself. "Monsignor, I
am returning his page," was all he said.

"One moment."

The line went silent.

"Rindt?"

"*Si*, Your Eminence."

"His Holiness has invited this Peter, or whoever it is, to
join him on his Saturday radio broadcast."

"I see." Rindt waited.

"How could you let this happen? How could you let him
get away? I pay you a prince's ransom. I put the wealth and
power of the Church at your disposal so that you may prevent problems. Now you have become the problem!"

"Would you have had me shoot him in the piazza under
the pope's window?" Rindt asked dryly. "Even that was
not an option. My handpicked operatives followed Sabatini
and Shepard back to her apartment, but Peter was not with
them. His Holiness, it seems, decided to take him on a tour
of the excavations, to show him the place of his interment.
They entered alone, at the pope's insistence, and no one saw
them leave. Apparently one can take the boy out of Belfast,
but one can't take Belfast out of the boy."

"What is that supposed to mean?" Cosa snapped.

"It means your tame pope is no longer sleep-walking, Eminence. He is aware of danger, though he may not yet know its source. Obviously he let Peter out a side entrance, where he went on his way. Whether he speaks on the radio or not, the damage is done."

But Cosa wasn't listening. "You must stop him. He has filled His Holiness's mind with strange ideas. He—"

"I will take care of it, Your Eminence."

"He's going to create chaos!" the cardinal wailed.

Rindt had never heard the cardinal lose control. It was unnerving. *Tactics, tactics, was there never any time for strategy?*

"Your Eminence"—he inhaled—"I will handle this. But I cannot waste time in constantly reassuring you at every step."

"I don't care what you have to do, he must not appear with His Holiness!"

"I understand, Your Eminence," Rindt acknowledged crisply, quickly adding a casual warmth. He knew the cardinal's moods; no matter how far their swing, they always responded to confidence, and Rindt excelled at such emotional subtleties. "Consider the matter resolved."

A bell strained weakly through the thick wall behind the headboard, muffled in the dense apartments in Prati. Nula sat up. She heard a voice from the next apartment—a tone, really—the murmur of some vital information to a distant ear, perhaps a relative, one of the everyday sounds of her life.

Peter lay asleep in a tangle of her best sheets, one leg above the waves for air, his powerful head heavy on the pillow, eyes still, mouth closed.

Nula leaned on one elbow and gazed at him fondly. *Thank God he doesn't snore!* she thought, smiling as she remembered.

Outside, Rome stirred more genially than usual. She felt young again. What had begun as guileless talk with a dangerous man, an animal off his range, so sensitive and gentle . . . she couldn't have suspected . . . it was a miracle. No one had ever matched her desires. Men had failed her. Not many—a few beaus in her teens, then her numbing marriage, no one after that. It wasn't their fault when it came to the wonders that a woman was capable of feeling. They were yearning in their way, too, striving for ideals they weren't sure even existed. But most gave up too easily, content to take their own pleasure, impatient with hers.

But this man, he understands women! she smiled to herself. Peter saw the spirit inside, not just the body, although he was passionate about that, too!

She ran a finger along his arm, curled under his whiskered jaw, and recalled how she had responded to his fervor to possess her, his desire to adore every aspect of her being, his need to give her pleasure of the spirit and the heart as well as the body, which he did with infinite attentiveness.

He had renewed her desire for life, for love. He almost certainly wasn't aware of what he had evoked in her. How could he have been aware that when he combined his erotic spontaneity with such adoring tenderness, he would transform her? She sat up, looked at Peter, and felt excitement stirring again.

How could the priests call what they'd done a sin? It was natural, and God, having created everything that is natural, surely created the pleasure they had found in one another. So if God created their need, how could what they felt and the way they fulfilled that holy need be sinful? What did priests know? How dare they condemn what God created?

Peter opened his eyes, stirred by the impact of a dream bumping up against waking thought. He grinned, memory quickly catching up with his senses. Had it really happened? He stretched his sinewy limbs and enjoyed the rush of blood and feeling into his mortal tissue.

Nula watched, affected by his every movement. *"Buon Giorno, Pietro."*

"Buon Giorno," he growled warmly, then admired her, remembering. He pulled her down into his arms and recaptured her warmth against his own bed heat. "I am hungry."

"I have no doubt," she replied mischievously. "After . . ." She traced her memory on his full lips.

"You are not?"

"Oh, I got up and ate a little last night. I couldn't sleep." He raised his eyebrows in surprise.

"Were you troubled?"

She shook her head no.

"I don't do this as a rule, you know," she said seriously.

"What? And you think I prowl the streets for defenseless women?"

She laughed richly. "No. I know you don't. I knew that immediately. And I am not 'defenseless.' I just want you to understand that this is the most reckless, most wonderful thing that I have ever done."

He tightened his embrace in answer. "I'm happy for you. But I'm still hungry."

She noticed the clock on the stand and scrambled out of bed. "I'll fix you a frittata. You must get ready; there's not much time!"

After they showered and dressed, she sat with him as he ate. He grew stronger before her eyes, fueled by her food. It gave her an extraordinary feeling of purpose. She wanted to live like this, with Pietro. She wanted him to stay forever, but of course she couldn't tell him this. She felt so right. How could it be anything but exactly as it was meant to be? Yet it was too soon for these thoughts.

"This is history, living history, Pietro!" she exclaimed. "Vatican Radio has broadcast papal messages ever since Enrico Marconi himself went on the air in 1931 to introduce Pius XI! Never has a pope requested an average person to join him in these messages!"

"Imagine!" Peter agreed, humoring her.

"Why you, Peter? Not that you're average. Not in any sense of the word!" she quickly backfilled. "But if you had told me you knew Dottore Sabatini I would have known she could arrange an audience." She was growing nervous. Why should she be nervous? Maybe last night was catching up with her. "I would not have made a fool of myself, bringing you to the piazza to watch him bless the crowds—!"

"You were anything but foolish, Nula!" Peter reveled in her excitement. "You were generous and helpful. I myself didn't understand the rules that day."

"Yet now you're so calm!" Nula scolded him. "Radio Vaticano links listeners all over the entire world, from young boys listening on shortwave in New Jersey to pensioners in

Glasgow to villagers in the remote African bush! How can you be so unaffected?''

"I guess it just hasn't sunk in yet," he said quietly, still smiling.

She checked the clock and then quickly cleared the table. Her gown fluttered like wings. Before he knew it she was holding his jacket for him. "You mustn't be late, it wouldn't be *corretto*. Tell me again where you are to meet them?''

"The Gasparone, near Trevi. Now, listen to me," he started to say, but she interrupted him.

"Pietro, I have been thinking."

"Hmm?"

"Maybe you should not go. Once the world hears your voice they will fall in love with you and I won't be enough for you anymore."

He laughed heartily and held her close. "I must do this thing. Then we will go away together. What do you say to that?"

"I say we go now."

"You stay here, doors locked, do you hear? Don't even answer the phone."

"But what if I need you?" She tugged playfully on his jacket lapels.

"I'll come to get you when it's safe. Tell me you'll stay here."

She gauged his concern, judged it was genuine, and decided to trust him. "*Si*. I will stay here. But you come back to me, and quickly."

Peter kissed her deeply and slipped out the door.

She stood for a very long moment, her hand on the knob, forehead pressed against the door. When she didn't hear his footsteps moving down the hall, she knew he was still standing there. She reached for the chain and pushed the bolt. "There!" she said to him through the door. His footsteps began again and faded down the hall.

He avoided the main streets and made his way through alleys. It would take longer to reach their rendezvous, but Rindt had proved he was serious, so Peter was forced to play stealth against Rindt's force. He passed behind apartment buildings and shops and restaurants. As he elbowed his way down a particularly crowded walkway, he came out into an intersection where he had no choice but to cross an open piazza. Fortunately it was filling with stalls and farmers who were off-loading breads and ripe apples, greens of every sort, squash, potatoes, and peppers. A hawker emptied whitefish from a bushel basket onto crushed ice and swore when a large, shiny *eglefino* slid onto the cobbles at Peter's feet. Peter bent down, brushed it off gently, and returned it to the merchant.

"*Grazie, Signore. Grazie.*"

"*Prègo, Signore.*" Peter glanced at the fish, its unseeing eyes watching him leave it to its fate.

Peter walked faster, yet he kept seeing the haddock. *How much men are like fish,* he thought. *They follow one another in large schools, with no real connection to each other or the sea in which they swim, they just bite blindly at bait, are reeled in gasping, their eyes clouding over as they wait in fear for the end and hope for mercy!*

Every time Peter went his own way without telling them where he was going, Andrew worried that they'd never see him again. If Giuliana shared his fear, she didn't show it. She seemed to accept Peter's attitude that he was here for a purpose and that that purpose would be fulfilled no matter what.

"There he is!" Andrew spotted Peter as they entered Via del Muratte and waved to get his attention. He seemed relaxed, even reflective as he joined them.

"*Buona mattina, i miei amici!*" he brightened as he accepted Giuliana's greeting kiss.

"*Bene,* Peter!" she praised him. "Your Italian is *molto bene!*"

They continued walking to the restaurant, happy to be in one another's company again. Giuliana linked arms with the two of them. As they turned into the nameless alley that led to the Gasparone, however, she froze. Peter and Andrew then saw what she saw. Several guards waited around the front entrance of the restaurant, their eyes scanning the passersby. One of them noticed the trio, set his coffee down on one of the outdoor tables and began striding toward them, calling out imperiously: "*Fermate! Aspetti un momento!*"

Giuliana stepped in front of Peter and pushed Andrew away from her. "Run!" she ordered both of them, beginning to run herself. "We meet at Raphael's Tomb in Pantheon at ten o'clock. Go!"

Andrew started to run alongside Giuliana, but she pushed him away. Her fear and determination told him all he needed to know. They scattered in three directions and quickly vanished into Rome's labyrinthine streets.

Andrew ran into Piazza Barberini, up the hill along Via Veneto and then doubled back to the Ministero Industriale, where he flagged a cab and traveled north toward Piazza del Popolo. He walked the block to the Flaminio Metro and rode south to Colosseo station. He was zigzagging, moving back and forth across the ancient city without a clue what else to do. Thirty-five minutes to go before ten o'clock. Checking his pocket map, he calculated that he was forty minutes' walking time from the Pantheon. He looked around the side streets for a cab, a bicycle, anything that might get him there on time.

Twenty-five minutes. Traffic buzzed around him. Towering tour buses rumbled past. Romans zoomed in and out of side streets, never stopping long enough to give him an opportunity to ask for a ride. The cabs seemed to have vanished. A courier stopped and parked his Vespa before a government building and was nearly to the door before Andrew caught up with him.

"Hey! Excuse me? *Mi scusi, signore!*"

The young man stopped and turned to face him.

"I want to buy your Vespa."

The man looked at his scooter, then back at Andrew, not comprehending.

"How much? For your Vespa?"

"*Si tolga dai piedi!*" the young man snarled.

Andrew didn't need to understand Italian to know he had been told to take off.

"*Per favore, signore? Per favore!*" Damn! Why didn't he learn to speak the language? He pulled out all the cash he had in his pockets and wallet, a few hundred thousand lire.

The man must have understood Andrew's desperation, or

else Andrew had offered him more money than he realized. He dug into his pocket, handed the key over to Andrew and stuffed the money into his jacket. Mumbling *"Buona fortuna,"* he disappeared inside.

Andrew had started the Vespa and was darting through traffic before he remembered to check the time again. Seven minutes until ten o'clock.

Traffic moved so swiftly that he missed a turn and was three blocks past the Pantheon before he could turn around. Finally, breathless and disheveled, he pulled up and parked the Vespa between columns under the Pantheon's portico. It was 10:02.

He found Peter and Giuliana on the far side of the rotunda near a low, flower-bedecked tomb. Relief at seeing Andrew showed on Giuliana's face.

"We'll have to get going," he said urgently.

"Si, we must hurry," agreed Giuliana. They started for the doors.

Too late. The massive bronze doors swung resoundingly closed. Perhaps a dozen men in black suits appeared out of nowhere, instructing everyone in several languages to remain calm and move to the center of the temple. A routine matter, they assured; no one need worry.

The one in charge looked over the group and approached, his boots echoing off the vast marble floor.

"Swiss Guard," Giuliana whispered to Andrew. This time she moved closer to him, pointedly not looking at Peter.

"Dottore Sabatini. Dr. Shepard. I am Tenente Rozzanni," the man announced with what he thought was an affable smile. "I have come to escort you and Peter to the Vatican."

"Is all this necessary?" demanded Andrew. "You scared the hell out of us!"

"Where is Colonel Rindt?" Giuliana asked, a strange tone in her voice.

"Detained." The *tenente* hesitated. His instructions had been minimal. How much did Dottore Sabatini know? "He—ah—ask me do this for him. Now where is Peter, *per favore*?"

Andrew began to protest, but Giuliana interrupted forcefully. "I was going to ask you, *Tenente*. Dr. Shepard and I, we are also searching for him!"

The officer surveyed the twenty people assembled in the temple and looked carefully at each person.

"Hey, mate, what's all this, then?" bellowed an Australian as he moved to confront the officer. A younger man in black blocked his path.

"No cause for alarm, *signora e gentiluomini*. This is an official matter. Stay calm, do as I say, and we'll have you on your way in no time."

A dark young man bolted for the door but was knocked to the floor by another guard before he was halfway there. A collective gasp resounded in the large rotunda, then settled into a nervous silence. The *tenente* motioned to all the women.

"*Signora*, please step over here behind me."

The women, including two frightened preteens in ponytails, did as they were instructed.

The *tenente* looked over the eight men remaining and focused on the oldest of them. There was a gaunt pensioner with a British Airways shoulder bag, a stocky, white-haired bulldog-faced laborer in his Sunday suit, and Peter.

"Your name, *signore*?" the *tenente* asked the laborer.

"Holshein, Johan."

The officer considered the man for a moment. "Where are you from, Herr Holshein?"

"Stuttgart. What is this about?"

The *tenente* didn't answer. He was scrutinizing Peter.

"And you?"

"What business is it of yours?"

"American, I see."

"And proud of it!" Peter boasted convincingly.

"Good for you. Now what is your name?"

"Austin, Will Austin," he answered, clearly irritated. Andrew winced.

The *tenente* watched him closely. Peter didn't blink.

"Where are you from, Signore Austin?"

"Before Montana, Rome."

"Montana?"

"Yep."

"Do you know this man?" The officer pointed to Andrew.

Peter shook his head no.

"This woman?"

Giuliana's eyes widened.

"Nope. But if I were a little younger, I wouldn't mind getting to know her better!" Peter winked. Giuliana relaxed.

"You're telling me your name isn't Peter and you don't know who this *signore* and *signora* are? I have trouble believing you. You look familiar to me."

"Never seen 'em before now. Never seen you before, either. And if you want my opinion, I don't care if I ever see you again."

The *tenente*'s attempt at intimidation was blunted.

"Say, what's with all of these guns, mister? In Montana we don't pull a gun if we don't intend to use it!"

The *tenente* shook his head, dismissing this annoying American with a wave of his hand before turning to Andrew and Giuliana. "I will take you to Radio Vaticano now."

Now it was Giuliana's turn to give him a hard time. "Do you really think that's necessary, *tenente*?" she demanded, her voice calculatedly loud. "Do you expect us to lead you to Peter? Or perhaps we are hiding him in our back pockets?"

"Dottore Sabatini, *per favore*." The *tenente* was distinctly uncomfortable. He gestured to one of his subordinates to unlock the bronze doors and let people file out one by one. "Is it necessary to create a disturbance? We are only attempting—"

"It is you who have created the disturbance, *tenente*! Locking the doors, herding these people about, frightening them half to death—!" Out of the corner of her eye, Giuliana watched Peter stroll through the doors with a mock salute to one of the Guards. "I intend to report this incident to Colonel Rindt, if the tabloids don't do it for me. In the meantime, escort us if you wish, but we are perfectly capable of finding our way on our own!"

She took Andrew's arm and swept out of the Pantheon ahead of Tenente Rozzanni, who signaled to one of the youngest Guards to follow a few respectful steps behind them. It would seem that Giuliana had won this round. Only Andrew could feel her trembling.

• • • •

Luke John arrived early at Radio Vaticano's studios. The startled staff of nuns and lay engineers dropped what they were doing and welcomed him, hiding their irritation under artificial smiles and polite banter. They were so flustered they failed to notice his high spirits, the glow of his cheeks, the flash in his gaze. They couldn't know the source of his excitement.

He, Stephen Parnell, Pope Luke John, would in a few moments have the privilege of introducing to the faithful around the world the father of their Church. He would be the humble man who had the vision and faith to stand up for a miracle and testify to the world that here was Peter, returned to earth. He would risk his entire career, his life if it came to that, to build the bridge between man and the Word, between earth and heaven.

He went into Studio A to be alone with his thoughts, to pray for wisdom in this moment for which he now knew he had been born. He settled into the comfortable armchair by his usual microphone, but when he looked across the table and noticed for the first time that the guest chair was a cursory wooden affair with scant padding, he quickly rose again and changed places.

Waiting, praying in fits and starts, he took in the soft lights, the padded walls, and thought of the history that permeated the place. He had a special affection for this magnificent facility. It had fed his imagination as a youngster in war-torn Belfast, where he had listened in on a medium-wave radio to the late broadcasts into the wee hours, all the way to the papal blessing and hymn at signoff. The radio had become his link to the world outside his own.

Although Gindman still expected Andrew to return to BioGenera, Will Austin knew better. Andrew Shepard had seen another, better world and would choose to live there. As for Will, he was on his own now, his apprenticeship over. He was free to achieve his own significance.

In the wee hours of the morning, the layered tangle of T cells on the slide resisted his efforts to count them, but he was determined. He peered into the microscope and his mind focused like a laser. He was working on something with potential even greater than memory resurrection—a

DNA computer, a way to make more computations than all the computers currently in existence with just a few quarts of DNA—not artificial intelligence, but the real thing. In the next room, Niko had been whining and yapping about something all evening; the sounds tickled the edges of Will's concentration but couldn't distract him. At first.

The slide blurred for an instant and he sat back, rubbing his eyes. It was well after midnight; he ought to knock off and get some rest. Well, maybe a beer in town and . . . What the hell was eating Niko?

"Okay, son, I'm coming. Jeez, what's the matter with you tonight?"

The chimp was perched high on his cage bars and reaching for Lucy, trying to wake her. She was deep in slumber on her raised sleeping shelf, oblivious to his efforts.

"Andrew?" Will called to the monkey. Since Niko's transformation, "Andrew" was the only name to which he would respond. Will had felt ridiculous at first, but he'd gradually gotten used to it. "What's the matter?"

Niko didn't react. He stretched his arm farther between the bars and caressed Lucy's head, sighing and cooing as he attempted to groom her.

"Andrew?" Will said again.

No reaction.

"Niko?"

Niko craned to look at Will, bared his teeth in greeting and returned his attention to his mate. As for Lucy, who was still grieving over the replacement of her mate by a stranger, the grooming brought her gently out of her dream. She opened her eyes slowly, sadly. When she saw who it was that touched her, she was instantly awake and at the bars scrutinizing him to assure herself that it was really her Niko. She reached over and touched his face.

"Niko!" Will exclaimed as he watched them. "Damn, it's you! You're back, buddy!" he exclaimed, happy to have his familiar presence back in the lonely laboratory. "Where've you been, fella?"

Niko laughed and screeched as it all came back to him: the laboratory, Lucy, Will. He whooped and leapt from bar to bar, desperate to be freed from the cage.

Will opened the door and was practically knocked off his

feet as Niko exploded to freedom. The chimp bounded around the lab on all fours, swung from shelves, and celebrated in a raucous, discordant rush of screams and breathless cries. Finally he arrived back at Lucy's cage, trying to hug her through the bars.

"Well, it's good to have you back," Will beamed. He retrieved some bananas from the cupboard and opened Lucy's cage so the two could have the run of the lab and apartment. Niko and Lucy made the most of it, and for fifteen minutes joyous chaos ruled.

"Is this a private party or can anybody join?" Delphine asked from the doorway.

Will looked chagrined. "I hadn't meant to stay this late, but I guess there was a reason why I did. Niko's back."

"The personality from Andrew's DNA is gone," he explained. "Either it's gone into remission or it's just plain gone."

Delphine sat on the edge of the desk and considered what this might mean.

"We have to tell Andrew."

"Agreed." Will showed her the notes he'd been typing in spite of the chimps' antics. "I've been sending him update memos every couple of days, but he's not picking up his e-mail."

"He's not answering his pager either," Delphine reported. Will gave her a quizzical look. "Some information on religious debates I downloaded and thought he might use, but he never responded. It's like he and Giuliana have dropped off the face of the earth."

30

TEN-THIRTY. RINDT WAITED WITH TWO SUBORDInates in a freshly washed Alfa on Via del Borgo Pio at Via de Porta Angelica, watching the morning rush. This was the dangerous time, he knew. Two days without sleep. Relying too much on youth when youth was draining from his arms, legs, and will. He used to take it in stride, but the unrelenting stress, fuzzy objectives, and frustration were taking their toll.

He looked at the crush of foot traffic competing at the intersection with the flood of merging cars and trucks and forced himself to focus on the facts. Romans were not predictable in a close-quarters frenzy, but his men were well trained. Rindt was confident they could handle all contingencies.

The radio crackled, and a voice crisply announced that Peter had been sighted walking west on Via dei Gracchi. He would arrive in the piazza across from the colonel's position in five minutes. For an operation of this urgency, Rindt had insisted he have as many men as possible at his disposal; he had a man stationed at virtually every Metro station and others watching the bus routes, all of them armed with copies of a photo of Nicolao Soares that the colonel had acquired by surreptitious means. The men did not need to know who this man was, only that he was to be monitored, his every move reported to Colonel Rindt. He might be a murderer, a potential assassin stalking the pope. The thought visited Rindt with a brief, ironic smile.

Peter would turn south on Via Ottaviano, then Via de Porta Angelica into Piazza San Pietro.

Five minutes. Half the pain in life is waiting, Rindt thought. Long ago he had disciplined his emotions, relegating them to remote corners of his psyche. The discipline to wait without restiveness, however, had eluded his best efforts. There was no control he could exert over its power on him. It was absolute, like the earth's rotation and the tides. Cause and effect.

Jesus, Rindt! He shifted irritably: *Concentrate!* The driver, a twenty-two-year-old who was far wiser than his years, glanced at him, then resumed his watch. For the first time in his intense career Rindt experienced something approximate to disgust. He didn't particularly want to do any harm to Peter. He liked him. But it had been his mistake to befriend him in the first place. His job was the only reliable aspect of his narrow life. It was always there when all the rest evaded him. So he returned its loyalty.

He shifted in his car seat and squinted, then chuckled coldly. Man is the only animal that remains friendly with his victim until the moment he devours him. The thought made him feel stronger, purer, more efficient. Surely there must be a reason for this edge given to man! Above all else, Rindt required reasons.

The door to Studio A opened, the rush of sounds from the corridor an unwelcome interruption. Cardinal Cosa swept in with the air of importance that had once irritated Stephen Parnell. Since he had been elected pope, however, Cosa's idiosyncrasies had become less relevant.

"Have you seen Peter?" Luke John asked, checking the clock and seeing that there were still more than twenty minutes left before 10:55, the time to which Peter had agreed the previous day.

Cosa lifted his shoulders and his bejeweled hands in a universal shrug. It was nonchalant, ostensibly intended to calm the pope, Stephen guessed. He didn't care much for the cardinal when Cosa patronized him.

"Perhaps he isn't used to morning traffic," Cosa offered. He noticed that the typed pages of the pope's comments lay in the center of the table and arranged them before the comfortable chair. "You will be sitting in your usual place, Your Holiness?" He looked across the table, a little too nonchalantly, thought Stephen. Something was up.

"No. I will sit here. Peter will sit in my usual chair." Luke John reached over and pulled the radio address papers to him. "He is looking forward to this almost as much as I am."

Cosa considered the pope's decision to sit in the guest's place. "Are you certain? Perhaps he has decided not to join you," he ventured.

"He will be here. I know this."

Cosa remained quiet, gauging the pontiff's temperament.

"It would have been wiser to insist that he stay in the Apostolic Palace," Cosa ventured, a told-you-so edge in his voice. "To leave him free to roam the streets unescorted—"

"You don't believe he is Peter, do you, Adeodato?" Stephen asked the cardinal directly.

Cosa turned and busied himself with the angle of the microphones. He remembered how this annoyed the studio engineer, retracted his hands into his waistband, and paced slowly. "What I believe has no relevance, Your Holiness."

"Oh, I think it does. A man of your determination has a

great deal at stake in a historical moment such as this.''

Cosa paused and looked at the pope. Stephen looked for a clue to Cosa's thoughts but saw only the studied blank expression of a diplomat.

''I need not remind you, Your Holiness, of the importance of allowing God to do his work whether we comprehend his ways or not,'' the cardinal said evenly.

Stephen held up Cosa's response in his mind for any hints of a fault line but found none. This was Cosa's game. No one could better him at semantics.

''Exactly,'' he replied simply.

The two men were silent in the muffled air of the studio's voice booth, each treading water, gauging the other against the moment's potential.

Stephen knew the next line in the argument for faith. ''When you surrender to his will, only then will you find peace. Can you surrender to his will, Adeodato? Are you capable?''

''What kind of a question is that, my friend? I am a man, mortal and imperfect. But I think I am as capable of saintly surrender as''—his gaze challenged Stephen—''the next man.''

''We can never know until we are confronted with the choice,'' cautioned Stephen. ''I believe this is such a choice.''

''Do you? What choice?''

''A choice between hubris and subjugation to the unseeable, untouchable.'' He looked squarely at his most trusted subordinate and instinctively understood the danger that now threatened Peter.

''You must be under a great deal of stress, Adeodato,'' the pope said, not unkindly. ''No doubt you rue the day you received that first request from BioGenera. What you thought was a simple matter, a commendable way to bring the Church into harmony with the technology of the times, has become your greatest trial.

''If you publicly commit yourself to Nicolao as the resurrected memory of Peter, you verify his authenticity, his right to speak for a return to the simplicity Jesus intended. Is there a place for a man like you in the Church that Peter envisions? Do as your heart tells you to do, you lose your comfortable position and place your career in jeopardy. And if you are wrong and this man is not Peter, you disgrace and discredit yourself. A little like faith in heaven, wouldn't you say? Live for the day and risk eternity. Live for eternity and risk the day.''

Stephen noticed that his friend was listening intently, perhaps grateful to have his private turmoil in the open between them, yet still not willing to confess to it.

"Or, you can pass. Neither endorse or condemn. That's the safe thing to do,'' Stephen observed thoughtfully, "but it's not like you.''

Cosa massaged his jaw thoughtfully, distantly.

"And finally, there is the strategic move that avoids any potential embarrassment, the political expedient. After all, we have all confronted the devil's logic at one time or another: surely, it must be better to sacrifice one man than the entire Church.

"Have the burdens of leadership worn you down, my friend?'' Stephen asked, his voice warm with compassion.

Cosa exhaled wearily. He sat in the armchair where Peter was to sit. It sighed under his great weight. "Would that surprise you, Your Holiness? After all, institutions tend to outlive their tenants. The Vatican is better at it than most.''

"True.'' Stephen nodded agreement, outwardly calm but now perspiring under his linen robes. "But perhaps one last mission is asked of you.

"You see, I believe every soul has a mission and if we are lucky, we will recognize the crucial moment of that mission. For some it is a mission of hardship in which the spirit may grow. For others it is a confrontation with evil to test and strengthen. And for some, it very likely is evil itself.''

They were longtime associates, if not exactly close friends. Each realized the significance of their conversation and chose to stay in the region of the theoretical, the intellectual dialectic.

"Holiness, it seems to me that the reason men need the Church is because it is not always easy to discern evil for oneself,'' Cosa suggested. "If you tell me as pope, ex cathedra, that Nicolao is Peter, then I must acquiesce. Otherwise, you must allow me the voice of my own conscience.''

"I would never presume to do otherwise,'' Stephen assured him. "However, I suggest that without help from faith to see beyond the evil—and the pride that unbroken success can breed—it can be devilishly difficult to choose." He fingered the pages of his address. "I would think that such a cycle of self-deceit can be great indeed, greater than the memory of God, difficult to break without help."

The cardinal locked his jaw and was uncharacteristically silent, Stephen thought.

"In the depths of every heart there is a Tullianum, a dungeon where secrets are kept under lock and key," the pope suggested. "We try to stay vigilant and keep our weaknesses hidden away, but we are only human. We cannot stand watch without occasional rest, and in the small hours of the night we know that the errors we have committed must be answered to. Perhaps you are tired, Adeodato. Perhaps it is time to open your heart and answer."

"There is much to lose!" Cosa murmured, as if to himself. "The consequences . . . We must protect ourselves, the Church . . . It is not a matter of individual choice but of the greater good . . . My mentor understood . . ."

The pope froze. "Votto?" he said, horrified. "Oh, no, Adeodato. Not Votto!"

"We are the true faith, Parnell!" Cosa rose from his chair like a volcano, his strength renewed. "The world is complex and the old ways don't work anymore. When Catholics achieve a majority, they can influence the State—"

"To restrict other faiths?"

"To work for the betterment of the human condition. We must protect what the Church has gained!"

"No, Adeodato. We must protect the human soul."

Lost to some private dilemma, Cosa seemed not to hear him.

"Adeodato, I want to lead souls, not steal them."

For several minutes silence owned the room.

Suddenly Cosa pulled the door open and rushed out.

"*Cum tacent clamant . . .*" Luke John murmured, a quote from one of Cicero's orations against his enemy Catiline. " 'When they remain silent, they cry out.' "

He could get used to this walking, Andrew decided as he and Giuliana threaded their way down Via de Porta Angelica. He enjoyed how connected he felt to Rome and Romans when he walked. Californians needed the isolation of their cars. Romans needed community.

He watched Giuliana as she walked ahead, her handbag strap slung across her right shoulder, the bag rhythmically stroking her right hip, away from light fingers. Her hair bounced with the pace and her skirt flowed in the morning stillness. There was nothing about her that didn't fascinate him.

"*Avanti*, Andrew! Hurry!" she called over her shoulder, looking back to make sure he was still with her. Then she saw his expression and frowned. "Hurry!" she repeated and finally smiled.

They crossed the street as they approached the terminus of the Number 64 bus line to avoid the crowds. Andrew spotted Peter about fifty yards away, walking through Porta Angelica and into the Piazza San Pietro, beyond a passing white Lancia.

"Peter!" he shouted, but Peter couldn't hear him. The traffic was getting more dense. Andrew stepped into the street with Giuliana and looked for an opening in the traffic. To his right a line of compact cars was poised for clearance, all of them coated with Rome's film of dust except for a freshly washed car farther down. Newness stood out amidst so much antiquity.

Finally they passed under the Porta Angelica and into the relative openness of the piazza, where they had a clear view of Peter thirty yards ahead. Peter walked quickly across the vast circle, past the obelisk, and was nearing the Arch of the Bells when Andrew saw Cardinal Cosa running toward them, toward Peter. What was he doing?

Andrew held Giuliana's arm as he began to run after Peter, who still hadn't spotted them. They were only twenty yards away when a roaring engine behind them caught Andrew and Giuliana's attention. Cars were never allowed onto the piazza. The wail of the engine and its slapping tires on the cobbles profaned the peace of this place. They turned around to see the shiny car pressing up parallel to them and a man in the back leaning out the window, pointing something in Peter's direction.

Andrew pushed Giuliana to the ground and yelled: *"Peter!"*

Peter turned, saw Andrew, and waved. Then he read Andrew's expression and saw him lowering himself to cover Giuliana, waving frantically, gesturing for Peter to get down. Peter didn't understand. He stood and stared.

"Coming about!" Andrew shouted in desperation.

Without thought or calculation, Peter instantly bent over at the waist and crouched down, his sailor's reflexes instinctively avoiding the lethal arc of a sailboat's boom. Once down at the level of the cobbles, he seemed puzzled. Was Andrew joking? Then something flew past his head. He felt the *whoosh* a few millimeters from his cheek, and the narrow medieval bricks of the Vatican wall behind him exploded.

Cosa pounded down the paving stones like a lumbering jumbo jet straining for flight. Had his fears been realized?

He saw Peter standing frozen, Andrew and Giuliana falling to the pavement beyond. Then he saw Peter fall.

Rindt knew he had failed. The Carabinieri were scrambling from their post at the Porta looking for the source of the gunfire. Two plainclothes Swiss Guards lunged from the Arch of the Bells and raised their weapons. One stood staring in disbelief at the blue Alfa and the man in the front passenger seat.

There was no time. Rindt had to act decisively. He aimed his 9 mm Berretta at Peter and pulled the trigger twice in quick succession, before the driver wrenched the wheel hard to the left . . .

Andrew looked at the hurtling car as it passed.

"Rindt!" He saw the smoke before he heard the report.

Cosa swerved to place his body between the chaos he had created and its victim.

What was Andrew trying to tell me? Peter asked himself. Suddenly someone was shouting, *Coming about!* and he had ducked without thinking. An explosion rocked his brain, and he felt cold daylight where the left side of his skull had been.

Dark liquid blinded him in the left eye. Then there was a flash of light and he fell. There was no end to the fall. He tumbled, then floated into a deep starless pit. Soon everything went away. The commotion eased. The explosion stopped echoing. He let himself go.

The gunman in the backseat responded to Andrew's shout with a burst of gunfire in his direction. The wall behind Andrew boiled with explosions. A sharp blade sliced through his shoulder like lightning.

It occurred to him like a distant childhood memory: There was power in the heart of lightning. It went beyond terror and force and danger. It was somehow superior to life itself, primal and timeless, spectral and colorless, deafening and mystically silent. The rules of life are immolated for an immeasurable instant and possibility—both heavenly and hellish—existed simultaneously. Anything could happen. The world could reduce to a cinder or new life could be created. It could go either way. How he reacted in that moment could define a lifetime and change history.

The bright flash faded and the air turned misty red. He heard a rush of air escape from his throat and knew he needed to scream, but nothing came. His arm had either exploded into a million bits of tissue or simply fallen away to the sidewalk. He didn't have the stomach to look. Then he felt the spreading warmth down his chest; it was saturating his shirt and pants. A terrible chill followed.

He inhaled for control, but it only made him dizzy. The street spun out of control and he blacked out across Giuliana's shoulders.

The last thing Peter saw before Cardinal Cosa's body was thrown back onto him, blocking his view, was the blue car careening toward the Via della Conciliazione.

When he came to, a hand was holding his head and another was wrapping the top of his skull in soft clouds of dull cloth, which the hands then tightened until it pinched.

"*Lei va bene*. It's just a nick. You're going to be fine. I was a nurse in the army,'' she said with practiced calm.

His body lurched violently and he inhaled gallons of fresh air. Then he felt his pulse start again as if someone had suddenly released the clutch while his engine was racing. But it worked; his vital functions were restarting.

He opened his eyes but could only see from the right eye. His left eye was glued shut.

"Molto sangue, poco scapito," she assured him.

Surprising the Samaritan who was holding his head in her lap, Peter tried to pull himself up far enough to look for Andrew and Giuliana. He saw some flowing robes.

Peter sat bolt upright, a small involuntary groan the only clue to his pain.

"Peter . . ." It was just a whisper.

"Adeodato!" He grimaced as he saw the damage to Cosa's chest. Paramedics were working on him, but without much urgency; they knew. "What in God's name were you doing?"

"Peter . . ." He gasped for air and then winced. One of the paramedics muttered something about a collapsed lung. Surrender replaced Cosa's pained expression as he focused on Peter's face. "Forgive me?"

"Save your strength." Peter sat on the stones and supported him. "Save your strength."

"Please, I beg you. Forgive me?"

"Of course I forgive you," Peter tried to comfort him.

Cosa's eyes widened, and he looked directly into the high sun. His smile melted into a child's expression of simple joy.

"Go, Adeodato," Peter spoke quietly into the cardinal's ear. "Go in peace. I'll see you again."

The nurse who had tended him was dumbstruck by his brute strength in light of his still-bleeding head wound. She watched in awe as Peter stood and walked unsteadily over to where Andrew lay at the base of a wall, a fan of red sprayed across its bricks at shoulder height.

People still crouched on the sidewalk shouting at Andrew, motioning him down when he regained consciousness. He was already down, wasn't he?

"Get down!" a man shouted nearby.

An American, thought Andrew. *Where am I?* he wondered.

He reached for Giuliana and felt her respond by his side.
"Giuliana?"

"I'm all right." She took his head in her hands and embraced him.

"Easy!" he complained as his shoulder exploded in pain
again.

He was surprised when he saw his own left hand reach
out for her.

He looked toward where Peter had been. Then he saw the
face of his friend looking down at him with concern.

Later, at *l'ospedale*, Peter and Andrew needed only X-rays,
an MRI scan for Peter because of his head wound, a dozen
stitches, antibiotics and painkillers, then the *polizia* reports,
and they were free to go.

When Peter called Pope Luke John to explain, the pope
already knew most of the details. He said he had wanted to
come to the hospital, but his security people objected. Could
Peter perhaps join him for a broadcast in the afternoon?

The three received a motorcycle escort back along the
route they'd walked earlier. Andrew held Giuliana in his
good arm, content not to look too far into an uncertain future. On his left Peter sat forward, admiring the monuments.
Andrew sat between heaven and earth in a place that until
now had existed only in his imagination. Outside the car,
Michelangelo's dome passed in front of the low sun and
cast a cooling shade on them. He was happy in that light
with Giuliana, Peter, and his career's great purpose. A trinity
of his own.

God made man in his own image, he recalled the nuns
telling him in catechism classes so many Saturday mornings
ago. Man as God, God in man. God's Holy Trinity, Andrew's trinity. Wholeness grew within him until he felt he
couldn't contain it. Why him? He had no particular quali-
fications. He hadn't committed his life to the service of others or suffered biblical hardships. He was an ordinary
mortal, who loved a woman more than God! Then why was
he so blessed?

"Don't waste time asking questions that have no answers in this life." Peter spoke quietly. His dark eyes looked beyond Andrew's bandaged arm, beyond Giuliana's deceptive calm. He saw into their thoughts and the forces at work in them.

"You have more than you realize. Use it."

"If we live long enough," Andrew quipped and instantly regretted saying it. It sounded petty and self-indulgent.

Peter ignored it. "I died once before, Andrew. It taught me not to fear death again, even now." The car passed out of the dome's shadow into bright sunlight. "Dying cured my need for control. Once I let go, I had total control."

The car slowed for identification by the Coppo Di Guardia at the Arco della Campana. There, waiting anxiously, was Nula.

"Nula!" Peter opened his door.

"Pietro! Oh, my God, what happened to you? What's going on? I was so worried! I heard about the gunshots in the piazza and I knew; I just knew! By the time I got to l'ospedale they said you'd gone!" A torrent poured from her as she flew into Peter's arms. Two Swiss Guards moved to protect Peter, not understanding Nula's English.

"It's all right," Peter gestured quickly. "Va bene. Va bene!" He laughed as Nula first showered him with kisses, then scolded him. Finally he said, "We'll be late, Nula. Stephen Parnell is waiting."

She squeezed into the car beside Andrew and nodded through the introductions. Peter wedged himself in again, forcing the door closed, and the car accelerated under the Arco. Having seen their charge safely onto Vatican state territory, the polizia stayed behind.

They drove across a small courtyard, under another arch, past the entrance to the Ufficio Scavi and the plaque marking the original site of the Heliopolis Obelisk. Nula noticed that Giuliana crossed herself as they passed the site of Peter's crucifixion and asked why.

"This is where Peter was martyred," explained Giuliana, glancing at Peter.

Nula smiled her understanding but was puzzled when Giuliana gestured toward Peter. She caught him watching her closely and laughed uncomfortably, then frowned. It was preposterous, of course. They were playing with her.

Then she remembered all the coincidences. She recalled his fascination with Nero's fate and his curiosity about Pope Luke John. No, it wasn't possible!

She looked to Andrew for a clue to save her from her misunderstanding. Then to Giuliana. They were admiring the gardens outside. Then she looked back to Peter, who still watched her, now with more concern.

"I'm sorry, Nula."

"Sorry?"

"I meant to explain, but there was never time. I didn't know how to tell you."

"Tell me what? That you're Saint Peter!?" she gasped, blushing even as she said the words.

He nodded, holding her eyes as the car ascended a gentle grade that wrapped around the massive stone foundations of the basilica. Nula joined the silence of the others as the verdant gardens consumed them. She had a thousand questions for Peter, but she couldn't think of a single one. A voice deep within her told her that she had known all along. Of course it was San Pietro; who else would Pope Luke John honor with a Vatican Radio broadcast? She had fallen in love with Saint Peter. How? She took his hand in her own.

The slopes and hollows of the red clay Vaticanus Hill, once the site of graves for the poor, mosquito-infested marshes and Christianity's best-kept secret, was now a verdant emerald Eden. Meticulously kept pocket gardens of evergreens and perennials bordered stands of cypress and Italian stone pines, cathedrals of scented peace and tranquillity at the heart of a chaotic world.

The car purred down vacant paths, passing first into cool shade, then through showers of sunlight slanting brightly through the open car window. Their eyes could barely take it all in. Birds lifted their song into the silence and the four passengers silently reveled in this sensation of exquisite mortality, this lightness of being that hinted at another existence.

A building appeared on the right in a large clearing. "L'Governatorato," gestured the driver.

As it fell away behind them and the car began climbing

again, Andrew thought he saw the antenna tower far ahead, then it too was swallowed by more trees.

"What do you plan to say to the world, Peter?" asked Andrew.

Peter thought back to his dialectic with Luke John. They had said it all that afternoon, had they not? It remained now only to share it with the world. He noticed that Giuliana was watching the play of emotions on his face. She was remembering their own dialectic on the *Kestrel*, how they had solved the world's problems in a single afternoon at sea, and nodded knowingly. He was not the only one here who could read another's thoughts.

Peter winked at Giuliana. "Oh, I have a fair idea. And I have something to say to all of you, too." He took Nula's hand between his own. "Andrew, Giuliana, I have decided something."

They waited expectantly.

"I am staying here with Nula. I got it wrong the first time, you know. Now that I have a chance, I will treat this woman properly."

"Peter, there's no telling . . ." began Andrew.

"It's a hard decision and I have made it," Peter cut him off. "Congratulate me and be happy for me, or go away and leave us alone. Do not fight me on this."

The car followed a sweeping arc to the right into a long tunnel between dense stands of more evergreens. Their eyes eventually adjusted as they moved through it, and they saw a roan buck standing lightly on damp moss, chewing, gazing at them. It was hardly more than a shadow, but everyone saw it. Distant birdsong echoed. The car's engine idled gently, a cat's contented purr on a lazy afternoon.

As they emerged again into the sun, the light seemed all the brighter for the darkness before it. Everyone squinted in the glare. The driver slowed for safety.

Andrew rubbed his eyes. When he was able to focus again, he checked the others and saw Peter with his head in his hands, adjusting his eyesight also.

When Peter looked up, he panicked momentarily, like a man waking up in a strange room.

"What the h—?"

"Pietro?" worried Nula.

But when Peter looked at her, he was different. The sparkle in his deep black eyes was missing. He scowled fearfully, not recognizing her. He shook his head and the sparkle glimmered falteringly, then flared brightly again. He looked quickly at Andrew and Giuliana for an explanation.

"Driver, stop the car!" shouted Andrew.

"*Alto, per favore!*" Giuliana translated.

The driver did as he was told and pulled the car to a stop on the shoulder.

"Andrew? My head—I can't stop the spinning, Little Brother!" complained Peter as he leaned forward, struggling for control of his wandering senses.

By this time Andrew and Giuliana had gotten out of the car on their side and run to open the door by Peter. Andrew grabbed Peter's wrist and took his pulse.

Peter smiled to comfort Nula. He eased himself down, his head in her lap. "Just a little rest, that's all I need." He let his eyes close. Then they snapped open. The sparkle was gone again. He saw Andrew and calmed down a little.

"What's going on, Doc?" It was Nicolao. Andrew recognized the growling dialect.

"Nicolao?" he asked.

"Nicolao!" repeated Giuliana, her eyes wide with horror.

"Dr. Sabatini!" Nicolao grinned, happy to see another familiar face. Then he looked around, saw Nula looking down at him and quickly raised himself. "Who are you? And where in Neptune's name are we?"

He began to panic. It crept into his expression like a nightmare.

"Nicolao, you're all right," Andrew said with forced calm in his voice.

"Nicolao?" Nula cried, as bewildered as the man beside her. "Who is Nicolao?"

Nicolao's fear began to multiply. He wrested his hand away from Andrew and started to climb out of the car.

Andrew held him back, slapping him to get his attention; he collapsed again into Nula's lap.

"What's going on?" Nula demanded of Andrew, holding on for dear life to the man she loved.

"Peter's memory, it's fading . . ."

Nicolao's eyes opened, and when he looked at Nula he was calm, with fire in his eyes.

"Nula. Nula, listen . . ."

Nula responded immediately to the familiar power in Peter's voice. She caressed his face.

"Take me as I am, Nula, a stray visitor, a spirit passing through a moment in your life. I am accustomed to open spaces and invisible codes. I am unfit for the confinements of this life," he confessed. He knew his time was near. The next world was pulling him home. "So much I wanted to say to you."

Nula accepted his meaning. It was a miracle, she would come to believe later, that she knew not to question but to accept him in that moment, to give him the peace he craved with her.

"Pietro!" She began to weep, cradling his magnificent head between her breasts, rocking him. "Oh, Pietro *mio*!"

He placed his palm over her heart. *"Petros Eni,"* he whispered.

He blinked, and Nicolao's terror returned. He closed his eyes tightly.

"Quo Vadis, Domine?" He focused on a distant face in a time long, long ago. He shook his head again and glanced at the others once more before settling down to rest.

"I am with you," he whispered, his gaze focused on the sun through the trees. *"Consummatum est . . ."* His face relaxed and he fell still.

Peter thought of Stephen Parnell. He wanted to go to him, to tell him that he had done well; it just wasn't meant to be, not yet. But he had done well. He had believed when others did not. Yes, he would go to him.

And he was before the pontiff, who waited in the hushed sound booth. He didn't know yet.

Peter moved closer and listened to Stephen's thoughts. He was giving thanks and asking for wisdom to do the right thing.

"Adeodato, poor Adeodato," Stephen murmured. "He is with the angels now. Maybe they can explain why he faltered . . ."

Peter touched Stephen's forehead.

For no apparent reason Stephen felt new hope and certainty that all was as it was meant to be. He sensed a new peace.

He remembered the Gobba. He would go to her and invite her to the evening meal with him.

When the eyes opened, the energy in the face that had been proof of Peter's presence lapsed into an enveloping fatigue of loss. It was as if Nicolao's former self could not be extinguished. It was restored.

"Nic?" asked Andrew.

"Hmm?" was all the reply Nicolao could muster.

"Peter," Giuliana whispered, reaching out and smoothing the old man's hair.

31 NICOLAO SAT BENT OVER IN THE COURTYARD OF the papal residence at Gandolfo, squinting at the shining Apennine ridges.

"You're saying I'm cured?" he asked Andrew.

"The tumor's no longer in remission, it's disappeared," Andrew explained. "It started shrinking while you were still in the lab at BioGenera, right after we began the procedure, but it seemed premature to say anything until we were sure. Then again, who would I be talking to—you, or—"

"—or the other guy," Nicolao finished for him. Neither of them would say the name.

"When we were in the hospital in Rome, they did an MRI scan. I just got the results today and they're, well, extraordinary. I actually called and asked them if there'd been some mixup." Andrew reached for his briefcase, which he'd left beside the bench. "I'll show you—"

Nicolao shook his head. "Nah. Why spoil a good thing? A miracle's a miracle." He blinked away tears. "You saved my life, Doc."

"No, not me, Nic." Andrew laughed dryly. "Not me."

The old man rested his calloused hands on his knees, squinting at the mountains again.

"So what's it mean? I get to live out a normal life now?"

"Pretty much." Andrew nodded. "We all have to die of something."

Now it was Nic's turn to laugh. "Well, at least this time I'll see it coming!" He grew thoughtful. "I've changed, Doc. Don't know how exactly, but I know things. Things maybe I shouldn't know. Things that make all that back there seem unimportant."

"I think I understand," said Andrew. "What will you do now, go home? Your family must be wondering."

"That I don't know yet," the old man growled. "I'm an ornery cuss, used to going off on my own. They won't worry about me for a while. I want to go somewhere where no one knows me, somewhere where I can prepare for what's to come. I've got a whole new life to think about now, you know?" He looked at Giuliana, then Andrew. "The pope's made arrangements at a monastery up north."

"North?" Andrew asked, thinking he meant Northern Italy.

"Ireland."

"Skellig Michael," Giuliana explained.

"Ireland," Nicolao grew more enthusiastic. He would find peace there in the currents of a sparse existence.

Luke John had advised that Nic tuck himself away where Rindt would not find him. He might still be in danger.

Where there is one Cosa, there are a dozen Cosas, thought Andrew, reading between the lines of Luke John's advice. Where there is one Rindt, there are a hundred Rindts.

The pope also wanted Giuliana to take sanctuary with the Dominican Sisters in the Cloisters in Firenze. Later he planned to secrete her in Rome to confer with him. He was asking her advice on how to alter the Church's course!

Giuliana insisted on staying in Rome. The work would go faster that way, she insisted. The pontiff didn't need to know that she would be reunited with Andrew sooner that way, also. To mollify him, she agreed to keep a low profile in the nearby Handmaids of Jesus Crucified Convent. In the meantime, Andrew would escort Nic to Ireland, then go into hiding and wait for her. Encrypted e-mail would be their lifeline.

* * *

Skellig Michael. For a hundred years in antiquity, between domination by the Roman Empire and the long night of the Middle Ages, monk-scribes preserved humankind's library of Greek and Latin civilization here. Western culture survived the darkness by clinging to a pinnacle of rock eighteen miles from the Irish coast. The future of the Western world was written by Celtic monks with quills atop a seven-hundred-foot rock outcropping.

When Andrew and Nic drove up to the windswept monastery at Michael Head opposite the now abandoned Skellig Michael, Andrew understood Nicolao's attraction to this end of the world. A bullying wind off the North Atlantic ripped at the stones, carrying away anything not firmly rooted, including a man's regrets. This wasn't a place for worldly comfort; it was a haven for struggling spirits.

Nic caught Andrew off guard when he hugged him. It wasn't something he'd expected of the fisherman. There were a lot of things he hadn't expected from the old man.

"So long, Doc," Nic whispered hoarsely. "I won't be seeing you again."

"My loss."

Nic lifted his bag and headed toward the small lancet passage into the chapel. He paused to take in the low-slung, weather-beaten structure, then turned and grinned. "Ain't exactly St. Peter's, is it?"

Andrew laughed. As he watched Nic vanish into the squat spirit fortress, he replayed the old man's last words and the laugh drained out of his expression. Had Nicolao been aware of what had gone on while Peter occupied his mind and body? Had he shared Peter's perceptions? His experiences?

"Nic!" he shouted. "Peter!?"

But the wind carried his voice away like down across the heather. He considered going inside after him but decided against it. Leave the man some peace; he'd earned it.

There was another hour before the day passed into night. Andrew walked to the edge of the cliff and leaned into the howling westerly. It brushed past his ears, swept around the distant chapel, and picked up the day's prayers for the hereafter.

He tried counting the 572 steps, dating from the sixth century, that led to the monastery, but he lost count. Did a spirit have as many trips to earth as there were stair steps below? Were there as many enemies of understanding as there were molecules in the waves below? Andrew's thoughts were grim; he tried to shake them off. The stitches in his shoulder itched, reminding him of how close he'd come to death, how fortunate he truly was. Tucking his neck into the collar of his jacket, he moved on.

Nic entered the small chapel and paused to let his eyes adjust to the soft radiance of a candlelight mass that was under way. A knot of monks, dressed in shapeless dark wool robes, stood at the center, in front of the altar.

Off to the side were a few of the local poor, each with a lighted candle. One weathered-looking man had a little girl at his side. She too held a candle proudly, and when the others began to sing a hymn, her voice carried above them all, a clear lilting note interwoven with their more somber tones. She turned to study Nic, holding him in her gaze. Only then did he feel how cold and tired he was, and older than the world.

The only seats were up front with the monks. He didn't feel he'd earned a place with them yet. He sat alone and tried to become invisible.

Gregorian chant filled the small chapel. It seemed as familiar to him as the solitary beauty of a night watch under a midnight clear. He couldn't remember the Latin verses from boyhood, yet his heart swelled at the sound.

Something pulled at his coat sleeve. It was the child, tugging lightly with one hand, a candle held out for him in her other. He smiled and shook his head, refusing her offer with a wink before once again facing the altar. She tugged again. Glancing at her father, who tried to suppress his pride without much success, Nic surrendered. He accepted the candle and hummed along with the monks.

From Riva there is a road that winds beside Lago di Garda, skirts the cliffs of the Rocchetta, and passes through several mountain tunnels before it reaches the remains of a remote Bronze Age settlement near Pieve di Ledro. Andrew explored the abandoned excavations while waiting for Giuliana in this high mountain hamlet. It passed the time and kept his intellect in the game.

The Vatican had forwarded a letter from Margaret. She'd seen the news reports about Cosa's murder, heard Andrew's name mentioned, and assumed that it was over. She was back in the house in La Jolla, she wrote to him. She hoped he was safe and well, and wished him a happy future. There was a finality to her letter, and Andrew knew she wouldn't expect a reply.

Considering his own life for the first time since the adventure began, Andrew decided that he knew as much as he wanted to know. He hadn't been looking for religion necessarily, just something beyond himself to believe in. It had been inside him all along, waiting. When it broke the surface and blossomed, he came to appreciate it, marveled at how quickly it grew strong. Like cactus, it survived on the sparsest elements and grew taller, casting shade against sun, protecting against the harshest evils of a barren existence.

The wind shifted and Andrew thought he heard Gregorian chant carry across the mountainside. It was only his own thoughts, somehow more real now that he was free of regret, free to live.

The more deeply we allow ourselves to accept our inner darkness, he realized, the more we settle into our true selves, beyond the noise of relationships and society's codes, closer to the bones of that which makes us unique. We can accept faith.

What was he to do now? He considered the flight back to La Jolla and BioGenera, eight meridians back to PST, Pre-Sabatini Time. He'd wanted another chance. Here it was, new and challenging. Home was wherever he wanted it to be.

He longed for Giuliana. He missed her desperately. But rejoining her too soon would put her in danger. He would have to content himself with notes on the small laptop screen until he could be sure the threat had subsided.

She had glowed like a contented ember their last night together, knowing they would have to be apart for a time.

"I had a dream," she breathed into the darkness. "A dream about a stranger. For the very first time—I was beginning to think it might never occur for me—I allowed myself to open completely . . . for him. And like a miracle I was whole again. So I surrounded him with everything I am, ever was, and will be, and he was happy. That stranger was you," she whispered. "It is you."

They held each another, caressing, memorizing. "I feel as if I now know what Peter knew," she whispered as she watched dawn's light slide down the wall and illuminate Andrew's hair, creating a familiar aura. He remembered the look on her face when she saw herself reflected in his eyes.

The pope had given them his personal access codes to the ciphering lines into and out of the Vatican. Besides using them to maintain contact with Giuliana, Andrew would use them to update Delphine, Will, and Gindman. He hadn't yet reached out to them, hadn't even read their e-mail. He didn't know exactly how to tell Gindman that he wouldn't be returning to BioGenera. Knowing Gindman, he'd probably figured it out for himself already. The news about the spectacular initial success of memory resurrection, as well as its ultimate failure, would have to be enough. Gindman would consider Andrew's departure as a chance to cut his own losses, hire someone new, no hard feelings.

Sooner or later, he thought, you find out and you know. You know what to agonize over and what to accept, what to change and what to eliminate. You know when the time comes to take care of yourself, for yourself, to become more whole. It's never too late to have a life. It's never too late to be loved the way you want to be loved.

Why had it taken him forty-five years to realize what was before him all that time?

His experiences had taught him that the latter half of his life would necessarily consist of unlearning most of what he had learned in his youth. The years ahead would truly be his growing years.

A faint buzz whispered through the wind. He unclipped his pager from his belt, held it out at arm's length and squinted to read it. The words "I love you" appeared on the tiny LCD screen and brought a wistful smile. He pictured her in her cell in the convent typing those words into her laptop, thinking of him.

A flutter of sunlight flashed and subsided into a deep lavender. There in the lee of gnarled scrub, a patch of wild violets blossomed impossibly in the punishing mountain wind. He touched their petals, remembering a sweetness on the tip of his tongue, marveling at their simple, complex beauty.

How many other secrets did creation hold? The more he looked into the evolutionary adaptations hidden in the helical strand of DNA, the more rich and mysterious, the more deeply saturated with life and purpose it became. Each tentative foray into the chaos of man's impact on his universe became more humbling.

He had felt the foundations of life shiver when he unlocked the door to mortality.

He had discovered a new world within himself in the arms of a stranger he had always known.

He had looked into the vision of a time traveler and felt the warm wind of compassion against his soul.

He knew that the miracle in which he had participated had limits. The door had opened, but then it had closed. The procedure was imperfect, like its creator.

Knowing that there were secrets to be discovered and very likely secrets that could never be revealed reassured him. If ever there was a grace to failure, he hoped he had now captured it. At least that.

He was about to leave the overgrown, rubbled site when he spotted a jagged shard. Barely visible above the red soil, it was only a splinter, dun and dull, yet enough to catch his attention. He brushed the dirt away and lifted the object free. It was a bone. The wind had uncovered a remnant missed by the archaeologists. It looked like a metatarsal, possibly metacarpal, but definitely human. And it was definitely very, very old. Prehistoric? Bronze Age?

Andrew examined it with his expert eye and considered whether or not he should report it to the authorities. Finally, he carefully wrapped it, put it in his pocket, and returned to the hotel to wait for Giuliana.

Giuliana dressed once, then twice, and again.

"Come straight away, *Dottore*," he had said.

Her heart had stopped. Had any woman heard a pontiff's voice so vulnerable, so—human?

"I'm after history this morning, and the truth is I'm as wobbly as a new colt."

She had arrived early, conscious of the sound of her shoes on the stones, the sound of history embracing her. She had looked up at Cardinal Cosa's window and realized with the shock of recognition that it was now hers. Peter would be pleased. Andrew would be proud. She wanted to share it all with him. Life was so short, and they had so much to experience together.

The pope's reinvigorated humanity revealed itself to her in his new dependence upon her. He shared with her the exhilaration of his newborn faith, his irrepressible Gaelic humor, his affection for Peter's salty approach to life, and his struggle with this morning's stage fright.

As with everything else about the hours since Peter had left them, truth now dictated the pace of discovery and her reactions to it. Truth would not be deferred any more than her love for Andrew or her duty to Peter's Church.

She had first dressed in a stylish linen suit, then a more muted silk ensemble and, finally, a fine lightweight navy suit with a crisp white blouse underneath. Colors of the Virgin.

She had fantasized about being needed someday by the Pontifical Academy of Sciences, by Cardinal Cosa, but she had never imagined being important to His Holiness. Neither had it ever occurred to her that a saint could use her skills or that God could depend upon her. When she was a child she had prayed for significance, for a visit by Mary, an opportunity to be like Bernadette, but those dreams had faded with adulthood. And never—not once—had it occurred to her that any male in the hierarchy of the Church would bless her with such purpose as Luke John required of her here.

The pope's private apartment seemed brighter than she expected it to be. She went to the window and, being careful to avoid the cameras, peered out at the gathering sea in the harbor of Piazza San Pietro. Waves of souls washed against the barricades. Behind those already gathered, still more arrived, until hundreds of thousands spilled out onto Piazza Pio XII and through Bernini's colonnade onto Via del Sant' Uffizio.

Where had they all come from on a weekday? It was she

who had arranged this appearance—his first not to be scheduled months in advance, choreographed, scripted, and staged with the precision of a moon launch—but she hadn't expected such a turnout. The usual diplomatic machinery of the pope's staff, the aides and assistants and media liaisons had been dismayed by Luke John's short notice, yet he hadn't backed down. He would speak to the world, he decreed. His sudden reliance upon Dottore Giuliana Sabatini? That was not open to discussion.

Had he gone completely mad? they blustered. What could possibly be so important to him that he would abandon two thousand years of tradition and protocol? And why *her*? Luke John listened to their howls for an hour before silencing them and expelling them from his plan-making with Giuliana.

She heard his measured footsteps on the parquet in the next room. Then he was in the doorway, wearing the simple black cassock of a parish priest. Only the heavy pectoral cross distinguished him as pope. Even the papal ring was gone. His snow-white hair floated like an aura; his scholar's fingers, absent their gaudy jewelry, were as refined as old ivory. He beamed when he spied her, brightened as if lit from within.

"I've never seen such an audience, Your Holiness," she smiled.

"Aye." He raised himself up on his toes in the center of the room away from the window and looked over the masses. "Think they are ready, Giuliana?"

"No more than you or I were ready, Your Holiness."

He winked at her and strode briskly across the room, past the prie-dieu and the deep leather reading chair. When he reached the edge of the runner by the foot of the bed he pivoted, stood and admired her. From Eve to the Virgin, the traditional Church had typecast Woman, looked at her askance, alternately reviled and revered her, but always kept her at arm's length. No more. Luke John consciously received Giuliana's presence as a blessing in his newly brightened existence and gave thanks.

Her Tuscan grace and Roman formality were somehow different from what he was accustomed to, he noticed. Some Italians who are well traveled accept the pomp and para-

phernalia of the papacy with good-natured distance, a lack
of conviction. There was something unique in Giuliana's
manner, however. Not condescension—there wasn't a hint
of that in this attractive and intelligent woman—but self-
possession, an assured sense of metaphysical parity, of balance. Luke John liked it very much.

Odd, thought Giuliana, how natural this new sense of belonging and purpose felt after so many years of restless ser-
vitude in the Apostolic Palace. Maybe it wasn't just her
feeling. His Holiness also seemed more sure of himself, em-
boldened by some spiritual certainty that reconciled human
doubts. It was as if he was experiencing personal miracles,
one after the other. Was it generosity that impelled him?
No, it was more than that. More freely shared, without a
thought of return. It was—love. Yes, that was what it was:
love. The same overwhelming sense she had of how simple
life can be when one surrenders.

Giuliana basked in his admiration in silence, then spoke.

"Andrew tells me that Nicolao will outlive us all. The
tumor in his brain is gone without a trace."

"Splendid!" Luke John said, but then his face fell. "If
only we could be sure the colonel is gone also."

"I don't think we need worry about him, Your Holiness.
He is not a believer in the cardinal's cause, only a soldier.
It is over; he knows this. The only motive he has left is
pride."

"Pride keeps fighting after the battle is over, Giuliana,"
Luke John said with the wisdom of Belfast. "No armistice
can satisfy it in some men. The colonel is not like Adeodato."

He longs to be spiritual, Giuliana thought, *but he must be
pope also.*

"I've seen the cardinal's tomb at Santa Maria's in Trastevere." Giuliana changed the subject. She didn't want to
think about Rindt. "It's quite beautiful."

"Fitting that a man of Cosa's medieval tendencies should
spend eternity among the best art of that rigid and unyielding era," Luke John uttered sadly. He smiled tightly at Giuliana, embarrassed at having allowed his disappointment in
his old friend to surface.

Giuliana nodded sympathetically; she understood.

They sat in two matching armchairs listening to the sea-swell of the gathering crowd below. Luke John glanced at the old Gruen on his wrist. "Just a few minutes," he mused. "So much will change . . ."

Giuliana consulted her own wristwatch and smiled. "I will tell you when it's time, Your Holiness."

They fell silent in the calm before he was to step outside. "I miss my island," he said quietly.

Giuliana understood. She remembered the quizzical look on Andrew's face that morning in La Jolla when she'd told him she missed Italy even when she was there. No one should pass through life without missing a place where they felt at home.

"For a long time, Giuliana, I did not understand the concept of order. The neat symmetry of these magnificent gardens irritated me on some level. The alignments of the Guard in the square, the diplomatic protocols, they all inspired ungenerous thoughts in me. Whether they pushed me to God's discipline or it was I on my own who fled to the harsh interpretations of the Gospels, I don't know. But I can say that I have walked in this pope's life aware of my imperfections and still managed. That's a sign of honesty in a person, don't you think? When one tends toward what he can never achieve?"

Sunlight glimmered on the carved legs of the table at his side, lifting a reflection onto the wall. The universe moved, indifferent to human dilemmas. Giuliana did not know how to respond. She had never thought of the pope as a person who doubted. Before she had known Peter, the thought might have frightened her, yet now she could allow her childlike need for heroes to fall away. Either all men had the potential to be heroes, or none did. Everything was happening as it should. The naive, openhearted self within was more potent and true than all the outer armor collected during a lifetime.

"To what extent my spirit has been imprisoned by my fears, my errors, to what extent my knowledge—no, my understanding of life—has been inadequate, I can only trust the best part of myself and others to forgive . . ." Luke John went on. He was guileless, allowing Giuliana into his innermost thoughts. "Now, I have remembered how to listen.

There is still time for me—for us—to make right what has been wrong. It will take more than the years I have left," he concluded pointedly.

"I understand, Holiness."

There was no need for small talk. Each recognized that they were equals joined by circumstance at a crossroads. The choices were larger than either of them had confronted before, but they were ready. In any other situation there might have been a need for discussion, but in the wake of Peter, these two disparate individuals were of one mind, facing a new future. All that remained was to work out the details.

Luke John had wanted to appoint Giuliana as his new Chief Pontifical Adviser. She had had to persuade him that the Church was not yet ready to accept her in that role. It had proved to be the only sticking point. He had rather stubbornly hinted that he had such plans for her. She would, she assured him, assist in the selection of the new adviser, and she would always be available to him to serve Peter's Church, but she insisted that her profile remain discreet for the present.

In the meantime, until this critical period of transition was over, she had agreed to supervise the establishment of new commissions within the Curia to reconsider the Church's stand on what had heretofore been preached as dogma. A conclave of cardinals would be summoned as soon as possible to attend to the thousands of other details necessary to move the Church forward on the course Peter had charted for them. Her responsibility was the simplest and most complex of all—to make certain that Luke John, and whoever succeeded him, did not falter on that course.

Giuliana checked her watch again.

"It's time," she said.

Luke John drew himself up, adjusted his cassock, and moved toward the open doors to the balcony. He tried to appear solemn, but he could not stop smiling. He shrugged good-naturedly and stepped up into the bright morning on the balcony.

A roar lifted into the air and grew louder, until the entire palace shook with its thunder. It lasted for endless minutes despite Luke John's attempts to subdue the adoring masses.

Eventually the cheers subsided and there was a splendid quiet. Giuliana held her breath.

Luke John cleared his throat. Several moments passed without a sound. The air was electric with anticipation, and still he didn't speak.

It was unbearable. What was happening? Why didn't he begin?

Suddenly Giuliana sensed a shift in the current. The tension broke and silence spread throughout the city. Calm settled over every living being. Even the cooing of doves was stilled.

Then a vast sigh rose like a whisper from the masses. There were smiles everywhere, some of them shining through tears.

At last Luke John spoke. His words came from the stillness, as Peter had come from the heart of eternity. They carried warmth and hope like dawn across the piazza, echoed down alleys, filtered through apartment windows, soared beyond the seven hills to touch waiting hearts everywhere.

EPILOGUE

SHE HADN'T BEEN FEELING WELL SINCE SHORTLY AFTER PETER left. She missed him; that was a big part of it. There were times, alone at night in the bed they'd shared so briefly, so joyously, when she'd curl herself up in a little ball and rock in silent grief. Other times, during the day, she would find tears in her eyes and not know how they'd gotten there. Were they tears of mourning or of remembrance?

She had grieved before, but never like this. Still, something in her staunch peasant spirit told her that, no matter how acute the pain, it would ease to a dull ache in time. But she had also grown physically ill, and that began to trouble her even more. Sleeping was difficult, she couldn't eat. She was beginning to wonder if whatever was making her feel so terrible would get the better of her.

Her *dottore* was kind, but his concern went only so far, she guessed. He didn't seem to be worried. After asking some questions and running several tests, he sent her home with a prescription to ease her nerves, and advised her to avoid wine and coffee until the tests came back. He called her at work the next day to tell her that there was nothing wrong with her that wouldn't work itself out by Christmas.

"*Natale?*" she snapped, unable to mask her irritation.

"*Si, Signora,*" he responded, enjoying this rare aspect of his work. "You are *gravido e favorire*, my dear."

"*Que?*"

"*Pregno, Signora.*" His smile lifted his tone. Such news

was a particular source of joy in Italy, regardless of the circumstances. In this case, he considered it a miracle. She was well into middle age. It wasn't unheard of, but it was unusual.

"Pregno," she repeated quietly, unable to believe what she was hearing.

"Si, and at your age, with a first pregnancy, I must say you are blessed. I will watch over you and your *bambino* carefully, very carefully."

They didn't speak for a few moments. Nula's hand dropped to her belly as she remembered her night with Peter.

"Miracolo . . ." her doctor suggested.

"Si, miracolo," she whispered. *"Miracolo."*

Consummatum est